PRAISE FOR JANE PORTER

MRS. PERFECT

"A poignant exploration of the pressures modern moms face today, both from without and within, but ultimately it's about supporting each other in our choices, no matter what."

> —Melanie Lynne Hauser, author of *Confessions of Super Mom* and *Super Mom Saves the World*

"Jane Porter strikes a fine balance in the follow-up to her hit *Odd Mom Out*, MRS. PERFECT, a novel about losing 'The Good Life' only to discover what the good life really is—funny, thought-provoking, affecting . . . and highly recommended."

> —Lauren Baratz-Logsted, author of *Secrets of My Suburban Life* and *Vertigo*

ODD MOM OUT

"Jane Porter nails it poignantly and perfectly. This mommy-lit is far from fluff. Sensitive characters and a protagonist who doesn't cave in to the in-crowd give this novel its heft."

> —*USA Today*

"A poignant critique of mommy cliques and the plight of single parents."

MRS. PERFECT

ALSO BY JANE PORTER

Odd Mom Out
Flirting with Forty
The Frog Prince

MRS. PERFECT

JANE PORTER

NEW YORK   BOSTON

Copyright © 2008 by Jane Porter

5 Spot
Hachette Book Group USA
237 Park Avenue
New York, NY 10017

Visit our Web site at www.5-spot.com.

5 Spot is an imprint of Grand Central Publishing.
The 5 Spot name and logo are trademarks of Hachette
Book Group USA, Inc.

Printed in the United States of America

First Edition: May 2008
10 9 8 7 6 5 4 3 2 1

Library of Congress Cataloging-in-Publication Data

Porter, Jane
Mrs. Perfect / Jane Porter. — 1st ed.
p. cm.
ISBN-13: 978-0-446-69924-2
ISBN-10: 0-446-69924-1
1. Single mothers—Fiction.   2. Working mothers—Fiction.
3. Stay-at-home mothers—Fiction.   I. Title.
PS3616.O78A79 2008
813'.6—dc22
2007041321

For Jacquelyn Gaskins
1934–2007
The boys miss their grandma and I miss my mother-in-law.
Jackie, you knew how to laugh, live, and wear red lipstick.
We miss you. This one's for you.

Acknowledgments

A huge thank-you to my agent, Karen Solem, for making this fourth book for 5 Spot a reality. She's an extraordinary agent and I'm lucky to have her.

Another huge thank-you to everyone at 5 Spot/Grand Central Publishing for their tremendous support. I'm lucky to work with such talented, creative, and dedicated people in publishing. I am especially grateful to my editor, Karen Kosztolnyik, for understanding where I want to go with my stories and making sure I get there. To Elly Weisenberg, my 5 Spot publicist, and all the sales, marketing, and art department folks who always make sure I look good and my books are where they need to be. Thank you, thank you, thank you.

I'd also like to acknowledge my Bellevue friends who helped my research, notably former ad exec Denise Bocezk, preschool teacher Wendy Lange, and life coach Kristiina Hiukka, for their wonderful insights, inspirations, and brainstorming. There are so many other Bellevue friends who have been here for me over the years. You know who you are. Thank you.

To fellow 5 Spot authors Liza Palmer and Megan Crane,

thanks for becoming such good friends. I love talking books with you and just hanging out. I'm lucky to know you.

To my boys, Jake and Ty, thanks for understanding that Mom needs her words but loves you both dearly.

And finally, to my guy, Ty Gurney. You're my sugar and salt. You make life taste better.

Chapter One

Zooming into the country club parking lot, I snag a spot close to the club pool. Okay, technically it's not a spot, but there's nothing else close and I'm late.

Nathan says I run late often, and yes, sometimes I do, but not always. It's just that my schedule all summer has been ungodly. I've always been busy, but in the past year I have taken on way too much, sat on far too many committees, agreed to assist too many organizations.

The problem is, everyone needs help, and I hate inefficiency, I really do, which is how I got to be on so many committees in the first place.

I know how to get things done. I've always known how to get things done, and for me, it's relatively easy organizing functions and raising money. And as we all know, everything these days is about raising money. As well as improving the quality of life for the kids.

It really is about the kids, isn't it?

I sign in quickly at the poolhouse's front desk and wave at a passing mother—never do remember her name, though—and emerge into the late afternoon light that already streaks the pool.

Scanning the area for my girls, I tug my top over the waist of my white tennis skirt. I wish I'd showered and changed before heading to the pool, but I was afraid of being even later. It's Friday, Labor Day weekend, and my nanny hoped to leave early today to go camping with her boyfriend.

I feel bad that Annika, our Finnish nanny, didn't get to leave at three-thirty as requested (it's nearly five now), but today was hellacious. Morning Pilates, two-hour auction committee meeting, afternoon on the tennis court before quick grocery shop. Then it was a rush home to get the salmon steaks into the bourbon marinade for dinner before another rush out to pick up the girls from the club.

Pulling my sunglasses off, I spot the girls. Tori's in the baby pool, Brooke's lying on her towel on the lawn, and my eldest, ten-year-old Jemma, swims in the deep end with her friends. Annika sits in the shade near the baby pool, her purse on her lap. She's ready to go, which annoys me.

I don't like being disapproving, but I do resent being made to rush and then feel guilty. It's Labor Day weekend. She has Monday off. It's not as if she won't have three full days of vacation.

Annika spots me. I lift a hand, letting her know she can go. She leans down, kisses Tori, and, with a nod at me, leaves. Quickly.

"Taylor!"

It's Patti calling my name. I turn, spot her and a cluster of women at one of the pool's round tables, and indicate that I'll join them in just a moment. First, I have to get something cold to drink.

Something preferably with alcohol.

A few minutes later, I collapse in the poolside chair with my gin and tonic. Nice. Sliding my sunglasses on top of my head, I sip my drink appreciatively. Day's almost over. I'm almost free.

Suddenly Annika reappears on the pool deck, dashes to a table near the baby pool, and rifles through the stack of beach towels they brought earlier. She's looking for something, and it's got to be her car keys or her cell phone—she couldn't survive without either.

It's her cell phone.

I'm not surprised. What twenty-two-year-old girl doesn't live on her cell?

Annika leaves again, and I watch her dash back out. She's worked for me for over a year now, and we almost never talk. I leave her to-do lists, and when she goes home at night she leaves the lists behind, everything done, all the chores checked off.

Sometimes I feel a little guilty for not ever having a proper chat, but what would we talk about? My girls? My house? My laundry? No, thank you. I have enough on my mind without having to discuss the above with a foreign teenager.

What a day. Not bad, just long and busy. Pilates nearly killed me, I killed my opponent in tennis, and the committee meeting…well, that went so much better than I expected.

"Have you been here long?" I ask the group at large, dropping my sunglasses back onto my nose.

"An hour," Patti answers.

Monica grimaces. "Since two."

"Noon," Kate adds.

Noon? I make a face. I can't imagine sitting here for five hours. My God, doesn't she have anything else to do?

"You should have gotten a sitter," I say, glancing at my children, praying they'll be content for another half hour at least, an hour if I buy them an ice cream. Tonight I would buy them ice cream, too, if it meant I could just leave my feet up for a while and relax.

Kate sees my grimace. "I couldn't get a sitter," she explains. "Labor Day weekend. Everyone's going away."

True. We were going away, too, and then Nathan begged off at the last minute, said all he wanted to do was stay home, enjoy the girls, and maybe get in a round of golf.

"Actually," Kate continues, crossing her legs, tugging down her straight twill skirt that looks like Eddie Bauer but I know is Ralph Lauren, "I feel like I got off easy. The kids really wanted to go to Wild Waves, but I convinced them they'd be better off just spending the day here and saving the money."

Saving money? *Kate?*

I struggle to keep a straight face. Kate Finch is loaded, one of the area's old money, and then she married Microsoft money—and not one of the little Microsoft millionaires who pop up everywhere, but Bill Finch, head of the games division—so the Finches are set for life.

"How did you convince the kids to do that?" Patti asks, leaning forward to get out of the sun's rays. Petite and brunette, Patti Wickham has endless energy, a vivacious personality, and the inability to take no for an answer.

"Bribed them." Kate sniffs. "Told them I'd give them the cost of the admission ticket and what I would have spent on gas if we could just come here. Worked like a charm."

Thank God for money.

Hate to admit it, but I'd do the exact same thing. Who'd want to make the drive from Bellevue to Federal Way—what is that, forty minutes each way?—and then spend hours worrying about the kids getting lost or abducted before driving back home in rush-hour traffic? No, Kate's right. Far better to take advantage of the Points Country Club pool before it closes for the summer.

My youngest daughter, Tori, who has just recently turned four, remembers I'm at the pool and comes running over to give me a wet hug. "Mama, Mama, Mama! I missed you!"

I hug and kiss her back. "Having fun?" I ask, rubbing her bare tummy.

She nods, her blond curly ponytails like piggy corkscrews in the sky. "I'm hungry."

"We're having dinner soon."

"Can I have some French fries?"

"We're going home in twenty minutes—"

"I want French fries."

"Honey."

"I'm starving." Her lower lip thrusts out. "*Starving.*"

Oh, why not? It's Friday. Labor Day weekend. I'm tired and don't want to get up. If French fries will keep her happy, let her have them. "Tell Brooke to go with you to order. She's right there, in the shallow end."

"'Kay."

"'Kay."

Tori runs off in her pink two-piece, her still chubby thighs making little slapping noises. "Is that bad?" I ask, looking at my friends. "French fries right before dinner?"

"It's the end of summer," Patti answers with a shrug.

Exactly. Kids will be back in school in just days, and it'll only get harder, what with homework and sports and meetings. Being a mother is a full-time job. I couldn't work outside the home even if I wanted to.

"Mom! *Mom! Taylor Young!*" My middle daughter, Brooke, shouts at me from the pool, resorting to using my name when I take too long to answer.

I put a finger to my lips, indicating she's too loud. "Come here if you want to talk to me," I stage-whisper. "Don't shout across the pool."

With a sigh, Brooke drags herself out of the pool and splashes her way to our table. "Did you tell Tori I had to go order her French fries?"

"She's hungry." I'm not in the mood to deal with Brooke's attitude now. For a middle child, Brooke is extremely strong-willed. "You can share her fries."

"I don't want fries."

"What do you want?"

"Ben and Jerry's ice-cream bar."

"No—"

"You said." She gives me her "I'm seven and going into first grade" look. "You did, Mom."

"What about a Popsicle?"

"Why does Tori get fries and I have to have a Popsicle? Why does she always get everything she wants? Because she's the baby? When I was her age I could order my own fries—"

"Fine. Get your ice cream." I give up. I just can't do this today. Not without another drink. "Help Tori and get what you want."

She flounces away, and I see the face she makes at me. I don't call her on it, though. I'm too tired, and as the parenting experts all say, you have to pick your battles. I want them to get good grades, so I suppose I've picked mine. Besides, they're not as lippy with Nathan. They wouldn't be. He doesn't put up with it, not like I do.

"Good meeting today, Taylor," Patti says as Brooke grabs Tori by the shoulder to haul her into line at the snack bar.

Patti is co-chair with me for the Points Elementary School auction, and we held our first meeting of the year this morning at Tully's on Points Drive.

I was worried about the meeting, but I needn't have been. Our committee of seven is amazing. We've got the best parents this year, the best moms hands down.

"I heard so many great ideas during our brainstorm session," I say, squeezing the rest of my lime wedge into my gin and tonic. "I have a hunch that this year's auction is going to just blow everyone out of the water."

And it will with what we're planning.

We've got some *spectacular* live-auction items already lined up, including a trip to Paris—first-class on Air France—and a week on Paul Allen's private yacht...in *Greece*, no less. I suppress a shiver of excitement. Corny as it is, I get goose bumps just thinking about it. "Patti, we can make this happen."

"We are making it happen," Patti corrects. She might be tiny and pretty, but she's a workhorse. "We've already got chairs for each committee, and everyone's experienced—"

"On the *ball*," I add.

"And as we know, experience makes all the difference."

Isn't that the truth? I just love Patti. We're on the same wavelength. It's not just that we're friends, but we've served on practically every school committee possible, and there's no way I would have tackled the school auction if Patti hadn't suggested we co-chair it together.

The school auction is Points Elementary's biggest annual fund-raiser. The phone-a-thon, walk-a-thon, and wrapping paper sales all bring in money, but they don't come close to generating the kind of money the auction does.

A strong auction nets a quarter million dollars. A fabulous auction nets a hundred thousand more.

Patti and I think we can hit four hundred thousand this year. At least that's our goal.

"Anything juicy happen at the meeting?" Kate asks, pulling up another white chair to stretch her legs on. Her legs are thin and tan, but they're always tan. Kate plays a lot of golf, and she and Bill routinely sneak off to Cabo.

Patti and I look at each other, try to think. There wasn't a lot of chitchat. We were pretty organized, and the auction meeting isn't the place for gossip. It would look bad. Unprofessional.

"I know something juicy," Monica chimes in eagerly.

I shoot Patti a "here we go again" look. Monica Tallman irritates me. She isn't poor, and she's not unattractive, but she's pathetically insecure and compensates for her feelings of inferiority by trying too hard.

The truth is, Monica needs a life. And she needs to stop copying my hairstyle.

Monica throws a hand into her hair, showing off her most recent highlights, which are nearly identical to mine. "The Wellsleys separated this summer," she announces loudly.

"The Wellsleys?" Kate gasps.

Monica nods, sips her wine cooler, pleased to be the bearer of horrible news. "Apparently Lucy was having an affair."

"*What?*" We all turn, shocked, to stare at Monica.

Patti frowns, a deep furrow between dark eyebrows. At least I know she doesn't do Botox. "I don't believe it," she says. "I can't believe it. Lucy would never do that. I've known her for years—"

"She's on the altar guild at St. Thomas," Kate adds.

Monica shrugs, lips curving. "Jesus loves a sinner."

Unbelievable. I drain the rest of my gin and tonic and immediately crave another. Too bad I can't send one of my girls for the drink, but they don't sell liquor to minors here.

Monica gives her wine cooler a twirl. "Pete's going after custody."

"*No.*" Now this is going too far. It really is. I know Lucy, too, and she's a great mother, a good wife, and it would destroy her not to have the kids. Kids need to be with their mother, too.

Well, unless their mother's a nutcase.

Like mine was.

"Pete thinks he's got a case." Monica sounds smug.

I hate it when she's so smug. I really think she needs to work out with her personal trainer a bit less and volunteer a lot more.

"You can't take children from their mother," I defend.
"Courts don't do that. I know it for a fact. Are you *sure*
she's having an affair?"

"I imagine it's over now that Pete found out, but Pete's
embarrassed. He paid for her lipo, the implants, the
tummy tuck, the eye job, the laser skin treatments, and
now he finds out it wasn't even for him? Fifty thousand
later he feels a little cheated."

Patti's outraged. "Lucy didn't even need the work.
She did it for him. He's never been happy, especially
with her."

I nod my head in agreement. Lucy was really attractive,
even before all the surgeries, and you know, you couldn't
tell she had that much work done because it was subtle.
We knew, because she'd told us, highly recommending her
plastic surgeon to us. And in the plastic surgeon's defense,
he was very, very good, and the only way I knew Lucy had
done her eyes (before we knew about the plastic surgery)
was because she just *looked* happier.

Apparently, she was happier.

She was getting laid by someone who wasn't her fat
husband.

That's not a nice thought, and I shouldn't think thoughts
like that, but Pete *is* big. He's gained at least thirty-five or
forty pounds in the last year or so. Maybe more. When I
saw him at brunch a couple of weeks ago, I almost didn't
recognize him. Nathan, who never notices anything like
that, leaned over to me and said Pete was a heart attack
waiting to happen.

Did that stop Pete from filling up his plate at the buffet? No. In fact, he went back for seconds and thirds—

piles of sausages, cream cheese Danishes, eggs Benedict, blueberry-and-sour-cream crepes, strawberries covered in whipped cream. You could hear his arteries hardening as he lumbered back to his table.

I can't blame Lucy if she didn't want to sleep with Pete. I wouldn't want to eat with him, much less do the down and dirty, but an affair...?

I wonder if the sex was good.

God, I hope it was, especially if she's going to lose the kids.

Shaking my empty glass, I listen to the ice cubes rattle. I want another drink but can't make myself move. Not just because I'm tired (which I am), but because if I go get another drink, it's more calories.

I weigh the pros and cons of another drink, knowing that I'm in good shape, but it's something I work at. Image is important, and the closer I get to forty (oh God), the more I care about my appearance. It's not enough to be fit. You've got to look young, and that's some serious time and money.

Lately, I've been thinking about getting some work done. Nathan says he loves me as I am, thinks I'm perfect, and doesn't want any artificial bits of me, but if it'd make me better, wouldn't the pain be worth it?

I tune back in and realize they're still discussing Lucy and Peter.

"—says he feels like she humiliated him in front of the whole community."

"Well, I didn't know until now," Kate says.

Me either, and my fingers itch to take my phone and call Nathan and see if he's heard. He used to be in Rotary with Pete. They were both in the Friday morning group that met for breakfast at the golf course across town.

Patti's frowning. "She's like us, a stay-at-home mom. So who could she be sleeping with? A UW student? A pool boy? Who?"

"Someone's husband." Monica looks like a cat. She's so pleased with herself that even her ears and eyes are smiling. "Apparently Pete has told the wife, too, and so that's two families wrecked."

Wrecked.

The very word conjures up horrible memories, and I suddenly touch my stomach, checking to see if it's flat. It is. I can feel my hipbones. Good.

The thing to know about me is that I hate fat almost as much as inefficiency, which is why I'm always hungry. I want to eat, but I don't. Nathan thinks I'm too thin, but he doesn't know what it's like always having women look at you, compare themselves with you.

"So where is Lucy now?" I ask.

"I think she's still in the house. Pete tried to kick her out—and she left for a couple nights—but she returned. Said she wouldn't leave, that it was her home, so Pete took the kids and left." Monica stretches, yawns. "God, it's a gorgeous day. Can you believe this beautiful weather?"

Kate and Patti exchange glances. "So where *are* Pete and the kids staying?" Kate persists.

"Their place in Sun River."

But they've got to be coming back soon. School starts on Tuesday, and Pete has to work.

Those poor kids. They must be so scared and confused.

I look around the pool for mine. My girls are just yummy.

I really shouldn't brag, but all three are beautiful—you can tell they're sisters, they all have the same golden skin, long honey blond hair, and big blue eyes. People are always stopping me, telling me the girls should be models. Maybe they will be. I don't know. We're just so busy as it is.

"Mom! *Mommy!*" Tori wails tragically at the edge of the grass, her big beach towel bunched at her feet, her paper plate upside down in her hands. "I dropped my French fries!"

I sigh. My friends chuckle. They know what it's like, they know what I'm going through. "Go get some more," I call to her. "They'll remember you at the counter."

"Come with me," she pleads.

"You can do it. Besides, Brooke's still over there. Catch her before she leaves. Tell her Mommy said to—" But before I can finish, Tori's running past me.

"Daddy!" she screams, rushing toward Nathan, who has just appeared at the pool.

Smiling, I watch Nathan swing Tori into his arms. We've been married eleven years, twelve on Valentine's Day, and I still think I married the sexiest, greatest man. It's not just because he has money, either. We're *happy*. We have a great life together. I'm lucky. Blessed. Really and truly.

Nathan's a wonderful father and an amazing provider. You should see our home—as a little girl, I dreamed of someday living in a house like ours—and our three little girls are gorgeous, and Nathan spoils all of us. Constantly. So much so that I feel a little guilty sometimes.

"There's my beautiful wife," Nathan says, walking toward us with Tori still in his arms.

Nathan is a vice president for Walt McKee's personal holding company, McKee being the founder of satellite communications, and that's the name of the game here in Seattle: technology. Bill Gates, Paul Allen, Steve Balmer, and Walt McKee are all practically neighbors and if not close friends, acquaintances. I'm not trying to name-drop, it's just that this is my world, the one I live in. I see the Gateses and McKees and the Balmers everywhere. Our kids play together on the same sports teams, dance at the same ballet studios, swim at the same country club pool, and sometimes attend the same school.

Nathan leans down and kisses me before turning to greet my friends. In the late afternoon light, he looks even more golden than usual, his brown hair sun streaked from swimming, surfing, and playing golf, his warm brown eyes almost bronze. I think he's more handsome now than when I first met him.

"Hello, honey," I answer, reaching out to capture his fingers. "How was your day?"

"Good." He shifts Tori to his other arm, oblivious that Tori's damp little body has left his shirt wet as well as stained with a splatter of ketchup.

Tipping my head back, I smile up at him. "I didn't think I'd see you for another hour or two."

"Escaped early." He puts Tori down, glances around. "I see Jemma. Where's Brooke?"

"Eating something somewhere," I answer.

He nods and pushes a hand through his thick hair—I'm so glad he still has his hair. "I'm going to get a beer. Anybody want anything?" he asks my friends. "Kate? Patti? Monica?"

They all shake their heads, but I can see their eyes feasting on him. I can't be jealous, either. Let's face it: Nathan's feastworthy. Six three, very broad shouldered, and with very nice abs. He works out daily, always has.

"How about you, darling girl?" he asks, turning to me. "Gin and tonic with lots of lime?"

I smile up at him. "I love you."

"I know you do."

I watch him walk away, thinking again that I'm so lucky that it sometimes makes me feel guilty, having so much. I certainly didn't have any of this growing up. Growing up...

Growing up was a nightmare.

I shudder, push the thought away, telling myself to focus on the here and now. Everything's good today. Everything's great. And it's not as if I just fell into this amazing life. I worked to get here, worked to make it happen. Now if only I could relax and enjoy it more.

"Oh, my God." Monica leans forward, grabs Kate's arm. "Lucy's here."

"What?"

Monica nods across the pool. "She's just walked in, and she's got the kids."

Our heads all swivel toward the pool entrance, and Monica's right. Lucy Wellsley is walking around the deep end of the pool, a beach tote bag over her shoulder, a stack of colorful striped towels in her arms as her three kids, two boys—fraternal twins—and a little girl, all run ahead.

"Should we invite her to join us?" Patti asks, glancing at me.

"I don't know." I mean, I feel bad for her, but infidelity? Affairs? This is bad. Really bad.

"She's brave," Kate mutters. "I wouldn't show my face here."

"Well, I don't think we have to worry about extending an invitation," Monica practically purrs. "Because Lucy's on her way here now."

Chapter Two

Lucy stands next to us, her arms still bundled around the thick stack of fuchsia and turquoise beach towels. "Hi," she says brightly. Too brightly.

I feel for her, I do, especially as she has to know that everyone's talking about her. God, what a nightmare. I'd rather die than be discussed by all the other moms.

Patti stands and gives Lucy and her towels a quick hug. "Hi, stranger," Patti says. "How are you?"

Lucy's gotten thin, and not attractively thin. Her eyes look huge in her face, the skin pulled too taut across her cheekbones and jaw, ruining the effect of all her expensive work. "Fine. What are you girls up to?"

"Not much," I answer, and really, my troubles are nothing compared with her drama.

"When did you get back in town?" Monica asks.

Lucy appears momentarily rattled. "I've been here." There's a pause. "Was I supposed to be out of town?"

Monica has the grace to blush. "Sorry. I was thinking of Pete." No one says anything, and Monica adds even more awkwardly, "He was the one out of town. He had the kids, right?"

Lucy's fingers tighten on the towels, her fingers and knuckles shades of purple and white. She swallows hard. "They've just come home." Her voice has dropped and deepened, reminding me of bruises. "It's been a month since I've had them. Or seen them."

I can't help glancing toward her kids, who are in the pool, jumping and diving as though they haven't a care in the world, and my chest tightens.

They're pretending. Kids do that so well. Pretend to forget. Pretend you don't feel. Pretend you don't remember.

We had to do that in our family, too, when my parents divorced. Act like you're just a kid and you don't hurt. Act like you feel nothing and all you care about is your TV show and your bowl of ice cream. Because you are only a kid, right, no real feelings developed yet. . . .

Nathan returns just then with our drinks and welcomes Lucy with a genuinely warm hug and hello. "Hello, Lucy," he says, handing me my drink before leaning down to kiss her cheek.

She stands stiffly, her body at an angle as though afraid to be caught touching him.

"Hi, Nate," she says, using her husband's nickname for Nathan. I'd never call Nathan "Nate" in a thousand years, but for some reason all Nathan's friends shorten it up.

"Sit down," he says, gesturing to our grouping.

Lucy looks at us, her eyes nearly as lavender blue as her voice. She's depressed. It's there, all over her face. I bite down, uncomfortable. "That's okay," she answers, sensing correctly that she's not wanted.

Nathan shakes his head. "No, I insist. Let me get you a chair."

"Nate, no. I can do it. Honestly. I'm not sick."

But Nathan's already gone to locate a chair, and once he's returned we all settle into a rather stilted conversation about the coming school year and the start of soccer, although Patti's boys have been playing football for nearly three weeks already.

Our kids appear periodically with requests for food and drink and ice cream, requests we all manage to resist to varying degrees.

"Hey, isn't our book club meeting soon?" Patti asks with a small self-satisfied stretch. It's nice just sitting here, feet up. The kids are happy. We're happy. There's nothing we have to do.

"One week," I answer. I'm hosting the September meeting. Haven't even thought about book club in a while. "I guess I better get reading."

"You haven't read *The Glass Castle* yet?" Monica's lips purse disapprovingly.

I flex my toes. "It just sounds so depressing. Another memoir about a dysfunctional family. I mean, haven't we read that already?"

"Book club isn't genre reading, Taylor. We're not just reading for the plot, but the beautiful prose."

"I don't find poverty, abusive parents, and alcoholism beautiful. No matter how one writes about it." I'm irritated now. I don't know why everyone gets such a vicarious thrill out of reading about childhood pain. I certainly don't. "I wish we'd pick some different books this year. More uplifting subjects, maybe even some nonfiction."

Monica rolls her eyes. "*The Glass Castle is* nonfiction."

Monica so annoys me. I can't even believe that we pretend to be friends. I don't know why she does it. I do it because she's Patti's childhood friend, and Patti says she has a good side, although I haven't seen it.

"The point is," I answer, folding my hands neatly in my lap, "that we've read lots of stuff like this before, and I thought we could maybe read something more uplifting."

Monica laughs. "Like what? *The Secret?*"

My face suddenly feels hot. She knows I've been reading the book and have it on DVD, too.

Thankfully, Nathan saves me from having to answer by placing his palm on my bare thigh. "We should head home." He lightly rubs down to my knee. "Feed the kids dinner."

Grateful, I cover his hand with mine and squeeze. I'm ready to go. My little gin-and-tonic buzz has abruptly worn off, and all I want to do is escape. Rising, I start gathering the girls' things, organizing the sundresses and sandals to expedite getting to the car. It's while I tuck suntan lotion and little-girl sunglasses into the tote bag that I hear Nathan invite Lucy over.

"We're just throwing some salmon steaks on the grill," Nathan is saying to Lucy, "and I can pick up some burgers on the way home for the kids. Why don't you join us?"

My head jerks up.

Lucy for dinner? Lucy to our house...*tonight?* After the day I've had? No, Nathan, no. I don't want company over. I'm not in the mood to entertain, and if I was in the mood, it wouldn't be Lucy.

"That's so nice of you, Nate," Lucy answers, "but I don't want to put you and Taylor out—"

"If it were an inconvenience, I wouldn't have offered." Nathan smiles down at her. "We haven't seen much of you lately, and it'd be good to catch up."

"Let me go talk to the kids. We were just going to hang out here until they kicked us out, but it'd be fun to go to your house. We...haven't seen much of our friends this summer."

She disappears, and I just stare at Nathan. He sees my expression. "What?" he demands quietly, hands outstretched.

My friends turn their heads away while I just keep staring at Nathan. I hear Patti start talking about the back-to-school brunch as Nathan crosses to my side.

"I thought she was one of your friends," he hisses.

"She is," I hiss back. But my tone isn't convincing. I don't know if Lucy and I are still friends. Angrily, I stuff Brooke's terrycloth jacket into the tote. "It's just been a busy day, Nathan—"

"They're going through a hard time. Just look at her, Taylor. She's obviously very lonely."

"I *know*, but I'm tired, Nathan, and you and I need some alone time. We need to destress, and having Lucy over isn't going to destress me at all."

"This isn't about your mom, is it?" he asks, a deep furrow creasing his brow. "Because this is completely different. Your mom ran off—"

"*Nathan.*" I cut him short, shoot a swift side glance at the others, but they've segued from the annual brunch to discussing Tuesday's Welcome Coffee at the school. I lift the tote bag, sling it over my shoulder. "Okay, yes, I'm concerned about having Lucy and the kids over. I'm concerned

about the fallout for our kids. If there's going to be sides
drawn, I'm not sure we should be taking Lucy's—"

"That's ridiculous."

"It's *not* ridiculous." My voice trembles, and I find myself
clenching my hands. He doesn't know what it's like to be
rejected by everyone. I do. I have. And I won't allow that
for my children. "I'm protecting our girls."

"You're *over*protective, Taylor."

"The house isn't even clean—"

"It's spotless. It's always spotless."

"There are dishes in the sink and toys scattered on the
lawn."

"I guarantee Lucy and the kids won't notice." His tone
softens. "Taylor, honey, they need us. Look at them."

Reluctantly, I glance past him to where Lucy is corral-
ling her kids, her arms wrapped around the shoulders of
her twins, her head bent as she talks to them. She seems to
be having quite the heart-to-heart with them. She's always
been a good mom. It would be tragic if she lost the kids.

"Fine…" I sigh. "We'll all have dinner."

The Points Country Club is only a mile or so from our
home in the tiny town of Yarrow Point. Yarrow Point is
just that, too, a point of land that juts into Lake Washington with loads of low waterfront footage. You pay to be
on the water, though. I honestly don't think you can get a
house on the water for less than four million right now. I
could be wrong, but I think even that price is low.

After taking a left off 92nd Avenue NE, I turn down
our small lane that dead-ends in front of our house, a
big sprawling shingle house highlighted by glossy white

paint, true divided light windows, a steep shingled roof, and long-columned covered porches.

Every time I pull up, I feel a stab of pride and possession. I love my house. I helped create this house. I was part of the design process—indeed, much of the design was my ideas and my pictures and drawings. During the eighteen months it took to build the house, I was on the job site nearly every day, checking on the progress, talking to the contractor, discussing details with the head carpenter. I loved every aspect of building the house, from the muddy lot in the Seattle December rain, to the immense framing stage, to walking through the space with the electrician, placing each of the outlets.

I was there when they poured the concrete and there the morning the drywalling began and again for the finish painting. It's hard not to fall in love with a house when it's not just a house but a part of you.

But it's not just the house I love. Everything is magical here—the garden and rose-covered trellises, the huge lawn that rolls right to the water with the sandy beach, private dock, and darling boathouse.

As I turn off the engine, the girls fling open their car doors and spill out in a flurry of terrycloth towels and bright sundresses, their sandals falling out and slapping the ground.

"Take everything to the laundry room," I tell the girls as I dash inside. "Don't leave one towel in the car. Everything goes in the laundry basket."

While the girls strip off their wet suits in the laundry room—a room that Patti once said was bigger than most people's living rooms—I get the miscellaneous dishes from the sink into the dishwasher, the white Carrara marble counters wiped off, and some of the pink roses from the garden in a vase of water before Lucy and her children arrive.

"How gorgeous," Lucy says, spotting my arrangement of lush roses on the counter. Keys still clutched in her palm, she bends to sniff them. She lifts her head, clearly disappointed. "No smell."

"No, they're not fragrant, but they look beautiful and they're far more disease-resistant than the older varieties."

Lucy gives the roses one more disappointed sniff. "Disease-resistant is important, especially in the Pacific Northwest with all of our black spot and mildew, but a rose just isn't a rose without its spicy scent."

Inexplicably annoyed with Lucy, I yank open the refrigerator with more force than necessary, rattling the jars in the door. "Would you like something to drink?"

She stares at me. "Are you drinking?"

From one of the many kitchen windows, I can see Nathan cross the back patio to light the barbecue. "I'll probably have a glass of wine."

"Wine sounds perfect."

"White or red?"

"Whatever you're having."

"Lucy, we have both." My irritation shows, and her expression crumples. I don't know who I dislike more right now—her or me. Taking a deep breath, I try again. "We're hopeless wine snobs, Luce, you know that. I have loads of wine, and I'm happy to open a bottle of red or white. Just tell me what you want—"

"Red." Her cheeks are a dark, dusty pink.

God, I hate myself. I'm such a bitch, and I don't want to be. I don't mean to be. My patience isn't what it once was. Maybe it's the long summer with the kids out of school. Maybe it's the start-up of the auction meetings. Maybe it's the tension I've begun to notice between Nathan and me. Nathan sometimes seems like a stranger. We used to agree on everything. Lately, we agree on almost nothing. Maybe that's marriage. Maybe that's life. Maybe he and I just need to get away for a few days and spend some real time together. "Shiraz, Merlot, Cab?"

"Shiraz or Merlot," Lucy answers quickly. "I love both."

I open an Australian Shiraz that Nathan favors. I pour three glasses, hand Lucy one, and pick up the other two. Lucy follows me outside.

I carry a glass of wine to Nathan. "You'll like this," I say, simultaneously giving him the glass and a kiss. We're good, I tell myself as he kisses me back. We're fine. No one agrees all the time. People have different points of view. Life's bound to have ups and downs.

"I have some groceries in the car," he says, taking a sip from his glass before putting the goblet on a table near the barbecue. "You girls relax. I've got dinner under control."

He heads for the garage to get the groceries he picked up on the way home. Lucy watches him go. "You're lucky," she says wistfully as he disappears into the garage.

"Because Nathan grocery shops?"

"Because he obviously still adores you."

I don't know what to say, because I am lucky. I've always been the first to admit it. I knew when I met Nathan that big things would happen. I saw right away that he had the potential for something big and knew it was my job to bring it out in him. It's not that I didn't believe in me. I just realized my skills would be best put to use supporting him. To drawing out his potential and helping however I could best help, whether it's opening doors or keeping them open.

Good wives are a tremendous asset.

You shouldn't ever underestimate the power a good wife brings to not just marriage, but careers and life in general.

When I look at couples who've divorced, you see what they've lost. Not just materially, but socially. Their bank account has taken a hit, but more important, so has their clout and respect.

Which brings me back to Lucy, but Lucy's turned to face Lake Washington, the Seattle skyline, and the Olympic mountain range. During summer, the sun sets on the far right corner of the mountain range, giving us the most amazing red-and-hot-pink sunsets on the lake.

"It's beautiful here in summer, isn't it?" she says on a sigh.

"My favorite time of the year."

She nods agreement. "I always wanted to be on the water. And you have such a nice dock, too. Perfect for your boat."

"It does make it convenient," I agree, lifting a hand to shade my eyes. The boat is Nathan's toy. He likes to go out on the lake a few times a week during the summer, just cruise around with a great bottle of wine. He doesn't go out in the boat as much as he used to, though. In fact, lately he's started to talk about selling the boat, something I don't understand, as Nathan loves boating almost as much as he loves golfing.

Turning, I catch Lucy watching Nathan through the kitchen window where he's standing at the sink, rinsing something. Lucy's expression is wistful. So wistful that for a moment I wonder if it's Nathan she's been sleeping with.

Immediately I push the horrifying thought out of my head. Don't want to think like that. Can't think like that. Nathan wouldn't have an affair. He just wouldn't. I know him too well.

"Let's see what the kids are doing," I say, injecting cheer into my voice as I lead Lucy into the house and up the curving staircase in the hall.

The hour before dinner passes, and then we're all sitting at the table on the terrace, enjoying our meal beneath strings of twinkly lights. After dessert, the kids dash off, disappearing upstairs into the big bonus room again. Nathan lingers for a bit before excusing himself, leaving just Lucy and me at the table.

It's a quiet night on the lake, and silence envelops the table. I get the sense that Lucy wants to open up, have a real talk, but I won't let it happen. I'm sure Lucy's confused and fearful and probably in some pain, but it's not something I can deal with. My mother's affair destroyed our family and killed the relationship I had with her.

"You're angry with me," Lucy says in a small voice, her words so faint that they're nearly swallowed by the night.

I open my mouth to disagree but end up saying nothing.

"It wasn't what Peter's telling everyone. There wasn't this big affair. It was one night. One mistake. A terrible mistake."

It feels as though she's dragging her fingernails down a chalkboard. My skin crawls. I want to get up, walk away. "What were you thinking?"

For a moment, I don't think she's going to answer, and then she whispers, "I thought he loved me."

I'm silent, my throat thick, my chest aching.

"I just wanted to be loved again," she adds even more softly.

"Now you've lost everything," I blurt out.

"Hopefully not my friends."

"Hopefully," I echo after a moment.

She nods and a minute later plants her hands on the tablecloth and pushes to her feet. "It's late. I should get the kids home and into bed."

"Thank you for coming," I say stiltedly as I rise.

"Thank you for having me," she answers just as stiltedly.

I stand at the door as she drives away and then slowly head into the kitchen, where Nathan's tackling the dishes.

"She seemed like she had fun," he says, scraping the appetizer plate and putting it in the dishwasher.

He has no clue. And I can't bear to clue him in.

I met Lucy seven years ago at First Pres's preschool Christmas pageant. We'd both been pregnant, and we both had a four-year-old wise man—in my case, my daughter Jemma—bearing gifts for the infant king.

"The kids did have a good time, didn't they?" I answer, dumping what's left of my wine into the sink. "So tomorrow what are our plans?" I ask, changing the subject. "Are we still going boating with the Prices, and if not, can we sneak away to Vashon?"

Nathan picks up his glass and takes a drink. "I'd like to play a round of golf. Don made us a ten a.m. tee time."

"We're not going to do anything as a family?"

"We do things as a family all the time."

I press my lips disapprovingly.

"Take the girls to the pool," he says. "Or down to the beach. You know how much Tori loves it."

"I also know there's something in the lake water that gives Jemma hives, so no." I give him a dark look. "We should have gone to Vashon for the weekend. Anything but stay here. I need to get away."

"Honey, you're never home. You're either at the Bellevue Club or the Seattle Tennis Club—"

"You like me working out! You want me in great shape. You've said so yourself."

He sighs, exhaling slowly. "Can I just play golf, Taylor? Can I please do this without fighting? I don't ask a lot. I really don't."

"Go. This isn't jail. You're not my prisoner." Then, realizing things are just too tense, I go to him, wrap my arms around him, and kiss him on the lips. "You're not my prisoner. Yet." And smiling, I kiss him again.

Tension broken, Nathan kisses my forehead. "You and the girls go have fun tomorrow. Have a girls' day. Hit your Asian nail place and have manicures, pedicures, and lunch. The girls love that."

Nathan sees the light in my eyes. "But no shopping," he adds. "The girls have enough. Deal?"

"One outfit?"

"Taylor."

"A cheapie outfit?"

"Baby, you wouldn't know cheapie if it hit you between the eyes."

I grin. "You like my good taste."

"I like being able to pay the bills, too."

I reach for him, wrap my arms around his lean waist. "Fine. Cheapie nails and cheapie outfit." My hands slide down to his still amazing butt. "How about we leave the dishes until morning?"

An eyebrow quirks. "You're not too tired?"

"Not if you turn off the water right now."

"What about the kids?"

"That's never stopped us before."

Making love with Nathan is as good now as it was sixteen years ago when we slept together for the first time. Nathan was always good in bed. He was a USC quarterback after all, and he'd dated a lot of women before he ever met me. Although I wasn't crazy about all the women chasing him, I secretly liked that he was experienced. He knew how to please me. He's always pleased me. Sometimes I worry that I enjoy sex more than I should. I know a lot of my friends don't have sex with their husbands anymore. Lucy being a case in point.

"Are you awake?" Nathan asks, running his hand down my back.

"Mmmm," I answer sleepily, shifting in his arms, putting a little more space between our warm, sticky bodies. I love making love. I'm just not as good at cuddling afterward. It's hard for me to sleep when Nathan holds me too close.

He's still stroking my back. "We need to talk."

I open my eyes, stare at the bedroom wall and the window with the taupe shades drawn against the night. "About what?" I ask, immediately wondering again if it was Nathan Lucy was sleeping with.

"Our finances."

A wave of relief rushes over me, and I almost laugh. "What about our finances?"

"We're spending too much money." He's found the small hollows in my lower back, and he traces them lightly over and over. "We're living way above our means."

My relief is replaced by a sharp twinge of guilt. He's seen my credit card statements, then. I was hoping to hide them for another week or so. "I know. I'm sorry."

"We're killing ourselves, Taylor."

My guilt deepens, the twinge turning to a flood of shame. I've had trouble with spending for years. I'm compulsive about it. I buy too much and then hide the bags in my closet, vowing to return everything, and sometimes I do and other times I just go buy some more. I don't even like half the stuff I buy. "I'll stop. I promise."

He doesn't say anything, and my insides churn. Nathan knows me better than anyone. Nathan knows the truth. I might look great on the outside, but on the inside I'm a disaster. Obsessive-compulsive, control freak. I shop too much. Eat too much. Work too much. Work out too much. "Nathan," I whisper.

I can feel his shrug.

"Nathan, what's wrong?"

He takes a long time to answer. Finally: "I'm worried."

"About what?" I ask in a small voice.

His hand stills on my back. "Everything."

"You're just tired, Nathan. You're working too hard. This is why I wanted to get away. You need a break. You deserve a vacation." But even as I talk, I can feel him pulling away, physically, emotionally. After a bit I run out of words, and I lie next to him in the dark, wondering why I can't comfort him. Wondering what's happening to us.

"I have full confidence in you," I say after a moment, trying again. "Everything's going to be all right."

He says nothing.

I nestle closer, curve my body around his, and hold him as tightly as I can. "It is, Nathan."

Several minutes pass, and he doesn't relax. Finally, he rolls away from me to climb from bed. I watch as he walks to the window, where he lifts one blind. The pale moonlight illuminates his broad shoulders and lean, naked torso. I usually love the sight of him naked, but tonight it fills me with fear. What if I lose him?

"What are you doing?" I ask as he steps into a pair of boxers.

"I'm going downstairs."

"Why?"

"I'm not sleepy."

"What will you do?"

"Read. Work."

I sit higher up in bed. "It's almost one-thirty."

"I know, but I won't be able to sleep." Then he leaves.

Chapter Three

After Nathan goes downstairs, I lie in bed and practice breathing, the way I learned in yoga. But it's hard to calm myself. My chest squeezes tight. I'm worried, too. Nathan's different. He's changing. We're changing.

Breathe, I tell myself. Just concentrate on your breathing.

But even as I breathe in and out, I feel the panic build inside of me. I'm too damn busy lately. I'm juggling too many balls. I shouldn't have agreed to co-chair the school auction this year. I barely got through last year in one piece, and last year I was only the silent auction procurer chair.

It's going to be fine, I repeat. Nathan and I have just hit a little rough patch. That's normal, it happens to all couples, even couples like us.

Maybe that's why I'm panicking.

Nathan and I never used to have problems. Nathan has been my godsend.

Life before Nathan was a bitch. I might look like All That now, but it's something I've worked for, something I still work for, and I can't imagine my life without him.

Truthfully, I never thought my life would turn out like this. Growing up was a nightmare—you don't want to know all the sordid details—but despite the disaster at home, I excelled in school.

I did the whole cheerleader/homecoming court/student body thing in high school before spending four years as an Alpha Beta Pi at USC.

I first met Nathan (Nathan Charles Young III) while we were both undergrads when we were set up for a fraternity/sorority dance. I was a sophomore and he was a fifth-year senior, as he'd redshirted for the football team. Move ahead sixteen years and you have us today living in our lovely home in the Pacific Northwest with three gorgeous girls—ten-year-old Jemma, seven-year-old Brooke, and four-year-old Tori.

Despite once having an interesting career in PR and communications, I'm now a full-time mom by choice. Nathan and I agreed from the beginning that I'd stay home with the children. He was making great money in his career, and we didn't want our children raised by anyone else.

I wanted to be the kind of mother my own mother couldn't, or wouldn't, be. Room mom, PTA president, office volunteer. Of course, there are days when I long for some peace and a less structured life, but for the most part I have no regrets. I like the power. I want the power. And don't think being a stay-at-home mom isn't powerful.

I can bring a school board to its knees. I heard via the grapevine that I once made a principal cry. But I've never been malicious. I'm in this not for me, but for my children. I want the best for my children. I want to help them get ahead. I want them to have every opportunity.

The only drawback?

Our lives are really jam-packed. Sometimes too stressful. But then I look at the great friends we have, and our lifestyle—Christmas at Sun Valley, February at St. Barts, and Easter usually in Hawaii, while summer vacations we head to Jackson Hole.

I don't think we ever meant to travel this much, but it's what our group does, and the kids love being with our friends, and it's hard staying home when you know what a fantastic time everyone else is having. Which reminds me. We were supposed to be gone this weekend, escaping for the three-day weekend to Vashon.

Sighing, I reluctantly put thoughts of relaxing on Vashon Island out of my mind. We're here this weekend. We might as well make the most of it.

Nathan's up and gone by the time I come downstairs in the morning. I heard him shower earlier—he must have already hit the gym—and he left a note in the kitchen saying he's gone to have breakfast at the country club with the guys before they tee off.

With Nathan gone, I let the girls lounge in their pajamas until ten, when I insist they finally turn off the TV and computer games and get dressed if they want to go have lunch at Bellevue Square and do a little shopping.

Jemma immediately begs to go to the Cheesecake Factory, while Tori pleads for Red Robin. "It'll probably be the Nordstrom café," I say.

They groan.

"What's wrong with the café?"

"Nothing," Jemma answers unhappily, "but we always eat there, and it's boring. I want to go somewhere fun."

"Yeah, fun," Tori adds, and Brooke nods.

"We'll see," I answer evasively, thinking I'm not about to lug our shopping bags throughout the mall. The café is close and convenient, and I can charge our lunch on my Nordstrom's card.

On the way to the mall, we swing by the school so Jemma can check the class lists one more time before school starts on Tuesday. She heard that she's got Eva Zinsser in her class again, and she wants to see for herself.

I park my Lexus SUV in front of the school, and the girls scramble from the car. Stepping out of the car, I pray that Paige is wrong. I can't bear another year with the Zinssers. Jemma feels the same way. Last year was a bear, a real struggle, and I refuse to go through another school year like that.

"Paige was right," Jemma shouts, standing in front of the window and scanning the names. "We're in the same class again." She turns around and groans. "Why, Mom? Why me?"

"It'll be fine," I say unconvincingly, hating that there are now two strikes against the new school year.

First, Jemma's been assigned to Mrs. Osborne's class—something I'm just dreading, as it's rumored that Mrs. Osborne piles on the homework, although not as much as Mrs. Shipley last year. Nathan might say it's good for the girls to have hard teachers, but he isn't the one who helps with homework every night, and he's not the one devoting hours to overseeing the reports and projects, either.

I'd been hoping Jemma would get Miss Tanzey for fifth grade. Miss Tanzey arrived midyear last year, replacing Mrs. Jenkins, who was going out on maternity leave, and everyone who had Miss Tanzey just loved her. Miss Tanzey didn't assign homework during winter or spring break—not like Mrs. Osborne—and she was, by all accounts, a much easier grader, which would be so much better for Jemma, who has begun struggling in school.

It's not that Jemma's not bright enough, but she's just not motivated, and last year her grades really dropped, which sent Nathan through the roof. He took Jemma's cell phone away from her and grounded her from the computer for nearly a month, but Jemma just sulked and then used Annika's phone behind her father's back.

I vowed this year would be different. I vowed that we'd start school on a more positive note, but it's hard to be as optimistic knowing that we've got to deal with the bizarre-o Zinssers again.

"Come on, girls, let's go shopping."

The rest of the weekend passes in a blur of picnics, barbecues, and swimming dates at the lake and the country club pool. Kate and Bill have us over for dinner Saturday night. Patti and Donald have a pre–Labor Day party Sunday night. Then some people I don't know well invited us to a big shindig Monday afternoon, and I wouldn't have gone except that Gary Locke, the former governor of Washington, was going to be there with his wife and children.

By Monday night, I'm so tired of small talk and smiling that it's a relief to put the kids to bed.

In our bed, Nathan reaches for me in the dark and I'm about to refuse, citing extreme exhaustion, but then

I remember our odd night Friday night and the tension over money. I don't want tension over sex.

I give in to his kiss. He is such a good kisser, and as his body sinks into mine, I know that at least I'll climax. I always do. Nathan wouldn't have it any other way.

The morning arrives along with tears and tantrums. Tori doesn't want her big sisters going off to school and leaving her alone. "But you're not alone," Brooke tells her imperiously. "You'll be with Annika." Which of course leads to more tears.

Brooke's upset because her hair isn't holding a curl.

Jemma's upset because her hair won't stay straight.

I'm upset because I've got to get ready, too, and I can't get dressed or do my hair with everyone screaming in every upstairs bedroom.

But finally by seven forty-five we make it to the car. I'm driving the girls this morning instead of having them take the bus so I can formally introduce myself to Brooke's and Jemma's teachers. It's something I've done every year since Jemma started kindergarten, and now it's a tradition. I always take a little welcoming gift, too. It just helps start the year off on the right foot.

But today I also have the PTA's Welcome Coffee, and I stack my purse on top of my binder in the backseat of the Lexus. The PTA board puts on the Welcome Coffee for all the parents every year on the first day of school, but usually only a dozen or so women attend. I've never understood why more moms don't attend. It's an ideal chance to get to know the PTA board and to find out more about this year's activities and available volunteer positions.

I glance at my watch, wondering where Annika is, even as I recall how several years ago I was responsible for filling all the school's volunteer positions. *That* was a job. You'd think more moms would want to be involved. You'd think they'd care.

The girls are in the car, howling that we're going to be late. I'm standing between the garage and kitchen doors, trying not to scream, and suddenly Annika arrives, sweeping into the house in a flurry of apologies. Instead of jumping on the breakfast dishes, she scoops up Tori and sits on the couch with her to watch *Dora*. Tori's getting a little old for *Dora the Explorer*, and the kitchen needs attention, but I bite my tongue. I just want to get out of the house at this point, and time is of the essence.

By the time we reach Points Elementary, the parking lot is a zoo. Everyone has come today, and I squeeze in next to another car, hoping I'm not so close that I'll get the Lexus's paint chipped. I'm proud of my Lexus. I've had it two years, and it still looks brand new.

We hustle across the parking lot and enter one of the outside buildings where the second-grade classes are held. Brooke has one of the new teachers, a Miss Johnson, and from what I understand, Miss Johnson is young and inexperienced. I believe this is her first year teaching, although I don't know why the school district would hire such a green teacher for Points Elementary. Living in Yarrow Point, we pay a fortune in property taxes. The girls deserve a great education, and I'm determined they'll get that education. That's one reason I volunteer as much as I do, and of course I'm volunteering as a room parent for Jemma's and Brooke's classes again.

I've already e-mailed both teachers, letting them know I'm available and interested in helping them out. I do this every year in August as soon as the class rosters are posted, and it works. Teachers have a lot to deal with at the beginning of the year, and they shouldn't have to worry about managing all the parent volunteers.

In my e-mail (I saved it in my Outlook box a couple of years ago so it's easy to resend every summer), I tell the teacher a little about myself and explain why I'm so qualified.

First, I'm experienced. I've done this every year since Jemma started kindergarten, and I know what needs to be done.

Second, I'm a full-time mom, and I've dedicated myself completely to my kids' future.

Third, I'm committed. When I say I'll do something, I do it.

Fourth, I'm good. Every class that has me as head room parent has a great year, guaranteed. They have the best parties, the best field trips, the best class projects for the school auction. But I don't help just with the fun stuff. I'm there in the classroom helping out, too. I read with the children, I photocopy handouts, I sort homework, I help with bulletin boards.

In the past, teachers have always been so grateful for my assistance (well, except for Mr. Smythe, the PE teacher, but he's not a normal teacher, he's a retired marine), and I love making a difference in my children's education.

It's important that I know what they're learning, whom they're playing with, what's going on at school. Nathan once said I should have become a teacher myself and brought home a paycheck since I spend so much time at school, but that's just him teasing me. He's proud of me, proud of all I do.

In Brooke's first-grade class, I greet Miss Johnson, a cute young blond teacher who looks just like what she is, a corn-fed midwesterner. She lights up on hearing my name.

"Thank you so much for your e-mail," she says warmly. "That was wonderful, and I definitely welcome all the help I can get."

She's going to be my kind of teacher. "You've got my e-mail and phone number. Call me if you need anything this week."

I wave farewell, leave a small welcome gift on her desk, and walk with Jemma to her class. The first bell has already rung, and the second bell will ring any second.

I spot Mrs. Osborne at the front of the class, and it's not until I'm hurrying forward that I see she's talking to another mother, one with long loose dark brown hair, wearing jeans and flip-flops and a faded black T-shirt. Marta Zinsser.

I stiffen, my spine straightening as I glance around the room until my gaze settles on a thin girl with thick black hair cut in a chic bob, but the stylish cut does little to hide the mouth that looks too big for her face.

"Her hair's longer," I say to Jemma.

"It's a good cut," Jemma answers grudgingly.

"Kind of Katie Holmes Cruise–like."

I give Jemma a quick kiss good-bye. "I'm just going to say hello to Mrs. Osborne and then I'm out of here. Have a good day."

Marta leaves as I approach. She doesn't look at me. She's probably intimidated by me. She shouldn't be, although I know some of the other women are. I can't help that Nathan's so successful.

The second bell rings, and before I can introduce myself to Mrs. Osborne, she's politely but firmly calling the class to order. I hate interrupting her, so I hurriedly tell her my name, although it doesn't seem to spark the recognition I'd hoped. I let her know what I said in my e-mail, that I'd be happy to be head room mother and do whatever I could to make her year the most successful it can be.

Mrs. Osborne thanks me, and I feel reassured. For a moment, I'd almost gotten the impression that I'd annoyed her somehow, but as I leave, I drop the gift I bought her—a Starbucks drink card—on her desk and head out. It's going to be a good year, I tell myself, far better than last year.

With that thought in mind, I retrieve my phone and dial Nathan's cell. He answers right away. "Hi, hon," I say, "girls are settled and I'm just entering the school gym for the Welcome Coffee, and then I'm off to the gym to work out."

"Girls okay? Teachers seem nice?"

"Everything seems great. I met both teachers. I think it's going to be a really good year."

"That's great. Can't wait to hear all about it at dinner."

"All right, sweetheart, have a good day."

"You too."

I make a kiss sound into the phone and hang up. I really am very lucky.

* * *

The Welcome Coffee is in full swing when I enter the school gym. Laura and Joan, mothers of second-grade daughters, wave as I walk in. I smile back and move through the small throng until I find Patti, who happens to be standing with Kate and Monica.

"That's a cute shirt, Taylor," Kate says by way of greeting.

"Thank you," I answer, leaning forward to give everybody the customary kiss-kiss.

Monica looks me up and down. "Isn't it the one you got at the Tory Burch trunk show last spring at Nordstrom's?"

I nod, my hair falling forward to brush my cheek. "I splurged that day, but God, her clothes were gorgeous. I couldn't help it."

"Well, you look positively gorgeous in the tunic," Monica says almost enviously. "You're so slim, you can wear everything."

"Look who's talking," Patti flashes. "You're so thin, Monica, you're about to disappear. If you lost any more weight, you wouldn't even be here."

Monica shakes her head even as she tries to hide her pleased smile. Being too skinny is one of the best compliments you can be paid. "Speaking of down-to-earth," Monica says, changing the subject as she likes to do, "I heard that Martha Stewart is about to become a neighbor. She's apparently buying a house in Medina."

"Not just a house," Patti corrects, "three. They're going to tear them down and build a big compound, kind of like what Gates did."

"You can't build megahouses anymore," Kate replies firmly. "Medina's passed a number of ordinances since Gates's house went up."

"I think they're able to get around the building code, as it's a megaestate, not a megahouse. Martha wanted to leave plenty of open land for her gardens."

My eyebrows lift. I hadn't heard anything about Martha maybe moving to Medina until now. "Is she moving here with her daughter? Or a boyfriend?"

"Her daughter is grown, and her 'best' friend already lives here. Charles Simonyi."

"Charles who?" I ask.

Monica sighs with exaggerated patience. "*Simonyi*. He was born in Hungary and became a billionaire after helping design Microsoft Word and Excel."

Patti touches my arm. "He's the one who spent two weeks in space with the Russian astronauts."

I grin at Patti. "Don't they call them cosmonauts in Russia?"

Kate frowns. As her husband is a mucky-muck at Microsoft, she often knows the inside scoop before most people. "I didn't know he and Martha were that close."

"Apparently they're *very* close," Monica adds in her precise know-it-all voice. "They're building a house together."

Kate lifts a hand to slow the zinging conversation. "I don't think they're building a house together. I think Martha's just looking for a change of venue. After all her problems on the East Coast, she might be ready to start over, you know?"

We're nodding sympathetically when Patti suddenly

leans forward and whispers, "Hey. Looks like we've got a new daddy among us."

"Where?" Monica demands, head swiveling around rather like Linda Blair in *The Exorcist*.

"By the cafeteria door," Patti answers. "Six feet, short dark hair, good build. He's either a French doctor or a cyclist."

Monica stares at him. She has no shame. "God, he's gorgeous."

"You think so?" I ask, trying to see the gorgeousness in the new dad. He's too narrow, too lean, for my taste, but Patti's right, he does have the hard, sinewy look of a long-distance runner or a cyclist.

Monica practically licks her lips. "Yes. Yummy."

"I wonder what he does," I say.

"I'll go find out." And Monica's off, flipping her hair as she stalks toward him.

While Monica's off grilling the new dad, Kate, Patti, and I make an effort to mingle. I'm not a big fan of mingling. All that chitchat is exhausting, but the point of the Welcome Coffee is to make new and returning families feel welcome, so that's what I do. Mingle, shake hands, kiss cheeks, and effusively greet. Patti and I work the room in opposite directions so we're near each other as we come full circle. I have no one left to greet, but Patti is still talking to a very petite, very thin brunette in a gray dress and black knee-high boots.

Patti waves me over. "Come meet Amelia," she says. "They transferred into Points this year, and she'll have a kindergartner here next year. Her daughter and Tori might be in the same class."

"Wonderful," I say. "Where did you move from?"

"Not far. Just the Plateau. We decided we couldn't handle the traffic any longer." She smiles a very small smile. "And you? Are you a native Washingtonian?"

"No. I'm a California girl, although I've lived here thirteen years now."

Amelia's expression is curious. "Where did you go to school?"

"USC."

"No way. So did I."

"Were you in a sorority?" I ask.

"For a year," she answers, nose scrunching, "but then I dropped out. Hated it. So fake." She pauses. "Were you?"

"Yes."

"Ah."

Patti feels the sudden awkwardness, too, and she rushes to fill the silence. "Amelia's an actress."

I smile stiffly. "How did you get up here, then?"

"My husband was offered a job here, and we thought it'd be good for the family to get out of L.A. It's hard to raise children there, hard to be normal when everyone's trying to make it in the industry."

I nod as if this is every woman's problem. "Where does your husband work?"

"For the McKee family."

My ears perk up. "Mine does, too."

"Who is your husband?"

"Nathan Young."

Amelia frowns, thinks, shakes her head. "I've never heard of him."

"He works for the holding company." I hesitate and then delicately drop in, "He's a vice president."

Amelia's brow furrows more deeply. "So is mine. I'm surprised I haven't heard of him. I'll have to ask Christopher."

There's something about her tone that makes me feel defensive. I smile more broadly, do my best to nod graciously. "I'll ask Nathan about Christopher." And then, turning away, I spy Monica. She's heading toward us and walking like a lioness who has just taken down a kill. Patti and I meet her halfway across the room.

"His name is Leon," Monica announces coolly. "His wife's a neurosurgeon, and he's Mr. Mommy now. They moved from Philadelphia, he's an avid cyclist and marathoner, although he's recently discovered yoga. Best of all, he's going to co-chair Fun Day with me this year."

Patti arches her eyebrows. "Wow. Impressive. That's quick work."

Monica laughs, giving her once dark hair that's now full of honey highlights another small toss. "It's not every day we get new blood in the PTA. What should I have done? Let him get away?"

The first week of school goes as smoothly as a new school year can. The girls don't have too much homework, just the usual getting-to-know-you essay assignment stuff. I help Brooke with hers—she can't really write yet—and stay on Jemma until she gets four paragraphs completed. Jemma's not much of a writer, and it's always a struggle to convince her that a paragraph must be three sentences long.

On Thursday, I'm in the school office making photocopies for the next auction committee meeting when I happen across a sheet of paper with the volunteers for each class this year.

I skim the sheet—Taylor Young, head room mom for Miss Johnson's second-grade class—and then I check to see who will be working with me in Mrs. Osborne's class. But when I check Mrs. Osborne's class, it's not my name there.

I can't believe what I'm seeing, and for a moment, I think I have it wrong:

"Fifth Grade, Mrs. Osborne, Head Room Mom, Marta Zinsser."

Marta Zinsser?

I'm beyond shocked. That can't be right. I must have read the wrong class or the wrong name. I check again, but no, it still reads, "Fifth Grade, Mrs. Osborne, Head Room Mom, Marta Zinsser."

Dropping the paper on the corner table, I stand there stupefied. Marta Zinsser is going to be the head room mom for Jemma's class?

You've *got* to be kidding.

Marta Zinsser doesn't even know where Yarrow Points Elementary cafeteria is. How can she be not just a room mom, but head room mom?

That's like making SpongeBob SquarePants president of the United States.

Marta isn't just seriously unqualified, she's *weird*. She makes me feel weird, as though there's something wrong with me and I just don't know it. But the fact is, she's the one who doesn't fit in. She's the one who wears totally inappropriate clothes for a woman her age. She wears her hair down to her butt. She likes stiletto heels and/or clogs, depending on her outfit. It's so obvious she doesn't care what others think of her, and she doesn't even try to get along with others. Marta comes late to school meetings, leaves early, sits at the back, and although she doesn't exactly sit there filing her nails, she does look damn bored.

Oh. Just thinking about her makes me crazy. *She* makes me crazy.

I start the copy machine and then head to the front where the secretaries sit poised to deal with tardies and lunches and the principal's requests.

"Alice," I say, approaching Alice Dunlop, the secretary with most seniority, "I saw the room parent assignment sheet—"

"Oh, I'm sorry, Taylor, that's not public yet."

Well, good, if it's not public yet, it's not too late to make some changes. I'm already feeling better about things. I lean on the counter, smile hopefully. "I think there was a typo."

"Really?" Alice looks up at me, brows furrowed. We've worked together over the years and have an excellent relationship.

"It has what I'm thinking is a typo. Marta Zinsser, head room mom, fifth grade?"

Alice's expression doesn't change. "No, that's correct."

"Really?" I'm back to just being stunned. I can't fathom how this has happened. What did Marta do, waltz into Mrs. Osborne's class and announce she wanted to be in charge? I honestly don't understand. "Does she know?"

"I'm calling all the new room moms today."

"Yes, but—"

"I believe you're the head room parent for Miss Johnson's class. She requested you."

"And Mrs. Osborne didn't?"

Mrs. Dunlop, being the model of professional diplomacy, reveals nothing. "As you know, it's important to involve as many parents as we can."

"Yes, but *who* made the decision to choose Marta Zinsser instead of me?"

Alice Dunlop smiles kindly. "I really don't know, Taylor. I wasn't involved in the selection process. And I know you need your copies. Were you able to make them, or did the machine jam again?"

Chapter Four

Later that afternoon, I'm sitting at the dining room table giving Brooke her spelling words, but I'm unable to concentrate.

I'm still angry about Marta being chosen as head room mom for Mrs. Osborne's class. It's not just that I'm more qualified and better suited to the job, but the decision is also unfair.

Marta hasn't even paid her dues. She never donates to the auction, doesn't attend, doesn't spend, doesn't support the school financially the way Nathan and I do.

I don't see how Marta can just waltz in at the last minute and announce that she'd like to be a head room mom, and presto, that's that.

I work hard at the school. I read with the kids who need support. I put in hours in the computer lab when there aren't enough parents willing to volunteer. I do recess duty and supervise at lunch. Movie night? I organize. Big class project? I implement.

"What's the next word, Mom?"

It's not that I'm looking for a blue ribbon or a tangible reward, but it doesn't seem right that someone who has never cared enough to sign up to bring anything but paper goods for the class party should now be the mom in charge of everything.

"Mommy."

I look up. Brooke's chewing on the ends of her ponytail. "Is that all?" she asks. "Only six words?"

Glancing back down, I see there are at least fourteen more. "No. Lots more."

She groans, her elbow sliding across the table. "I hate spelling!"

Not as much as I'm going to hate working with Marta Zinsser.

It's nine-thirty and the girls are in bed, hopefully asleep. I'm in the bathroom, washing my face with my special antioxidant foam wash and then applying the antiaging serum from collarbones to hairline and finally smoothing on a layer of moisturizer. But even as I spread the lotions, I find I can't stop thinking about Marta. I know it's shallow and unkind, but I don't want her on my auction committee, and I don't want her to be head room mom.

Leaving the bathroom mirror, I walk into the bedroom, where Nathan's climbing into bed. "I don't know what to do about her, Nathan, but she's making me crazy—"

"Because you're letting her make you crazy," he answers, reaching for the hardcover book on his bedside table and turning on his reading light. "You don't even know Marta very well. She might be a very nice person."

I glare glumly at Nathan. He's too nice, especially when it comes to women. "Have you seen the way she dresses?" I don't even wait for him to answer. "She wears smocks,

Nathan. Full-on smocks and painted clogs, and have you seen her hair?"

Nathan gives me an apologetic look over the top of his book. He loves reading in bed. He does this every night and has since we were first married. "I actually don't have any idea who we're talking about."

"I know. Because if you did, you'd see why I can't have her on the auction committee—"

"Why would she be on the auction committee if she's just head room mom?"

"Because she'll be responsible for the fifth-grade class project. And that means she'll be working with me. And I can't. I can't work with her, not this closely, not talking every day."

"Then don't talk every day."

I sit on the edge of the bed next to him. "I *have* to communicate."

"Use e-mail," he answers, picking up his book again.

I stare at the spine of his book. Another nonfiction historical battle book. Why Nathan loves reading about war is beyond me. "Isn't that the book you were reading last Christmas in Sun Valley?"

"It's the sequel."

"Oh." I return to the bathroom, where I study my face and neck in the mirror. Small, fine lines at my eyes, a deeper line between my eyebrows, and creases in my forehead. Probably time to get more Botox. Last year I did it only twice, but this year I might need it more. "Speaking of Sun Valley, if we're going this year, we should make our reservations. The airfare only goes up the closer we get to December."

"Mmm..."

I rub lotion into my hands and up my arms, paying special attention to my elbows. "Remember how last year we waited to the last minute and we paid almost six hundred dollars for our tickets? That's the same price you'd pay for Hawaii over the holidays." I squeeze more lotion into my hand and begin smoothing it over my legs and bare feet. "Ridiculous when you think about it, since Sun Valley is just a twelve-hour drive and Hawaii is, what? Five thousand miles?"

"About twenty-six hundred," he answers from behind his book.

Reaching for more lotion, I catch a glimpse of my profile and the skin near my nose. I lean toward the mirror, peer more closely at my reflection. My pores are getting bigger. How is that possible? And I'm beginning to find the odd straggling hair on my upper lip and chin. Scary. "Should we let the girls invite a friend this year, or would it be better to just keep it us?"

I hear a heavy sigh in the bedroom, and then Nathan closes his book with a thud. "What if we didn't go to Sun Valley this year?"

I lean back and look around the bathroom door. "What?"

"What if we did something else?" he repeats patiently. "Something...closer to home."

"But we always do Sun Valley—"

"Maybe it's time for a change."

"But all our friends go. It's what our friends do."

"And don't we see enough of them without having to go on every vacation with them? Wouldn't it be nice to just do things with the five of us?"

I stand there and think about it for a second before shaking my head. "No. It wouldn't be as fun. I like our friends, and I like the dinners and the cocktail parties. I like how you dads go skiing early and my friends meet up at Java before we go skiing—"

"Or shopping," he interrupts flatly.

I shrug and return to the bathroom, where I pick up my jar of La Mer eye cream and take out a small dollop with my fingertip to pat gently below my eyes and then above on the brow bone. "The point is, it's fun—"

"And expensive. Dinner for just the two of us each night is at least three hundred dollars, and that's not including the baby-sitting or feeding the girls."

Maybe I need to buy the La Mer cream for my throat. "Okay, it's expensive, but it's fun, and you know it. You love getting drinks at the Roosevelt, and you're the first one on the slopes every day."

"But maybe this is the year we take a break and try to conserve. Protect our finances."

I lean back around the door. "Are our finances in trouble?"

His chest rises and falls, and I notice for the first time that he's not quite as muscular as he used to be. "We took a pretty hard hit in the stock market."

"How hard?"

He shrugs. "Enough that we can't afford to pull out. We've just got to ride it out and hope for the best, and stocks are cyclical. They'll turn around. They always do. It just might take a couple of years."

A couple of years?

I purse my lips. "You're saying we can't go on vacation for a couple of years?"

"Of course we can go on vacation. We just have to be careful, that's all."

"So we can go to Sun Valley."

His heavy sigh doesn't escape me. "If you can find a way to do it for free."

Monday morning, I'm at Tully's for the first auction meeting with the new head room moms. Patti and I met with the auctioneer earlier in the summer, and he had such great insights into making the live auction as interesting and effective as possible that I want all the new moms to learn what we learned.

Unfortunately, Patti isn't attending this meeting, and I'd hoped to have this one—since it's so important—at the school in the library. But the library is being renovated, so Tully's on Points Drive it is.

Tully's is great, though. It sits on a little triangle lot between Medina, Yarrow Point, and Clyde Hill and has plenty of parking as well as a huge lobby with a conference table, fireplace, leather club chairs, and dozens of tables. And then there's the staff. They take such good care of everybody. I love them all, especially Joel. He knows my drink and always has a smile for me, which honestly helps.

I pull together a few round tables since the conference table in the corner is already filled with men and their computers. Once the tables are together, I get organized, stacking the binders and folders so that I'm ready for everyone, even as I dread the moment Marta Zinsser arrives.

I force her out of my mind, and having nothing else to do, I sit down with my iced coffee and check my Black-Berry. No voice-mail messages. No text messages. I cross my legs, check my e-mail. An e-vite for our wine group and a notice of a secret sale for special customers at Neiman Marcus.

I'm so on top of things that I just have to sit back and relax, something that is hard for type A's to do.

I like being prepared. I'm always prepared.

If you looked at my appointment book, you'd see that I schedule my hair appointments six months out, color every four weeks and cut every eight weeks.

I get my eyebrows waxed the same day I do my hair and have a pedicure and manicure every two to three weeks, depending on if I have a special event coming up or not.

I'll hire a new nanny two months before my current one's contract is up.

Our vacations are always booked four to six months in advance.

Not having anything else to do, I study the woman at the window. She has a small coffee and bagged bakery items, and as I watch, she pulls a thick slice of pound cake from the paper bag and places it in the middle of a napkin. Using a wood coffee stirrer as a knife, the woman carefully cuts her slice of cake in half and then carefully cuts one of the halves again into excruciatingly small squares before sliding the second half into the paper bag to take home.

Once the second half is bagged, she begins to eat each minuscule bite of cake from the first half until there's nothing left.

My insides squirm as she licks every crumb off the napkin with a moistened fingertip and then every crumb from her improvised knife and then a few off the table itself.

I want to tell her to just eat the other half of cake.

I want to tell her that it's okay to eat a slice of pound cake at one sitting, but who am I to tell her anything? Until recently, I still kept a journal where I wrote down every morsel—every calorie—that passed between my lips.

The front doors open. The first of the room moms have arrived.

The doors open again, and there she is. Marta Zinsser. Her long dark hair is loose, and she's wearing black jeans, biker boots, and a gauzy orange smock that reaches her thighs. Of course. Why would Marta attend a parent meeting in anything else?

It takes everyone a few minutes to settle with their coffees and teas at the tables, and I do my best to ignore Marta, who has taken a seat almost directly across from me, which puts her in my line of vision no matter where I look.

Thank goodness I'm focused and prepared, or Marta's cynical smile would completely undo me. But I am prepared. I've put together binders with pertinent info for the new room parents, and I swiftly cover the auction goals and the room moms' responsibilities.

"Our fund-raiser is significant," I continue, "and the children's class projects are one of our biggest ticket items, too. Parents actively bid on them, which leads to bidding wars, resulting in even more money for the school."

I take a breath and glance around, checking to see if there are questions. There are none, so I press on. "If you aren't familiar with our annual auction, we do the traditional 'turn the auction into a party' event, with great food and drink—with emphasis on drink as alcohol—playing a huge part in creating the right environment for active bidding—"

"How do you put an emphasis on alcohol?"

It's Marta who has interrupted me, and I sit a moment, loathing her for having to make yet one more meeting confrontational. "I'm not sure I understand your question."

She smiles with excessive politeness. "It's a school event, and yet you're pushing alcohol?"

I take in her mocking expression and smile back, every bit as polite. "We're not *pushing* alcohol, we serve it, offering free cocktails when the guests first arrive during the silent auction hour and then switching to a cash bar once dinner begins." My gaze meets hers and holds. "We want multiple bids on items, and if alcohol helps 'juice' the competitive nature of our moms and dads, more power to the bartender."

I pause, stare at her, challenging her. If she wants to have another go at me, now is her chance. But she doesn't say anything. I smile faintly. Taylor Young, five points. Marta Zinsser, none.

With the Monday committee meeting behind me, I've now got to get serious about finishing the book before tomorrow night's book club meeting. But instead of reading *The Glass Castle*, I curl up in the chaise in my bedroom to pore over *W* magazine.

If I could, I'd be like one of the gorgeous golden girls featured in *W*. A New York or London It girl, one of those with long sleek hair and endless legs who wear fitted slacks and slim jeans paired with Manolo Blahniks or Jimmy

Choos. I want the effortless grace of Tory Burch, Brooke de Ocampo, Cosima Pavoncelli. I want effortless grace. I want control.

I have no control.

Disgusted with myself, I drop *W* and reach for the newest issue of *O, the Oprah Magazine*. I always feel guilty for reading *W, Town & Country*, and *Vanity Fair*. I never feel guilty reading Oprah, though. Oprah's good for me. Oprah's determined to save women. Not from men, but from ourselves.

But after I've spent ten minutes leafing through *O*, my conscience gets to me again.

I'm supposed to be finishing the book. I have to read the book. Dammit.

One day later I'm still in my room, struggling to finish the novel and prepare for hosting the group.

Who would have ever thought that book club would be stressful? When I joined two years ago, I'd imagined interesting conversations among relaxed friends. Instead, book club freaks me out. It's not enough to read the book. I've got to get online and research what all the critics are saying, including positive and negative consumer reviews. I need not just the Amazon reviews, but those from the *Seattle Times*, the *Los Angeles Times*, and the *San Francisco Chronicle*.

I don't even like most of the books we pick. They're dark and sometimes so damn boring that I can barely plow my way through the paragraphs.

Every now and then, I just wish we could read something fun. A Jennifer Weiner novel. Jane Green.

Nancy Drew.

I pick up the book with its murky vintage photograph cover. It's the newest big hit. It's being read by everyone, and of course there is terrible suffering and loss. A book club book wouldn't be a book club pick if it wasn't achingly poignant or heartrendingly bittersweet.

I toss the book back down and head to my closet, feeling crabby all the way to my bones. I'm just so damn tired of trying so hard. So damn tired of trying to keep it all together—not just me, but Nathan and the girls, too.

Nathan's home early, and he's promised to take the girls out so we can have the house to ourselves for the book group tonight.

"What's wrong, honey?" he asks, catching sight of me standing motionless in our walk-in closet.

"I don't know what to wear." I'm wearing just a bra and thong as I face the rows and rows of clothes. "Nothing I ever wear is right, either."

"Taylor, you're always impeccably put together."

"And it's so much work. I'm sick of it."

"Don't let your book club do this to you. It's supposed to be fun."

"Monica says I never read the book."

"Do you read the book?"

"Yes! Maybe once in the entire last year I didn't finish it, but I still participated. I still did the research. I tried."

"So don't let her upset you. Monica's in competition with you. She has been ever since you first met."

He's right, but it's small comfort when Monica will be holding court in my living room in less than an hour.

I reach for Roberto Cavalli animal-print jeans and his silky black fitted blouse. With the right shoes and my hair drawn back into a smooth ponytail low on my nape, I hope I'll strike the appropriate note for discussing yet another tortured, dysfunctional American family where dad drinks too much and mom takes to bed and no one protects the children.

"God, Taylor, you always look so amazing," Suze exclaims as I greet her at the door sixty-some minutes later.

I kiss cheek-cheek with Suze and then Jen, who have arrived together. They're Medina moms, not that that's such a big deal, but last year when we had the whole kindergarten fiasco, quite a few of the Points moms weren't talking to the Lakes moms. Fortunately, everyone's moved on to other things, and the kindergartners in question survived and are now happily well-adjusted first graders.

Nathan and the girls haven't left yet, so Nathan's uncorking wine and pouring drinks. After Jen and Suze, Ellen arrives. Ellen is an Atlanta transplant who lived in New York before the South and brings her East Coast edge with her.

After Ellen, it's Patti, Raine, and then Monica close behind. Kate and Lucy also show up at the same time, and I wonder if they've driven here together. Lucy looks as though she's been crying, and Kate keeps her close at her side. Two more women arrive—prospective members?—and they're talking animatedly as they drop their purses and books on chairs and then head for the appetizers and wine.

I'm in charge of the main course, Jen has appetizers, Patti dessert, and Kate has wine.

The appetizers are a tad ethnic for my taste. I was raised on the best of the 1950 cookbook—hot crab dip, artichoke-and-spinach dip, chilled shrimp and cocktail sauce—but Jen has brought Thai spring rolls and other vegetarian dishes.

"What are we drinking?" one of the women asks, dipping a spring roll in sauce.

"Pinot Gris, Columbia Valley, Château Ste. Michelle," Kate answers, flashing the bottle's label. "Bill and I have really been into this wine this summer. This and rosé—"

"Rosé?" Monica repeats, scandalized.

"It's making a comeback," Kate answers calmly, filling another glass. "Rosé is really hot right now."

"I can't see Bill drinking rosé," Monica protests.

"You're thinking of those Gallo jugs you used to buy in your twenties. But rosé's gone upscale. It's a perfect wine for the summer."

"I like Muscat for summer entertaining," adds Raine, reaching for one of the tomato slices. "Or a late harvest Riesling."

"Gewürztraminer if you're serving Indian food," Monica answers, jumping right back into the middle of the discussion. Monica can't stand being less than an authority on everything.

God, I wish I liked her better.

"Suze, wine?" Kate asks, lifting the bottle.

"No. Can't." Tall, blond, gorgeous Suze grimaces. "I'm in the middle of a detox cleansing. Just water and green tea for the next forty-eight hours."

"You're kidding." Ellen stares at Suze agog. "Just water and green tea?"

"There are some natural herbal supplements, too. And then on the last day you get a series of colonic treatments. Positively life changing."

"What is it supposed to do?" Lucy asks uneasily.

"Recharges your metabolism and makes your skin look and feel fantastic. Afterwards I just glow."

Monica nods. "I've read about them quite a bit but didn't know anyone who actually did them."

"Oh yes, there are quite a few of us in the area who do the detox and colonic cleansings. But it's not something you talk about at parties, if you know what I mean."

I do. I'm disgusted. As much as I wrestle with my weight and body image, I can't imagine having anyone squirt anything up my backside.

"Why don't we move into the living room?" I suggest, ready for a change of subject.

Unfortunately, the self-improvement topic follows us to the couches and chairs, but Monica finally wrestles the book into the conversation and for the next hour holds court on agonizingly boring literary comparisons and useless literary theories.

Finally, the book has been discussed as much as it can be by women who have consumed numerous glasses of wine.

Now it's the tricky part of book club: scheduling the next month's meeting. Once upon a time we had a fixed schedule, but that proved impossible with the crazy demands on us.

"How about the first Thursday of October?" I suggest, my BlackBerry calendar open.

"Uh, Boy Scout pack meeting," Jen answers, looking

up from her BlackBerry. "What about Wednesday, the day before?"

"There's a Little Door parent education class," Monica answers, her pen poised above her appointment book.

A wrinkle forms between Kate's brows. "You still attend parent education classes?"

"The school brings in top-notch speakers and specialists to discuss hot topics," Monica answers, nose lifting slightly with her ever-present superiority. She has two kids, and they attend different schools. "We're discussing bullying."

"God, that topic's been done to death," Jen mutters.

Either Monica doesn't hear her or she chooses not to respond. Jen attended Harvard and is one of the only moms Monica defers to.

I hear the garage door open. Nathan's home. We definitely need to get the next meeting scheduled before the girls come in. "How about Tuesday of that week or Thursday the following week?"

"Thursday the following week would work for me," Raine says.

"Me too," Patti agrees.

"It's a busy day for me, but I think I could do it, too," Suze answers.

"Look at your day!" Monica squeals, catching a glimpse of Suze's calendar. "Hair, hair, facial, wax, wax, pedicure, manicure, massage? You're kidding, right?"

Suze's lips curve wryly. "It is a long day, but Jefferson loves it, especially the after-the-wax results."

"How much do you wax?" Raine asks curiously.

Suze's slim, straight shoulders lift and fall, her long hair a perfect streak of pale gold. "All of it. Jefferson likes me bare and baby smooth."

"And how often do you get it done?"

"Every four to six weeks."

Raine points to Suze's crown. "What about that hair?"

"Every four weeks on the dot."

"Pedicure and manicure?"

"Every two weeks." Suze, seeing the wide eyes, laughs. "I wouldn't do it, or be able to afford it, if it didn't mean so much to Jefferson. He loves me to be groomed."

"Groomed, yes," Ellen answers with a faint frown, "but that's...that's...some serious time at the salon and spa."

Suze glances around. "But don't you all get your hair colored and blown out every three or four weeks?"

Most of us murmur agreement.

"And nails? Come on, I know we all get regular pedicures. I've seen your toes all summer!"

Patti sighs. "I'd do more massages if I could. Facials do nothing for me, but massages...Ah. Heaven."

"God, I'd pay for a happy ending, too," Ellen whispers with a wicked quirk of her lips. "I don't know if it's being in my mid-thirties, but I'm revved up all the time. Unfortunately, Mark's not interested. I suppose having just me in his bed for the past eighteen years has dulled his appetite considerably."

"It's the stress of the job," Jen says with a shake of her head even as she puts her hand on Ellen's forearm. "Anthony is so tense all the time. The only time he wants sex is when we're on vacation."

Heads nod. "Vacations make sex new," Kate agrees.

"Hotel rooms make it new." Suze giggles. "This summer when we were at the house in Canon Beach—" She breaks off abruptly, her gaze fixed to Lucy's face.

We all turn and look at Lucy. Her lips are slightly parted. Her expression is stricken. She looks as though she's being skinned alive.

Swiftly I go over the conversation. What could have upset her? And then I realize: sex, husbands, and hotel rooms.

Just then my attention's caught by Nathan's shadow in the hall. He's directing the girls up the stairs to their rooms.

"We'll meet Thursday, then," Ellen says quickly. "Jen, it's your turn to host, right? And Raine, your book pick. Have you selected a title, or will you let us know by e-mail?"

"I'm still trying to decide," Raine says, clicking her pen. "I'll send out an e-mail and let you know sometime this weekend."

"Great!" Patti answers with a little more enthusiasm than necessary. She closes her minicalendar and slides it back into her purse. "I look forward to the next meeting, and now I better get home. I promised Don I'd help tuck the kids into bed."

Everyone's on her feet, quickly gathering purses and books before giving hugs and kisses, and then in one big group they're out the door and heading for their cars.

As the front door closes, Nathan comes back down the stairs. "How did it go?" he asks.

My shoulders lift. "Good. I guess." I glance toward the door and picture Lucy's silent agony. "I think Lucy's having a hard time, though. I should call her. Make sure she's all right."

"You should."

I'm about to turn away when I suddenly remember the Welcome Coffee and my conversation with Amelia. "I met someone last week, Nathan, at the Welcome Coffee. She said her husband works with you. Christopher. He's apparently a vice president at McKee, too."

Nathan's expression is blank. "What's his last name?"

"I don't know. They moved from L.A. I guess they've been up here a while, but until recently they lived on the Plateau."

Nathan shrugs, heads up the stairs. "Don't know, hon."

"Well, find out. If the girls are going to be in the same class next year, it might be good to get to know them better. Have them over for dinner or drinks."

He mumbles assent, and I follow him up the stairs, turning out the lights as I go.

I tuck in each of the girls and then wash my face, doing the nightly skin repair routine before climbing into bed. Nathan's not reading tonight. His light is already out. I turn out my light and curl up next to him, but he's asleep and doesn't respond.

Lying there in the dark, I see Lucy's face. No matter how hard I try, I can't make it go away. I see her eyes, the open lips like a silent scream, and I shiver.

How horrible to be so alone, so naked.

Chapter Five

It's Tuesday morning one week later, and tonight's Back-to-School Night. I'm giving one of the welcoming speeches, which means I've woken up feeling as though I've already drunk ten cups of coffee even though I'm still lying in bed.

Things are good, I tell myself. I'm doing good. No need to stress. I just need to relax.

I wish I knew why I have such a hard time relaxing. It's almost as if I'm afraid something bad will happen if I'm not constantly in control.

Voices waft from downstairs. From what I can hear, Nathan's in the kitchen trying to get the girls to eat their breakfast. He's usually patient with them, but unfortunately this doesn't seem to be one of those days, and Tori—or is it Brooke?—begins to wail.

Grimacing, I pull on the nearest thing I can find—my Juicy tracksuit—as I think about my day. I'm supposed to meet Patti at noon to discuss the auction and the auction chair meeting scheduled for next week. I'd normally have yard duty, but I traded with another mom so I could meet with Patti. The morning's more or less free, and I consider taking an exercise class. I need some exercise.

In the walk-in closet, I glance at myself in the full-length mirror. In my tracksuit I look fine, but the soft fabric can hide the truth, so I pull up the jacket and pull down the bottoms, exposing my stomach, hips, and boobs. I do this almost every day. Sometimes what I see is okay, sometimes I can see only ugliness, can see only where my waist might be thick and how I'm slightly round across my stomach where I know it should be flat.

Now I touch my stomach, try to suck it in even more, looking for definition, turning to the side to check my width.

The most fashionable women, the truly stylish women, are all thin. Every month when my new issue of *Town & Country* comes, I leaf through "Parties" to see if I know anyone. And to see if I look better than anyone.

I don't like that I do this. But I'm so afraid that if I don't keep on top of the situation, of me, I won't matter.

Usually all the couples in "Parties" are well-known, society staples and celebrity faces, and nearly every woman looks like a greyhound that's just come from a spa. Their skin is taut and glowing, and they're all racehorse thin. But every now and then one woman looks a little bigger, sturdier, than the rest of the stick figures in their couture gowns, and I breathe a little sigh of relief— I'm not that fat!—even as I feel a prick of pity that she's not as skinny. Privately, I don't understand this preoccupation with weight and figures. I never even think twice about the men in the "Parties" pictures. It's a nonissue if a man is stout in his tux, or narrow through the shoulder, or thinning at the scalp. Men don't have to be model perfect. Men just have to be men.

Tugging up my bottoms and yanking down the jacket, I tell myself I should go to Pilates this morning. It'd do me good. But it's LuLu in the studio today, and LuLu's style doesn't work as well for me.

Instead, I drop to the carpet next to my chaise and go through a couple of yoga poses, hoping that five minutes of floor work will equal an hour of Pilates. Closing my eyes, I take a pose, focus on breathing, focus on stretching, focus on being present and in the moment.

Less than two minutes into my routine, Jemma crashes through the door, interrupting my Downward Dog. "I can't find my butterfly hair elastic," she cries, her long blond hair caught in one fist.

"Did you check your room?" I ask, turning my head to peer through my arms at her as I inhale slowly to a count of three.

"Yes, and it's not there."

I exhale slowly to a count of three. "Then it's probably in your bathroom."

"It's not there, either. I've looked. Everywhere."

I'm inhaling again, and it takes me a moment to answer. "Then I don't know what to tell you."

"Mom."

I stand, brush off my hands, trying to ignore the low blue feeling that engulfs me. "Jemma, it's your hair elastic."

"And you're my mom," she flashes before flouncing off.

Fifteen minutes later, I've got the girls rounded up, backpacks on their backs, lunches in hand, and I walk them to their bus stop. Nathan's upstairs in the bathroom, shaving at his sink when I return to the house.

Our bathroom is enormous, a true spa retreat with heated marble parquet floor, his and her counters and sinks, glass shower, whirlpool tub, and heated towel bars.

"You're heading to work late today," I say, leaning against one of the brown-and-white marble counters. This marble is probably my favorite stone in the house. Dark cocoa richly veined in white. It's glamorous and masculine at the same time.

He makes a face in the mirror. He's shaving his neck now and pauses to tap his razor in the sink. "I'm actually heading to the airport. I have an eleven o'clock flight."

"You're going out of town?" I can't quite suppress the sharp edge in my voice. "Why didn't you mention it before?"

"I wasn't sure I'd need to go until last night and you had book club and then I fell asleep."

I frown. His explanation is suspect at best. "I'd think you would have told me first thing this morning, then."

"You were asleep and then I was getting the kids ready for school."

"Your leaving town is more important than feeding the kids Froot Loops!"

He looks at me in the mirror. His brown eyes hold mine. "I'm sorry, Taylor."

He sounds sincere, but at the same time something doesn't feel right. "But it's Back-to-School Night tonight."

He uses a washcloth to wipe away shaving cream residue. "You've got it down. You don't need me there, and I need to be in Omaha."

I shake my head. "Arkansas two weeks ago. Omaha today. What's next? Bakersfield?"

He rinses his razor, takes his time answering, and when he finally speaks his voice is pitched low, his tone almost excessively patient. "I'll try to get back tonight, but if I can't wrap everything up today, I'll be home tomorrow night. Either way, I'll call you and let you know when I know more."

I don't know if it's his tone or his expression, but I feel something small and hard and sharp form in my gut as he combs his hair and then heads for our closet.

He's my Nathan, but he's also a stranger.

"Don't you want to hear more about the girls' teachers and their year?" I ask, following him.

"You'll tell me," he answers, reaching for his suit jacket. "You always do."

His answer perplexes me, and I stand there, arms at my side, my brain racing to make sense of what he's saying and what he's not saying. This isn't the Nathan I know. This isn't the devoted dad who never missed anything pertaining to his children. "Are you okay? Are you not feeling well?"

"I'm feeling fine." But he's picking up his briefcase and a small overnight bag, and I can't help it, I feel as though he's shutting me out.

The cold, sharp knot in my gut grows bigger, and I open my mouth to ask what I really want to know.

Are we okay?

Is there someone else?

Will you always love me?

But I don't. I can't. Instead I kiss him and let him leave.

For a long moment, I don't know what I feel. I don't know what to do with myself, either. I have a half hour before I have to drop Tori off at preschool. I should go sit with her. She's just lying on the floor of the family room, watching cartoons. Instead I sit at my laptop computer in the little room off our bedroom that serves as my home office/ wrapping paper/scrapbook room and get on the Internet to check out the flights to Sun Valley for the winter holiday: $380 each. Not bad. Not great. But it could be worse.

I know Nathan said we couldn't go this year, but he can't be serious. Sun Valley is the place to be, and I love the town of Ketchum. Tons of our friends have houses or condos there. We usually book two hotel rooms, but this year we won't go to a hotel. We can just stay with Kate and Bill. Their house is enormous—a seven-bedroom, seven-bath, ten-thousand-square-foot lodge—and they've asked us to stay with them every year. I book the five tickets and then reserve the car. By saving on a hotel, it's almost free, isn't it?

Back in my room, I strip off my Juicy tracksuit and rummage through my built-in wardrobe drawers, searching for my tiny pink Cosabella thong panties and the matching pink bra.

Years ago when I bought my first $200-plus bra, I felt guilty and sick. But $200 for a bra is nothing now. All of my lingerie is expensive. It's Italian and French.

Nathan claims that no one in his family ever spent that kind of money on underwear and that people with real money don't blow it. The truly rich are far more conservative with cash than those who want to prove they're successful.

Living here in Bellevue, I'm not sure I agree, but I do know that Nathan's family isn't like mine. They have money, lots of money. They also detest me, at least his mom and sister. Nathan's dad seemed to have a soft spot for me, but he died five years ago, and his mother and sister have just grown closer. And colder.

It never crossed my mind that Nathan's family would despise me. I'm an overachiever, former born again, straight-A student, and cheerleader. I wasn't the most popular girl at Muir High (being born again had its drawbacks), but I was well liked enough to be put on the homecoming court and respected enough to be named ASB president.

I didn't get the same respect at USC. UCLA students mocked us by saying USC stood for University of Spoiled Children, but the truth is, I was there on full scholarship. A lot of us there were on scholarship, and I had a virtually free ride through a university that cost others over $30,000 a year in tuition alone.

Nathan should have never told his parents about my scholarship. It prejudiced them against me. They were sure I was after his money.

His mom said so to my face: "You do know under California state law that whatever assets one partner has before marriage remain with the partner after marriage."

I simply stared at her, and she added, as if clarifying her position, "If you marry Nathan, you'll never have one penny of his trust fund. If you divorce him, you'll have even less."

Even today, I'm just one step above poor white trash in their eyes.

Nathan's family is wrong, though. My family wasn't affluent, but we weren't white trash. At least, we weren't until my mother fell into the gutter, but that was her choice, not ours.

I step into slim, pale gold Adrienne Vittadini slacks topped by a pale gold Adrienne Vittadini knit top that has a long matching car coat. Scraping my hair back from my face into a tight, low ponytail, I study my reflection.

There are times like now where I realize I'm pretty. I'm grateful that God gave me this face. It's what attracted Nathan in the first place. Dark blond hair. Strong eyebrows. Angled cheekbones. Good mouth. Great body. But I work it. I work it every day. Why?

I like being Taylor Young. I need to be Taylor Young. I never want to be Tammy Jones again. That was my name on my birth certificate. That was who I was growing up.

I change purses, choosing a white Coach bag with a natural leather trim to match my natural leather pumps.

We weren't always the most dysfunctional family on my block. We just turned out that way. Dad was religious, a deacon in the church. We attended church services twice a week as a family, and then in summer Cissy and I attended vacation Bible camp, first as campers and then as teen leaders.

Growing up, we read a fair amount of the Bible. For all the scripture we read and all the verses we had to memorize, you'd think we were a good family. And to be fair, we were, at least until my mom, the deacon's wife, started sleeping around. Before long, everyone in South Pasadena knew it but my dad.

Four months into Mom's affair, I went to my mom and told her if she didn't tell Dad what was going on, I would.

Mom decided she might be better off breaking the news, and she did, which resulted in a divorce. Dad got custody of my sister and me, and for two and a half years we tried to get on with things. But then Mom wanted back in. She missed us, and her fling had flung, so she begged Dad for another chance. Dad, being Christian, forgave her the way Christians should. They remarried when I was fifteen, and for two years we pretended nothing untoward had happened. Unfortunately, Mom couldn't stay put. Two years later, she ran away with Ray, a truck driver who ended up getting arrested my senior year at Muir, serving serious time for assault with a deadly weapon.

Interestingly, Mom stuck with him throughout his twenty-two-month prison stint.

I could almost admire her for that.

Purse over my shoulder and binder tucked under my arm, I head downstairs to wrestle Tori into shoes and drag a hairbrush through her blond curls until they're shiny and smooth. "We're running late," I tell her. "We have to hurry and brush your teeth so we can go."

"I don't want to go."

"It's not a choice."

"I want to watch *Blue's Clues*. It's on next."

"Teeth, now."

"I'm not going to go."

I grab the remote, power off the TV, and look at her. "You have one minute to get upstairs and brush your teeth or you lose all TV privileges for the week."

Tori stomps her way up the curving staircase and down the hall to her shared bath. "I hate brushing my teeth."

I don't answer. Arguing is pointless, and I need to get her to preschool on time. It's a great preschool program, but they are rather firm on pickup and drop-off times. Apparently, children suffer more separation anxiety if they see other kids arrive late and/or leave early.

Once Tori's buckled in her car seat, I hit number 5 on speed dial. Voice mail is number 1. Nathan is number 2. School is number 3. Baby-sitter is always number 4, and my friends take up 5 through 10, with Patti always my top friend.

"Patti," I say, backing my pale gold Lexus out of the garage and into the September sunshine, "could we do an early lunch? I know we agreed on noon, but would eleven-thirty work for you?"

"I can do that."

"Where do we want to eat?"

"How about 520 Bar and Grill on Main Street?"

"Great."

The 520 Bar & Grill was opened by the Brazens two years ago beneath their real estate office, and the restaurant still draws a good lunch crowd. Fortunately, Patti is close friends with Rondi Brazen and can always get a table at a moment's notice.

With two hours free between dropping Tori off and meeting Patti, I head to the mall to get a little shopping done. My sister has a birthday coming up, and I want to get her present bought, wrapped, and mailed soon.

I bump into Kate on the first floor of Nordstrom's, right next to the shoes.

Kate has a daughter in second grade, too, but she and Brooke are in different classes. "How is it going so far?" I ask as we stop to chat.

"Fine. So far."

"We'll be working together on the second-grade class auction project," I say, pulling my purse strap higher on my shoulder.

"That's right. As head room moms, we have to coordinate that ghastly class project. I hate that thing, I do." Her freckled nose creases. "It's the worst job for someone who isn't creative. I glue and staple fabric instead of sew."

"We'll figure it out together. Don't worry."

Kate shakes her head in admiration. "You're so good with all of that. I don't know how you do it. Chair the auction and help out in the classroom."

I shake my head right back. "It's because I have no life outside of the girls and school."

"Well, thank God for that. If we didn't have you, I swear, the school would fall apart."

Kate is exaggerating. She's even more important to the school than I am. Her husband, Bill, is second in command at Microsoft, and she's pretty, not in that fake plastic surgery way, but in a healthy natural strawberry blond way that makes you think of skiing, golf, and quick getaways to Kauai. She's nice, too, something you wouldn't expect when your husband earns several hundred thousand a year, with annual bonuses of up to a million dollars.

A million-dollar bonus. Not bad for a year's work. And if it weren't for her massive diamond ring—five carats, I think—and her Medina waterfront house, you wouldn't know she's rich. It's not as if she drives a yellow Hummer like some of the mothers I know. Her car is a discreet navy Mercedes, a classic model with the original tan leather interior.

Kate, as you can imagine, is every teacher's dream room mom. Can you imagine not wanting Microsoft's number two wife as your room mom? Can you imagine the technology benefits? The *software*?

We chat a little more, and then we both glance at our watches at the same time. "Better go," Kate exclaims. "I've got a women's lunch over at the club. These things always sound fun until I actually have to go."

"I know what you mean." We kiss good-bye, and we're off.

I stop in at Kit's Cottage, a cute little place filled with adorable things that I find nearly irresistible. I love all the beach house items—the glass jars filled with gorgeous seashells and tied with aqua ribbon, the quaint painted signs pointing to the beach, the ornate oversize picture frames made from sand dollars.

I buy a bracelet as a gift for my sister and then some cute frames for the girls' rooms and a little painted sign to put in my potting shed. As the sales clerk rings up my purchases, I dash back and grab a few scented candles and a pretty potted topiary.

"That's it," I say, slightly breathless and feeling rather triumphant as I pull out my checkbook. "I better get out of here before I'm late to meet my friend."

Unfortunately, parking isn't easy on Main Street in Old Bellevue. I circle the block twice before finally locating a spot at a lot near the downtown park.

I walk quickly to 520 Bar & Grill and find that Patti's already there. She's secured us a table outside on the patio beneath a shady tree. "How's your day?" she asks as I slip into a chair opposite hers.

"Good. I bumped into Kate at the mall."

"How is she?"

"Good. How's your day?"

"Insane. Bellevue Schools Foundation meeting. Hearing and vision screening meeting at school. An hour in the classroom afterwards. Sometimes I feel like I never left school."

"Oh, I know. Today's easy for me, but tomorrow's going to be a nightmare. PTA board meeting, reading with the second graders, Pilates, errands, lunchroom duty. I dread it already."

"You need to stop with the lunchroom duty. I gave it up years ago and haven't regretted it once."

"But no one else volunteers."

"Because it's a miserable job." Patti's iced tea arrives, and I signal to the waitress that I want one, too. "You're too good an asset to waste on monitoring lunch trays and wiping up spilled milk."

"I don't know that the school thinks I'm all that valuable," I answer, flashing back to the moment when I discovered Marta would be head room mom in Mrs. Osborne's class. "Seems like they'll take anyone for any job."

"Don't fool yourself. Not just anyone can chair an auction that raises a quarter of a million dollars. In three hours, no less."

"You and Kate always make me feel like a million bucks."

"You are! Taylor, you're an achiever. You're fiercely dedicated to your causes. I don't know anyone who does as much for the school as you do."

I shrug even as I flush. It's hard for me to accept a compliment. I never believe them. How can I? I wasn't raised like my friends. I've gotten where I am by the skin of my teeth.

We order our meals—salads with dressing on the side—and then I peel off my coat and let it hang on the back of my chair.

"Let's talk about what we want to accomplish at the next auction meeting," I say, stabbing a shrimp with my fork once the salads arrive. "In my opinion, the chairs need to set goals. I want to hear what they're going to do this month, and then we need to follow up with them in October to make sure they were able to accomplish their goals."

Patti nods. "Last year we netted a lot of money, but it was too chaotic. No one communicated, and until the last minute I didn't know if Nel was going to be able to pull the auction off."

I stab another pink bay shrimp with my fork. "I'm a control freak. But you know that. Communication's everything. We have to know what everyone's working on, and we need to know if they're having problems."

"Right."

I eye the small bay shrimp clinging to my fork. I dread even bringing this up. It upsets me so much every time I think about it. "We do have a small glitch."

Patti's brows furrow. "How small?"

I take a deep breath. "Enatai is using our theme for their auction, too."

"What?"

The women at the table next to us glance our way, and Patti drops her voice and leans toward me to whisper furiously, "We had our theme set for over a year. Since before last year's auction. They didn't even have a theme till this summer!"

"They claim they didn't know."

"Bullshit." Patti tosses down her napkin. "We should talk to them—"

"I've tried. They've already printed their save the date cards."

"*So?*"

The waitress stops to refill our iced tea, and I reach for a packet of sweetener, tear off the corner, and sprinkle some into my glass, waiting to continue until she leaves. "I've taken this all the way to their school principal and got my hand slapped by our principal. We've been told to gracefully accept defeat and come up with a new theme. Fast."

"Unbelievable," Patti groans.

"I know."

"So when are we going to tell everyone?"

"Soon. We have to print our own save the date cards in a month's time."

"We'll discuss this at the meeting next week."

"Where are we going to meet?"

"Let's do it at your house." Patti pushes away her plate, her salad virtually untouched. "It's perfect for entertaining, and it's always a thrill for the new moms to go there. You earn instant rock star status, and the new moms feel like princesses."

The bill arrives, and Patti and I both pull out our wallets. I snatch the bill away. "I've got it," I say. "It's my turn."

"You always say that," she answers with a laugh.

"I want to treat you."

"But you don't need to treat me. It's fun just seeing you. You don't have to pay for everything."

I slide my card into the black leather folder and hand it to the waitress. "I don't."

As the waitress walks away, we talk about the kids' fall sports schedule. My two older girls both play soccer. Patti has three kids, two boys with a girl in the middle. Her oldest son is an amazing athlete, plays quarterback and wide receiver for the Bellevue Wolverine program, while her younger son is playing football for the first time this year.

I prop my elbows on the table. "Ray's only six. Isn't that too young?"

"They don't do a lot of hitting at this age. Mostly drills, running, teaching them fundamentals."

"And he likes it?"

"Hell week was rough, but he's doing better. They've had two games already and won both. The coach says Ray's another natural, just like his big brother."

"Mrs. Young," the waitress interrupts, reappearing at our table with the black leather folder, "I'm afraid there's a problem with your card. It was declined."

I stiffen, mortified. "That's impossible." My voice rises as heat surges to my cheeks. "There's nothing wrong with this card. I use it all the time."

She shifts her weight uncomfortably. "We can take another form of payment. Rondi's here, and she says a check is fine, another credit card—"

"I've got it," Patti says. "Here." She hands the waitress her card, a black Platinum card.

The waitress hurries away and, utterly humiliated, I look at Patti. "This is ridiculous. There's nothing wrong with this card. This is my signature card. It's the card I use for everything. It has a fifty-thousand-dollar limit and there's no problem with it. There's never been a problem with it."

"It's probably just early fraud prevention warning," she answers soothingly. "It happens to me all the time."

"It's embarrassing," I mumble, my face burning.

Patti puts a hand on my arm, squeezes. "It happens to everyone. Don't take it to heart."

I glance up at her, grateful, but duck my head as soon as I see the waitress return. I just want to escape and call the credit card company. I'd call here and prove to everyone my credit is fine, but it's too personal. The last thing I want is for anyone to know I had a card declined.

Lunch paid for, Patti and I exit together. We say goodbye on the street, and as Patti walks one way, I go the other, heading for the parking lot near the park my children used to call "the castle park" because of the castlelike play structure in one corner. As I walk, I dial my credit card company's toll-free customer number.

I tersely explain my situation to the credit card's rep once he's on the line. "I was just now turned down for a forty-eight-dollar purchase, and I want to know why."

"I need to first establish whom I'm speaking with. May I have the last four digits of your Social Security number?"

Suppressing my impatience, I rattle off the numbers.

"And your date of birth?"

I don't want to lose my temper, I really don't, but I'm growing hotter and angrier by the second. But I give that information, too.

"And your mother's maiden name?" he continues.

I'm so embarrassed, just so embarrassed. "Meshinsky. M-e-s-h-i-n-s-k-y."

"Yes, Mrs. Young, how can I help you?"

At last. I feel a margin of relief. "I was just declined for a small purchase, and I want to know why, and then I want this sorted out—"

"Mrs. Young, your account is over its limit."

A wave of heat hits me. "Over limit?"

"Yes, ma'am."

I grow warmer still. "How?" I choke, knowing Nathan never, ever missed a payment—for anything. He's timeliness personified, something I've faulted him for when it came to social events (I hate being the first to arrive for anything) but value when it comes to our finances.

"You're nearly eight thousand dollars over your limit and you're two months behind on payments. Your card has been frozen, ma'am."

Chapter Six

Standing next to my car in the parking lot adjacent to Bellevue's downtown park, I hit speed dial 2 for Nathan. I'm immediately dumped into his voice mail, and I leave him a hasty, panicked message. "My Platinum Visa was declined today at 520 Bar and Grill. In front of Patti Wickham. Rondi was there, too. Apparently the waitress said I could write a check, but it was mortifying. Patti paid for lunch, but I was supposed to be treating. Call me."

I hang up. My heart's still racing. My blue mood returns, weighing heavy on me.

Why do I always feel like I'm one step from disaster?

Still standing there, I check my messages, and while listening to the second one, I spot Lucy Wellsley driving by on 1st Street. She looks so little inside her big black Suburban, her light blond hair almost white against the glossy black exterior. She's wearing sunglasses so I can't see her eyes, but her lips are pressed down, her mouth small and tight.

Impulsively, I go through my contacts and dial Lucy's cell number.

"Hey, it's Taylor," I say when she answers. "I just saw you drive by."

"Where are you, the park?"

"The park's parking lot. What are you doing? I wondered if you wanted to grab coffee or an ice tea."

"Oh, Taylor, that's so nice of you, but I'm supposed to meet with my attorney this afternoon and I'm already late. I'm lost and can't seem to find his office."

"Is he a good lawyer?"

"I hope so." She draws a shaky breath. "I can't lose my kids."

"You can't. You're a great mom."

I hear her exhale in a *whoosh*. "Thank you."

Guilt weighs even more heavily on me. I have not been a good friend. I haven't been as supportive as I should have been. "Use me as a character witness if you need one. And if this lawyer doesn't seem like he's the right one, let me know. Maybe Nathan and I can do some research, find someone else."

She's silent so long that I think the call's been dropped, and then I hear a sniffle and realize she's crying. "Why are you being so nice?"

She means, why am I being so nice now, because Labor Day weekend I wasn't nice and we both know it. Maybe it's my lunch humiliation, but I take a quick tender breath. "Mistakes happen. You know?"

"Thank you, Taylor." She's crying harder.

I feel worse. "Lucy, please don't. Please."

She can hardly talk through her tears. "I better go."

"Okay. Good luck, Lucy."

"Thank you, Taylor." She hangs up in the middle of a sob.

Standing in the parking lot in front of the park, I feel a thousand years old.

A lump fills my throat as I do nothing but stand there. I see the fountain and the gleam of sculpture and seniors sitting on the benches beneath big green leafy trees, and my self-loathing grows.

Do you think I like being this way?

Do you think I want to be wound so tight? Worrying all the time? Projecting ahead to see every crisis before it happens? Monitoring every nuance around me so I'm ready to leap the moment something breaks free?

I *hate* being this way.

I hate my need for control, I hate my fears. I hate the flood of cortisol, the way my heart starts racing and tension roils through me, building until I feel as if I'm either going to kill someone or explode.

Only Nathan and the girls know I can get really sad. I'd never let anyone else know. It'd be too damaging all the way around.

Glancing at my watch, I see I have an hour and a half before Annika picks up Tori from preschool and takes her home. Brooke and Jemma will arrive on the bus forty minutes after that.

I don't want to go home, though. I don't want to be alone in that huge house of ours. I love the house, but sometimes I feel lost there when no one else is home.

I fish out my keys from my purse and spot the gift card for the massage that the girls gave me for Mother's Day. I've been carrying the card in my purse to remind me to use it before it expires, and suddenly right now seems like the perfect time. I'm stressed out of my mind. Depressed, too. I want to eat. Eating comforts me, but I know I can't eat. I don't want to be fat. But I didn't eat a lot of lunch.

Just get the massage, I tell myself. You'll feel better and will be calmer for tonight.

That's right. Tonight is Back-to-School Night, and who knows when Nathan will be home. He hasn't called yet to say whether he's arriving home tonight or tomorrow.

I call the spa. They could get me in at two for an hour Swedish massage. Perfect. I take the appointment.

The massage is heavenly. Not too much pressure, nor is the touch too light.

During the first half hour while I lie facedown on the table, I breathe slowly and deeply to a measured count of one, two, three. I'm so relaxed that I'm nearly asleep when the masseuse's quiet voice says, "Okay, Mrs. Young, you can turn over now."

The sheet above me lifts discreetly, and groggily I flip onto my back and the masseuse drapes the sheet back over me.

She continues working her magic, and again I nearly drift to sleep. Twenty-five minutes later, I leave a $20 tip and float out of the day spa. I feel so good right now, so calm and relaxed. This is how I want to feel tonight: calm, relaxed, confident.

Back home, I greet my girls, say hello to Annika, whom I unfortunately need to remind that Brooke and Jemma should be doing their homework before they turn on the TV, and grab the pile of mail off the hall table.

I carry the mail upstairs to my desk. Magazines, bulletins, bills. Most of the bills have Nathan's name on them, but my credit cards have my name. I open the credit card statement that arrived in today's mail. It's not my Platinum Visa. It's my Platinum American Express.

The statement is long, two and a half pages. Chewing my lip, I glance to the top to see how much we owe.

Fifteen thousand.

My God.

I sink into the chair at my desk and flatten the statement pages. This is bad. Bad, bad, bad. How could I have spent this much? Fifteen thousand in one month?

Again?

Three months ago, Nathan—who never loses his cool— lost it with me. I'm lucky, too, I know it. I have the best husband in the world, and I hate to upset him, I really do, and I work so hard to be the good wife, but I've got these... things... that keep me from being the perfect wife.

My impulsive spending.

And my compulsive dieting.

Most people don't know about my inability to budget and my obsession with my weight, and I try to hide both from the girls. Nathan knows, of course. After all, he handles the finances and sleeps with me, so he knows the things I'd never want others to know.

And I promised him, I *promised* I wouldn't lose control again. I thought I'd been better, thought I'd watched the expenses, but obviously I forgot just how many purchases I'd made in August.

I do this, and I'm not sure how, but I forget the money I spend, and looking at the statement, I see that some of it is on me: hair, $300; skin care, $1,000; dermatologist, $1,000; shoes, $1,500; swimsuit and new yoga outfits, $500; personal trainer, $1,000 (and I didn't show up for half but was billed anyway); pedicure and manicure, $100; dinner with the girls, $200 with tip.

The other $10,000? Five thousand on back-to-school clothes for the girls at Nordstrom's. Ballet lessons. Tap shoes. Lunch at Red Robin. Dinner at California Pizza Kitchen. Birthday party at Build-a-Bear.

Airline tickets for our March trip to Disneyland. Flowers for a friend's birthday. Catered lunch for another friend's birthday.

Gas for the car, Amazon book purchases, groceries, wine, household stuff from Crate & Barrel, more household stuff from Pottery Barn, Starbucks gift card, Kodak Gallery online photo store, cute nothings from Kit's Cottage, and oh, jewelry to accessorize a new outfit.

Nathan's going to kill me.

I put my head down on my desk and cry. And then when I'm done crying, I go downstairs and rummage through the cabinets, looking for anything chewy, gooey, and sweet. I'm on my fourth Double Stuf Oreo when the phone rings.

I pick up the cordless handset off the counter. It's Nathan's cell.

I should answer. But I don't. Instead, the phone rings three more times before switching to voice mail.

I'm eating my sixth Oreo when I realize what I'm doing. Disgusted, I spit the rest of the Oreo in the sink's garbage disposal and turn on the faucet, washing down what's left of the cookie.

I have to get a grip. I can't eat my way out of this.

I pick up the phone and check messages. The first is from the housecleaner. She can't make it in to work tomorrow.

The second is for a playdate for Brooke. Nathan's message is the third one. He's not going to be able to fly out until tomorrow, and he promises to call the credit card company tonight, but I'm not to use the card anymore until everything's sorted out.

I can't use my Visa, and I'm afraid to use my American Express. That means I have no more plastic. It's an odd thought, an uncomfortable one, as I never carry cash. I've gotten used to using my credit cards for everything.

Annika wanders into the kitchen while I'm standing there. I tell her Nathan won't be home until tomorrow and I need her to sit tonight. She says she already has something planned. I then promise her twice her hourly wage if she stays late so I can attend Back-to-School Night. Annika wants to be paid cash tonight, then. I agree.

Back-to-School Night ends up being anticlimactic. I deliver my speech without note cards, getting laughs where I intended to get laughs, and then I'm done and handing the microphone over to the vice principal.

I note the applause as I walk off the stage, but it doesn't really sink in. I'm supposed to be a good speaker. I'm supposed to be helpful, interesting, entertaining. I'm just doing what was expected of me.

I visit Miss Johnson's classroom first and then, in the three-minute break, hurry to Mrs. Osborne's, but instead of trying to push to Jemma's desk in the front, I stand in the back. Mrs. Osborne sent me an e-mail earlier in the week saying she'd moved Jemma up to the front to try to help her "focus." From the back of the room, I stare at

Jemma's empty desk, only half listening as Mrs. Osborne covers the curriculum highlights for the coming year.

They'll be reading three novels, plus units on short stories, poetry, and nonfiction essays. They're doing advanced math that was once taught at the junior high level and science involving microscopes and writing carefully researched and annotated papers.

As I listen to the curriculum, my mood sinks lower. Jemma won't possibly be able to accomplish half of the above without tremendous parental support. Thank God Brooke is still in second grade. It'll be a nightmare once Brooke and Jemma both need help with essays and reports.

How do other parents do it? How do they manage the soccer practices and Saturday games, music lessons and dance lessons, along with hours of homework? I have Annika because I can't be in three places at once, and sometimes all three girls have to be someplace at the same time. If not the dance studio, then at tutoring; if not at tutoring, then at the soccer field; if not at soccer, then at piano.

Growing up, we didn't run around like this. We couldn't afford a life like this. The only music lessons I ever had were the ones I got in school. In fourth through sixth grades, all children were assigned an instrument, which the school supplied along with the teacher. We had orchestra practice on Tuesdays and Fridays, and then twice a year we performed for our parents. Although orchestra was mandatory, I actually loved the violin. I practiced every single day, just the way we were instructed. Most of the kids didn't. They never progressed. I ended up playing quite well by the time I reached high school. Unfortunately, I stopped playing the violin around the same time I discovered cheerleading.

As if Mrs. Osborne can read my mind, she segues into the fifth-grade music program. "As you may have already heard from your child, fifth grade is the year all students learn to play an instrument." She pauses as the parents begin to talk among themselves, waits for them to quiet. "Our music teachers will ask for your child's preference, but you should know, they do some aptitude testing, too. There's no point in a tiny girl playing the bass if her arms won't reach around the instrument, or a boy playing the tuba if he can't blow enough air into the mouthpiece. Instrument assignments happen the end of this month. More information will be coming."

Books, reports, essays, musical instruments. The list overwhelms me. Not because kids shouldn't learn and do these things, but because I know Jemma, and just like last year, this year she will fight me every step of the way. I excelled in school. Jemma either can't or won't. As I learned last year, Jemma will do anything to get out of homework, including lying about her assignments.

I close my eyes, exhausted. Blue. I don't even know why I feel blue. I have everything I ever wanted, and as a sixteen-year-old I wished for a lot. Beauty. Wealth. Success.

I wanted a handsome, rich husband, one who was good in bed but not so sexy that I'd worry about him. I wanted him to have good values and a great family. I wanted him to be ambitious and successful. I wanted us to live in a big, beautiful house and know beautiful, glamorous people. I wanted 2.5 beautiful children; the .5 was a baby. (In my mind the baby never grew up, just gurgled and cooed like a precious pink or blue bundle in the pram, and it was a pram because we were going to be a family like those in *InStyle*, people who could afford a proper English nanny, and the proper English nanny would of course want one of those huge, solid English prams.)

I wanted all this. And jumping ahead sixteen years, I realize, I've got it.

All of it.

The gorgeous husband, the house, the 2.5 kids (although the baby did grow up; she's four and a half now). I even got the nanny who once pushed the proper pram.

And the problem—if there *is* a problem, and I even hesitate to call it a problem—is that this life, my life, looks good from the outside, but it's not so fun on the inside. On the inside, it's intense. On the inside, it's endless stress.

Sighing softly, I look up, straight into Marta Zinsser's eyes. I don't know how long she's been watching me, but our gazes collide and then lock. For a moment, I feel like crying. The day rushes at me: Nathan leaving abruptly, the declined credit card, the conversation with Lucy, the American Express statement. But just as quickly, I remember my friends and my commitment to the school and my family. I lift my chin, square my shoulders. I've got nothing to apologize for. I'm doing the best I can.

Marta looks away. Good.

The next morning when my alarm goes off, I hit snooze twice. I don't want to wake up. And then I remember that Nathan's not here. I roll out of bed and stumble down the hall to wake up the girls, still wearing the pink-striped nightshirt the girls gave me for Valentine's Day. It has a big heart on the chest and another big red heart low on the back hem, the heart dancing just over my butt cheek.

Brooke is my light sleeper and morning person. I wake her first because it's easy. Tori rolls over to go back to sleep. Jemma glares at me, her thick honey hair a tangled mess on her pillow. "I don't want to get up," she says, her beautiful face creased by her frown.

"I didn't want to get up, either," I answer, "but I did."

"I hate school."

"You don't."

"I do."

"Come on." I haul the covers off her. "Be downstairs in ten minutes."

"And if I'm not?"

I look at her over my shoulder. Her skin is a light gold from the last of her summer tan, and her long hair has shimmery sun streaks. With her dark lashes and light eyes, she's pretty, too pretty. She's going to wrap the wrong people around her little finger, I think, people who will cater to her instead of teaching her right from wrong. I have to teach her right from wrong. "You're on your own for homework. No help from Annika. No help from me."

"Mom!"

I ignore her shout and head back to Tori's room. "Get up, little girl. It's late. We've already overslept."

Downstairs, I look in the cupboards and try to figure out what I can make that everyone will eat. Unlike Nathan, I don't feed them junk. Having lived with an eating disorder for nearly twenty years, I wouldn't want to wish my craziness on anyone else, much less my daughters.

At the back of the pantry I see the red-and-white canister: Quaker Oats. Oatmeal it is.

Tori is delighted by hot oatmeal for breakfast. Brooke less so. Jemma makes retching noises.

I'm not in a good mood, and Jemma isn't helping things at all. "Eat it. It's good for you."

"It's disgusting," Jemma whines, shoving her bowl away.

"It's not if you put brown sugar and raisins on it," Tori says, heaping a second spoon of brown sugar into her small bowl.

"I hate raisins."

"We don't say 'hate,'" I correct wearily, "it's not polite. We say 'I don't prefer.'"

Jemma looks at me disdainfully. "You say 'hate' all the time."

"I'm wrong, then. And just because I do something doesn't make it right."

Brooke dumps some sugar on her oatmeal and then nearly drowns it with milk. "Dad makes us good stuff in the morning. Eggs, pancakes, French toast."

I pour three little glasses of orange juice. "Your dad is more of a morning person than I am."

"He just loves us more," Jemma replies, draining her juice.

I pour myself a thimbleful. "That's not true."

"Yes, it is."

I give up. Fine. "Okay, yes, he does. Feel better? Now finish your breakfast, brush your teeth, and go to school." And I smile. It's a feral smile, but at least it makes me feel good.

Chapter Seven

With a half hour to go before I drop Tori at preschool, I head upstairs to shower and do my hair.

Blowing my hair dry with the big round brush, I realize I'm due to have my color done. I know the appointment has already been made, but I'm not looking forward to going and sitting for two hours for the color processing. I have good hair and have always taken care of it, but like everything else, it takes effort.

Once my hair is dry, I dress. I'm wearing a black fringed Chanel blazer today with a pair of True Religion jeans and black Gucci loafers.

Back in the bathroom, I twist my hair back before switching my wallet and keys and lip gloss from yesterday's Coach bag to a year-old black-and-pink Chanel purse. Sliding on my oversize sunglasses, I go back downstairs to herd Tori to the garage. She looks adorable in her gray plaid skirt and white Peter Pan–collar blouse, and as I lift her into the car, I can't resist covering her face with kisses. "My darling little girl."

"Ew," she giggles.

"Watch your hands," I say, adjusting the straps of her car seat.

She lifts her hands into the air and out of harm's way. "When is Daddy coming home?"

"Late tonight," I answer, shutting her door and heading to the driver's side. "We'll all be asleep when he gets home," I add, sliding behind the steering wheel, "but at least he'll be here when you wake up in the morning."

I start the car and am backing out of the garage when she asks, "What's a affair?"

I hit the brakes harder than I intend and turn to look at her. "What did you say?"

Tori with her cherubic round cheeks, blue eyes, and blond ponytails shrugs innocently. "Jemma said she hoped Daddy wasn't having a affair. But I don't know what it is."

My heart's pounding. My hands suddenly feel damp on the steering wheel. "Daddy's not having an affair."

"But what is it?"

"It's…" I swallow, grip the steering wheel tighter. "It's…an adult thing. But Daddy's not."

Tori smiles at me, small dimples appearing in her cheeks. "'Kay."

'Kay.

My eyes burn and I turn around to finish backing out. Nathan wouldn't have an affair, I tell myself, feeling anything but okay. Nathan wouldn't. He's not the type. He loves us. All of us. Including me.

Nathan and I met at a Lambda Chi fraternity party at USC. The party was a costume party with a cowboy and Indian theme, a fact I wouldn't have remembered if I didn't have a framed photo of that night of me and two of my sorority sisters and Nathan. I didn't know Nathan at the point when the photo was snapped. He was the friend of my friend—her older sister had apparently dated him the year before—and there we all were arm in arm and grinning our smashed-out-of-our-mind grins. My Pocahontas top is sliding off my tan shoulder, and my eyeliner is slightly smudged along with the war paint stripes on the bridge of my nose and across my cheekbones.

But I'm young and thin and tan and smiling.

I think of the Nathan I met at the party and how dazzled I was by him then. He wasn't just a USC quarterback. He was drop-dead gorgeous and Mr. November in the "Men of USC" calendar.

I'd been bulimic only four months at the point I met Nathan, bulimia as new to me as the USC campus itself, learning it from the older, wiser girls in the house. I didn't even have a name for it in those early years. Everybody did it. Eat a big breakfast, barf. Eat too much, barf. Eat dessert, barf. You barf until the barfing becomes habit. You barf until you barf even when you don't want to.

I thought it was a fast, cheap weight control technique. I had no idea it would become the new center of my universe.

In the meantime, Nathan and I began to see a lot more of each other. He was my best friend Lindy's big brother at the fraternity, and he'd drop by the Pi Phi house to see Lindy and then, according to Lindy, ask about me.

The next Lambda Chi party was the autumn formal, which was essentially a prom for the university Greek crowd, and Nathan, USC second-string quarterback, asked me to be his date.

I was over the moon. So nervous. So worried about what I'd wear. Lindy and I went shopping for a new dress for the formal, but nothing seemed right. In the end, I bought a vintage Dior cocktail dress. It cost less than a new dress. In the black sheath, I felt very sophisticated and nothing like Tammy Jones.

Nathan and I danced all night, slow dancing even to the fast songs, and by the end of the evening, I was head over heels in love.

I've been in love with Nathan ever since.

Instead of driving straight to Points Elementary, I stop in at the Starbucks on 8th Street across from the mall. I don't know why I chose this location. It's always so busy in the morning, and as usual, the line stretches to the door. But I wait my turn, trying to ignore my growling stomach, telling myself that a coffee is sufficient even as I eye the other women in line to see who is slimmer.

No one. Good. Yet I feel so empty today, empty and hungry, but I sternly remind myself that being hungry has benefits. Being hungry means I can keep my figure.

Yet what is the point of keeping my figure if I can't keep my husband?

Nathan *has* been distant lately, and he has traveled to odd cities, cities that seem awfully far off the McKee radar. But what do I know about McKee business? The McKees are mavericks, billionaires who do business out of the box.

The line moves, and I reach the long glass case of bakery goods. The cookies, rolls, and cakes tease me, tempt me. Maybe I could eat a low-fat crumb coffee cake without doing too much harm. The problem is, I don't want a low-fat crumb cake. I want the enormous chewy molasses cookies or the chocolate mint frosted brownies. I want dark fudge brownies with dark fudge icing.

"What can I get for you?" the barista asks me.

"Short skim, no foam double latte," I answer.

"Anything to go with that?"

"No." Thank God I still have a little control.

I'm in the office after lunch duty ends, grateful I wore flats today after the past hour and a half on my feet. Now I'm in the copy room, where we're copying and collating Friday's school bulletin, which all the kids take home in their Friday folders. Fortunately, I don't have to tackle the daunting task alone. Kathleen and Lori are also in the copy room with me, and having worked with both of them before, I at least feel like I'm among friends.

"Did you see that article in this morning's paper? The one on the value of stay-at-home moms?" Kathleen asks as she fills the copier with lime green paper. "According to recent studies, stay-at-home moms are worth close to a hundred and fifty thousand dollars a year."

Kathleen has just one child, a son named Michael, who was in first grade with Brooke last year. Kathleen apparently used to have a mucky-muck job until her son was born and has been a stay-at-home mom since. I've always gotten the feeling she's not entirely happy being home.

"If stay-at-home moms were paid," Lori retorts, grimacing. "And if we were paid for all we do, I wouldn't have to work. But that's not the case." Lori has three kids, three restaurant locations, and a brand-new "counter" in the Microsoft campus cafeteria. Her daughter, Jill, is Jemma's age. She also has a son named Mike, but he's still just a preschooler.

"Either way we're seriously undervalued," Kathleen continues, punching in the number of copies needed. "According to the study, working moms are putting in forty-four hours a week on their career job and 49.8 hours a week on their 'work' at home, while the stay-at-home moms clock 91.6 hours. Nearly two more hours of work a week."

"Is this another study the media is turning into the 'mommy wars'?" Lori asks, opening the ream of red paper that we'll use next. "Because I find these studies highly suspect. Working moms often do everything stay-at-home moms do. It just means we've got to juggle two or three things at one time. Folding laundry while we book our business travel. Help with homework via the phone while we commute."

Kathleen stiffens. "I'm not criticizing working moms, I'm just sharing the results of the study, and according to the study, stay-at-home moms are undervalued and underappreciated."

"In that case, I think *all* moms are undervalued and underappreciated," Alice Dunlop, the school secretary, interjects as she enters the copy room to give us another page to be copied for the newsletter.

My phone vibrates in my purse, and checking the number, I see it's Nathan. I leave the copy room to take the call in the quiet outside.

"Good morning," I greet him, gently closing the front office door behind me, my insides suddenly all rumbly as

I remember Tori's question this morning about the meaning of an affair. "Long time no talk."

"I know. I'm sorry. It's been extremely hectic."

"Things not going well?"

"No, things are going extremely well, but it's one meeting after another, and by the time I get a free moment, you're either in a meeting or still sleeping."

"The time difference is hard," I agree, wanting to believe him, wanting to believe that everything is as good as it's always been. Nathan and I are solid. We're the perfect couple. Everyone knows that. Even I know that. "So we'll see you late tonight?"

"That's why I'm calling. It doesn't look like I can wrap everything up by tonight. In fact, I don't think I'll be home until Friday—"

"That's two more days!"

"Honey, it's not by choice."

I picture him in bed with a sultry brunette, a gorgeous Salma Hayek–type seductress. My fingers ball into a fist. My stomach aches. "We miss you," I say huskily.

"I miss you, too, darling. I'll call tonight, once the girls are home from school. Okay?"

"Okay." Hanging up, I stand there for a moment, phone clutched in my hand, my insides on fire. For a moment, I swing wildly from despair to calm to despair again.

I'm still standing frozen, lost in the horrific fantasies of Nathan making love to a luscious, passionate woman I can't even compete with, when the office door opens and a little girl bounds out.

"Hello, Mrs. Young."

Shaking away the pictures, I turn to see Eva Zinsser standing in front of me, smiling her shy smile. I force a smile. "Hello, Eva."

"I like the fringe on your jacket," she says. "And the buttons, too."

"Thank you."

She's still studying me. "Is it a designer jacket?"

She's such a strange thing, so serious that it always unnerves me a little. "Yes, it is."

Her gaze sharpens. "Is it Chanel?"

"Yes, it is." I'm astounded. Not even my daughters would know such a thing. "How did you guess?"

She shrugs. "I like fashion, and it has the Chanel details. The buttons. The fabric."

I want to remind her she's just a fifth grader—she's not supposed to know such things—but Eva's suddenly being called.

We both turn and spot Marta, Eva's mother, approaching. "Eva, we're late," Marta calls. "We have to hurry."

Marta, unlike her daughter, knows nothing about fashion, dressed in her usual antiestablishment wardrobe of camo pants and a long white men's workshirt. Her black hair is loose. She wears taupe flip-flops. She's not hippie as much as f-you. It's the f-you part that drives me nuts. How can she get away with it? Why doesn't she care more?

Eva takes her mother's hand. "Mom, Mrs. Taylor's jacket is Chanel. Isn't it beautiful?"

A mocking expression crosses Marta's features as she turns to look at me. Her gaze coolly sweeps over me. "Yes, it is beautiful."

I stiffen. I can't help it. Marta has that effect on me. But I force a saccharine smile. "Nice to see you, Marta."

Marta sees through my smile. Her eyes glint back at me. "Nice to see you, too, Taylor. Things going well?"

"Fantastic."

"Wonderful."

We stand and smile at each other, even as I think, I hate her, I hate her, I hate her. "We'll have another auction meeting soon," I say.

"I can't wait," Marta answers. And with one last condescending smile, she walks into the office with Eva to sign her out of school.

The next few days are busy as always. All three girls have soccer practice on Wednesday afternoon and then dance on Thursday. Because of their different ages, they're all in different levels and classes, which means nonstop carpooling from three-thirty until seven. I split the driving with Annika, and while one of us drives, the other oversees homework.

On Thursday, while Annika takes Brooke to ballet, I'm home with Jemma and Tori. Tori has a friend over from her preschool, and they're playing dress-up in her room. Jemma's at the dining room table, grumbling through homework. I'm sitting with her at the table, sending e-mails from my laptop computer to the auction committee, when I'm suddenly reminded of my conversation with Tori yesterday morning.

I sit back from my computer. "Jemma, why did you tell your sisters that Daddy was having an affair?"

Jemma starts guiltily. "I didn't."

I stare at her steadily. "You did."

"I didn't."

"Tori didn't just dream this up. She's four. She doesn't even know what the word *affair* means."

Jemma slouches in her seat, her mouth pursed petulantly. I'm not fazed. We can sit here all day. And we do sit, for several very long, uncomfortable minutes, until Jemma squirms. "I didn't say Dad was having an affair. I said I *hoped* Dad wasn't having an affair."

"Why would you even think that?"

She looks at me defiantly. "Because that's why the Wellsleys are getting divorced. Mrs. Wellsley had an affair, and now the kids are going to have to live with their dad instead of their mom."

I sit, trying to piece this all together. Part of it makes sense. Part of it doesn't. "But if Mrs. Wellsley had the affair—and we don't really know if she did, do we?—why would you say you hoped Dad wasn't having one?"

She squirms again, more miserable than defiant now. "Because if Dad had the affair, then we would have to live with you."

I think I'm beginning to see where she's going with this, and I don't like it. "If Dad and I divorced—which we'll never do—you're saying you'd rather live with him?"

She looks away from me. "Yes."

I shouldn't persist with this line of questioning, it's only going to end badly. But I can't seem to help myself. "Why wouldn't you want to live with me?"

She shrugs. "He just loves us more."

My expression doesn't change outwardly, but I'm reeling on the inside. I couldn't love my girls more. "Why do you think that?"

"Because he just does. It's obvious."

"Jemma, your dad's a wonderful father, and he does love you, very, very much, but I do, too."

She makes a face, a sassy face that cuts even more than her words do. "I'm thirsty," she says, jumping up. "I'm going to get some water."

I don't stop her. There'd be no point. It's not as if I can force my love down her throat.

Friday night, Nathan returns home in the middle of the night. He's so quiet that I don't even know he's back until the sheets lift and he's sliding into bed beside me. I mumble a sleepy hello, and he wraps his arm around me. Usually I don't like being held closely, but tonight I cover his hand with my own.

I fall back asleep cocooned in his arms, and when the phone rings five hours later, I'm still nestled close.

The phone rings again, and Nathan, usually the lighter sleeper, is dead to the world. I get up to grab the phone before it wakes him up. He didn't get in until nearly four in the morning. He needs his sleep.

"Hello?" I whisper, leaving the bedroom with the phone and closing the door behind me.

"Uh, Mrs. Young?"

Still groggy, I rub the back of my head. "Yes?"

"This is Charlotte Frankel. I wanted to call and introduce myself. I'm not just a Realtor. I'm a relocation specialist—"

"Excuse me," I interrupt, "but who did you say you were?"

"Charlotte Frankel. I've been assigned to work with you on your move."

"I'm sorry. You must have the wrong number. Young is a fairly common name—"

"Nathan and Taylor Young."

I lean against the wall. "Yes, that's us."

"Well, I'm Charlotte, and I'm most anxious to help make your move as easy as possible. I understand you have three little girls—"

"Charlotte."

"Yes, Mrs. Young?"

"Where are we supposed to be moving to?"

"Omaha," she says gaily.

My stomach rises. *"Nebraska?"*

Charlotte laughs, a surprisingly tinkly laugh for a woman with such a deep voice. "The one and only."

"When?" My voice is all but inaudible.

"To help expedite things, I've pulled a number of listings for you. I've tried to find neighborhoods comparable to your current neighborhood, and your husband has been most helpful. He said good schools would be your number one priority."

"Charlotte, I haven't had my coffee yet, and Nathan has only just gotten home. Could I call you back, please?"

"Of course." She rattles off a phone number I don't even try to write down or remember. "Give me a call once you've gotten your caffeine."

"Right. Thank you. Good-bye."

For a long moment I just stand there in the hall, the phone pressed to my chest. Move. Move? Move to Omaha?

Is Nathan out of his mind?

*   *   *

My first reaction is to go drag him out of bed by his hair. My second is to go downstairs, make some coffee, and calm myself down. Before I go drag him out of bed by his hair.

I shake as I fill the coffeepot with water. I'm shivering by the time I start measuring the tablespoons of freshly ground coffee.

This isn't happening. This isn't. Nathan wouldn't move us to Omaha, especially not without talking to me about it. Nathan would never take a job without discussing it with me. We're partners. Lovers. Best friends.

Brooke wanders into the kitchen, her long flax-colored hair in tangles down her back. "Hi, Mom." She wraps her arms around me in a great bear hug.

Still shivering, I hug her back. I'm cold on the inside, cold and numb and scared.

"Can I watch TV, Mom?"

I give her one more squeeze before letting go. "Yes."

She turns to look at me as she heads for the family room. "You okay, Mom?"

Brooke's my bookworm. My confident, athletic, independent daughter. Also my most perceptive daughter. I manage a faint smile. "I'm fine."

Her brows knit. She has more olive in her skin than the others; it's Nathan's coloring, and coupled with her fair hair, she's stunning. "You sure?"

I force a bigger smile. "Yes. I just need my coffee. You know me in the mornings, all grumpy and mean."

Reassured, she laughs and heads for the other room. I hear the TV come on and the ridiculous cartoon voices.

I'm still shaking as I stand in front of the coffeepot, waiting for the brew cycle to complete.

How could he?

How could he?

I give up on the coffee. I can't wait. I have to know what this is about right now.

My heart races with every stair I climb. In our bedroom I shut the door, wishing yet again we'd installed a lock on the door.

"Nathan," I say, standing next to the bed. My voice comes out curt. I swallow, cross my arms, and try again. "Nathan, wake up."

"Hmmm?" He lifts his head sleepily.

His hair is sticking up all over his head, and he has enormous bags beneath his eyes. I almost feel sorry for him. "We have to talk."

"The girls...?"

"No. No." I don't know how to do this. I don't know how to say this. Nathan and I are nonconfrontational. Nathan and I are happy. We have a good marriage. I thought we had a good marriage.

He rolls up onto an elbow. "What's wrong, honey?"

I have loved this man so long that he's part of me. But how could someone so close to me keep a new job in a new city secret? "We had a call this morning from a Realtor who is supposed to help with our move." I take a quick sharp breath. "To Omaha."

He's sitting all the way up, the sheet low on his hips. He doesn't look surprised or confused, just wary.

He knows what I'm talking about.

Oh, my God. This Omaha job is real.

"What's going on, Nathan?" God, I'm freezing. So cold.

"I've been offered a really good job, and I've accepted."

He doesn't even blink as he delivers the news. No softening of his voice, no apologetic tone. If anything, he sounds resolute. Proud.

"But school began three weeks ago. The girls are settled. They've gotten adjusted to their new teachers and classes and routine. They're doing homework and playing soccer."

"They'll adjust to life there—"

"But why should they have to adjust to life there when we live *here*? Their friends are here. *My* friends are here. Our life is here. Why would we even contemplate moving?"

He rolls out of bed and walks to the window, where he lifts one blind. The sunlight illuminates his broad shoulders and lean, naked torso. I usually love the sight of him naked, but this morning it leaves me cold. "Because I'm the breadwinner," he says, turning to look over his shoulder at me. "If I don't go to Omaha, we have no way to pay our bills."

"What about your job with McKee? Vice president. Big salary. Amazing benefits."

He says nothing.

"Nathan!"

His jaw hardens, and he looks at me with pain and fury. "I don't work for them anymore, Taylor."

"Can't you get your job back?"

"No."

"What do you mean, no? Have you even tried?"

I don't know if it's the hysterical edge in my voice or my questions, but, swearing softly, he goes to the closet and yanks a T-shirt out of a drawer and then a pair of baggy sweatpants. Dressed, he turns to face me. "I quit, Taylor."

I sit on the edge of the bed. *"What?"*

"Seven months ago."

My mouth opens in protest, but I don't make a sound. I'm too shocked, and there aren't any words anyway. He's been unemployed for over six months?

No. No. This is all impossible. This can't happen. This can't be.

Nathan's been getting up and getting dressed and going to work every day. He's been tied up in meetings and busy on conference calls. "Nathan," I plead.

He shrugs once, a weary shrug, and walks out of the room.

No. *No.* You can't just drop a bomb like this and walk out of the room. Absolutely not. I wrench on my robe and fly after him.

Downstairs, I find him in the kitchen, pouring a cup of coffee. He sees me and reaches for another cup, fills that one, and pushes it toward me. I ignore the coffee, bundle my arms over my robe. "What exactly happened?"

He adds a splash of milk to his coffee. "Is this an accusation?"

"I just want to understand."

"I did my best, Taylor."

"But you were making good money. You had a good job—"

"I was redundant, and instead of waiting to be let go, I quit. I thought it'd look better when I was job interviewing to say I'd moved on to better things instead of being fired."

"But if they fired you, there would have been a severance package, wouldn't there?"

Nathan looks through me. "I had my pride."

"But pride doesn't pay the bills."

He clears his throat, pain and frustration written in the lines of his face. "Hindsight's always twenty-twenty, isn't it?"

"And you haven't had a job since when? Last January?"

"February fifteenth."

My legs nearly go out beneath me. Since February? It's late September now.

Thinking back to February, I remember our winter vacation, the trip to Maui with Patti and her family. We stayed at the Four Seasons, next door to the Grand Wailea, and the kids were so disappointed because they didn't care for the beautiful groomed Four Seasons resort and pool. The girls wanted the enormous pool and water slide complex at the Grand Wailea and the fancy morning buffet. Both hotels were pricey, over $450 a night before room tax and room charges like cocktails, spa appointments, meals. "You never once said anything on our trip to Maui."

He shrugs. "I didn't want to ruin our vacation, and I was confident that I'd get something soon."

I hear what he's saying, but my uneasiness only increases. Something doesn't fit. Something doesn't make sense. "Didn't you ever want to talk to me about not having a job? Didn't you ever feel like...sharing?"

"Every day."

"But...?"

He laughs, shrugs. "I didn't know how to talk to you."

I jerk, stung. "You didn't know *how*?"

"I was afraid."

I just look at him, my jaw dropping.

"You have such high standards," he adds bitterly. "You're on this quest for perfection, and I'm not perfect. No one's perfect."

My throat feels scratchy. "I'm not perfect."

"No, you're not, and that's why you hate yourself. You hate whatever's not perfect." He draws a deep breath. "And I didn't want you to hate me."

"Hate you? How could I hate you? God, Nathan, you're my husband."

"You hate your mom, and she's your mother."

I don't know how to answer. In fact, I can't possibly answer. I can't even look at him, my eyes closing at the pain. Only those who know you well can hurt you badly. And Nathan has hurt me. Maybe even badly.

Suddenly everything is too raw, too painful, and I turn away so he can't see my face.

"See?" he continues. "How can I talk to you, Taylor? You just shut me out when you don't like what you hear."

"I'm not shutting you out," I say hoarsely even as my heart feels as though it's falling, falling, falling. I shoot him an intense look. "You're the one who hasn't worked in seven months. You're the one who hid the truth, shut me out—"

"I didn't want you worried. When you worry you starve yourself or binge and purge—"

"*Nathan.*"

"It's true. The moment there's any stress you're in the bathroom sticking your finger down your throat—"

I turn away and walk out, walking quickly to keep from hearing what he's saying. But I hear it anyway. This is my fault. I'm messed up, and I'll always be this way.

Chapter Eight

How amazing that just one phone call can change everything.

I'd so looked forward to Nathan being home. I was so ready to have just a relaxing weekend with the five of us, but the day is horrendous. What's happening between us is horrendous.

Nathan and I haven't spoken in hours. Earlier, he took the girls to the club to play some tennis, but now he's back, closeted in his office, and when he does emerge he doesn't speak to me.

By four I can't take it anymore. I'm in knots, my nerves absolutely shot.

I enter his study, bringing him a peace offering in the form of a beer. "Feel like something cold?"

He just looks at me.

"Besides your wife?" I try to joke.

He doesn't even smile.

"Nathan, we have to talk about this."

"Yes, we do," he agrees.

Leaning forward, I set the unopened beer on his desk. "There has to be another option, honey. There has to be—"

"I've been interviewing for months, Taylor. I've been putting on the dog-and-pony show for anyone who would give me the chance, and now I've been given a chance. A chance to work again. A chance to pay our bills again."

"But Omaha?"

"You say that because you know nothing about the city. Omaha has some beautiful neighborhoods. It's an interesting city with a strong arts community, and most important, it's a great opportunity for me."

I rub my upper arm, glance around his dark-paneled office. The wood paneling cost a fortune, $35,000 for this one room alone. But I wanted the best for Nathan. I wanted him to have a proper study that could also be his library. He loves books so much. He's always buying books. You should see his side of the bed.

"But this is home, Nathan," I say in a small voice. "This is where we live."

His expression doesn't alter, yet I feel him pulling away emotionally. "Taylor, I've already accepted the job. I've been introduced around the office and spent Friday in meetings with my department. I've promised to be back in their headquarters—permanently—by Thursday."

"This coming Thursday?"

"Yes."

"What about us?"

"Charlotte's a relocation expert. She's done this dozens of times and will orchestrate the move. She swears she can have you moved out of here and into a new place in less than two weeks."

"Just like that?"

He stares out his window. His study overlooks the back lawn and has a spectacular view of the lake. I wanted him to have the best view. "It doesn't have to be complicated, Taylor."

"But it is complicated. We agreed to move here, live here, because the quality of life was superior to other places. We checked out the different school districts, looked at the different schools—"

"I've looked into schools in Omaha. They have great schools and soccer programs, too. We'll get the girls enrolled this week, and by Thanksgiving it'll feel like home."

"You can't be serious."

"I've never been more serious." He pauses. "The cost of living is considerably lower, too. It's the best thing for us. It really is."

I shake my head. "No, it's not. It isn't, Nathan."

He's silent a moment, and then he looks up at me, his handsome features utterly expressionless. "I'm sorry you feel that way, but the decision's made. I've taken the job. Charlotte will have a moving company come on Monday to schedule the move. The company is paying for the move. The company is handling all the relocation expenses, including three months temporary housing in Omaha—"

"I'm not going."

"Taylor—"

"I'm not going." I reach for the beer, grab it back. "I have commitments here, Nathan. I have friends here. I never agreed to move. I never agreed to any of this."

As I walk out, I drop the beer in the trash. It shatters in the metal garbage can, but I don't care. The can at least has a plastic lining.

We eat dinner in different rooms and sleep apart, the first time we've slept apart in the same house in years. Sunday morning, Nathan wakes early and grabs his clubs and heads to the golf course. He doesn't call, and I won't try to phone him. After feeding the girls lunch, I let them invite friends over.

Now I sit on a lounge chair and watch the little girls play on the lawn while the older girls are in the house on the computer. I hope they're not on MySpace. Or Facebook. Or any of those other Internet places. Too many perverts hang out there.

Friday, Raine e-mailed with the title of the new book club selection, *The Memory Keeper's Daughter*, which we'll discuss at Jen's, although I wish Raine had picked an Amy Tan novel, since Jen is hosting. Jen's Chinese. Her parents were both immigrants, and she's living the immigrant dream. I'd very much like to hear more about life, particularly life in America, from someone who isn't white.

But *The Memory Keeper's Daughter* it is, and I give the opening chapter thirty minutes of undivided attention before I close my eyes. The writing's beautiful. It's going to be depressing.

I don't think I can do depressing right now.

I'll wait. I'll read it later. I'll just look at magazines now.

Fortunately, I've brought some magazines out with me,

so I drop the book and leaf through the newest issue of 425, a glossy quarterly magazine devoted to the upscale lifestyle we enjoy here on Seattle's Eastside.

There are new reviews of spas and restaurants, including a review of the Redmond location for Lori's restaurant, Ooba's. I've been there only a couple of times, but everyone raves about the chicken enchiladas, grilled salmon soft tacos, and shrimp quesadillas.

Just reading the reviews makes me even more determined to remain here. I love Bellevue. This is home. It's everything I ever wanted in a city, too.

I'm reading a profile of a Seattle Mariner player who has chosen to live in the area in the off-season when I hear Nathan's car. He's back. I'm suddenly a ball of nerves again.

However, I nonchalantly continue to read my magazine for another half hour. Then Kate calls to say she'll come pick up her daughter, who has been playing with Brooke. "I'm out in the back," I tell her. "Come have a drink with me."

I fix Kate our favorite drink, the good old gin and tonic, a drink she lovingly refers to as "mother's little helper."

Outside, we curl up on two padded lounge chairs. Kate is usually sunny and poised to tell a wicked joke. But she's pensive today, and for a moment we just sip our cocktails and sit in companionable silence.

On the lake, a motorboat speeds by. Pretty girls laugh from the back of the boat as it hits a wake and bounces hard.

"Do you ever go out on your boat?" Kate asks, watching the sleek speedboat disappear.

"Not as much as we used to."

She sighs. "Isn't that the way it goes? You spend a fortune on second homes and toys, and one day you wake up to realize you're tired of your vacations and your toys."

"Thinking of selling one of your homes?" I ask. Kate has vacation houses scattered all over the world. Over the years, they've either bought or built houses in Cabo, Sun Valley, and Scottsdale, a condo in Maui, a time-share in Las Vegas, and something in Carmel or Monterey so Bill can fly in and golf for a day.

"I don't know. It just seems like a lot of work lately. I'm tired of fielding phone calls from staff regarding the need for repairs. It gets expensive and time-consuming. Sometimes I think we're better off just selling everything and going back to staying in resorts."

I make a sympathetic noise even as I wish I had Kate's problems. Her husband has a stable job. Her husband is worth millions, maybe even a billion by now. "You'd have to pack suitcases again that way, and you hate packing, remember?"

"That's true." She takes a long sip from her cocktail. "This is just what I needed. You know, you now make a better gin and tonic than I do. What's your secret?"

"Lots of lime."

Kate's daughter spots her from the upstairs bonus room and leans out the window to shout hello. Kate waves back. After her daughter's head disappears back into the bonus room, Kate says, "I've been so upset all day. My mother has invited herself, and her husband's entire family, to Sun Valley for Christmas. Twenty more people to feed and entertain."

I guess this isn't the time to bring up the fact that I'd

hoped we could stay with Kate and Bill in Sun Valley for the holidays, too.

"It wouldn't be so bad," she continues, "if my mom would even ask me. Instead she assumes I'm dying to host all of Larry's children. They're so ungrateful, too. Just because their dad married my mom doesn't mean I owe them anything. We were all adults when Mom married Larry. I wasn't looking for another father or another family."

I nod and concentrate on listening. Sometimes we just need someone to listen to us. Men don't seem to understand that. They think we want them to solve our problems when we just want to share.

"Don't you have a stepfather?" Kate asks.

"Yes."

"Is he as bad as Larry?"

I think of my mom's husband, Ray, the trucker convict. Mom's been married to him for fourteen years now. Almost as long as she was married to Dad. "Worse."

"Where does your mom live?"

"All over." I make a face. "Ray's a truck driver," I add delicately. "They pretty much live out of Ray's cab."

"That must be interesting," she answers just as delicately.

I've never really talked about my mom before, and I'm not sure why I shared what I did just now. I'm sure we all have our family skeletons, but they're safest in the family closet. "It is." I pause, wondering how to close the topic and smooth it over. "We don't have a lot of contact. The children haven't seen her in years."

"Not much in common?" Kate guesses.

I nod, and we move on to other subjects, but the shame

lingers. Shame is a heavy burden, too, which is why my kids don't see my mother.

The girls don't really understand why not, either, as Mom sends a card with checks for the girls every birthday and Christmas, but I don't try to explain. I deposit the checks in the girls' savings accounts, have them write a brief thank-you, and that's that. The girls don't need to understand everything now. It's enough that they know I don't approve of her and that I don't believe she's someone they need in their lives.

After another drink and another half hour of chatting, Kate leaves with Elly, and I start dinner.

Dinner the next night is nearly unbearable. It's been a terrible Monday and I'm so upset with Nathan that I can't even look at him, can hardly tolerate being in the same room with him.

He's not who I thought he was, and I thought I knew him well.

If it weren't for the girls' silly chatter about their day at school, there would be no conversation during the meal. I couldn't talk if I tried. I feel as though I'm losing my mind. Nathan can't be serious. He can't be. Move? Move to Omaha?

My throat seals shut, and I battle the threat of tears. Can't cry in front of the girls. Can't. Can't. Must maintain control. Must keep it together.

But later as I wash the dishes, my throat gets that horrible squeezed feeling again. I can't go to Omaha. There's nothing for us in Omaha. We know no one there, either.

Bellevue's home. This is where we live. This is where the kids go to school. Besides, I'm committed to co-chairing this year's school auction, and there's no way I can leave the auction in the lurch. It's the school's biggest fundraiser, and it's a huge job. I couldn't walk away now. It wouldn't be fair.

I go to bed first tonight, and when I wake in the middle of the night to use the restroom, I discover Nathan's sleeping in bed with me. He's not lying close, though. He's practically sleeping on the edge on his side.

Good. He can stay there. In fact, I hope he falls off.

In the morning, Nathan gets the girls breakfast and I dress so I can walk them to their bus stop. When it's time for Jemma and Brooke to leave, I fill the tall red thermal cup I've bought from Tully's with coffee and carry it with me as I escort the girls to their stop.

It's chillier this morning than it has been, the late September morning a misty gray. Standing at the bus stop with the other moms, I chat about everything and nothing, and it's comforting. They're all as frazzled and frustrated as I am. At least, I think, I'm not alone in my mountain of worries. All women seem to worry about being good enough, doing enough, trying enough.

I kiss Brooke good-bye as she climbs on the bus. Jemma allows me to blow her a kiss. I watch the bus chug down 92nd Avenue as it heads toward school.

Back at the house, I dress Tori and then pack my workout gear in my gym bag. I'll do the Pilates class today. God knows I need it.

Nathan sees me with my gym bag. "Where are you going?"

"Taking Tori to school and then to the Bellevue Club."

"What about the Bekins rep that Charlotte's arranged to come meet us today?"

I shake my head disbelievingly. "Why won't you listen to me? I'm not moving to Omaha, and if I did move, I guarantee it wouldn't be until you've been on the job at least six months. Maybe this summer I'd consider moving. Maybe once we get through this year—"

"Taylor, you're the one not getting it. We can't afford to live separately. Hell, we can't even afford to live here. We have no money."

"But what about our money?"

"What money?" He laughs.

I pull the gym bag strap tighter on my shoulder. "The rest of our money."

He pauses for a split second before answering. "There is none."

"But our savings?"

"We've never had a formal savings account. We've had stocks, real estate, investments."

"So we do have something more."

"I've liquidated what I could. The rest is gone."

I look at him, trying to process this but failing. Nathan's rich. He comes from money. He made good money. What is he saying? That we have no money? That we're...broke? "Our house must count for something."

"No."

His flat, hard answer leaves me stunned. "Nathan, it's a five-million-dollar house—"

"Mortgaged to the hilt. We can't get any more money out of it. Not without selling it."

I laugh. "Sell the house?"

He just looks at me, deep lines etched at his eyes and mouth.

I abruptly stop laughing. "Is that the real reason we're moving? Because we're broke and might have to sell the house?"

He doesn't answer, and I feel a terrible lump fill my throat. It grows and grows and presses down so that I want to gag. Gag and throw up.

I've been through this before. I lived this as a kid. I refuse to live this now.

But Nathan isn't my dad. I'm not my mom. This can't be happening. This can't be happening again.

"You'll get another job here, a great job," I tell him low and clearly. "But until then, we'll cut back. We'll cut back on whatever we can—"

"It's too late for that," he says. "It's...unfixable."

Tori wanders into our room, her thumb popped in her mouth, her eyes wide and a frightened blue. I haven't seen her suck her thumb in at least a year. It means she's heard us arguing and she's nervous. Scared. That makes two of us, baby.

I scoop her into my arms. "Let's go to school," I say with false cheer, and step around Nathan without looking at him.

I try my best to focus on the exercises and lengthening and breathing during the Pilates class, but my mind races and I keep turning the same thought over and over in my head. *What does unfixable mean?*

Nathan said the situation is unfixable, but I don't understand what unfixable is. I don't accept unfixable. I believe things can be fixed. I believe. I believe.

It's not until I've showered and dressed and am leaving the club that I check my BlackBerry calendar and remember I'm hosting the auction meeting at my house tonight.

Nathan's going to have a fit.

Wearily, I call him to give him fair warning. He's definitely not happy. "Can't you at least wait until I'm gone?"

"The date's set, Nathan. Everyone's made arrangements for child care. I can't change it now."

"Why is the auction so much more important than your family?"

Stung, I fall silent. My mouth opens and closes before I manage to find my voice. "How dare you say such a thing? I only volunteered to chair the auction to help the girls—"

"Oh, please, Taylor. You can fool everyone else, but you can't fool me. The auction is nothing but a huge ego booster and we both know it."

My eyes feel gritty. A lump fills my throat. "How long have you hated me?"

"I don't hate you, Taylor, but I know you and I know your games."

Games? What games? "I have to go," I say thickly. "I'm supposed to be helping in the computer lab."

"Of course. Taylor Young, queen of everything."

I'm shocked at his bitterness. I've never heard him speak to me like this. How long has he felt this way?

Shaken, I stop by Starbucks on my way to school and get my usual latte, but instead of passing on the sweets, I buy a pumpkin scone with the maple glaze. I scarf down the scone sitting in my car. I eat as fast as I can, eat until every crumb is gone. And then I pound the steering wheel.

I hate myself.

I hate myself.

I hate what's happening all around me. But I feel so helpless. I want to fix this. I want to make things better. But moving to Omaha isn't the answer. It can't be the answer. This is home. This is where we live. We have to find a solution here.

Nathan takes the girls out to a movie while I host the auction meeting. He doesn't say good-bye when he leaves. Brooke and Tori give me a kiss. Jemma shouts from the doorway that she loves me. Thank God. I couldn't bear it if the girls turned on me, too.

The meeting is set for seven p.m., and everyone arrives promptly. I've opened bottles of good Chardonnay and Merlot, believing that a fund-raising meeting is so much more civilized with a great glass of wine.

We spend ten minutes socializing before I call the meeting to order. "As you know from my e-mail, we need to come up with a new theme, as Enatai took ours. Patti and I met last week to brainstorm ideas, and I sent you all our top three. Can I have some feedback on the new suggested themes?"

"I'm not crazy about any of them," Louisa says candidly, "but of the three, my favorite is the Côte d'Azur."

"Do you really think the Côte d'Azur is a good theme?" asks Carla, leaning back in her chair, her pen pressed to her chin. "Will everyone get the whole South of France thing?"

"Everyone knows about Cannes," I answer firmly. "The

film festival is renowned. We can decorate with palm trees and white tents and red carpets, really working the glamour of the film industry. Big spotlights, select live auction destinations blown up and framed like movie posters."

"Or we track down vintage travel posters depicting some of our destinations like Greece, Paris, Sun Valley," Patti adds. "Honestly, I think it would be fun and glitzy, kind of a holiday party in the middle of March."

A debate ensues and then turns heated, as it often does. So many of us are strong women and opinionated. Give us all leadership roles and there's bound to be conflict.

Patti eventually calls for a break. "I don't know about you, but I could use some more wine," she says with a self-deprecating laugh.

She takes my arm as we all rise and head for the dining room, where wine and appetizers wait. "Are you okay, Taylor?"

I nod briskly. "Of course. Why?"

"You don't seem like yourself. You're sure everything's all right?"

My chest squeezes tight, and I fight the most ridiculous urge to burst into tears. I would love to confide in her, but I can't. This isn't something I can talk about, isn't something that can be shared. "I'm fine. Just concerned about the auction."

"Don't be concerned. We'll do the Côte d'Azur theme, everyone will have a ball, and we'll raise buckets of money, okay?"

I struggle to smile. "Okay."

Patti offers to top up my wine, but I cover my goblet.

One glass is enough. I have to be careful about drinking. It's not just the calories. If I drink too much in one week I sometimes feel more blue, and I have enough trouble not being sad as it is.

The others aren't holding back, though. The two bottles are nearly empty, and I go to the kitchen to retrieve a third. As I return to the dining room, I overhear part of a conversation taking place between Patti and Barb, one of the new first-grade moms.

"There's definitely a mystique about Sun Valley," Patti says with a laugh. "Maybe it's because there are four distinct groups that gather in Sun Valley at Christmastime. The locals, the Seattle people, the L.A. people, and the celebrities."

"Celebrities?" Barb asks curiously.

Patti glances at me before answering. "Well, you don't talk to the celebrities—that's a definite no-no—but they all go during the winter holidays. Bruce Springsteen, John Kerry, Bruce Willis, Demi Moore, Ashton Kutcher." Patti glances at me again. "Who am I forgetting?"

This should be easy—I've been going to Sun Valley for the past ten years. But I can't think of anyone. My brain doesn't seem to be working. I frown hard, concentrating, trying to picture faces I've seen the last few years. "Um, Arnold Schwarzenegger and Maria Shriver last year, and oh, Clint Eastwood and Robin Williams, too."

"Tom and Rita Hanks," Patti adds.

"Bode Miller," I chime in, feeling utterly ridiculous for even having this conversation when my world is spinning wildly out of control. Nathan's right. Why am I hosting this meeting tonight? Why am I doing this now? He says he's moving. He says we have no money. He says we're broke. I nearly sway on my feet.

Patti shoots me another worried glance. I pretend I don't notice, and the young first-grade mom, Barb, definitely hasn't noticed. She's dazzled by what she's hearing. "And you just...hang out...with these people?"

Patti shrugs. Her tone is casual, dismissive. "If they're at the evening parties, and they usually are."

"Is it hard to get invited to the evening parties?"

"Not if you know people, and ski."

"Skiing is essential," I agree, trying to pull myself together. "The people who ski like to get together in the evening for a cocktail party, and every night it's a different house and party. Of course, the party is never 'planned' in advance, but is a spur-of-the-moment thing while on the slopes."

"But don't you believe they're all that impromptu." Patti laughs. "The cocktail parties are usually catered, and some people bring in chefs to cook for their friends."

Barb is hanging on every word. "Are kids included?"

"Most kids stay home with the nannies, although there are evenings where kids are included. It's not the norm, though, and you don't want to take your kids to an adults-only party. Big mistake."

They continue talking, but I can't listen, can't do this anymore. It's starting to hit me, really hit me. Nathan hasn't worked in months. He isn't a vice president at McKee. We've been living on borrowed money. We're out of money. *Broke*, he said.

That's the part I have the hardest time with. How can we be broke?

I'm hit by an icy wave of panic, and then another. I'm

shivering again, uncontrollably. I look around, trying to figure out how to escape. Patti grabs my arm, walks me into the kitchen. "What's wrong?" she demands, her voice no-nonsense. "Tell me. I know something's wrong. I've known it all night."

I want to tell her. I want to tell her everything, but the problem is, I don't understand everything. I don't understand anything. My husband's lied to me. My husband's been living a lie. We've all been living a lie. We've been going on trips and spending money and buying expensive bottles of wine when we had no savings and Nathan didn't even have a job.

My stomach heaves. I put my hand to my mouth, afraid I'll throw up.

Patti suddenly understands. "You're sick."

I nod, my hand pressed even more tightly to my mouth as I battle to get my sensitive stomach under control.

"Go upstairs," she orders. "Get in bed. I'll wrap up the meeting, send everyone home." She claps her hands as if I'm a wayward child. "Go. Now. I'll call you tomorrow."

I dash upstairs and climb into bed fully dressed. My head aches. My stomach continues to heave. I'm shivering like mad.

I can't believe this is happening. I can't believe Nathan's been lying to me. Not just once, but again and again. For over seven months he's deceived me. Gotten up and "gone to work" and allowed me to believe that everything's okay when it's just the opposite. Nothing's okay. Everything's changed. We're facing disaster.

Chapter Nine

Nathan returns with the girls a little after nine. I get up and put the girls to bed and then robotically wash my face and prepare for bed.

As I leave the bathroom, I find Nathan standing at our bedroom windows, looking out. The clouds have again cleared, and the lights of Seattle sparkle across the low purple lake.

"Do you know what it's like trying to provide for a family of five in Bellevue?" he asks as I turn off the bathroom light.

"No."

"Did you ever wonder?"

"You never talked about it."

"But then again, it's not as if you wanted to be bothered," he answers.

The coldness is back in his voice, the sharp tone that makes me feel as though we're balancing on a knife's edge.

"You're oblivious," he continues brutally. "You've no idea how expensive it is here. No idea how pressured I've felt. I barely sleep at night. I wake up early and go work out to keep from having a nervous breakdown."

I sit on the side of the bed, slide my hands beneath my thighs to hide how much they shake. "I wish you'd tried to tell me."

"I did." He turns to face me. "I said, Taylor, stop spending. Taylor, we're tight on cash. Taylor, don't buy things. Taylor, Taylor, Taylor."

He did. I hang my head, the guilt and shame so dark and deep that I can hardly breathe. I feel lost and scared, the same fear I felt when I was fourteen and ashamed of my mother and ashamed of my father and ashamed to be Tammy Jones.

"Why didn't you listen?" he demands, walking toward me. "Why didn't you care?" His hands bunch at his sides. He's furious, and he's shaking, too. Nathan isn't a fighter. He avoids conflict like the plague.

Just like my dad, I think, and my dad's conflict avoidance meant he ended up becoming the laughingstock of Pasadena. Dad didn't want to fight with Mom and did everything he could to avoid the truth, which included admitting that he was married to a woman with no moral fiber.

But this isn't about my parents, it's about Nathan and me and our life together. A life that seems as fragile as a sandcastle.

"I did care," I whisper. "I do."

"Then why didn't you stop?"

I can't answer him. He already knows I'm compulsive and obsessive. He knows the reason I try so hard to be perfect is to make up for my failures.

"Maybe it's better if you don't go to Omaha," he says after a moment. "Maybe it's better if you and the girls stay here. Better to keep the girls settled until you and I sort out our thing."

I lift my head to look him in the face. "What do you mean, *our thing*?"

"Us. You and me. It's not really working anymore, is it?"

He's taken my heart in his hand. "I still love you."

"And I love you. But—" He pauses, rifles his hair, his expression stricken. "But what good is love when it turns us into this?"

Chest burning, eyes burning, I look past him to the night and the lake and the lights of a boat slowly sailing by.

"Face it, Taylor, we're not living in reality. We haven't been in years. We both buy stuff to keep us busy. To keep from feeling empty."

My eyes are watering. I'm trying to hold back the tears. I don't want to cry.

"Taylor…" His voice drops, persuasive. "I know you're not happy. I don't make you happy—"

"But you do," I interrupt, desperation making my voice too loud. "You do," I repeat, more gently. "I love you. I love you more than I've loved anyone or anything. That's what makes our girls so special. They're you and me together. They're us."

He just shakes his head. "I can't," he says finally. "I realized this afternoon I can't do this anymore. I don't want to do this anymore. I need to get back to work, get back to earning money and paying the bills. Get back to the things that matter."

"I don't matter?"

"The family matters."

I hear such a strong "but" in there. "But it's not the girls you want to get away from. It's me."

He gives me a side glance, his expression remote, shuttered. "Taylor, you're still not listening. I love you, but I can't do this right now. I need to think. I need some time."

Nathan goes to bed, but I can't sleep. I pace downstairs. I eat four white-cheddar-flavored rice cakes. A handful of almonds. A couple of Oreos. Half a pint of ice cream.

Nathan has said things he's never said before. He's said the very things I've feared my whole life. I'm too flawed. Too broken. Unlovable.

My hand presses to my eyes to stem the tears. I wrap the other arm around my middle, holding in all sound. I have to keep it together. Have to keep me together.

I get scared when I hurt like this. So afraid there's something really, truly wrong with me. None of my other friends ever talk about hurting. None of them talk about fear and shame. I went to counseling for a number of years after I graduated from USC. I was tired of being bulimic, tired of hating myself. The counseling did help. Maybe I need to go again.

At one, I make myself go upstairs and climb into bed. Nathan sleeps with his back to me. His shoulder is so wide, his legs so long. I creep toward him, lie curled just behind him, as close as I can without actually touching him. I need his warmth. I need his love. But most of all, I need him.

In the morning, I get the girls to their bus stop and return home to tackle the breakfast dishes, only to find that

Nathan's already done them and is now sitting with Tori on the couch, reading her one of her favorite stories, the Berenstain Bears' *The Bears Picnic*.

I hover in the doorway, listening to Nathan read. It's a story I've heard a thousand times before. Jemma never really took to the Berenstain Bears stories, but Brooke and Tori just loved them. Tori has her dad read them at least once a week.

When Nathan finishes the story, I drive Tori to preschool and come home instead of heading to the gym. Upstairs, I find Nathan packing. He's dragged out a suitcase—a real suitcase, not one of those overnight bags that hold a few things. This suitcase could empty his closet.

That's when I get it. Nathan's leaving. Really leaving. Permanently leaving.

I lean against the doorjamb, my legs weak. "When do you fly out?"

"Tonight."

"The girls—"

"Already know. I told them last night. I've promised them I'll call every day. I told Jemma to keep her cell phone charged, as I'll call the girls daily on that."

"You don't want to use the house number?"

"You're not usually at the house, and I don't want to risk missing talking to the girls. This way they know they can always reach me, too."

I bundle my arms across my chest. "You make it sound like we're getting divorced."

"That's the last thing on my mind. I love the girls. I care about you. But for now, I have to focus on getting my life back on track. I've had a hard year, Taylor. Things weren't great at McKee before I quit, and I just want to start feeling better about myself again."

I nod. I can understand that. "Do you need help?"

"No."

I find it hard to just stand by and watch, though. "Do you want some coffee or a cup of tea? I can make you a cup of green tea. It's really good for you—"

"Taylor." His voice is sharp, and it silences me. "I'm fine."

I nod, but I don't leave and I don't speak again as Nathan grabs more shirts and slacks and sweaters.

I search my heart for the right thing, the perfect thing, to say, but nothing comes to mind. In my heart I know I have to be the one to fix this, but I don't yet know how. Instead, I watch as he selects a jacket. It's getting colder in Omaha. He'll need a heavy coat for the Nebraska winter.

I'm numb the first few days Nathan is gone. I don't sleep well. I have a hard time falling asleep, and then I wake up in the middle of the night to either eat or cry or do both.

I want to sleep, though. When I sleep, I forget. But then in the morning when I wake up, it all hits me again. Nathan's gone. We're in serious financial trouble. We might even get divorced.

Waking this morning, I roll over in bed and extend my arm where Nathan should be and grab air, amazed all over again at the empty space. He's been gone eight days now. He's talked to the girls daily, but only twice to me, and one of those times I think it was a mistake. I think he'd meant to dial Jemma's cell phone and dialed mine by accident.

For sixteen years, Nathan's been not just my lover, but my best friend. I've talked to him about everything, shared all the little details along with the big things, and now overnight he's gone.

I roll over onto my back, grab the pillow that would be his, and hug it to my chest.

What if he doesn't want to get back together?

Another thought hits me.

What if, like Peter Wellsley, Nathan wants the kids?

Tortured by the thought, I climb out of bed and go to the adjoining office with the huge arched window that overlooks the lake and dock and beautiful estates of Hunts Point.

The desktop computer is still on, and I click on Outlook and check my e-mail in case Nathan's written. He has.

I sit in front of the computer to read the e-mail.

I need you to gather up all the bills and mail and send to me here. They won't get paid just sitting there.

Give the girls my love. Hope everyone's doing well.

I close my eyes and press my forehead to my hand.

Nathan's got to come home. Or we have to go there. We have to be together.

I type a quick response before I can have second thoughts.

N, I can get a sitter for the weekend. Why don't I bring the mail myself? T

I push send before going to wake the girls.

While the girls brush their teeth after breakfast, I check my Outlook again. Nathan's answered me.

I nervously click to open his e-mail.

Taylor, I don't have the time and we don't have the money. Just put it in Express Mail. It'll be here tomorrow.

I read and reread the e-mail. I read it until my heart feels like it's on fire.

I go through the day on autopilot. I show up at school, woodenly fulfill my obligations, send out e-mails to the various committees, and read the e-mail reminding me that the next book club meeting is coming up. I haven't even looked at the book since that afternoon when I sat outside on the back lawn, watching Tori and Allison play.

I'm looking for the book when I remember Nathan's request to overnight the bills to him. Damn. How could I forget? Glancing at my watch, I see it's nearly five. Damn it again. Even if I rush to the post office now, the bills won't reach him for two days, as I've missed the three o'clock cutoff for Express Mail.

I go downstairs to Nathan's office and turn to his wood filing system on his desk. It's overflowing with bills. I pull them off the top and then reach into the middle shelf. There are more there. And more on the bottom. Envelopes opened and unopened, stacks and stacks with some dating back three months or more.

No wonder Nathan's depressed. He's been facing this mountain of bills for years.

Suddenly I need to know what we're dealing with. He might be the bill payer and the wage earner, but it's time I got informed about our finances, too.

Picking up an envelope, I wonder where to begin. Or how one should begin. I haven't paid bills for nearly thirteen years, since before Nathan and I were married, as he took over all finances the summer we were engaged. He'd wanted me to have great credit, not merely good credit, and he'd been appalled by my lackadaisical manner of paying bills, a system he considered hit or miss.

Nathan was the first person who made me realize that late was still terrible when it came to your credit score. Late meant a bad credit score, and it was better to make smaller but more frequent payments than my huge payments every now and then.

I don't know why I didn't understand the system before, but Nathan made it all clear. Nathan always made it clear. That was one of the things I loved most about him.

He took the time to explain things to me, filling those gaps in my knowledge base, and trust me, there were a lot of gaps. When you're a girl growing up in a dysfunctional family, you're far better at cleaning up others' messes than your own.

Nathan.

I close my eyes, hold my breath, try to keep the crazy emotions in.

I miss him. I really wish he'd let me come see him.

Reluctantly, I turn my attention back to the pile of bills, deciding I'll start by organizing them. I'll open all and then sort them by company, then due date, and then maybe finally I can see where things stand.

An hour later I've finished opening, stacking, and adding up what's owed, and I think I've added wrong, so I clear the calculator and start over adding again.

Mortgage payment: $5,600, times three (How can we have not paid our mortgage in three months?)

Lexus SUV car payment: $435, times three

Nathan's Porsche payment: $617, times four

Boat payments: $332—many, many times (six months late!?!?)

Country club golf membership and dues: $525 per month, times four

Bellevue Club membership, expenses, and dues: $675, times three

Landscape/gardening: $395, times three

Cell phone: $288, times two

House phone: $148, times two

DirecTV: $102, times three

Puget Sound Energy: $500, times three

Water: $600, times two

Nordstrom's: $1,400 minimum payment, times three

American Express Platinum card: $17,400 due

Alaska Airlines Signature credit card: $6,000 minimum payment

Discover Card: $3,300 due

American Airlines Citibank credit card: $2,800 due

Hawaiian Airlines Visa credit card: $1,900 due

Neiman Marcus credit card: $1,450 due

Macy's credit card: $800 due

Starbucks credit card: $375 due

Victoria's Secret credit card: $240 due

Eddie Bauer credit card (who knew? must be Nathan's…): $88 due

And there are more, miscellaneous bills from school, social obligations, medical, kids' orthodontics.

The rough total of what we owe—right now, this month, this moment—is $70,000. Or to be more precise, $70,756.

And even if we should miraculously pay that, four weeks from now we'll owe another $26,817. In fact, until we get rid of our credit debt, we're going to owe $26,000 every month, which means we need an income of over $300,000 this year just to meet our expenses...and right now we're not including food, new clothes, hair, travel, or entertainment.

Three hundred thousand just to pay for all the things we've bought in the past, never mind what we'll need in the future.

I'm beginning to see the whole picture, the one Nathan's been trying to make me see for a while.

I'm also beginning to see that Nathan can't do this alone. I'm going to need a job, too.

It's a bold decision and a good plan, but getting a job won't be that easy. At least, not getting a job doing anything serious that will help pay serious bills. Sure, I could work in retail. I could probably get a job today at Nordstrom's as a sales associate. I know fashion. I'm good with people. But being a sales clerk, whether it's at Nordstrom's or Ann Taylor, won't make a dent in the debt.

Each night for a week, I scan the classifieds. I overhear some of the moms at school talk about various home businesses. Tupperware. Creative Memories. Pampered Chef. Candles. Erotic toys. I look into several of the different opportunities but am more depressed by the opportunity than encouraged, especially when I discover nearly all require some kind of up-front financial investment.

What I need to do is find a good part-time position in my field. I studied communications and public relations in college. I worked for a PR firm here in Seattle after I married Nathan (not that I'd want to work for them again since all the owner did was hit on me nonstop), but there's no reason I can't get back into PR.

Confronted by a dwindling checking account and the sickening realization that we have no savings, I decide I need to put together a new résumé, a very good résumé, and make immediate, albeit painful, budget cuts.

I reduce the housecleaner from weekly to biweekly. She cries that she can't afford to be cut back. I calmly remind her that just months ago when she insisted on a pay raise, she threatened to quit if she didn't get it because she had so many families who wanted her, and they were all paying more.

I call the gardener, and I cut him back from weekly to once a month. He's upset, but fortunately he's cursing in a foreign language and I don't understand, and with a polite thank-you, I hang up.

Annika's a different story. It's hard to cut back her hours, especially with Nathan gone, but she's a huge cash drain, and if I keep her at her current hours, we'll have nothing for groceries soon.

Annika also complains at the reduction of hours. I offer to keep her at the same number of hours we've had her but reduce the pay. Grumbling, she opts to take fewer hours, and when she presses for an explanation, I tell her that with Nathan away I want to spend more time with the girls—which is true, as the children are missing Nathan terribly. They're all more cranky than usual, and Jemma is particularly volatile.

Bottom line, I'd rather die than let everyone know we're struggling financially. People would talk. And people can be so cruel.

As today is one of the days Annika doesn't work, I now sit with the girls in the dining room. They're tackling their homework while I face my laptop and slowly try to put together a résumé. It would have been nice if I could have found a copy of my last résumé, but no such luck. We've had so many moves since then that I've either tossed it out or buried it in a box in the attic.

It takes me three hours to put together the pieces of degrees, internships, and jobs held since graduating from USC as a communications major. I had two internships in Los Angeles, one while attending USC and one the summer after I graduated. The first was in radio (sales and advertising, which I *hated*; radio sales is the worst job in the world), and the second was for a talent agency. I loved the talent agency and the perks now and then tossed my way—parties, premieres, fetching coffee for bored stars and coked-up celebrities. Or maybe it wasn't the celebrities all coked up. Maybe that was my boss. Either way, it was fun and rather glam for a recent college grad. The only downside was they didn't pay, and I needed a paycheck.

My first paying job in Los Angeles was for a party-planning company. I look them up this afternoon online to get their details for the résumé, and I'm surprised to see they're no longer in business. Zelda's company, Invite, did fancy parties that we then worked hard to get good press for. One of Zelda's parties—a baby shower for a B-list star (but attended by three A-list actresses)—was featured in the April issue of *InStyle,* and for a month the phones didn't stop ringing. Zelda was over the moon. We all got a big fat bonus, and then later when the phones stopped ringing Zelda wanted the bonus back. I found out six months later that I was the only one who gave it back.

Nathan in the meantime had gotten a job in Seattle and was already working up there. We were dating long-distance. I hated being in a long-distance relationship, but I didn't pressure him. I knew how his mom felt about me. I also knew she was trying to introduce him to other girls, rich girls, because as we all know, rich girls have such great values.

Nathan surprised me by proposing on Christmas Eve. We were at his family's house in Hillsborough. When Nathan dropped to one knee, I swear to God, his mother screamed. It wasn't a happy scream, either. I'll never forget her grabbing at his arm, pleading for him to get up.

I guess it is kind of funny in hindsight. At the time, I was humiliated. I cried when I accepted Nathan's proposal and slipped the ring on my finger. But I was crying for the wrong reasons. I was crying because I knew I'd never be good enough for him, yet I loved him so much that I couldn't refuse him. Nathan was the first person to ever make me feel really beautiful, not just on the outside, but on the inside, too.

Maybe it's still not so funny.

I stop typing, close my iBook, take a deep breath and then another.

I look up, and Jemma's watching me. I give her a shaky smile. "You miss Dad," she says.

I nod. I do.

"Why did he have to take that dumb job in Omaha? Why didn't he get another job here?"

All the girls are looking at me now. I gather my pages of scribbled notes, stack them into a neat pile, and lay them on top of my computer. "It was a good opportunity. He's working hard to take care of us."

"Still," she snorts. "It's lame."

Brooke's expression darkens, and she shoves her spelling packet at Jemma. "Don't call Dad lame!"

"Well, he is if he expects us to move to Omaha!"

"I'd go to Omaha," Tori pipes up.

Jemma's jaw drops. "You would?"

Brooke's lips compress. "I would, too."

"You'd leave all your friends here and go someplace where you know no one?"

Her sisters nod, and Jemma turns on me. "Would you, Mom?"

I study my girls. I feel as though I'm seeing them for the first time in a long time. "Omaha wouldn't have been my first choice, no."

"See!" Jemma crows.

"*But*," I add emphatically, "I don't like living apart from Daddy. I love Daddy. I want us to be together. We should be together."

"So are we going to move to Omaha?" Brooke asks.

I stand up, move away from the table, as if I can

escape the wave of panic that's always threatening me. "I don't know. Maybe. We'll see. Depends if Daddy likes the company. If the job makes him really happy, I think we'll be happier being with him." And then I head to the kitchen. I want to eat something. Something bad. Something that will fill me up and make me warm and take away the pain.

Instead, I eat a nonfat light blueberry yogurt and make a cup of tea, using my instant-hot tap, and call Patti.

For five minutes, Patti and I discuss the auction and compare notes. How is procurement going? What about entertainment and decorations? Are the save the date cards now at the printers?

Business concluded, we switch gears. "Are you going to make book club this week?" Patti asks, her voice rising to be heard over a loud whirring noise.

"What are you doing?" I ask as the noise ends abruptly.

"Making smoothies. The boys have football practice from five until eight. Right in the middle of dinner hour." She hits the blender button again and shouts above the din. "So what did you say about book club?"

I wait for the blender to stop. "I don't think I can go this time. Nathan's away, and I don't have child care."

"It's probably time to replace Annika. She's becoming less and less reliable."

"Yeah," I answer, unwilling to admit that I'm the one who has severely curtailed Annika's hours rather than the other way around.

"In that case, just bring the girls here." The sound of Patti scraping the blender competes with her voice. "Our kids get along great. It'll kind of be like *The Brady Bunch*. My two boys and girl with your three girls."

"I don't want to create work for Don. Tori's still a baby. She can be a lot of work."

"Not to worry. I'll tell Suze she's the baby-sitter for the night and will promise her five dollars for helping watch Tori. Suze will love it. It'll make her feel like one of the big kids."

"You're sure?"

"I'm positive. Oops, it's late. I better run. If the boys arrive at practice late, the coach makes them do extra laps."

"Bye."

"Bye. See you tomorrow night. Bring the kids early and we'll drive to Jen's together."

"Deal."

After I hang up, I start downstairs but end up pausing on the curving staircase to look out the tall, multipaned window that stretches from the second floor to the entry.

It's so gray and drizzly. Typical November day, but it's not November yet, just the middle of October, and I'm not ready for the winter rain. Not ready for the months of dark clouds and gloom.

Grabbing my raincoat, I tell the girls I'm heading outside to get the mail.

Brooke looks up from her math workbook. "But it's raining."

I tug on my black slicker and pull up the hood. "I know, but if I wait for the rain to stop, I might have to wait all year."

The girls laugh, and there's something so innocent about their laughter that a lump fills my throat. I've tried so hard to protect them since they were born, tried to keep them from knowing about bad people and bad feelings, but it hits me almost violently that I can't protect them from the truth. Can't protect them from reality. And the reality is, we're in trouble. Big trouble. And it's not just money trouble, either.

The lump in my throat grows bigger, and I quickly head out the door, walk down the drive, my head bent beneath the chilly rain. I splash through puddles, my leather flats so low that my wheat-colored cords are getting drenched at the hem.

I use my key to open the mailbox and drag out the armful of mail. Catalogs, catalogs, magazines, and four inches of statements and bills.

I close the mailbox door, lock it shut, and stand in the rain, flipping through the statements and bills. The envelopes arriving aren't just white. A handful of the envelopes are pastel hued, shades of pink and purple and green. I open one of the colored envelopes with dread. I'm right to be worried. It's from a collection agency. They're threatening legal action. I know now what's in the other colored envelopes.

And it's not good.

Chapter Ten

The next morning I wake early, hoping if I call Nathan he'll pick up. He doesn't answer. I hang up furious and frustrated. But only seconds after hanging up, I dial again. "Nathan, we love you and miss you. Hope you can come home for a visit soon. I know the girls would love to have you watch them play in another game before the season ends."

I hang up once more. This time I bury my face in my hands and rage silently.

Maybe I did spend too much. Maybe I wasn't listening closely enough. But I didn't lie to him. I've never lied to him. He has no right punishing me like this.

He was the one who lied to me for over six months.

He was the one pretending to go to work even though he had no job. So where did he go for all those months? What did he do? Play golf? Internet solitaire? Gamble at Diamond Lil's?

Yet as angry as I am, I know I can't blame him, and I can't give up. I won't lose this house. I won't have my children embarrassed. I won't let us become a source of gossip and laughter for the neighbors.

Pulling my hair back into a ponytail, I take a deep breath and open the Word file containing my résumé.

For the next half hour, I work on polishing my résumé. Then, using last Sunday's classifieds, I write a cover letter for six different jobs I think I could do.

For each job application, I double- and triple-check my cover letter for spelling and typing errors before printing the letter on pristine Crane parchment paper. Then I rework my résumé for each different application, trying to refocus my résumé's objective statement to reflect what I could do for each company. Even to my eyes, my résumé looks sadly outdated. I haven't held a paying job since before Jemma was born. Over ten years without employment. Twelve since my last job search.

Scary.

I'm still working when the phone rings. I grab for it, see that it's Nathan.

"Hey, stranger," I say, sitting back in my chair.

"Hey," he answers, but his voice sounds strange. Strained. "I got your messages."

"You don't sound so good, Nathan."

"Just homesick."

"Then come home."

"I wish I could."

"Why can't you?"

"Taylor…"

"I'm going to get a job, Nathan, and when I do, quit that job and come home. You'll find another one here. We can make it work here—"

"I need to go, honey. Sorry."

"Nathan—"

"My appointment arrived early, Taylor. I'm sorry. Give my love to the girls." He hangs up.

I stare at the phone a moment before putting it down. What's happening to my life? I feel as if I'm starting to lose my mind.

I take a breath, and another, trying to slow my crazy pulse. I don't like feeling this way. I don't want to feel this way.

With a shaking hand, I press print and my résumés start to churn out, one after the other.

I will find a job. I will help out. We will get through this.

While the résumés print, I go wake the girls and do the morning routine. Once the big girls are off to meet their bus, I dress Tori and then head to my room to get ready for the day.

In my closet, I spot a long honey suede skirt hanging in the back. I pull out the skirt and see tags still attached. The skirt's been buried in my closet since last fall when I bought it brand new. I've never worn it, and I look at the tag. Michael Kors, $1,800.

With the way things are now, I'd take the skirt back if I could, but it was purchased in New York when I accompanied Nathan to a conference there last year. We stayed at the Four Seasons, ordered room service every morning to a tune of $75 a pop.

Play money. Monopoly money. That's what it was. I've lived on my credit cards, rarely paying cash for anything. I had no idea that Nathan was living the same way. It didn't cross my mind that we were living dangerously. That we could run out of money.

Tori wanders into my room, sucking her thumb. She's got her favorite stuffed green frog beneath her arm, holding it close to her body. She outgrew her thumb and the frog a year ago. "Going to wear that?" she asks around her thumb, using her pinkie to point to the suede skirt.

I start to hang the skirt back up. "No."

"Why?"

"I don't know."

"Like it." She looks at me, her blue eyes so serious. "Wear it. With boots."

Oh, my baby. I scoop her into my arms and hug her, kiss her. "Did you want to pick out a pair of boots for Mommy to wear?"

She nods and disappears into my closet. She's always loved my shoes, and she takes her time finding black stack-heeled leather boots. The toe is slightly pointed like a cowboy boot, but the black leather shines and the heel is four inches high and sexy. "These," she announces, dragging the pair to me.

I sit on the chaise to put on stockings and tug on the boots. "You've got good taste."

She stands in front of me as I finish dressing, watching as I pull an off-white sweater over my head and cinch the waist with a wide black leather belt highlighted by an enormous round buckle.

"Pretty," she says approvingly as I comb my hair straight, leaving it loose.

I put down my brush. "You think so?" She nods soberly, and I nod back at her. "Mommy thinks Tori's very pretty, too."

She adjusts Froggie under her arm. "I look like Mommy."

It's all I can do to keep from pulling her into my arms again. I'm so scared for her, so scared for all of them, but I can't let her see my fear. Nathan's going to call. Nathan's going to help me make everything right. "Yes, my darling girl, you look like Mommy and Brooke and Jemma. We're a family."

She nods once. "And Daddy."

Nathan. Nathan, call. Nathan, please come see us, please come home. "And Daddy."

I pick up my purse on the floor, not bothering to change it. It's mink brown and doesn't match my outfit, but suddenly I'm too tired and too busy to care. There are more important things on my mind, more important worries weighing on my heart.

It rains on the drive to drop Tori at preschool, rains during yard duty, rains during lunch duty, with no sign of letting up.

After lunch duty ends, I head to the office to copy and collate the bulletin. Lori and Kathleen aren't working in the copy room with me today. Instead it's a new face, a mom I haven't met yet but who seems to struggle with everything from working the copy machine to stapling the pages in the right corner to counting out the bulletins for the various classrooms.

I'm still trying to sort out the bulletins when my cell phone vibrates. I don't recognize the number. "Hello?"

"Mrs. Young?"

"Yes?"

"This is Cottage Preschool. We have Tori still here. Your nanny didn't show today, and we've tried her cell phone several times—"

"I'll be right there." I hang up even as I dash out the door. "Alice," I call to Mrs. Dunlop, "the bulletins aren't finished. My youngest wasn't picked up from school, and I have to go get her."

"Not to worry, I've got it covered," Alice answers.

I'm flooring it as I drive to Tori's preschool. It's actually not that far from Points Elementary, but my guilt is making the distance worse. There is no Annika today. I'm Annika today. I'm in charge of picking up Tori and meeting the school bus.

Thank God the school office is understanding, and after apologizing profusely, I buckle Tori into her seat.

"Annika forgot me," Tori says quietly.

I can lie to the school staff, but I can't lie to my own daughter. "No, she didn't. Mommy did. I'm sorry. I forgot."

At home we meet the girls' school bus, and after making them snacks, I get them started at the dining table on their homework. Jemma argues for the first ten minutes that she doesn't have any homework, and when I go online to the school Web site to show her that she does, she complains that she's too tired; and when I tell her she'll feel better when it's done, she says she wishes Annika were here instead of me.

"That's nice," I say, and shove her reading book in front of her face. "Now read. I'm going to quiz you on your reading when you're done."

Jemma howls with frustration, and I ignore it, offering Brooke a tight, overly polite smile. "Need Mommy's help?"

She looks at Jemma and then me and shakes her head. "Noooo."

"Great, then I'll just get my book and read in here with you two. It's book club tonight, and I haven't finished the book, either."

I've been reading off and on the last few weeks, but I haven't made great progress, and I'm honestly not sure I want to keep reading. I know it's the author's debut novel, but it's even more depressing than I anticipated, the story of a family torn apart over a husband's lie and how their lives all unravel, and I can't stop thinking about Nathan and us. How Nathan's lie—which became a secret—has pulled us apart whether he'll admit it or not. Nathan can be angry with me, but he's in this marriage, too.

I do like that the wife in the novel gets stronger. She was too broken for me in the beginning, made me uncomfortable. I know what it's like to be so broken, and it hurts. Books seem to be full of hurt. Fortunately, the wife does find herself. She develops a career and gains confidence. Only drawback? Her son now hates her.

I look at my girls. If I end up with a career, will my children hate me?

What a thought.

Fortunately, the phone rings. I'm happy to set down the book and take the call. Soccer practice has been canceled because the fields are too wet. The girls are thrilled to have an unexpectedly free afternoon. I'm not as happy. Now I have no excuse not to keep reading.

I pick up the book, try to concentrate on the story, but the rain drums on the windows and scatters my focus all over again.

I think about Nathan constantly. Obsessively. If only I could talk to someone about what's happening, but I've never had that deep confession kind of relationship with my friends here. To be honest, I've never had that kind of friendship with anyone. As a teenager, I was so embarrassed by my family that I dealt with problems by pretending they didn't exist and keeping everyone but my Christian friends at arm's length, and even my Christian friends didn't know about my life at home.

The idea that I could be someone else came to me my senior year. I'd somehow—miraculously—made the Rose Bowl court, and in interviews I became "Taylor" instead of Tammy. It was easy enough. People believe what they want to believe.

When I applied to colleges, I put my name down as Tammy Taylor Jones, and then once accepted to USC, I just quietly started dropping the Tammy off of everything until I was simply Taylor Jones by the time I graduated.

If I'd had close friends in high school, maybe there would have been someone to question my new identity—Taylor being far thinner, blonder, and more sophisticated than Tammy—but I had no one close. I'd never allowed anyone to get close. I couldn't, not with Mom moving in and out of our lives.

For the first time in a long time, I wish I had good friends, old friends, friends who could listen, counsel me.

Patti's my closest friend here, but I'm reluctant to open up to her. It's not a matter of trust. I know I could trust her. It's just that my Bellevue friends don't have "real problems." Lucy was the only one with a real problem, and look what's happened to her.

*   *   *

The kids are delighted to go to Patti's house and even happier when Don announces he's ordered boxes of Papa John's pizza and garlic breadsticks for dinner. Since Nathan left, the kids haven't been out much, and pizza is suddenly a big treat.

"Don't you feed your kids?" Don teases me. He and Patti have been friends with Nathan and me forever. We've practically raised our kids together. Don's another native Californian. He and Nathan grew up in Hillsborough together, went to different colleges, and then ended up in Seattle for work.

"You'd think not, huh?" I answer.

"So what's your husband up to? Haven't seen him lately."

Nathan hasn't told anyone about his new job. But then I'm not surprised. He didn't tell even his closest friends about being let go from McKee.

"He's working. Traveling."

"Well, tell him to call me. I've got some news to share."

"I will." I kiss the kids good-bye, and Patti and I head out the door.

I ride with Patti to book club. Patti's unusually quiet during the drive. I shoot her a worried glance. "You okay?"

"Yes." She hesitates. Her fingers tighten on the steering wheel. "I have news to tell you, too. I'm just not sure how to tell you."

"You're not getting divorced, are you?"

"No! God, no." Horrified, Patti shakes her head. "It's nothing like that."

"Then what?"

She frowns as she drives the short distance from Clyde Hill to Medina. "What if we talk after book club? Get a coffee and sit down. I just hate to spring it on you and then not be able to discuss everything properly."

I'm not at all reassured, but I can't force the issue. As we pull up in front of Jen's glass-and-steel home, one of those modern marvels that become features in architectural design magazines, I try to relax, but it's hard. I haven't read the book all the way through. I'm stressed out about things at home. And now I wonder what it is Patti wants to discuss with me. It sounds serious. I just hope it's not health related.

Jen's kids don't go to Points Elementary. Medina children go to Lakes, and if you think the Points parents are perfectionists, you should meet the Lakes parents. Seems like most of the moms are blond and fit and wear size 0.

Jen opens the door to her house. She's on a small lane tucked off Evergreen Point Road just a hop, skip, and jump from Bill Gates.

Although Jen's fit and an itty-bitty size 0, she's not blond, she's Asian—Chinese, actually—and of all the Medina moms, she's my favorite. First, she's smart, and second, she's funny. She has a proper laugh, too, the kind of laugh that makes a room happy. Her husband's a sexy surgeon who grew up in California's farmland. Even though they're both in their early forties, they look like lithe twenty-somethings.

"Welcome," Jen says, giving Patti and me each a kiss as we cross the threshold. "You know where everything is.

Help yourself to wine, Anthony's pomegranate martinis, and the nibbles."

Patti and I go with the pomegranate-tinis and snack on baked Brie, crackers, and delicate clusters of red grapes while catching up with Raine and Suze. Across the room by floor-to-ceiling plate-glass windows, Lucy is having a heart-to-heart with Kate and Ellen. I'm glad to see Lucy here, although she doesn't look well at all.

Monica arrives moments later, but tonight she's not alone. She's brought—God forbid—Marta Zinsser.

My jaw drops as Monica and Marta enter the sunken living room decorated in grays, pewter, and shots of icy lilac. I crumple the cracker in my hand.

What is Monica doing? Doesn't she know about the bad blood between Marta and me? Or is Monica too immersed in her younger son's world at $15,000-a-year Little Door, a point she used to work into almost every conversation?

Monica introduces Marta around the room, leaving Patti and me for last.

"Girls," Monica says with her too wide smile, "do you know my friend Marta Zinsser? She's a Points Elementary mom, although I think she would have loved Little Door."

As Monica talks, I keep thinking that something about her looks different. She still has my hairstyle, but her teeth aren't the same. They're huge. Long. She's had them capped. But the veneers are a little too big. They look like—gulp—horse teeth.

"It's nice that you're able to join us," Patti greets Marta.

I nod my head, my smile fixed. "Hello, Marta."

Marta's smile is just as superficial. "I didn't realize you were in a book club."

My eyebrows lift. Does she think I can't read? "I just show up for the wine," I answer coolly.

"That's not true," Patti contradicts. "Taylor started the book club. It was her idea. Then she enlisted me and I enlisted Kate, and the group grew from there. We've been together for how long now? Four years? Five?"

"I think Taylor likes the idea of being in a book club more than she actually likes reading book club picks." Monica laughs. "She thinks most of our selections are depressing."

I shrug. "I do. Sad stories of the poor and working class."

Monica laughs again. "Taylor can't relate to blue-collar America."

I wish I really were mean. I'd spill my drink on Monica's slouchy pale gold knit tank, a tank that looks suspiciously like one hanging in my closet. In fact, the whole outfit—tank, wide gold belt, and long gold skirt—is Chanel, or knock-off Chanel.

"Is that a new ensemble?" I ask Monica, shifting gears.

She preens. "My personal shopper located it for me after I told her about an ad I saw in a magazine."

Or on my body, I think sourly. "I have the same top, but I didn't buy the skirt. It was just a tad too glitz for me." I walk off to refill my pomegranate-tini.

Patti joins me at the table. She cuts herself a small sliver of pâté and spreads it on a cracker. "You do have that top, don't you?"

"Yes."

"I thought so."

Patti takes a teeny bite of her pâté and cracker. "You know, she's just jealous of you, Taylor. You've got it all—"

"My life isn't always what it seems."

"No, but it is pretty damn nice. Nathan is yummy. You have a brilliant marriage, and you live this beautiful, picture-perfect life on the lake with three picture-perfect children."

"Looks can be deceiving." I nibble on a grape. "Patti, do my teeth look like that?"

Patti stares at Monica a long moment before bursting into a fit of giggles. "Oh. My. God. What did she do?"

"I don't know, but it's not good."

"No." Patti's giggles subside. Her expression turns sober. "Do you think she knows they're way too big?"

"I just don't know why she did it. Her teeth were fine before." I sigh, suddenly exhausted by what we do to ourselves and how we try to impress. "Sometimes this is all too much. Too much work. Too much stress."

"What are you saying? That being Taylor Young is hard work?"

"Doesn't it ever seem like hard work to you?"

"Of course. But that's just life. Life is hard, don't you think? Now get your book and let's snag the couch before anyone else does."

I can't believe I'm saying this, but the book discussion tonight is actually interesting for a change.

I don't know if it's the copious amount of wine we're consuming or because Marta's sitting in tonight, but everyone participates, although I tend to once again be the dissenting voice. *The Memory Keeper's Daughter* is an unqualified hit. Except with me.

"I loved the opening," I explain, "and the first third seemed to move along all right, but then it just started to drag. I needed more character development. I needed change."

"There was change," Suze defended, "near the end where he helps that poor pregnant girl."

"After she untied him?" I shake my head. "I think that's when I stopped reading. It was too much. I couldn't suspend disbelief. Deliver your own baby, give away one child, keep a secret, don't confront your wife about her affair, but please, don't get tied up in a shanty shack in the South."

My words are met by a torrent of protests and comments. Shaking my hair back, I catch Marta's eye. I could almost swear she's smiling. *At me.*

Or maybe she's laughing at me.

Probably laughing at me. Oh, I don't care. It was a good book but not my favorite book, and I don't have to pretend to love it just to get everyone's approval.

A half hour later, the meeting is at an end. "You're picking next month's book, Lucy," Raine says, wrapping things up. "Do you have a title selected yet?"

Lucy nods and reaches into her purse and shyly pulls out a hardcover book. "*The Feminine Mistake* by Leslie Bennetts."

"No!" Suze groans. "No, no, no."

"I don't want to read that book," Monica adds flatly, "I've read enough on it already to know I definitely don't want it to be our book club pick."

"Why not?" Lucy asks nervously, putting the book on her lap and hiding the cover with her hands. "I thought

Taylor had a good idea when she said we should read some nonfiction this year."

"Memoirs, yes, but not feminist rhetoric," Monica answers sourly.

Marta's eyebrow rises, and she leans forward. "So you've read the book, then?"

Monica's shoulders square. "No, but I don't need to read it. I've heard all about it, and I'm sick of the Far Left attacking traditional family values—"

"It has nothing to do with family values," Marta interrupts. "It's about financial self-sufficiency."

"But it's a moot point for most of us," Suze protests. "Our husbands might be the breadwinners, but we make most of the decisions for the family—"

"Including financial?" Ellen interrupts.

"Not necessarily financial, but we're equal partners," Suze answers defensively. "We have our own division of labor."

"Which you don't get paid for," Ellen adds.

Suze shuts her mouth, shakes her head.

"If it's a really controversial book," Raine speaks softly, "maybe we don't want to read it. We have enough problems in life without adding to it."

Lucy sighs. "I don't want to force you to read a book you don't want to read, but I do think it'd be interesting. We could see for ourselves what the fuss is about. We'd be better informed about hot topics, too."

Suze looks increasingly unhappy. "I don't like hot topics. I don't like negativity. I want to focus on positive things—"

"But aren't the books we're reading depressing?" I can't

help interrupting. "Every one of the novels on this year's list is about tragedy and dysfunction."

"But they're well written," Monica protests.

"And so is nonfiction," Marta says. "And isn't being informed a positive thing?"

"Yes," I say firmly, reaching for the book and looking at the cover, surprised to hear myself agreeing with Marta.

Patti nods. "I say yes, too."

Jen and Kate are two more yeses. Marta doesn't cast a vote, which makes Monica anxious. "Do you think you'll want to come back?" she asks Marta.

"Probably not," Marta answers honestly.

Monica is crestfallen. "Why not?"

"It's not really my...thing."

Monica's even more perplexed. "But why not? You told me you read all the time."

"Yes, but this..." Marta glances around the circle. "It's not...me. It's a little too Stepford wife for my taste."

Suze gasps. Kate's surprised. Monica's beyond flustered. "It's not a Stepford wife book club. We've all been to college, and we've all had careers—"

"Good, then reading controversial books shouldn't be upsetting."

"So *The Feminine Mistake* it is," Jen says brightly, bringing the meeting to a close. "Kate hosts next month. See you in November."

Patti doesn't even wait until she's backed out of Jen's drive to drop the bomb on me. "We're moving," she says bluntly, heading east on 8th Street. "Don's been hired by a Bay Area investment firm, and they've asked him to start November first. He'll start soon, and then we'll move around Thanksgiving."

I'm stunned. It's the last thing I expected her to say. "I can't believe it."

"Don and I are both native Californians. We like it here and all three of our children were born here, but our families are in California, and to be honest, we miss the weather. We miss the sun." She looks at me. "And California's not that far. We'll still see you. You and Nathan will just have to pop down for the weekend, do some fun weekend trips like wine tasting in Napa or golfing at Pebble Beach."

I can't even imagine life here without Patti. She's been here as long as I have. "I can't believe it," I repeat numbly.

"I'm still kind of in shock, too. We've been really happy here, and while Don's from the Bay Area, I don't know anyone there. I'm nervous about starting over, trying to fit in, but this is a good move for Don and there's no way I could let him move without us. We need to be together."

Every word she says is a knife in my heart. This is how I should have been with Nathan. This is how I should have reacted. *Great, Nathan, I'm excited by the opportunity. I've always wanted to live in Omaha. . . .*

"How's the cost of living?" I ask tentatively.

"Terrible. Even worse than here. A million dollars buys nothing on the peninsula. We're already house hunting, and we're definitely going to end up with half the house we have here."

"But you'll have the sun."

"That's right. I tell myself we're paying for the great weather."

She falls silent, and we drive without speaking for a minute. "Taylor, I do feel terrible that I'm leaving you solely responsible for the auction, and if you weren't you, I'd worry about the auction, but you are you and you'll do an incredible job as chair. Let's face it, you don't really need me there."

"But I do." I'm sad, really sad. I don't want to do the auction without Patti. I would never have agreed to chair it if I thought I'd have to chair it alone. "I do need you."

Patti pulls into her driveway. Looks like we're not even doing coffee. My spirits sink about as low as they can go.

"You know you can run things by me anytime," she adds. "I'll just be a phone call away."

Nathan gone, and now Patti. I swallow hard. "I'm going to miss you. A lot."

Car in park, she reaches over to give me a swift hug. "You have so many friends, Taylor. You won't even know that I'm gone."

At home, after tucking the girls into bed and comforting Tori, who starts crying for Daddy, I sit at my computer and type a quick e-mail.

Nathan, just found out Patti and Don are moving. They leave before December. I can't stand it. And I can't bear to think about chairing the auction on my own. Help! What do I do?

I'm about to push send when I read it again and think about our financial crisis and the bills that just keep coming in.

PS. More and more collection agencies are coming at us now. I know what's in our checking account. There's no way to pay next month's bills. We need to talk.

Once again I reread the e-mail, and as I read my eyes start to burn. I don't want to e-mail Nathan. I want to talk to him. I need to see him. I need our lives normal again.

PPS. The girls miss you. It's not the same without you.

I push send.

Chapter Eleven

It's Saturday, and I've woken early again. There's no reason to get up before six on a weekend, but I didn't sleep well last night, and starting around four I'd wake up every half hour, look at the clock, and then force myself to go back to sleep. Finally at five-forty I got up and came downstairs to make coffee and have a look at the Saturday job ads. Only the morning paper isn't here yet, and it's wet out.

Please God don't let it be another long, wet winter. I can handle the Pacific Northwest as long as we avoid record-breaking rainfall.

At seven-thirty I dart outside to check for the paper. The rain has let up slightly, and I find the paper wrapped in bright blue plastic in the middle of a puddle on the driveway. I shake the plastic and, once inside, carefully peel the wet plastic from the paper.

After reading the headlines and the front section, I glance briefly through "Arts & Entertainment" before going to the classifieds, looking for anything related to PR, communications, and event planning. I see two possibilities and circle those. Just to be thorough, I go through all the sales positions as well, but nothing jumps at me. I'm still poring over the ads when the kitchen phone rings. It's Nathan. He must have gotten the e-mail I sent last night.

"Hi. Good morning," I say, picking up the phone and sitting on one of the wrought-iron bar stools. There are three stools, but we rarely use them. They looked pretty in the catalog, cost a fortune, and are ridiculously uncomfortable. "You got my e-mail?"

"Don and Patti are really moving?"

I get an immediate lump in my throat. "Yes. I guess Don starts work the first of November, then Patti and the kids move around Thanksgiving."

"Wow."

We're both low and blue, I can feel it. "So how did that appointment go on Thursday?"

"Fine."

But it doesn't sound fine. He doesn't sound fine. "You like the job, though?"

"It's good to be working again."

His cryptic answers do little to ease my sense of alienation. "When do you think you'll be able to come home?"

"I don't know. I'm working the entire weekend. It's a new industry for me, and I'm playing a lot of catch-up. Plus the company has some internal issues, and until those get resolved it's going to be hard to move forward." He pauses. "Can I talk to the girls?"

"They're still sleeping."

"They have games today?"

"Jemma at nine, Brooke at eleven. I don't know if you saw the e-mail I forwarded to you, the one from Brooke's coach. He says she's a natural. He loves her aggressiveness close to the goal."

"She's always been feisty."

"You can say that again."

"What about Jemma?"

"She's doing okay."

"Just okay?"

This is the longest conversation we've had in weeks. It's weird to think we don't talk anymore. "Mrs. Osborne is in weekly communication with me regarding her attitude."

"Is she being rude?"

"No." I slide off the stool and, with the phone tucked between shoulder and chin, warm up my coffee. "Her teacher would just like to see her make a bigger effort. Apparently she's underachieving."

Nathan sighs. "This isn't the first time we've heard this from a teacher."

"No."

He's silent and I hold my cup in my hands, aware of all the things not being said, aware of the distance between us.

"Nathan, we got some nasty notes in the mail this week. Collection agencies are now coming after us."

"Just put them in the mail to me," he says wearily.

"I've cut Annika back from thirty hours a week to seventeen. Imelda will only clean for us twice a month, and the gardeners are down to once a month." I wait for him to say something. He doesn't.

"I'm looking for a job," I add.

"Getting a job isn't going to change anything. You won't make enough money to help with the debt, and you'll just end up hiring more help so you can cope with the job demands."

"That's not true. I'll work in the morning after Tori's been dropped off and stop when it's time to pick her up."

"You'll work from nine forty-five till two."

"Yes."

He makes a rough sound. I can't tell if it's a laugh or a groan. "And who will hire you to work just four hours a day? McDonald's?"

"*Nathan.*"

"Seriously, Taylor, what company will hire you to work a four-hour day?"

I scramble, try to think of a good answer, but nothing comes to me. "Fine, I'll work more hours. Annika can pick the kids up from school. I'll work ten till five. That's seven hours. I can do a lot in seven hours."

His voice drops. "What about your auction?"

"I'll do it in the evening."

"What about the girls?"

I nearly scream. "I'll find a way. I'll make it work. They'll be fine. Everything will be fine."

He doesn't answer for a long time. Then he takes a breath, a deep, slow breath. "Taylor, I'm not trying to hurt your feelings, I'm really not, but I don't think you realize that we pay Annika more an hour than you would earn an hour."

"That's not true—"

"When you worked in PR, you were making what? Forty-four thousand? Forty-eight?"

"About that," I agree stiffly. "But that was ten years ago. Surely with inflation I'd be making more."

"Not for part-time work, and once you're hit by taxes, there won't be a lot left to bring home."

"So what are you saying? For me to do nothing?"

"Maybe we need to sell the house."

My heart falls, a sickening plummet down. I lean heavily on the counter. "Sell the house?"

"We'd use the equity that's left to pay off the bills. We probably wouldn't be able to buy another house right away, but in a year or two, we could find something comfortable."

He's talking, but I'm not listening. Every bone in my body, every fiber of my being, is protesting. I can't sell the house. I love this house. I love living here. "There has to be another way."

"Taylor—"

"I'm going to get a job. I will. This week. And it's going to be okay. You'll see."

Sunday night, the girls watch a Disney movie while I take a long bath.

I don't know that I'm depressed. I just know I can't get out of the bathtub. I've been here for the past half hour, floating in the dark, periodically topping off with more hot water.

Here in the dark I feel safe. Free.

Here in the dark I can almost pretend that everything will be fine.

We can't really lose the house. That can't be possible. Nathan's just trying to scare me. Trying to make me realize we're in trouble, like that program *Scared Straight* where they show troubled kids just what prison is really like.

Maybe that's what's happening here. Maybe I'm being scared straight. Maybe once the program ends I'll find out that everything is as it should be.

I'm still Taylor Young, wife of handsome, successful Nathan Young and mother of three adorable children living in a big beautiful shingle-style house on the lake, a house I designed myself. A house I love so much that it's become part of me.

Monday morning, I schedule an appointment with Maddox, one of Seattle's premier employment agencies. I know they're premier only because they said so in the phone book, and when I researched them on the Internet, they did come up with some high marks.

I'm meeting with one of their human resources specialists at the company's Eastside location in downtown Bellevue. I call and get directions. The office is located in one of the Bellevue Place Towers near Lincoln Square.

I wear a black pantsuit with a crisp lavender collared blouse. I carry a purse that could pass for a briefcase and wear black heels. With my hair pulled back in a low ponytail, I look serious. Successful. I look as though I can do just about anything.

The Maddox personnel specialist didn't see it that way. "Not to be blunt, but you're a dinosaur, Mrs. Taylor," she says, dropping my résumé and leaning back in her ergonomically correct chair. "You're virtually unemployable."

"How is that possible? I have worked. I have excellent experience—"

"A decade ago." She sighs. "Mrs. Taylor, you're competing with men and women who have just recently graduated from school. They're hungry, they're smart, they're ambitious, they're aggressive. They don't have spouses,

they don't have children, they don't have anything competing for their time or attention, and that's who employ-
ers want to hire. Smart, cheap, and available young
people."

I feel myself flush once and again. "You make me sound
old. Decrepit. But I'm thirty-six—"

"And you have what, two kids?"

"Three."

"I take it you've stayed home with them these past ten
years."

"Yes."

"But now it's time to go back to work?"

I'm shriveling up on the inside, and I don't know why.
"Yes."

"What do you have to offer my clients?"

"A good brain. Wisdom. Patience."

The young woman sitting across the desk from me
smiles. "How are your computer skills?"

"Good. I can use Excel and Word."

"How are you with PowerPoint?"

"I'm learning." I'm fudging the truth a bit. I'm not
actively learning, but I did help a little with a PowerPoint
presentation for last year's auction.

"You'd be available to work forty-, fifty-, sixty-hour
weeks? Weekends, evenings...?"

I sit taller. "I *know* there are companies interested in
part-time employees. I *know* companies job-share."

"In the big cities, for employees returning from maternity leave." She folds her hands, looks at me. "I'll be honest. I could probably get you a job, but it wouldn't be

part-time. It'd be full-time and you're not going to start at fifty thousand a year. You'd be lucky to make thirty."

"For full-time."

She nods. "You've been out ten years. There's a penalty for dropping out that long."

"Are men penalized that much?"

"You can't compare the two."

I look at her hard, finding it difficult to process everything she's saying. "I can't believe my prospects are that grim."

My Maddox employment specialist reluctantly smiles. "It's not all bad. It could be worse. If you were fifty-five or above, I'd have to tell you your chances for getting a white-collar job would be next to nil. Companies just don't want to hire 'old.'"

"But many 'older' employees are more experienced."

"Experience doesn't always excite companies as much as potential. And youth. You know in America, we worship youth."

A week has passed since my interview. On my own, I send out a few more résumés and cover letters, hoping that someone, somewhere, will give me a chance. Every day I check my phone and e-mail to see if I've gotten a response on any of the positions I applied for. I did get a form rejection in the mail last week from one, and an e-mail "no, thank you" from another as well, but the other companies haven't even bothered to respond. At least not yet.

The good news is that Nathan's finally coming home, even if it's a super-short trip for the weekend before Halloween. He's promised to take the girls to pick out Halloween costumes and carve pumpkins.

We drive to the airport Friday evening to pick him up, and I'm stunned by his appearance as he climbs into the car on the passenger side. He's thin and pale, with hollows and shadows beneath his eyes. "Hey, long time no see," I say lightly, leaning over to kiss him hello.

He gives me a small kiss. "It has been a while."

The kids all talk at once as I drive us home. Since it's Friday night, not Saturday or Sunday, there's no football game traffic to slow us down. Nathan yawns several times during the drive, and I catch him rubbing his eyes once, hard. He definitely hasn't been living the high life in Omaha, I think, merging onto 520 off 405 and moving into the carpool lane.

As we pull up to the garage, we crunch over piles of fallen red and brown leaves. Nathan frowns. "The gardeners aren't raking?"

I hit the automatic garage door opener. "They did. But it's been a couple weeks. They'll be back next week, though, and they'll get these then."

I can see Nathan giving the interior of the house a hard look. I'm suddenly glad I spent the afternoon cleaning. I made the girls help me. Jemma complained bitterly, but Brooke and Tori seemed to actually find it fun.

"Things look nice," Nathan admits rather reluctantly, sitting on the couch only to be smothered by the girls, who dive all over him for hugs.

"We're trying," I answer, sitting in the leather chair across from the couch. I watch the girls wrestle with him.

Nathan's tickling them and throwing them this way and that. For a moment I imagine everything's fine, everything's the way it's always been, but twenty minutes later Nathan pleads exhaustion.

"I'm beat, girls. I have to turn in, but we'll have the whole day to play tomorrow."

Brooke stops wriggling to look up into his face. "When are you going back?"

"Sunday."

"Sunday?" the girls all chorus loudly.

"But that's the day after tomorrow!" Jemma protests.

"You just got home!" Brooke adds.

Tori's in tears, and she flings herself around Nathan's neck and squeezes tight. "Don't go. Stay here. We need you here. Right, Mom?"

"Right," I answer, but Nathan's kissing Tori and doesn't seem to hear.

Nathan sleeps on the couch in the family room. He says it's because he doesn't sleep well anymore and he doesn't want to keep me up, but I feel utterly rejected as he leaves the room with his pillow and the plump satin quilt from the foot of the bed.

"Then take our room," I say, jumping from the bed and meeting him in the hall. "You're staying in some corporate motel. I'm sure the bed there can't be very comfortable. You deserve a good night's sleep."

He gives his head a shake. "I'm not going to kick you out of bed. I'm fine on the couch. Trust me."

"Nathan—"

"Do you know this is why I haven't come home? It's because I can't do this. I can't fight with you. It wears me out."

I look at him, hands clasped together even as I battle to stay calm. "But I don't want to fight with you, either. I just want you happy."

He suddenly leans down and kisses my forehead just above my left eyebrow. "I'm happy to be home. All I want to do is sleep. Okay?"

I will not cry in front of him. I will not cry. "Okay." I smile, nod. "I'll see you in the morning."

"Good night, Taylor."

"Good night, Nathan."

At breakfast, Nathan cooks the girls French toast and encourages Brooke to eat another piece of bacon. I refill his coffee cup and smile at them as though everything's normal, but in truth, on the inside I'm screaming.

On the inside I don't know who or what we are.

I did love Nathan. I still love Nathan. Unbearably, unbelievably. From the beginning he was my knight in shining armor, the hero of my story, the man who could do anything, who would do anything, who'd turn me into someone fantastic and beautiful, special and magical. Nathan was my answer to prayer.

But that isn't the Nathan here. This Nathan's different. He's the Iceman, and he's freezing me out. I'm slowly going all cold inside.

I struggle between anger and shame. Why didn't he tell me before it was too late? Why didn't he tell me how serious things were? Why did he have to be the savior, the answer guy, the fix-it-all-by-himself guy?

After breakfast, we spend the next four and a half hours watching Brooke and Jemma play soccer. Brooke is as aggressive as hell and scores four times for her team. Jemma actually plays better than I've seen her play all season, scoring one goal. She's elated, and after the game she leaps into her dad's arms.

"That was for you, Dad."

"Thanks, pumpkin."

It's one of those clear, cloudless autumn days where the sky seems extra blue and the colors on the ground extra red and gold. Nathan asks me if I mind if he takes the girls to lunch, just the four of them, a father-daughter treat before they go looking for Halloween costumes.

I'm glad he's so good with them. But as they drop me off at the house and I watch the four of them leave together, I can't help feeling a little left out. I want to have fun, too.

Four hours later, Jemma comes home with a red devil girl costume. Tori is—of course—a pink princess, and Brooke is a Bratz pirate. I didn't even know the Bratz dolls were now making costumes for real girls. I glance casually at the price tag from Jemma's red devil costume: $44, without the accessories. Have costumes always been so expensive?

While buying costumes, they also picked up pumpkins, one for each of us, and we line up in the dining room, the good table surface covered by thick layers of newspapers, and carve our pumpkins.

In keeping with the spirit of things, I heat apple cider on the stove, spicing it with cinnamon sticks, and find the CD of Halloween music that includes unforgettable favorites such as "Thriller" and "Monster Mash."

Leaning against the counter, I smile to myself as the girls dance around the family room, doing their version of the Twist.

This, I think, my mug of cider pressed to my mouth, is why we fall in love and get married and have babies. This. Three little girls shimmying and shaking and doing the Twist.

Chapter Twelve

Saturday night after the girls go to bed, Nathan and I sit in the family room watching an old movie. He's in the soft leather armchair, legs outstretched on the matching ottoman, while I curl up on the couch. We're not exactly talking, but I don't mind. It's nice just being here, together, like this.

An hour later, as the movie goes to commercial break, I look at him and see that he's fallen asleep. I'm not surprised, since he's on a different time zone from us. Quietly I turn off the TV, find the quilt he used last night, and cover him before dimming the lights.

I'm just leaving the room when I hear his voice. "It's been a good house, hasn't it?"

Standing in the doorway between the large, casually elegant kitchen and the spacious but cozy family room, I nod. "I love living here. The girls love it, too."

"Let's go Monday to talk to someone. I've got the number of a financial planner that specializes in situations like ours. Maybe he'll have some advice for us."

"I thought you were flying back tomorrow night."

"I can push the flight back a day. I think it's important we talk to someone sooner rather than later."

"Sounds good. Thanks. Good night, Nathan."

"Good night, Taylor. Sleep tight."

Early Monday afternoon, Nathan and I are to go see Michael Burns together at Burns & Bailey Financial, and I spend a long time standing in my closet trying to decide what to wear. We're seeking financial advice, so I know I shouldn't arrive dressed to the nines, but at the same time, I want to present a polished, even sophisticated image. We're in debt, but we're still successful people.

I settle on black, very straight-leg wool pants and a flame cashmere turtleneck sweater with my Miu Miu camel wool coat over all. My black patent Jimmy Choo heels are the perfect shoes and really pull the look together. It's appropriately autumn but still smart.

"You look nice," Nathan tells me as we get into my car, although he's driving.

"Thank you." I smile, yet I'm nervous. I cross my legs one way and then the other, struggling to get comfortable and thinking how odd it is to feel like a stranger with my own husband.

"You're sure Annika will be here this afternoon?"

I nod. "She'll pick up Tori and then meet the girls' school bus."

"God, I don't want to do this," Nathan mutters as we take 92nd Avenue to 8th Street.

It's not even a five-minute drive from our house to the Burns & Bailey office in downtown Bellevue, but it feels much longer. Nathan's tense. I'm tense. The strain is almost unbearable.

Burns & Bailey Financial is located on the twentieth floor of one of the Bellevue Place Towers adjacent to the Hyatt hotel. Nathan parks underneath the building, and we take the first of two elevators to reach the Burns & Bailey office.

Nathan and I are quiet during the ride up to the twentieth floor. Hopefully, Mr. Burns will be able to give us some guidance on how to start working our way out of debt without losing everything.

The office is large and plush in an understated financial decor sort of way—lots of soothing marine blue paint, a thick carpet on the floor to muffle sound, a series of framed black-and-white prints of Mt. Rainier and the Puget Sound on the wall.

The receptionist shows us down a narrow hall to an office at the end of the corridor. "Mr. Burns." She knocks on his door and then opens it. "Mr. and Mrs. Nathan Young are here for their one-thirty appointment."

Mr. Burns is actually a man our age, a little thick in the jowls and with thinning light brown hair. "Call me Michael," he says pleasantly, standing and gesturing for us to sit in the chairs facing his desk.

We sit. Sliding a pair of wire-frame glasses on his nose, Michael reviews the paperwork Nathan faxed earlier in the day. He studies it as though he's never seen it before, and maybe he hasn't, or maybe he has and his memory just needs refreshing.

After a few minutes, he pulls off the reading glasses and leans back in his chair. "You know, you aren't the first couple this has happened to. Lots of people are dangerously extended...."

Nathan shifts next to me, his jaw set.

"Americans have a love affair with credit. All it takes is one unforeseen tragedy, a death, divorce, a layoff—"

"So what do you suggest?" Nathan interrupts, his voice pitched so low that it's like nails on a chalkboard. He hates this. He's in his own personal hell right now.

"I'd file Chapter thirteen, reorganize your debts, and work on paying your creditors back."

I glance at Nathan. I don't understand. "Can we do that?"

Nathan's jaw thickens. "If we wanted to file bankruptcy."

I blink. "Oh. I didn't know that's what Chapter thirteen was. I thought Chapter eleven was bankruptcy..." My voice fades away as I realize it just doesn't matter. The fact is, this highly recommended financial guru is charging us $400 to recommend we file bankruptcy, and all I can think is, This is the best he's got?

"You'd erase a huge portion of your debt," Michael adds, "and you'd have a shot at protecting your remaining assets."

"What about the house?" Nathan asks bluntly.

"You *might* be able to save it. It's expensive property, but you've taken out numerous loans against the house...." Michael glances at our tidy stack of paperwork. "However, on the upside, Mr. Young, you *are* employed, and the fact that you are earning wages and wish to start repaying your creditors will certainly help as you work out a repayment plan." He pauses. "Of course, the court must approve your repayment plan and your budget."

Nathan glances at me. His misery is palpable. I feel the same way. Save the house, but publicly declare that we're shit at managing our affairs?

"It sounds worse than it is," Michael continues pragmatically. "Once the court approves your plan and you've been appointed a trustee, you'll have three to five years to pay back your creditors. You'll make monthly payments to the bankruptcy trustee, who will distribute the funds to the creditors. Once the repayment plan is completed, your unpaid debts are discharged."

Michael Burns makes it sound so easy. By filing Chapter 13, we'd buy time to reorganize our debt and then pay the bills as agreed in our approved plan. Piece of cake.

Except we're now treated no better than wayward children who've become wards of the court with a trustee appointed to watch us.

Michael must see the distaste on my face because he admits quietly, "It's tough on the ego, but consider your children. Maybe, just maybe, this is the best thing for your daughters."

Nathan stiffens. "How did you know we have daughters?"

Michael smiles kindly. "My daughter Maggie is in the same class with Jemma this year."

Nathan gets to his feet. "We'll think about it," he says.

We awkwardly shake hands and exit the office. Nathan doesn't speak as we ride the first elevator down to the lobby.

"I could use a drink," he says as we leave the elevator.

"Me too."

We walk through the Hyatt, heading for the hotel's new wine bar. It's still early yet, and the happy hour crowd hasn't arrived. We practically have the place to ourselves and sit at a small table not far from the bar.

The bartender comes out to take our order from behind the bar. "What can I get for you?"

"A glass of red," Nathan says.

"We have an extensive wine list by the bottle and the glass—"

"Syrah or Cab. The house wine's fine."

"The same," I say before the bartender can ask me.

As the bartender walks away, Nathan groans and rubs his face. "That was a waste."

"I'm sorry."

"Yeah, me too." We sit in silence for a while, and it's a companionable silence.

Our wine arrives. Nathan lifts his glass. "To unforeseen tragedies," he says in a mocking toast.

I warily clink my glass with his. "So is that what we do? Declare bankruptcy?"

Nathan sighs. "It'd give us time."

I nod.

"It'd have the least impact on the girls," he adds emotionlessly.

He's as dead as I am. "Won't people know?" I ask.

"I don't know. I've never known anyone who filed Chapter thirteen, or seven, or eleven."

Neither have I.

But then, when I was growing up, I never knew anyone who had money. If it hadn't been for my scholarship to

USC, I'd probably still be part of the struggling middle class today.

From dust to dust, I say silently, mockingly, ashes to ashes.

"What's that?" Nathan asks, and I realize I wasn't exactly silent.

Self-consciously, I repeat the passage. "It's from Genesis. The gist is that all our efforts, and all our striving, is in vain. We started as dust." I shrug. "And we'll end as dust."

Nathan cracks a smile. "Aren't you Debbie Downer?"

I smile back crookedly. "We can't say it wasn't fun while it lasted."

We sit so long, we end up ordering a blackened salmon Caesar salad to share along with another glass of wine. I'm not really hungry, so I let Nathan have the lion's share. I pick at a warm roll.

"When are you going to take your Porsche to Omaha?" I ask as the waiter clears the salad plate.

Frowning, Nathan slowly turns the wine goblet by the stem. "I'm selling it. I've got an ad in the paper and one on Craigslist."

"Oh, Nathan."

"I can't keep the car, Taylor. It'd be a joke. I'm a joke. What kind of man has a Porsche and no job?"

"But you have a job now and you need a car."

"The company's supplied me with a car for now, and someday when I buy another car, I'll buy something more practical." He takes a breath. "The boat, by the way, is gone. Bellevue Marine and Boat Sales bought it back from me."

My insides fall. "Did they offer a good price?"

He gives me a look. "I was six months late on my payments. I'm just lucky I got out of it."

Swallowing hard, I push my wineglass around. "But that still leaves us with a lot of debt."

"Between your car payments, the equity loan, and the credit card debt, we're in the hole about two million. And it grows every month we don't pay it significantly down. Unfortunately, we can't pay any of it down. All we can do is make minimum payments."

Two million in the hole. And the debt's just growing. My insides writhe. "If we sold"—God, this is hard—"the house. Would there be enough equity left after we paid off the second and third loans on the house to get rid of the debt?"

"It'd be close." He leans back, folds his arms tightly across his chest. "But it'd help. It would at least reduce the debt to something manageable."

Then that's all there is to it. I reach across the table, touch Nathan's elbow. "Let's sell the house. Let's just do it."

His features tighten. "It's a beautiful house, Taylor."

"It's a house." I can barely get out the words before my throat closes.

"I know how much you love that house."

"Let's not talk about it. It'll just hurt more if we discuss it." My eyes are burning. I won't be able to keep it together much longer.

He shakes his head, runs his hand across his face. Tears shine in his eyes. "That's your house. Your dream house. We built it for you."

I can't do this. I can't. What do they say when a limb has to go? Amputate it fast? "It's just a house," I choke. "We'll have another one someday."

* * *

So, it's settled. We're going to sell the house. We drive back home, and I'm keeping it together until we turn down the drive that leads to our house. The tall roof with the dormer windows comes into view and then the glossy white columns on the front porch and the elegant shingled facade. Hot emotion floods me, emotion so strong that I grip the edges of my seat to keep from making a sound.

We have to do this.

We have to.

There's no other way we can get the monkey off our back.

Nathan parks in the driveway instead of the garage. He leaves the car running and just looks at the house. "We don't have to do this."

Yes, we do. He and I both know it. "If we're going to do it, we have to do it fast. I won't be able to handle it if this drags on too long."

He turns off the ignition. "I should call Art, then," he says, referring to Art Whittelsey, our real estate agent.

Nathan still has Art on his speed dial, even though we haven't bought a house from him in a long time. But Art handled the four houses we owned previously in this area. Not just a savvy agent, Art has become a friend over the years. He helped us navigate the pricey, and at times ridiculously inflated, real estate market here on the Eastside.

Nathan and I bought our first house together the same year we married. It was a dark, tiny, windowless shoebox of a house in Clyde Hill, one of the coveted affluent Bellevue neighborhoods with proximity to everything—the bridges to Seattle, downtown Bellevue, Kirkland water-front, and, of course, great schools.

The exterior siding of our new house was painted brown. The exterior window trim was the same brown. Enormous cedar trees circled the house, blocking light as well as any curb appeal, and the backyard was a muddy swamp. I didn't know then what I know now about houses on hills in rainy cities. Don't buy a house at the bottom of a hill. Buy on the top. Water drains down.

That first year we were married, I'd come home from work and change into jeans and T-shirts and my work boots and I'd attack the yard. I had a professional tree company take out the massive cedar in the front yard, grinding the stump, and then prune the trees around the perimeter of the house, allowing more light to reach the house.

I dug up some of the huge overgrown rhodies and replaced them, whacked others down to size, and just removed others entirely. I removed wild ferns and hacked at thorny blackberry vines until my arms and wrists were scratched and bleeding.

One Saturday Nathan and I rented a rototiller and churned up the soil. The next day we tilled soil amenders into the freshly churned earth. The next Saturday we rented a roller to flatten the front smooth. The next day we seeded the front. Within three months we had a beautiful lush lawn that rolled from the front steps of the house and along the curvy walk to the edge of the street. The lawn was green, bright healthy green, and as it filled in I turned to the house and tackled the hideous brown paint job. It was April, and the weather was warming. I picked the sunny weekends and learned to use a paint sprayer. I wasn't great at spraying, so I learned to cover my splotches with a light, deft touch of a paintbrush.

The house, now a silvery gray, needed a new front door, and I bought one at Home Depot and painted it a gorgeous, glossy black. With a topiary in a pot by the front door and new brass house numbers on the side, it began to look like a real house, a house that was a home.

Every house we lived in, I did virtually the same thing. New garden, new paint, new doors and windows, new crown molding, new baseboards, new carpets, new hardwood floors, new fixtures, new, new, new, and I did most of it myself. I learned to plumb and wire and use a wet saw for tiles and a circular saw for chair rail and crown molding.

I would never have thought I could build anything. I'm not that handy. But desperation, and the desire to make Nathan happy, fueled my determination to learn.

I never told Nathan this, but I couldn't wait for his parents to visit. They'd see how hard I'd worked, how much I'd done for their son. I hoped they'd realize I wasn't just a good wife, but the right wife.

His parents, though, never came.

Art gets Nathan's message and he's over just before six. "What's going on?" he greets us, shaking Nathan's hand before leaning over to kiss my cheek.

Art's tall, the kind of man who looks like a former jock. He's all friendly and funny. Maybe that's why he's so successful. You like hanging out with him. You end up enjoying buying and selling houses, because along with the house, you get great company.

"We were hoping you'd list the house for us," Nathan says, not wasting time. He's still hoping to catch a late flight out.

Art glances back and forth at us. "This house?"

I suddenly can't speak. Blinking, I look away and shove two fingers into a tiny pocket on my black slacks, fingers curling against the fabric in silent protest. *I can't do this. Can't do this. Can't.*

"Yeah," Nathan says. "Can we do the paperwork now?"

"Sure," Art answers, and I see him glance my way, but I still can't look at him. This is so brutal. It hurts so much. "Let me just get my briefcase from the car."

While Art goes to his car, I go to the kitchen and crouch in the pantry and cover my head and open my mouth in a silent howl. Not my house. *Not my house.* I'd give anything if we could just keep the house.

But Nathan's stressed. Nathan's breaking. I can't have my husband fall apart. Can't have my family fall apart. *We can do this. We can do it. I can do it. I can.*

I stand and leave the pantry, close the door behind me, and step into the powder bath, where I check my face, wiping away mascara smudges and all hint of tears. I smooth my cashmere sweater's hem, slide my hands down my slacks.

I join Art and Nathan in the living room. They were talking quietly, and both look up at me quickly. "I'm sorry," Art says as I sit in a wing chair facing the couch.

I don't know what Nathan's said to Art, but whatever it is, it generates quiet sympathy. I try to smile. "Thank you."

With pen in hand, Art swiftly goes through the paperwork. We've done this so many times together, and Art
knows how we do business. We're not cutthroats, and
we're not petty. Nor do we believe in gouging people. Our
best offer is, indeed, our best offer. With that in mind, we
don't want others to play games with us, either. But Art
knows all that about us.

The questions Art asks are so very familiar. When do
we want the listing to go live in the computer? When
do we want to schedule our first Realtor open house? How
do we want to price it? What are we willing to accept?

I finally speak, my hands clasped before me. "We need
to get as much as we can for it. But at the same time, we
need it to sell quickly, too. Nathan's going to be gone, so
I'll be the one here while the house is being shown."

Art looks back and forth again. "You two are okay,
aren't you?"

"Yes," Nathan and I answer simultaneously, even as I
mentally add, Or at least we're going to be.

Nathan walks Art to his car. I go to the kitchen to start dinner. I'm numb as I go through the motions of measuring
the spices for the lime chili marinade I use for chicken faji-
tas. I'm numb as I whisk the marinade, numb as I pull the
package of free-range chicken out of the fridge and rinse
the six plump breasts. But it's okay to be numb. Numb, I
won't cry. Numb, I can cope with anything. It's how I got
through Mom leaving us. It's how I got through the whispers and snickers at school.

I've just poured the marinade over the chicken breasts
when Nathan enters the kitchen, opens the refrigerator,

and starts to pull out a beer but then replaces it. He pours himself a Scotch instead. "Want anything?" he asks, putting away the bottle of Johnnie Walker Black.

"No, thank you." I can't drink now. I'll end up morbidly depressed. Bawling my eyes out. Eating an entire package of Double Stuf Oreos.

Nathan takes a drink, exhales slowly, and then takes another sip. "We have to tell the girls," he says, leaning against one counter and rubbing the back of his neck.

I nod as I slice the red, yellow, and green bell peppers into narrow strips. I can't even imagine telling the girls. Brooke was fourteen months old when we moved in. And Tori came home here from the hospital. It's the only home she's ever known.

The house isn't just a status symbol. It's their home. It's where Nathan and I were going to make a storybook life for our kids and give them all the love, warmth, and stability we'd never known.

But there will be other homes, I remind myself fiercely, reaching for a sweet onion. It's not as if we won't have a home again. It'll just take some time.

Not that it'll make breaking the news any easier.

"How do we do this?" I ask Nathan as I finish chopping the onion. "Shall you tell them or shall I?"

He just stares across the airy kitchen, his jaw so tight that I can see all the tendons in his neck outlined. "I don't care."

I know him better than I know anyone, but we are both so alone right now, so isolated despite our efforts to come together, to work this out together.

Maybe we don't really want this to work out.

Maybe Nathan wants out. All the way out.

I can't think that way. Won't think that way. I refuse to make this worse than it already is.

"We'll just tell them together," I say, washing my hands and drying them on one of the French linen dish towels.

I should never have given up responsibility.

I should never have accepted financial dependency.

I should have remained aware, alert, an adult.

"We'll do it together," I repeat, and this time I move toward him, put my hand on the middle of his rigid back. He stiffens, but I leave it there.

We break the news after dinner before I serve dessert. I'm not sure why we chose that moment, but suddenly Nathan and I looked at each other and we knew. We had to. Had to get it over with.

"As I'm working in Omaha," Nathan says, "your mother and I have decided to make some changes. We've decided to sell the house. The house goes on the market a week from today."

There's a moment of incredulous silence, and then all the girls are talking at once.

Jemma's voice rises above the rest. "But this is our house. This is where we live."

I know exactly how she's feeling. I spent years looking at real estate, trying to find the right lot, the right place for our perfect future home. I spent another year drafting, planning, poring over magazines, talking to designers and architects, driving around neighborhoods, looking, thinking, dreaming.

Dreaming.

"I'm sorry, Jemma," I say gently, reaching over to cover her hand.

She rips her hand out from beneath mine. "Mom, no. *No.*"

"Jemma, I'm sorry, it's done."

"*Noooooo!*" Jemma's scream fills the living room. *"No! No."*

I don't even look at Nathan. I can feel his pain. He's in hell. He knows I love this house passionately. I know the girls love this house. We're giving up a part of our hearts, but that's the way it is. You spend too much, you live too freely, you fall too hard.

"Jemma." I say her name so sharply that she abruptly stops screaming.

All three girls look at me. Nathan looks at me. The thought comes: Only I can save us now.

I don't even know how I know, but it's the same thing that makes a little girl pick up a plastic doll and rock it and hug it.

Something somewhere inside me comes to life. I can do this. I know how to do this. I will rock us. Hug us. Love us. Things are just things. We are more than the sum of our things.

"We are not dying," I say crisply. "We are just moving to a smaller house. And we are going to be okay. It might not seem like it now. And it might not seem like it for a while. But we will be. We will. And that's all I"—I pause, look at Nathan, who has tears in his eyes—"I have to say."

After cutting me a check to get us through the next couple of weeks, Nathan stuffs the bills into his briefcase, and with the girls crying in the backseat, I drive him back to the airport for his Northwest Airlines flight to Omaha, connecting through Minneapolis. It's going to be another long night of no sleep on yet another red-eye for him, while I lie awake until nearly one-thirty, staring at the lamp on the table next to the bed.

Telling the girls we had to sell the house was worse than I'd imagined. I had thought they'd cry, but Jemma's reaction shocked me.

But what else do we do? File Chapter 13? Declare bankruptcy? My stomach turns over as I think the thought. The word *bankruptcy* is so horrible, it tastes like sour milk in my mouth.

It could save the house.

Everyone would know.

If we lose the house, everyone will know.

Either way, everyone will know. Everything.

I pull my pillow over my head and scream. I feel like my guts are being wrenched out one by one.

Chapter Thirteen

The bedside alarm keeps going off, and I just keep hitting snooze.

I can't get out of bed. Can't face the day. Can't face me. Can't face reality.

Five more minutes, I think, hitting snooze yet again and rolling over, burying my face in the pillow.

I try to fall back asleep, but a little voice inside my head is yapping at me. If I don't get up right now, the girls are going to be late. They'll miss their bus. I'll end up driving them. They'll get tardies.

I don't care.

Let them be late. Let them miss school. It's just elementary school. They're just children. And I'm just falling apart.

I must have fallen back to sleep because I'm suddenly being shaken awake by Brooke. "Wake up, Mom. School started a half hour ago.... Mom, get up. We're late."

I roll over onto my back and squint at her. "Is everyone else up?"

"Jemma's still asleep. Tori's watching TV." Brooke cocks her head and studies me. "You look sad, Mom."

I'm about to deny it, about to put on my happy mom face, when I can't do it. Can't fake it. Not now, not again. "I am."

"Is it about the house?" she asks carefully.

I nod a little. "And other things."

"Like Dad living in Omaha."

I nod again. "He's too far away."

Brooke reaches over to smooth my hair. It's a strangely maternal touch from my middle wild child. "I love you, Mom. You really are the best mom. Even if you do have too many meetings."

I catch her hand, kiss it. "Do I have too many meetings?"

"Yeah."

"If I worked, I'd have a lot of meetings."

"But I like that you don't work. I like that I can see you every day."

"If I worked, you'd still see me every day. You'd see me before school and after school."

Her small shoulders shrug. "But it wouldn't be the same, and most of the moms don't work. In fact, no one's mom works."

I roll into a sitting position and drop another kiss on the top of her head before sliding from bed. "Go wake up Jemma. I'll get dressed quickly and drive you girls to school. Tell Jemma to hurry and grab a Pop-Tart on her way to the car because we're leaving soon."

Brooke runs out and I strip in the bathroom, tie up my hair, and pull a shower cap over my head. I don't have time to wash my hair today, and even if I did have time, I don't think I could.

The old blue feeling is back, and it's stronger than ever.

I turn on the shower full blast, but it doesn't seem to help. I'm so sad, and I work so hard to not be sad. I work so hard to be up, on, optimistic, strong. I work endlessly at keeping a positive attitude when the truth is, I want to give up sometimes and give in to whatever it is dragging me down, pulling me under.

This morning I feel heavy with it, heavy and dark and slow. I can't tell anyone, not even Nathan, because people expect more from me, and now it seems Nathan expects the worst.

But he doesn't understand. He doesn't understand how it is to lose one's self, lose one's mind. Or at the very least, fear losing one's mind. And the mind is a tricky thing to lose. Lose your keys or your hat and you're a silly, head-in-the-sky dreamer. Lose your wallet or passport one too many times and you're careless. But lose your mind...? It's really not socially acceptable. Issues of mental soundness tend to make people uncomfortable. I have yet to hear mentions of nervous breakdowns in cordial cocktail chatter.

Somehow I end up dressed in a smart Ralph Lauren cashmere-and-tweed jacket and matching skirt, brown Wolford tights, and high-heeled Jimmy Choo brown buckle boots. I brush my hair hard before drawing it back in a low ponytail. I smile robotically at my reflection in the bathroom mirror. I still look good on the outside. No one will know I'm cracking.

I park in front of the school in the No Park zone. I'm running into the office for only a moment, and I'm not the only one who does it. All the moms leave their cars there if they need to dash into the school office for something.

I walk all three girls into the office. "I overslept," I tell

Alice Dunlop with a shrug as my girls take their tardy passes and dash off to class. It's not a good excuse. The girls' tardy will be unexcused, but I don't have it in me to lie.

"Not feeling well?" Alice asks.

"I didn't, no, not last night," I answer.

"We have to sell our house," Tori announces, standing next to me.

Alice's eyebrows lift. "You're selling your house?"

I wasn't ready for the news to go public, and while Alice isn't the type to gossip, walls in the school office do have ears.

"Nathan's taken a job in Omaha," I say lightly. "It doesn't make sense to have two big houses."

Alice leans on the counter, concerned. "Is this a permanent position, Taylor?"

"We don't know yet." I'm still smiling. "It was such a great opportunity for Nathan that we thought let's just go for it. See what happens."

"We don't see Daddy anymore," Tori volunteers helpfully.

I put my hand on top of her head. "Tori, Daddy was just home this weekend. He can't come home every weekend. Not from Omaha." I look at Alice, careful to keep my expression perfectly light and comfortable. "There aren't any direct flights from Omaha," I add for Alice's benefit. "It's a long trip back and forth."

"I can imagine." Alice tut-tuts. "It's got to be hard on all of you."

"It's a challenge, but we're doing fine. The girls are troupers." With my hand still on Tori's head, I steer her toward the door. "Now I better get this one to school before she's late, too." I wave good-bye and we leave the school office, Tori holding my hand, skipping next to me.

My BlackBerry beeps at me as I leave Tori's preschool. Auction meeting today at one p.m. That's right. The meeting is in three hours, but I'm not prepared. Haven't followed up on anything on my to-do list. I consider canceling the meeting, but I can't do that. The auction is in March. It's nearly November. Now is when we have to really get serious.

Sliding behind the steering wheel, I shut the door and then start the car. As I back out of the school parking lot, I get that crazy lost feeling again, as though I'm not here, not real, not going to make it unless I do something fast. Like take something, drink something...No, I'll just go shop. Shopping always makes me feel better. When I shop I get to be someone else: someone more interesting, more together, more powerful.

People wonder how you can get addicted to shopping, and it's like this: When you're making decisions—even decisions about what to buy—you feel strong. In control. I want this. No, I don't think so. Or, give me two of that, one in each color. As you make decisions, as you take charge, you feel empowered. You feel as though you matter. It sounds ridiculous, but when I'm at Nordstrom's or somewhere else, the salesgirls look at me, they listen, they hurry to help me.

But with only $1,200 in the checking account and no credit cards left, I can't shop.

Sorry

I guess I'm going to have to live with this heavy blue fog until it lifts.

I'm at Tully's early to push tables together. Patti arrives just after me and offers to put in our drink order. "That would be great," I answer, dragging a few empty chairs from other tables to our cluster.

"The usual? Short, skim, no foam latte?"

"Yep."

While she stands in line, I go to the ladies' room to wash my hands. My face catches me by surprise. I look hard. Brittle.

Old.

Little lines web my eyes. More lines frame my mouth. A deeper line is there between my eyebrows.

I practice a smile. I look marginally better. Next I rummage in my purse for my makeup bag and run warm autumny copper lipstick over my lips and add a similar copper blush to my cheeks. I darken my eyeliner. Smile at myself again.

Better. Younger. Brighter.

No wonder the cosmetic industry is so huge.

I put away my makeup bag, feeling like a faker. But faking it isn't all bad. In Los Angeles, fakers are called actors and they get paid big bucks.

After leaving the ladies' restroom, I discover Patti at the table with our coffee. A couple of the other moms arrive. Within another five minutes, everyone else shows up.

Unfortunately, five minutes into the meeting, Patti shares that she's moving Thanksgiving weekend and, regrettably, this will be her last meeting.

She turns to smile at me. "We're all lucky Taylor's the co-chair. She'll do a great job. She'll make sure this year's auction is the best ever."

My lipstick smile threatens to fall. I wish Patti had waited until the end of the meeting to share her big news. After her announcement, we never really get back on track, and the next ninety minutes slide by in one conversation after another.

I try halfheartedly to steer the discussion onto procurement and how we need a mix of items to generate the most interest, explaining that some auction attendees want to go home with an item that night, while others would rather bid on a future event; but when no one on the committee bites, I give up, sit back, and let everyone talk.

I so wish Patti weren't leaving. I don't want to chair the auction by myself. It's not that I can't do it, but it won't be the same. It was fun sharing the work, having someone else to bounce ideas off. And Patti always had a way of making me feel smart, clever. Without her I don't feel very accomplished at all.

Worrying about the auction, I watch people come and go, including the beautiful blond mother with thick Kim Alexis hair and a Christie Brinkley smile who walks through the doors with her towheaded preteen and her graying husband. The mother and daughter sit at the conference table while the dad waits in line. Soon he's with them again, and they enjoy their snacks and talk.

They look so comfortable. So relaxed. I find myself envying them. That's how it used to be with our family. Easy. Natural.

The front door opens again, and a woman enters with

three little girls all dressed in private school white blouses and plaid skirts. The mom is thinner than a sixteen-year-old even after three daughters.

The girls sit at a table, and the mom carries over a tray of snacks and drinks. As she passes around the small hot ciders, a man arrives with a baby and joins the family. He's wearing charcoal gray plaid pants, white button-down, tie, gold-rimmed glasses. He hands the baby to his wife. They don't kiss. They don't speak. They don't even make eye contact during the hand-off.

The mom returns to the counter for her own coffee, and she smiles at the barista when requesting a sleeve for her cup. It's the first smile I've seen from her since they arrived.

Now dad is leaving and the girls all chorus good-bye, but mom never once looks up, never says good-bye. He goes without saying a word, either.

Is this really how people live? Is this what happens when marriages go bad?

I think of Nathan. I think of how I still feel when he walks in the room, how everything in me lifts, so glad we're together, so glad he's mine.

I can't even begin to imagine life without him. I can't imagine me without him.

Things are going to work out. We'll be back together soon, back to the way things were. We will. We have to.

But what if we aren't?

The whisper of doubt undoes me, and abruptly I rise, suddenly, stunningly claustrophobic. "I'll be right back," I murmur before racing outside on shaking legs, nearly wobbling in my leather boots' four-inch stiletto heels.

Outside it's gray and cold and crisp, with massive gold and brown leaves blowing down the street. I walk to the side of the building where no one can see me and lean against the brown wall, my forehead pressed to the wood. I open my mouth and gulp in air.

I'm afraid. I'm afraid. I'm so afraid I can't survive this.

It's not just the loss of things. It's not even the loss of Nathan. It's the loss of pride. It's the loss of confidence. It's the loss of whatever protective layer I'd grown around me over the years, because that layer's now gone. I'm being stripped and it hurts and I ache.

Behind me, a truck pulls into the spot at the corner of the building. Car doors open and close. Footsteps sound and then stop.

"Taylor?" a female voice asks uncertainly, hesitating behind me.

I realize how ridiculous I must look in my designer suit and glamorous knee-high boots with my face planted against Tully's wood siding.

Straightening, I turn around. My heart falls.

It's Marta. Marta and her boyfriend, Luke Flynn, one of the auction's big supporters every year. He does a lot for disadvantaged kids, too, always helping underwrite local youth programs.

"You all right?" she asks. She's wearing faded jeans, her horrible combat books (Why? Why? Why?), and a black cable-knit sweater that hangs to her thighs. It looks like a guy's sweater, and from the size of it, I suspect it's Luke's.

"I'm fine." The words stick in my throat. I lift my chin, stare at her defiantly. "Thank you," I add pointedly.

Anyone else would back off. Go away. Marta just stands there, her dark eyebrows furrowed, her expression speculative.

Just go, I command silently. *Leave.*

She doesn't, and Luke, who stands a few feet behind Marta, looks away.

The wind tugs at Marta's long black hair, which hangs over her shoulder, past her breast. She's so damn sure of herself, I think bitterly, so goddamn untouchable.

I don't even know why I dislike her so much. I just do. She reminds me of Angelina Jolie. She even looks like Angelina Jolie, and I don't like Angelina Jolie, either.

Patti appears at the corner. She's holding my cell phone. "Taylor. It's Art Whittelsey. He says it's urgent."

Without looking at Marta, I walk toward Patti and take the phone. "Thank you," I say, my voice husky.

She nods and smiles, but her expression is concerned.

"Hi, Art," I say, phone to my ear as Marta, Luke, and Patti head inside. "How are things?"

"Good."

Art hesitates. Art's a good man, a kind man, and one hell of a Realtor, and I suddenly don't want to hear what he's going to say next.

I close my eyes, press a fist to my mouth. *Don't say it. Don't say it. Don't say it.*

"Taylor, we have an offer."

His voice is so quiet, so unbelievably gentle, that I know it's a good offer. And I know he's going to break what's left of my heart.

But I ask anyway, just to torture myself. "How good?"

"Very good."

Oh God.

"I've got a call in to Nathan," he continues. "I want to share the details with you both at the same time. Can I get you on a conference call as soon as he calls me back?"

"Of course."

After disconnecting the call, I go inside, collect my things hastily, stumble through quick good-byes. It's just two minutes to my house, and I park in the garage, leave my auction binder in the car, and carry my cell phone with me into the house.

"Hi," I call out, entering the mudroom from the garage. I call again for the girls once I'm in the kitchen, but there's no answer. The house is quiet. Annika and the girls aren't here.

I think. It's Tuesday. Where do they go on Tuesdays? Ah, piano lessons, right.

Deflated, I look around, see the beautiful custom kitchen cabinetry, the big window over the sink, the enormous Viking Range unit with the copper hood crafted for us in Spain. My phone rings shrilly. I fumble to take the call.

It's Art. He has Nathan already on the line.

"Taylor, I was just telling Nathan that you actually had two offers today, but the second offer wasn't nearly as good as the first, so it's the first I'm presenting to you."

"But we just started the paperwork yesterday. The house isn't officially even on the market yet. It's not even been available for a day," I protest.

"We priced your house well."

"Maybe too well," Nathan says quietly.

I'm more concerned about buyers who haven't even walked through our house yet. "How can these people make an offer on a house they haven't seen? Don't they want to see the inside?"

"They're a local family and familiar with your house." For the first time, Art sounds uncomfortable. "I believe they've been in your house before."

Oh, my God. It's someone we know. Someone we've entertained is taking our house from us.

Panic rushes through me, wave after wave, as Art presents the offer. As if sensing our misery, he goes through the details at a brisk pace.

"The buyers have agreed to your full asking price. They can close in thirty days. They've given their broker a check for eighty thousand in earnest money." Art pauses, takes a breath. "They do have a house to sell, but their offer isn't contingent on their house selling."

"Do you think the sale will fall through?" Nathan asks flatly.

"Honestly? No." Art then adds, "Don't forget, we have the backup offer, too. It's not as strong or as clean as the first, but it's a serious offer, and with a counteroffer, it could be acceptable."

I'm barely listening to the part about the backup offer, as I can't stop thinking about the people who've made the first offer, the best offer. "Who are they?" I blurt out. "Who wants the house?"

Arts clears his throat. "Their name has not been disclosed."

"Why not?"

He clears his throat again. "I'm not privy to their reasons, but you will find out at closing when you go in to sign the papers."

So anyone could be buying our house. For all I know, Marta Zinsser could be buying our house.

"So that's that?" My voice quivers. "The deal is done?"

"Only if you want it done," Art answers. "It's entirely up to you two."

"Taylor?" Nathan asks, giving me the power.

But I can't do it. In the kitchen with my hand over my mouth to stifle my crying, I shake my head, back and forth, back and forth.

No, no, no. Not my house. Please, not my house.

"It's everything you wanted," Art reminds us. "You won't have to show the house. You'll have thirty days before you move. The worst of it is over."

"Taylor?" Nathan repeats.

Art's words ring in my head. The worst is over. The worst is over. Just say yes and be done with it.

I let the blade drop. "Fine—" I choke. "Whatever you think is best. Now if you'll excuse me, I've got to go."

After disconnecting, I put down the phone and run out to the back garden and the swath of lawn partially hidden by fallen leaves.

My knees buckle as I race across the lawn, and I go down, to my knees and then all the way. Lying facedown on the cold, stiff grass, I stretch out my arms. With my palms facedown, I hold the grass and the soil and drink it in, breathing deep as if I could somehow suck the grass with the cool damp roots right in.

*   *   *

Thursday is Halloween, and I spend Wednesday night in the kitchen baking, even as I obsess over this mystery family that is buying our house.

Tori and Brooke help with the cookie dough, measuring and sifting and stirring, while I man the mixer. We're making homemade sugar cookies that I'll roll and cut into giant pumpkins, ghosts, cats, and bats. I'm in charge of activities for Brooke's class party, and one of the three projects we'll be doing during the party includes frosting and decorating their Halloween party snacks—the homemade sugar cookies—and then playing two games, Pin the Wart on the Witch, and Halloween Bingo.

The girls laugh and snitch bits of cookie dough while I use the cookie cutters and cut and lift the shapes onto baking sheets. They're having fun, and I watch them, acutely aware that this might be one of the last times we'll bake in this kitchen. It's a month before we have to move.

A month.

After sliding a cookie sheet into the oven, I set the timer. A month is nothing, especially when you love something so much. And I love this house. I know we're not supposed to love things. We're supposed to love people. But this house is everything I wanted when I was a little girl. A big, proper house with a big, proper kitchen for a big, proper family.

I squeeze the pot holder in my hand. If I'd been a better wife, none of this would have happened. If I'd paid more attention—

"We need some more bats," says Brooke, leaning on the marble counter, flour dusting her arms.

"And cats. Black kitty cats," Tori chimes in, pinching another little piece of dough.

"No more dough," I say, dropping the pot holder and returning to the work counter, "you'll get a tummy ache." I quickly smooth fresh flour over the marble before gathering what's left of the dough and rolling it into a ball. "Tummy aches aren't fun, and if you keep eating the dough, we won't have anything for cats and bats."

As I take the rolling pin to the dough, it hits me that I now have thirty days to find us a new place to live.

Never mind packing us up and moving us in.

I'm exhausted as I drive the girls to school Halloween morning. They're laden with costumes and party treats. I'm burdened with worry, dread, and guilt. I stayed up until two on the computer, looking at places to live. I want a house. I really want to find us a cute little house, something I can fix up and make ours like I used to do, but the market's so strong and there's nothing we can buy now. We're using all our equity to pay off the debt, and our credit is shot. No lender would touch us with a ten-foot pole.

It'll have to be an apartment or condo, something we can lease for the remainder of the school year, as I'm hoping that once school is out the girls and I will join Nathan in Omaha.

At Points Elementary, I pull over to the curb with the other carpooling parents, and Brooke and Jemma scramble out of the car and blow me good-bye kisses. Next I ferry Tori to her preschool and walk her, already dressed in her pink princess costume, to her classroom. She's skipping and grinning, and I carry the Tupperware container of sugar cookies with orange and purple sprinkles we made for her class. The preschool classroom is bright with Pokémon, Harry Potter, and Transformer costumes. So different from when I was a girl and everyone in my neighborhood dressed up as a ghost, a tramp, a cowboy, or an Indian.

Life was simpler then. Three TV stations. Youth group on Wednesday nights. Church and Bible study on Sundays.

Tori's running around the class showing off her costume and handing over the Tupperware container of cookies. I watch her for a moment.

I envy her. She's so happy right now, so blissfully unaware of our disaster.

Turning around, Tori spots me and runs back to my side to throw her arms around me. She squeezes me and squeezes me again. "Love you, Mommy."

"Love you, my baby girl." My hand slides over her curls, careful not to knock her plastic tiara of pink and lavender gemstones.

She breaks away and dances off. I walk away before I can feel an ounce of sadness or regret.

I'm scheduled to be at Points at eleven to help out with lunch duty before I set up for Brooke's class party, but first I need to stop at the grocery store and pick up the ingredients for my famous witch's brew, which is actually just green punch and dry ice.

I don't have more than sixteen items. It doesn't cross my mind that there could be a problem, so when my ATM card is declined for nonsufficient funds, I'm stunned. Nathan just gave me money, $1,000. My purchase today is $23.78. How can I have insufficient funds for a $23 purchase?

"Ugh, those cards and their magnetic strips," I say carelessly, reaching into my wallet and pulling out cash. I have $40. I hand two twenties to the clerk and try not to think about what will happen if we really don't have anything in our checking account and I have no cash, either.

I leave the store with the four plastic bags of juice and 7Up and sherbet, transfer everything to the back of my Lexus, and then get into my car. I sit for a moment, hands on the steering wheel, heart thudding, gut churning. The stress I feel is nearly unbearable. It's like earlier in the week when I stood outside Tully's and struggled to breathe. That's how I feel now. I can't breathe. I can't seem to get enough air and oxygen into my lungs.

The bills keep pouring in. The maxed-out credit cards that are now unavailable. The checking account without cash. Nathan gone. The girls so young.

I fish out my checkbook and look at the register. I'm careful about recording my checks. There's no way I've spent more than $800 in the last few weeks, so that means we should have $400 or so in the account.

I start to call Nathan but hang up and call our bank instead. I wait for one of the bank's customer service agents to get on the line and I explain our situation as calmly and clearly as possible.

"Have you included the automatic withdrawals?" the

bank agent asks helpfully. "Because that would explain the missing three hundred and eighty-five dollars."

"What automatic withdrawal?" I ask in a small voice.

"For COBRA." She pauses. "Your health insurance?"

"Ah. Thank you."

Off the phone, I put away my checkbook and close my purse even as tears burn my eyes. I didn't know we had any automatic payments to anything. I didn't know money could just disappear on its own.

I've been so careful, too.

Biting my lip, I start the car.

I need help.

I need help.

Oh God, I need help.

Somebody, anybody, give me a hand.

At school, I use the sun visor's mirror to touch up my makeup and reapply my lipstick before carrying the party goods into Brooke's class.

Brooke's Halloween party goes off without a hitch, and once her class is out parading in their costumes through the lower grades, I pop into Jemma's class to see how her party is going.

The classroom is dark, and all the kids are lying on the floor. They're watching the movie *Nightmare Before Christmas* and munching on popcorn balls and little bags of candy corn. In the back of the classroom, Mrs. Osborne sits at her desk grading while a mom mans the punch bowl and Marta slides photos into funky foam frames the kids must have made earlier today.

Marta looks up at me. I look away swiftly, glancing around the room until I find Jemma on the floor, curled up with a pillow she brought from home today. She doesn't know I'm here, and I watch her, feeling like an outsider. She's getting taller, older; she looks like the preteen she is.

Quietly I slip out of Jemma's classroom and return to Brooke's. I stay until the end of the day, clean up from the second-grade party, and then wait outside on the front sidewalk for the girls. When the girls find me, I double-check to make sure Brooke has all the pieces of her costume in her paper bag before driving them home.

As we pull up, we spot Annika in the front yard with Tori. Tori's in her princess costume, blowing bubbles from a tiny orange pumpkin party favor she got at school today.

Brooke bounds out of the car, grabs the bubble wand away from Tori, and tries to blow some bubbles of her own. Tori howls. Annika tells Brooke no. Brooke grabs the plastic pumpkin filled with bubble soap. Tori howls louder.

"Give it back," I say wearily, slamming car doors shut and scooping up discarded costume bags and book bags. "Jem and Brooke, homework. Tori, don't get your costume dirty. We'll have dinner and then go trick-or-treating when it's dark."

As the girls settle down at the dining room table to do their work, I go upstairs and call Nathan. I don't reach him, am sent to voice mail. I have to smother my frustration at being perpetually directed to voice mail. Once upon a time, my husband took all my calls. Once upon a time, he enjoyed hearing from me.

"Nathan, I know you just left me a check when you were here, but it's already gone. We've nothing in the checking account, and as you know, I don't have any credit cards. I don't have anything in my wallet, either." I take a breath, fight my panic. "I'll need at least a hundred and fifty dollars to get through the next week, and that's not counting what I'll owe Annika. Do you have anything you can deposit into our account? Do you know when you'll have another paycheck?"

Hanging up, I tap my phone against my chest. Need money. Need money. Need money.

I glance out the window. It's starting to rain. *Again.* Please God don't make me have to trick-or-treat in the rain.

I end up taking the girls trick-or-treating in the rain.

In ten years of being a mom, I've never had to escort them on my own. Nathan's always been there, and sometimes we've gone with other families so it's like a big party wandering down the street, house to house, door to door.

Tonight it's no party. It's cold and drizzly. The girls wear raincoats over their costumes and carry an umbrella to protect their candy. I carry an industrial-size flashlight as we trudge from house to house, the hems of my black cords getting wetter and wetter. I miss Nathan. I feel like half a person without him. I need him back so I can be myself again.

But as I stumble in a puddle I didn't see, falling to

the ground in an embarrassing heap, another thought hits me.

If he doesn't come back, if he doesn't want me back, what will happen to me?

What will I do?

More important, who will I be?

Chapter Fourteen

Nathan calls me Friday morning after the girls have gone to school.

He promises to deposit $100 in our account, but that's all he can do. He's paid bills and he doesn't have anything, either, until his next paycheck in a week, but at least some of the creditors and collection agencies should be off our backs.

But that's not the worst of his news. He's removing himself from our joint checking account. He says it's now my account for all my personal expenses, so I have to be careful, can't spend very much, since he's not making enough to support us both as he used to. However, he will have the COBRA payment moved to his account.

I listen as he talks, my brow wrinkling as I try to follow everything he's saying. He's talking fast, hard, as if he's prepared a speech and is determined to get through it.

He's been advised to file for legal separation but hasn't yet. He says the advice was given to protect me and the girls; that way, the creditors would go after him in the future. Of course, the banks would view our past debt as a joint responsibility, but he's determined to take care of it as he's head of the household and the breadwinner.

I close my eyes, listening hard.

The sale of the house will reduce most of our debt, but some miscellaneous bills will still come in, and he'll take care of the ones he can. He knows he told me I shouldn't get a job but thinks now I should look for something, even if it's just part-time. He also reminds me that the girls and I have to move by November 29, just days after Thanksgiving. I'll need to be prepared. Have I started looking for a new place yet? Do I need him to fly out and apartment hunt with us, or is this something I can take care of on my own?

As he keeps talking, I sink onto the side of the bed and then slowly, numbly, lie back. I stare at the ceiling as his voice washes over me in unrelenting waves.

He's divorcing me.

He just hasn't said it yet.

Saturday I wake up to high, thin clouds and hints of blue sky. Maybe, just maybe, it'll be a nice day.

And then I remember.

Nathan needs to put money into our—my—checking account, but he probably hasn't been able to do it yet. He's been advised to file for a legal separation but fortunately hasn't done that, either. He's promised to send us what he can, but there isn't much; he's not making what he'd expected, as apparently the company is giving an end-of-year bonus instead of a bonus up front.

Last night I was too shocked to cry. This morning I'm still numb, but I'm also getting angry.

I have three children. *We* have three children. What are we supposed to do? How could he go work for a company that refuses to pay what they initially offered? Why doesn't he just come home and look for a job here?

Tears start up in my eyes, but I refuse to give in to them. I'm tired of feeling bad. Tired of feeling bad about myself. Maybe I do have a spending problem, an impulse control problem, but I'm not a destructive person. I'm not a cruel person. I care about others. I try to help others. I really do.

Furiously, I rub at my eyes and then climb out of bed to splash cold water on my face. I am not going to cry. I am not going to fall apart.

I scrape my hair back and put on my pink Juicy sweats to head downstairs, where I discover the girls eating candy straight from their treat buckets. Butterfinger and Milky Way wrappers litter the floor. I love those candy bars, too. Also Baby Ruth, Snickers, Kit Kat, Reese's. In fact, if I had a bucket of candy, I'd be eating all of it right now.

Of course, I don't tell them that. I don't want them to end up like me. "Girls, candy for breakfast? Absolutely not. Give me your treat buckets. I'm putting them away."

Tori moves to give me her basket, but not before she sticks another fat Tootsie Roll in her mouth.

"Jemma? Brooke?" I extend my hand impatiently. "Come on, hand them over or I'll throw it all away."

"But there's nothing else to eat, Mom," Jemma answers, licking melted chocolate off her fingertips. "We're out of bread, and you don't buy Pop-Tarts anymore."

I pinch the tight muscles in my shoulders. Lord, I need coffee bad. "What's wrong with cereal?"

Brooke rises to give me her treat bucket. "We don't have any milk."

"We have milk. We always have milk." I open the fridge and reach in for the organic 1 percent milk carton, but as I lift it, it's so light that I know it's empty. Heart falling, temper rising, I turn to face the girls. "Who left an empty carton in the fridge?"

The girls just stare at me.

"Well, someone did."

The girls just stare at me some more.

"Well?" I wait, hand on my hip. "Annika wasn't here, so you can't blame her."

Jemma closes her eyes. "I did. I drank it. I was thirsty this morning. Okay?"

Okay, one mystery solved. I toss the carton. "Why didn't you just throw it away?"

She opens her eyes a little and peeks at me. "Because I didn't want you mad."

"Why would I be mad?"

The girls wiggle a little on the floor. None of them says anything. Now I am mad. "Well?"

"Because you have no money," Brooke whispers. "I heard you on the phone yesterday talking to Dad. You said we have no money and you don't know what we're going to do."

I sit on one of the miserably uncomfortable counter stools, the wrought-iron back digging into my skin. The girls look at me and wait. I'm not sure what I'm supposed to say next. Do I reassure them? Do I fib? Do I tell the truth that we're beyond broke?

"Money's tight right now," I finally say. "Even though

Daddy's working in Omaha, we have a lot of bills. We owe a lot of people money."

"We're poor?" Jemma asks, incredulous.

I grimace. "We're not rich."

Jemma's expression changes. "That's why we're selling the house. It's not because Dad's in Omaha. It's because we're broke."

My shoulders lift and fall.

"How did we go broke?" Brooke asks, scooping her crumpled wrappers into her fists.

Again I wonder what to tell them. I wonder what explanation would make the most sense. After a long moment, I take a breath and say, "We spent too much money. We bought too many things."

Brooke's gaze meets mine. "So let's sell them."

"I wish."

Jemma sits up on her knees. "We can do it on eBay."

I'd laugh if I weren't so damn tired. "I don't know anything about eBay. I've never bought anything on eBay before—"

"That's not true. You got that Barbie thing for Tori last year on eBay. You know, when you couldn't get it at Toys R Us."

"Yes," I agree, "but that was a onetime thing, and it's different buying something than selling. We'd have to list stuff and have people try to bid and send us money, and I don't know how, and right now, I can't deal with one more thing that I don't know how to do."

Everyone's quiet a minute. Jemma's looking around the kitchen and family room. "What would we sell if we could?"

"Toys," Brooke says. "I have lots of toys I don't play with. And our old bikes. We were going to trade them in, but we never did."

We do have things we don't use. We have closets of things we don't need. And there's an easier way than eBay. It's called the good old-fashioned yard sale.

My family used to have them when I was a kid. It humiliated me, putting our old worn things out there on a table for everyone to look through and paw at. The girls have asked if we could have a garage sale of our own, but I always refused. But it's different now. I'm not so proud. And I really do need the cash.

"We could have a yard sale," I say even as I mentally work out the logistics.

"When?" the girls demand.

I shrug. "We'd need to plan and post signs and put an ad in the paper. . . . Maybe next week?"

"No. Today." Jemma nods at the window. "It's nice today, Mom. Let's just make some signs now. I can go tape them up on the street. We can pull out the folding tables from the garage and just do it. Whatever we don't sell today, we'll sell tomorrow."

No, it's too soon. I can't imagine organizing and setting up a garage sale today. It's already nearly eight-thirty.

"We should really organize it right," I protest. "Get an ad in the paper—"

"An ad costs money," Jemma answers crisply. "We don't have money. Besides, people love going to garage sales, especially where we live. All we have to do is put a sign near the freeway off-ramp, and another one on the corner of Twenty-fourth and Ninety-second by the school, and everyone will come."

It's true. I don't have money. Not even $20 to my name.

"You think we can do this?" I ask. "Find stuff, set things up, make signs?"

They all nod.

"Okay. Bring me your treasures. Anything you're able and willing to part with, because if it sells, it's gone. It's not coming back."

They're on their feet and dashing up the stairs.

I make coffee and then head to the garage, open up all three car bays, and walk the perimeter, taking in everything we've got hidden in there. Three framed paintings lean against a wall. A Queen Anne armchair with a faded 1980s chintz fabric. I bought it two years ago at an estate sale and planned to reupholster it for Tori's room, but I've done nothing with it. Baskets of dusty silk flowers. An ornate wood birdcage. A rather bizarre bronze sculpture Nathan won at an auction. A box of outgrown girl clothes I was saving for Goodwill. A bag of my shoes I was going to give to Goodwill, too. Two boxes of books. Another box of mismatched kitchen pots and pans that I don't use because I use only Le Creuset now. And this isn't even counting the practically new clothes in my closet that I don't wear and probably won't ever wear.

So we do have stuff. A lot of stuff.

We can do this.

Seven and a half hours later, my feet are killing me, but our garage is cleaned out and the long tables in the drive-way are virtually empty, too. You would have thought we were having a carnival instead of a yard sale. The girls sold cups of hot instant cider and brownies they whipped up while I was pricing everything outside.

They taped little balloons to the street signs and used bright orange and purple and red tempera paint from the art cupboard to make a WELCOME poster for the driveway. Jemma proved particularly creative and industrious, free-hand drawing other signs that read BESTSELLING BOOKS!, STYLISH SHOES!, RARE ART!, KITCHEN DEALS!

She labored over every display, deliberating over the right colored tablecloth for each card table before arranging the display items on top. "We want it to look fun," she said to me. "If it looks fun, people will buy more."

I looked at my eldest daughter with a mixture of pride and wonder. I knew she loved to shop—we'd always enjoyed shopping together—but I had no idea she understood the retail side of things so well.

By dusk when we were finally forced to wrap up our day, we'd made some good money, too. I'm astonished by the cash in the little metal box I carry into the kitchen.

Over $2,000.

I count it again: $2,401.

The bizarre bronze sculpture ended up bringing in the most. Turned out it was a collectible piece, and someone handed me $400 for it, and then after I'd tucked the money in the cash box, he went on to tell me its value was ten times what he'd offered me.

I tried not to dwell on his good fortune as the other items sold.

The stuffed armchair went for nearly $300. The paintings brought in anywhere from $75 to $150 each. The bikes the girls had outgrown went for $15, $20, and $22. My shoes were popular items, each pair flying off the table for $25 a pop. Fifteen pairs of shoes times $25 equals $375—what I used to pay for a brand-new pair of shoes, but no matter. Can't look back, can only go forward.

After counting the money a third time, I give each of the girls $10. They want more, but I tell them if I give more, we won't have money for milk and food. Ten seems like a lot to them after that.

As I fall asleep that night, my body aches from all the lifting and hauling I did all day, but I also feel strangely peaceful. I did something good today. I did something positive. I'll be able to pay for groceries and child care this next week, and I did it without Nathan's help. I did it without his support. I did it by working with the girls.

We're going to be okay.

The girls and I will find a way.

Turning on my side, I smash my pillow up against my cheek. Now all I need is a job. And I swear I'm getting one this week, because if I don't, I'm going to end up hawking everything else I own.

Monday morning while I'm driving Tori to preschool, the Windemere real estate sign goes up in front of the house. I didn't know there was a sign up until I get a call from my neighbor.

I phone Art right away, ask him why we have a sign up when the house has already been sold. "You want to market the house until the escrow closes," he explains patiently. "It protects you."

By Monday afternoon I've had a dozen calls asking if it's true we're moving. I don't even bother to answer after the third call, letting them go straight into voice mail. It's hard enough putting the house on the market without having to explain it to all the neighbors.

With dinner in the oven, I sit at the computer and go through my e-mail, checking to see if anyone has responded to my job applications. I've mailed nearly fifteen résumés now. Followed up with phone calls. Someone has to have something for me. I'm not stupid. I work hard. I'd be an asset for the right company.

Tonight my persistence is finally rewarded. I have an e-mail. It's from the employment agency I interviewed with a month ago. They might have something that would be a good fit for me, but the interviews are tomorrow and only tomorrow. There is an eleven-thirty time slot open and a twelve-fifteen. The interview will be in the conference room at the downtown Bellevue's Barnes & Noble Starbucks. If I can make it, I need to confirm tonight so they can get my résumé over before the interviews begin tomorrow.

My fingers are trembling as I type a hasty reply. Yes, I can be there. Eleven-thirty is perfect.

I dress carefully for the interview, pairing a slim black pencil skirt with a very chic crisp pale pink Chanel blouse. I wear skin-tone hose and sleek black pumps and pull my hair back in a smooth low ponytail. With pink pearls at my ears and throat, I hope I look smart enough, sophisticated enough, and successful enough to win over the interviewer.

I take one of Nathan's slim black Tumi leather folders

and slide another copy of my résumé inside the left pocket, check to make sure the top sheet of the lined notebook on the right side is crisp and clean. I put a slim gold pen in the pen spot. There's nothing else I can do but go.

I'm nervous as I leave home, my stomach one big ball of butterflies. I get there twenty minutes early. I don't need another cup of coffee, so I order an herbal tea, something minty to soothe my nerves.

After a few minutes the door opens and a young woman walks out. She's dressed in a fashionable gray wool suit with a matching vest—no blouse, I notice—and wide trouser legs, very high heels. She's wearing strands of amber beads at her throat and is carrying a sharp lime green faux (I think it's faux) crocodile tote.

She breezes past me, all business and confidence. As I stand there, my hand trembles ever so slightly. I've got to be a good ten years older than this thin, tan, strawberry blond girl. Ten years older and yet a whole life apart in heartache.

I never thought I'd be back out here, job hunting, at least not hunting for a job that would actually pay the bills. I thought anything I did from now on would be artistic. Interesting. Something I did out of personal curiosity instead of financial need.

The door to the conference room remains open, and with a glance at my watch I see it's eleven-thirty now. Taking a deep breath, I head for the conference room, determined just to get the interview done and out of the way.

I'm shocked when I enter through the open door and spot Marta Zinsser sitting behind the conference table, a notebook on the table along with a pen and her cell phone.

I very nearly walk out.

"Hi," Marta says with a smile that's more professional than warm. She's actually dressed up today, wearing a St. John type of suit with a mandarin collar in cream.

"*You're* the one hiring?"

"Yes."

I stand in the doorway, my slim leather portfolio clutched to my chest, and I feel beyond foolish. I'm absurd. "I didn't know."

Marta gestures to the chair opposite hers at the conference table. "Have a seat, please."

"Marta—"

"Are you looking for a job or not?"

Swallowing my pride, or what's left of what was once immense pride, I nod and sit, perching carefully on the chair edge.

"I'm looking for a new office manager. My current office manager has a new position—a great position, and I'm very happy for her—but I need someone smart, organized, and reliable to take over when Susan leaves at the end of the month."

I nod.

"The job responsibilities include handling the phone, scheduling meetings, invoicing clients, following up with the printers on projects, and generally doing whatever we need done to keep the business going." She pauses, looks hard at me. "Can you do that?"

I'm mortified. Beyond mortified. Can I handle the phone? Schedule meetings? Pick up documents at the printers? I've raised hundreds of thousands of dollars for the school, organized virtually every fund-raiser the school has ever had, headed the PTA, represented the parents of Points Elementary at the Bellevue Unified Foundation.

My face flames. "Yes."

Her gaze rests steadily on my face. "It's a busy office with some intense, as well as creative, personalities."

Spine stiffening, I sit taller. "I have a degree in communications, and before I married I worked in event planning and public relations, two fields that attract the creative types."

She shrugs calmly. "You've been out of the workforce for over a decade."

"I might not have earned a paycheck, Marta, but I've worked every day this past decade."

Marta's lips twist, and she studies me for a long moment. "So why do you want this job?"

I can't quite manage to stifle my exasperation. "I'm not sure that I do." I see her eyebrows rise, and I add, "I want a job, and I know I can contribute. I've always been successful at whatever I do, but I'm going to be honest and say I don't know that I could work for you."

She doesn't even flinch. "Why not?"

I shouldn't say it. I need to bite my tongue, do some serious self-editing here, because I can't tell her that I don't like her. I can't tell her that working for her would be akin to drinking rat poison. "We don't have a lot in common," I answer as delicately as I can.

"I don't think having commonalities is essential in this position. I own the company. I'm the boss. You'd work for me." Marta stands, slides some brochures and glossy magazines across the table toward me. "Here's what we do. These are samples of Z Design's work. Take a look at them. Read up on us. If you're interested in being considered for the final interview, call Susan at the office. Otherwise, good luck, Taylor. I hope you'll find what you're looking for."

I've been dismissed. Hot color floods my face, and I rise on shaking legs to awkwardly gather the brochures and periodicals. "Thank you." My voice, pitched low, cracks as I head for the door.

"Taylor."

I stop, turn my head toward her but don't make eye contact.

"Eva heard at school about all the...changes...you're going through." Marta pauses. "I know it's small comfort, but I am sorry. It can't be easy for your children."

I leave Starbucks as fast as I can. I've got to get away. Have to escape.

It's too awful, too painful, too horrible at every level.

Marta Zinsser pities me.

I get the girls up and off to school Friday morning and am in the car now, driving Tori to preschool. As I drive, I clamp my jaw tight to keep from making a sound.

I'm lost.

Absolutely, terrifyingly lost.

My fingers squeeze convulsively on the wheel. My left high heel grinds into the floor mat. I've no idea who I am. No idea who this woman in this car is. I've no idea who is behind all this makeup and in these elegant, extravagant clothes.

Every day I dress myself and do my hair and put creams and lotions on my face, but I see now I've been creating someone else, someone not new, just someone better. It's as if there's a better version of me out there in the universe and I'm determined to find it, determined to make that better me a reality. Because God knows, the me that is, isn't good enough.

A small sound escapes from me. I press my lips together harder even as hot tears fill my eyes. Can't cry. Mustn't cry. Blinking very hard, I concentrate on driving.

"Mommy?" Tori's voice pipes up from the backseat.

I sniff. "Yes, honey?"

"You sad?"

I swallow hard, so hard that it hurts my throat. "No, honey. Mommy's just getting a cold."

After dropping off Tori, I consider going to the club. It's Friday. I could do one of the yoga or Pilates classes. It would help. It might make the yawning sadness go away. But I'm too sad to go to the gym, too sad to change, too sad to face people. I can't face anyone. I can't even face myself.

Instead I go home and unzip my black boots and strip off my lovely black knit Donna Karan sweater dress and climb into bed in my lovely black lace bra and panties. And in my lovely $500 bra and panties set, I cry.

How could I possibly have thought that a $500 bra and panties set would change anything? How could I have thought clothes, even gorgeous, expensive clothes, would change me?

Oh, my God. All this money spent. All these things we bought. For what? To feel what? Better? Happier? Different?

I'm still in bed hours later. I've slept for a couple of hours and am awake again, but I can't drag myself up.

I need a job. Marta Zinsser's company might have a position for me. If I wanted the job, I wouldn't have to interview anymore. I wouldn't have to worry anymore. I could start earning income right away. No more garage sales. No more worrying about Nathan and what he decides. I'd at least be able to provide.

But Marta. Working for Marta. Being Marta's assistant…

I squeeze my eyes shut as I picture her free-spirit ways, and maybe that's what I resent most. She's successful doing things her way. It's so obvious she enjoys being a renegade.

I'm still lying in bed staring at nothing, thinking too much, feeling absolutely desperate, when the phone next to the bed rings.

I don't want to answer it. I won't answer it. Voice mail can take a message. But as it rings a third time, I fight my own exasperation and reach for it, taking the call. "Hello?"

"Taylor?" It's Lucy, and her voice is thick with tears. "Are you busy?"

"No. No, I'm not busy. What's wrong?"

"Oh God, Taylor, oh God. What have I done?" Her voice rises to a keening, grieving pitch. "I've ruined everything, and I want to die. I do. I can't do this anymore—"

"Where are you?" I interrupt.

She sobs harder. "I don't know. On the 405 somewhere. I've been driving in circles. I don't know what to do, and I don't know where to go. I'm afraid to stop driving, afraid of what I might do."

She's hiccuping and sobbing, and I'm worried about her driving like this. It's dangerous. Glancing out the window, I see that the sky is a steely gray, but at least it's dry. There is no rain.

"Come over, Lucy. Come over right now."

"I can't," she gasps. "I can't. I've been crying so hard. I can't let anybody see me this way."

"There's no one here. It'd be just you and me—"

"You'd hate me like this. I'm wrecked, just wrecked, Taylor."

"That's okay, I'm wrecked, too."

"Not you. You're Taylor. Taylor Young."

I put a hand over my eyes. "Lucy—" My voice breaks. "Lucy, no one knows, but I'm in trouble, too."

"You are?" She sniffles, sounds surprised.

"Yes. So it's okay to have a bad day. I'm having a bad day. Maybe we should both just have bad days together."

Silence stretches, and she draws a shuddering breath. "I don't know, Taylor. I don't know."

I sit up, swing my legs out of bed. "Where are you, Lucy?"

"Um. Uh, somewhere between Woodinville and Mill Creek."

"So turn around. Head to my house. I'll see you in twenty to thirty minutes."

Chapter Fifteen

"People keep telling me it's going to get better, but it's not. It's been six months, and every month just gets worse."

Lucy sits curled in one of the wheat-colored armchairs in my living room, a butterscotch cashmere throw over her lap, clutching a cup of warm tea.

Her pale hair is loose and messy, as though she forgot to comb it this morning, and her eyes are nearly as pink and shiny as her nose. I'd never seen her without makeup until today.

"Everything hurts," she adds huskily, "and the only thing the doctor can suggest is medication. Something so I can sleep at night. Something so I can function during the day." She makes a soft, rough sound, and her eyes well with tears all over again. "I guess that's how we're supposed to cope these days. Pills and alcohol."

"Why didn't you call me earlier?"

She shakes her head, sips her tea.

"Lucy."

She shakes her head again even as a tear rolls down her cheek. "I didn't want anyone to see me this way. It's embarrassing. I'm a mom. I can't be falling apart. I have responsibilities—" She breaks off, takes a deep breath. "I didn't want to call you. But I didn't want to drive into a tree, either, and that seemed to be my idea of rational thinking earlier."

I sit facing her on my white linen couch. A slim glass-topped table separates us, but it might as well be a football field in terms of her despair. She's so remote, so incredibly broken. "You don't really want to drive your car into a tree, do you?"

She closes her eyes. "I want it back. I want my life back. I want how it used to be."

She's suffering, and her suffering undoes me. I thought my situation was bad, but hers is far worse. "Pete wasn't always the best husband—"

"Whose is?" Her mouth trembles, and she digs her teeth into her lower lip. "I was a fool. I'd do anything—*anything*—to undo the damage. I want things the way they were. I want to be in the same house with everyone. I want to sleep in the same bed. I want to wake up and find everything's the same, but it's not. And it will never be. I can't live like this, I can't. I hate myself. I—"

I'm off the couch and onto my feet, crouching at her side, my arms wrapped around her, rocking her as she sobs.

"Lucy, Lucy..." I'm rubbing her back and saying her name, and I wish I were a fairy godmother and I could do something to help her. We're just people. We screw up and we make mistakes, and then oh, how we suffer. We learn too late that we're not infallible, not indestructible, not untouchable. We learn too late that when things go wrong, we hurt.

Terribly.

Tears fill my eyes as I rub her back. "You'll get through this, you will. It's awful now, but it won't always be like this. Things do work out, things will improve. You'll see."

"Why didn't I realize things were good? Why didn't I know I was happy? That I was lucky? Why didn't I appreciate what I had?"

"I don't know, Lucy. I don't. Maybe none of us know what we have until it's taken away." I'm still rubbing her back and talking when Annika and the kids walk through the front door.

I don't hear the door open; instead I hear their voices. Turning my head, I spot them in the entry. They've caught sight of us, and they freeze. The children know Lucy well, but they've never seen her upset.

"What's wrong?" Jemma asks nervously, backpack sliding off her shoulder.

I sit up. Lucy hastily wipes her tears away.

"Nothing," I say. "It's nothing."

"But you're both crying," Jemma says.

"Jemma, it's silly. You wouldn't understand."

Her chin lifts stubbornly. "Tell me."

Lucy looks at me, and I take a quick breath. "Nordstrom had a special function for their level three and four reward customers and we both missed it," I explain sadly. "We could have met Donna Karan."

The girls stare at us a long moment. Jemma's brows wrinkle. "You're crying because you didn't meet a fashion designer?"

I gesture weakly. "There was a trunk show, too, honey."

Jemma rolls her eyes and walks out. Annika and the younger girls follow. Lucy waits for the girls to disappear into the kitchen to whisper, "I can't believe you! We're crying over a missed fashion event?"

I go back to the couch. "I didn't know what to say. I couldn't very well tell her we're bawling because we're miserable, unhappy women, could I?"

Lucy smiles halfheartedly and wipes her eyes again. "I guess I would be upset if I missed a secret Donna Karan trunk show."

"See?" But I'm smiling, and Lucy smiles wanly back at me. "We Bellevue moms have to have our priorities."

Lucy groans. "You're insane, Taylor."

"I know. But it's worked for me so far." I lift my tea and take a sip, thinking maybe it's time to tell Lucy about the chaos in my world. "Lucy..." But looking into Lucy's face, her light blue eyes red-rimmed, skin so pale that it's ethereal, I don't think I can do this. It doesn't seem right, or fair, to burden her now. She's so fragile at the moment. She's in such terrible pain. How can I add one more worry to her plate?

"Yes?" she asks, waiting.

No, can't tell her, I resolve, not yet, not until she's emotionally stronger. "You know, tonight's book club," I say, swiftly substituting topics. "I was thinking we should drive together."

"Oh God, that's right. I completely forgot." She looks at me, stricken. "And I'm supposed to be in charge of the discussion. I picked the book."

"Have you read it?"

"Most of it. Not the last chapter or two."

"So you're okay." I, on the other hand, have not read a lot of the book. What I did read was interesting as well as shocking. I've been having a hard time getting my head around the idea that so many women are ending up in dire financial straits.

Lucy's shaking her head. "But I can't do this. I can't face everybody. Look at me! I'm a wreck. I haven't slept in days. The bags under my eyes are too big for carry-on."

I choke on muffled laughter. "Was that a joke, Lucy Wellsley? Did I hear you make a joke?"

She cracks a reluctant smile. "I look like hell and you know it."

"Okay, you do look rough, but that's what our two-hundred-and-fifty-dollar lotions are for. Serious calming, soothing, and resurfacing. Depuffing, too."

I glance at my watch and note that we have four hours before book club begins. "Where are your kids?"

Her expression crumples. "Pete has them."

"No!" I hold up my hands to stop her. "That's a good thing. This way we have four hours to relax and repair and prepare. You need a nap. And then a shower and a little makeover. While you nap, I'll finish the book and then I'll be ready to help you get ready. Sound like a plan?"

She looks puzzled. "So you'll come to my house later?"

"No. You're going to relax and unwind here. You can have my room. No one will bother you. I'll draw the blinds and you'll have a lovely little catnap and then we'll get ready for tonight together."

"I don't want to put you out—"

"You're not."

She glances away, obviously uncomfortable. I wait

for her to say something, and it takes her a long time to speak.

"I'm not…Taylor, I'm not going to do anything." She swallows hard before looking at me. "If that's what you're worried about. I'm not going to do anything stupid."

"That's not what I'm worried about," I answer, finding this painful, too. "And that's not why I want you to stay. I want you to stay because I care about you, and I'd just feel better if I could do something for you. Maybe it's selfish of me, but I'd like to do something for you. It'd make me feel good if I could help somehow."

Heavy silence fills the room, and my insides knot so hard that my stomach actually hurts.

"Nathan doesn't live here anymore." My voice is quiet, yet to my ears the words crash and boom beneath the vaulted ceiling. "I've been alone a lot lately. I'd like your company." I pause, reconsider my words. "I'd love your company. I'm having a hard time, too."

While Lucy naps, I read. I sit beneath the butterscotch blanket on the living room couch and read for almost two hours straight. Now that I've started the book, I can't stop reading.

This is what went wrong in my life, I think. This is what happened to Nathan and me. I wanted to be taken care of, I wanted someone else to do the hard work outside the home so I could concentrate on raising kids, but in so doing, I became financially dependent and, worse, a burden.

When Lucy finally wakes up it's nearly six, and she creeps downstairs, her eyes dark and fuzzy with sleep. "I was out of it," she says, joining me in the kitchen where I'm helping Annika serve dinner for the kids.

"You needed it," I answer, setting the plates of meat loaf and rice in front of the girls.

Lucy eyes the girls' dinner. "You guys eat meat loaf?"

"You don't?"

She shakes her head. "It's eeew food in our family."

"I like it," I answer, grabbing the ketchup, which Tori has to have on everything. "They like it, too."

"How do you get Nathan to eat—" Lucy breaks off, realizing her mistake.

"Salt, Mom," Jemma sings.

I hand Jemma the salt and Brooke the pepper. "He likes it." I keep my tone deliberately casual. The girls don't know about the separation yet, and I don't want them to know. "The recipe I use calls for ground beef and Italian sausage. I also use tomato sauce and oatmeal instead of bread or cracker crumbs. It gives it a little more flavor."

Seeing that the girls are settled and happily eating, I gesture to Lucy. "Come on, we better get you in the shower. We need to go in less than an hour."

We drive to Kate's, as she's hosting book-club tonight. Her house, a three-story brick-and-white-columned minimansion, looks as if it should sit on a Mississippi riverbank surrounded by moss-draped oak trees instead of the tiny Clyde Hill cul-de-sac shaded by seventy-year-old cedars, but it is a striking home, stately and upright, just like old-money Kate and her Microsoft millionaire husband, Bill.

For all her sportiness, Kate is the quintessential suburban mom. She hangs seasonal wreaths on her front door.

Tonight the living room mantel is covered with orange candles and little Pilgrim and Indian figurines, while a fat fabric turkey sits on the kitchen counter near the Italian pottery cookie jar.

Her kids' art decorates the fridge, and the gold dish towels hanging on the eight-burner Wolf oven door are heavily embroidered with leaves, pumpkins, and cornucopias.

Kate is bustling around, pulling warm appetizers from the oven and making sure everyone has a glass of wine. The kitchen is huge, with a real used-brick floor and an old stone interior wall. Heavy beams run across the nine-foot ceiling, and copper pots hang in the stove's recessed alcove. I don't know if it's the kitchen's size or the fact that the living room seems so far removed, but at Kate's house, we always end up hanging out in her kitchen.

"Red or white?" Kate greets us.

"Red," I answer, sliding the plate of frosted brownies that the girls and Annika made earlier onto the granite counter. I wasn't asked to bring anything, but I feel guilty showing up empty-handed.

"Lucy?" Kate asks, holding up a bottle of wine in each hand.

"White, but just a little."

Lucy's voice sounds tight, and I glance back at her. She's still wearing her coat—my coat—and she has that "deer caught in the headlights" look again. I reach over, give her arm a little squeeze. She jerks her head up, meets my gaze, forces a smile.

"You're okay," I say, but it's not a question, it's a statement. She's going to be okay. We're all going to be okay. We're women, goddammit.

Kate glances from me to her and back to me again. "Can I take your coats, girls?"

"I've got it," I say. "You're busy enough in here."

I reenter the kitchen in time to overhear Monica discussing the pros and cons of Bellevue's athletic clubs. "They call themselves the premier club on the Eastside," she says bitterly, "but their tennis program is nonexistent and their swim team is hardly better—"

"That's not true," Suze interrupts. "Their team is highly ranked. They've had swimmers qualify for the junior Olympics."

"But not Olympic athletes," Monica counters.

Suze's eyes widen. Her children swim for the club, and she's one of the team's biggest boosters. "You don't know what you're talking about, Monica."

"I do, too. Phoenix had outstanding swim teams. Those clubs sent kids to the Olympics—"

"But I'm not interested in my kids swimming in the Olympics. I want my kids to develop skills, get exercise, learn sportsmanship. Studies show that children who participate on swim teams excel academically, particularly in math, language, and music."

Monica shakes her head and takes a sip from her glass, leaving a big coral lipstick mark on the rim. "You're thinking of tennis."

"I'm thinking of swimming."

Kate looks at me as I reach for my wineglass. I just shrug. This is the world as I know it.

Unfortunately, Monica isn't about to let the swimming

versus tennis thing drop, and after speaking exhaustively on the research she's read, she launches into an even more detailed critique of the area's tennis pros and then the playing surfaces before diverting to analyzing the massage techniques of the three best local spas.

Listening to Monica, I remember a story Patti told me. Apparently, when Monica and Doug were moving back here from Phoenix, Monica spent weeks and weeks researching all the Eastside schools. Academic excellence wasn't enough. Monica also wanted social prominence. Her daughter was two at the time.

I concentrate on drinking my wine. Twenty minutes and an empty glass later, which someone kindly refills, Kate shoos us into the living room to begin the book discussion. She's lit the pumpkin and bronze candles on the mantel, and the room dances with light.

As everyone settles into chairs, I hear Suze whispering to Jen about a party that took place in Clyde Hill last weekend. Suze attended, and apparently it included some serious wife swapping, something Suze wouldn't have believed if she hadn't been there.

"No way," Monica answers, having overheard the last. "That doesn't happen here. Absolutely not."

Suze, still prickly from her earlier conversation with Monica, is adamant. "Absolutely so. I don't know if Jefferson and I were invited because our hosts thought we were swingers, too, or if it was hoped we'd go along with the fun, but it was more than I could handle. Lots of sex, booze, drugs, and costumes."

I'm amazed. I've never been to a party like that, but then again, Nathan and I are pretty conservative.

Yet thinking about the moms who gather around the Points Country Club pool, I can't imagine any of them going to wild sex parties. They may be butt tucked, tummy lifted, and lip plumped, but they're moms and nice women.

Oh God. Nice women don't swing…do they?

"Maybe we should talk about the book," Kate says, settling on the needlepoint seat of a small antique side chair since everyone else has taken more comfortable seats. "So what would Leslie Bennetts say is the feminine mistake?"

I find it difficult to shift gears. I'm still trying to figure out who would go to sex parties. I don't even attend the parties where women buy erotic gifts and toys.

"The mistake is thinking a man will take care of you forever," Lucy answers, returning from the kitchen with another glass of Chardonnay and a handful of rosemary-dusted crackers. She sinks into one of the cushions on the love seat next to me.

"I might as well confess right now, I didn't read it." Suze shakes her golden hair back over her shoulder and crosses one slim, perfectly toned thigh over the other. "I didn't even buy it. I don't agree with it, and I'm not going to support a book like that."

"We don't have to agree with everything we read," Ellen says, looking at Suze. "But we should at least buy and attempt to read the chosen book."

Suze lifts a hand, lets her gold bracelets jingle. "I don't have to read it if the subject matter makes me uncomfortable."

"Taylor doesn't always read," Monica adds, "and no one minds when she doesn't."

I look at Monica and open my mouth to make a stinging retort when scripture pops to mind. *Why do you see the speck that is in your brother's eye, but do not notice the log that is in your own eye?*

I close my mouth.

Thankfully, Kate steers the conversation on. "What really struck me in reading this book was the idea that we women might unwittingly be putting ourselves at risk—"

"Not all of us are going to end up widowed young or divorced," Monica interrupts. "And if we do, we all have a great education and work experience to fall back on. I can return to business anytime."

"I could practice law again," Jen admits.

"Do you really think it's as bad as Leslie Bennetts indicates?" Patti asks, just now finding a seat in the living room. She arrived late and rushed in to drop her coat and get a drink before joining us. "Because I have to say, I was shocked to think there are that many abandoned women in this country, and we're not talking about women who were always poor, but women in the middle and upper class who are now living below the poverty line."

"It did make me uncomfortable," I admit.

"I don't believe the statistics," Monica responds. "And if it's true, then women are suffering because they made poor choices—"

"Bennetts isn't blaming anyone," I answer, glad I read as much of the book as I did. "Her premise is that women aren't getting the whole picture. They're not realizing what's happening to women in our society, and she wants to alert women to the facts so they can make better decisions."

"Oh, my God, Taylor!" Monica laughs. "Did you actually read the book this time, or did you get that little insight online?"

"What I found useful in the book," Lucy says quietly, her voice not entirely steady, "was that maybe it's time for women to think of themselves as marathoners, not sprinters. We need to expect we'll have fifteen stressful years juggling children and career, but fifteen years is just a drop in the bucket in a fifty-year career."

"Fifty-year career?" Suze pretends to faint. "Is that what some women do? Poor things!"

"I liked working," Ellen retorts. "I never intended to stop, but then I had to go on bed rest with J.D. After he was born, I returned to work. It wasn't easy. I wanted to be J.D.'s mommy, but I also wanted to be savvy, successful Ellen, the one who brokered big deals and earned outrageous bonuses. I liked that Ellen." She draws a breath. "I like her a lot better than who I am now."

"Shame on you." Monica wags a finger disapprovingly. "Being a great mother is the most important thing you'll ever do—"

"But what if you were a scientist and researching a cure for cancer?" Jen interjects. "Could that possibly be more important than being a stay-at-home mother?"

"That's different." Monica sniffs.

"Wait, wait, wait." Ellen slams her book shut so hard that it thuds. "You're saying that unless we do something like discover a cure for cancer, we should be home with kids?"

"What if you need the money?" Lucy demands.

"What if you don't, but you just enjoy working?" Jen retorts.

Kate clears her throat, and when no one seems to be listening, she clears it again. "Let's get back to the book. We all have opinions on parenting, but we're not debating motherhood. We're discussing the book. Does anyone have a chapter or passage that really resonated?"

There's a moment of awkward silence, and then Jen opens her book to a saved passage.

"What made an impression on me was the chapter about returning to work. I couldn't go back to work now and get my old job back. I've been home too long. And maybe I could get another job, but let's face it, if forced to hire me or an eager, competitive, fresh-faced twenty-something Ivy Leaguer with no husband and kids, who would they hire?"

"They'd hire you," Suze answers confidently. "You have real work experience, and life experience—"

"But they don't want to pay for that experience, particularly if it's dated." Ellen makes a face. "Don't think I like it, but I know it's true. Businesses are about making money. They make more money when they save money, and the new college grad will be a hell of a lot cheaper than me, and she probably will work harder, too. Let's face it, I'll never work fifty, sixty hours a week again."

"So we're safe as long as our husbands never die, divorce us, get sick, or lose their jobs." It's the first time Raine has contributed to the discussion tonight, and we all look at her. Raine isn't the most vocal member of our group, and she seems to spend more time wiggling her foot than paying attention, but right now she has all our attention.

"Matthew's MS has gotten worse," she adds carefully. "You probably don't know, but he hasn't worked in two years. The doctors say he'll never go back to work again. He was diagnosed at forty-four. He's forty-seven now. What do we do? I for one pray we can live off his disability for as long as we can."

Suze is astonished. "This has been going on for years?"

"Matthew didn't want people to know, but it's impossible to hide anymore." Raine's shoulders shift. "I grew up with a dad who had had polio, and now this. Funny how life is. I thought once I left home I'd never have to deal with a wheelchair again."

Everyone's terribly sympathetic. This sort of news just rocks you. If it could happen to Raine, it could happen to anyone...or, maybe because it happened to Raine, it won't happen to you....

"I'm sorry," Patti says quietly.

"Me too." Ellen leans forward to touch Raine's knee. "And know that we're here for you. If you need any help, or want anything—"

"I'll be fine." Raine cuts her off with a quick "I'm totally fine" smile. "We're fine."

I look at Raine, so petite and striking in her russet suede coat, a color that plays perfectly off the copper highlights in her long, sexy shag, and I think, I know that tone. I know those words.

I'm fine. We're fine. Don't bother yourself. We don't need anything.

When what we're actually screaming is *Help me, help me. Oh God, someone help me.*

Why can't we accept help? Why can't we ask for help? Why are we afraid of not having it all together?

"Raine, you have to know you're not alone," Monica says kindly. "You'd be surprised at the number of husbands not working." She pauses, and there's something in her pause that gives me pause.

Slowly Monica turns to look at me. "Lots of husbands are unemployed. Like Nathan. Taylor, he didn't work this last year...did he?"

I hear a strange noise, like a roar of sound, and I think it's because everyone's talking—but after a second I realize no one's talking. They're silent. The noise is in my head. It's me silently screaming.

"I wondered why you were selling your house," Monica continues. "Because it didn't make sense. It's a beautiful home, and you always threw the most gorgeous parties. I couldn't imagine why you'd sell that house unless you and Nathan were divorcing or were in serious financial difficulty—"

"Shut up, Monica." Lucy has shot to her feet, and she's standing there, eyes blazing, features pinched with fury.

Monica pales. "What?"

"You heard me. Shut up. Stop talking. Stop saying horrible things. I used to think you just lacked sensitivity, but it's not that. You *like* being mean. You enjoy making people squirm. Well, I've had enough of it. I've had enough of you and your rumor mill. Talk about me if you want, but for God's sake, leave Taylor alone."

The room's gone deathly quiet, and all you can hear is the tick-ticking of the antique grandfather clock in the hall.

Monica is the first to speak. "Lucy, what a goose! No one's making fun of Taylor. It's okay if Nathan hasn't worked. And it's okay if they have to sell their house—"

"No, it's not." I'm on my feet, too, and I'm gathering my book and glass of wine to carry to the kitchen. "It's not fine that we're selling our house. It's not fine that Nathan's now working in Omaha. It's not fine that my girls are losing the only home they've ever known. But that's life. Shit happens, right?"

I look one by one at Patti and Kate, Ellen, Jen, Suze, and Raine, before staring pointedly at Monica. "And just so you don't hear this from anyone else, I'm going back to work. I'll be working full-time, and I'm not ashamed of it. My only regret is that I wasn't working earlier. I should have never become totally financially dependent. It wasn't fair to Nathan, and it wasn't fair to me."

I can see by Patti's stunned expression that she had no idea I was going through any of this. Kate doesn't look as surprised, but that might just be her boarding school stiff upper lip coming through. The others...quite frankly, I don't care what they think. The last few months have peeled my skin off, turned me inside out, and left me bare. It sucks to take such a hard hit, and to have it made public, but that's how it is.

Gathering my tattered pride, I turn to Lucy. "I think I'm going to go home now."

She nods quickly. "I'll go with you."

"This is silly," Monica protests. "What are you doing? It's book club, and we're discussing your pick, Lucy, this was your book. You can't leave like this."

"Yes, I can," Lucy answers, lifting her purse.

"No." Monica rises and gestures to the room. "No, you can't just have a tantrum and walk out. That's immature. You're being very immature."

"Kate, Patti, girls, I'm sorry." I look around the room. "I'm sorry to ruin tonight's party, but this isn't the right place for me. This isn't fun for me. And now that I think about it, I won't be coming back—"

"You're quitting book club?" Monica's voice rings out sharp and loud.

"Yes." I hadn't really thought about it until now, but book club hasn't been a good place for me. It's negative and competitive and just makes me miserable. "I like all of you individually, but I don't enjoy book club—"

"Maybe because you don't like reading," Monica answers savagely.

I shake my head. "No. I like to read. I just don't like discussing the books the way we do. It's not your fault that I don't find it fun. But it's pointless to continue with something I don't like."

"I couldn't have said it better," Lucy says, rising. She's smiling, the first smile I've seen from her all day. "I'm quitting, too."

"*What?*" Monica practically shrieks.

Lucy shrugs. "I want reading to be fun again. I want to like the books I read. And while you're all my friends, book club really isn't that friendly." She lifts a hand, waves. "Good night, everybody."

As we walk out the door into the night, Lucy turns to me, slides her arm through mine, and gives it a little squeeze. "That was fun!" Then her expression changes. "Well, the last bit, anyway." She pauses, squeezes my arm again. "I'm sorry, Taylor, she's just plain mean. There's no excuse for her, there really isn't."

We walk to my car, and as I press the unlock on the keypad on my key chain, I turn to face Lucy. "But why? Why is she always poking at me? What did I do to her?"

Lucy shrugs helplessly. "Maybe it's because you make life look so easy."

Chapter Sixteen

Lucy's asleep in the guest room, and I sit on my bed eating Honey Nut Cheerios straight out of the box.

I make life look easy? *I* do?

What a joke. That's the biggest laugh of all.

I munch on another handful of Cheerios. I don't even know how much I've eaten now. A quarter of a box? A half box? All I know is that I can't stop. I have no desire to stop. I'm going to eat until I pop.

I've never found life easy. It's always been a fight. Push, push, push. Work, work, work. Smile, smile, smile. And I push because I'm afraid. Afraid of everything that's happened before, everything that could happen again. I work to make sure I won't be trapped, won't be lost, won't be forgotten.

Of course, I don't let others see my fears. It'd be dangerous. I'd be vulnerable to everyone and everything. As it is, I'm so vulnerable at home.

I love my family. I need my family. I need us together again.

Realizing the Cheerios box is almost empty, I drag myself off the bed, close the box top, and go down the stairs to return the cereal to the kitchen cabinet.

To make sure I don't eat anything more, I brush my teeth extra long before rinsing with Listerine Whitening.

But in my bed with the lights out, I feel the crunchy crumbs from the Cheerios and my stuffed stomach and am very glad no one can see me now.

The next morning, I call Z Design after Lucy returns to her house. It was nice having Lucy stay over. I enjoyed having company, and I think it was good for her, too.

Just as I planned, my call to Z Design goes to voice mail and I leave a message on their office phone for Susan, asking her to let Marta know I'm interested in the job and would appreciate the opportunity to interview again.

Marta calls me back two hours later. I can hear a child's voice and TV noise in the background and realize she must be phoning from her house. "I got your message," she says, her voice crisp, precise, as though we're back in the conference room at Starbucks. "But I'd like to hear more from you about why you want *this* job."

My heart takes a nosedive. I'm beat and feel beat up. I honestly don't know if I have it in me to razzle-dazzle anyone right now. "I need a job," I answer slowly, "and this position sounds like a good fit for me."

Marta is silent at the other end of the line.

I struggle on. "I'm also impressed by Z Design and the quality of your company's work." Which is the truth. Earlier today I read every brochure, every document, everything I could about Z Design. I even researched Marta. She came from a prominent Laurelhurst family. I didn't know that. "It helps, too, that your office is close. I'd be able to work and still be close if the kids needed something. That's always a worry for me."

"You don't mind the clerical aspect? Your position is really a support position for the Z Design team."

"Not at all. If you think about it, my volunteer work is all about supporting the school and the teachers and the PTA. Most of the work is administrative—photocopies, phone calls, e-mails, and mailings."

"That's a good point," she agrees. "So, were you able to take a look at the benefits package? After three months you'd qualify for medical and dental. We're working on adding vision to the health plan. We don't have it yet."

"I saw that. Right now we're on COBRA, but that will change." I pause, aware that my throat is closing. "And I should have insurance of my own. Just in case."

Marta exhales. "So. Any questions for me? Anything else you want to know?"

I actually don't have any questions. I don't know why. Maybe it's because I'm too overwhelmed. I'm talking about a job, a job with set hours and a detailed job description. A job where I must answer to someone and meet expectations.

I've liked my independence.

I've liked setting my own hours.

I've liked being my own boss.

"No." I close my eyes briefly, force myself to look forward, not back. "I just...appreciate...your time, and I know I could be an asset to your company."

Silence stretches over the phone line. It's almost as though I can feel Marta digesting and processing what I've said. Would Taylor be a good employee? Would Taylor get

along with everyone? Would Taylor contribute to the bottom line?

I'm suddenly desperate to fill the silence, to blurt out
something stupid, tell her that although we're not friends,
I can suck it up and behave like a professional. I want to
reassure her I'm not the diva she thinks I am and, at the
very least, confess that if I have issues with her, they're my
issues, not hers. But I don't say any of that. I've already
told her I want the job, and I don't want to be perceived as
groveling.

"Taylor, I know we talked about a late November start
date, but Susan's getting pressure to begin her new job
sooner. If I hired you, when could you start?"

"Monday." Then I remember yard duty, lunch duty,
reading, office help. "As long as I could sneak away now
and then to fulfill my obligations at Points Elementary.
I intend to cut back on the hours I volunteer, but I can't
drop everything. I'm the auction chair—"

"I know." She sounds almost kind. "And I wouldn't
expect you to drop everything. You might need to cut
back on some of the volunteer hours to protect your san-
ity, but otherwise, I support volunteer work. Susan's pretty
involved at Points, too."

We both fall silent. Then I realize what we've just been
discussing.

"Are you hiring me?" I ask.

"I think I am."

"Really?"

She laughs, a deep, throaty sound that matches her crazy
camouflage pants and combat boots. "Do you want it?"

"Yes."

"Good. Consider it yours. What if you take the first few days of the week to sort things out at your end, and we'll look forward to seeing you here Thursday morning at nine?"

"How's nine-fifteen?" I counter nervously. "Tori's pre-school doesn't start until nine, and it'll take me a few minutes to get to your office after...."

"That's fine. The kids come first."

My eyes suddenly burn. "Thank you."

"See you Thursday."

"Yes, thank you again."

"Take care of yourself, Taylor."

I hang up quickly before she knows she's undone me completely. I've been anti–Marta Zinsser so long that I don't know what to feel now that I can't be anti-Marta anymore.

Humble? Grateful?

All of the above?

I'm no sooner off the phone than the doorbell rings. I go to the door to find Patti standing there.

"Hey." She smiles uncertainly and tucks a strand of hair behind her ear. "Can I come in?"

In all the years we've been friends, she's never asked permission to come into my house before.

"Of course." I open the door wider, gesture for her to come inside. "How's it going?"

"Good."

I shut the door, turn to face her. She's wearing a trench coat, but she doesn't bother to undo any of the buttons. "Want some tea? I could make a fresh pot of coffee?"

"No. I'm good." She frowns, her dark arched eyebrows

wrinkling. "Taylor—" She breaks off, and her frown deepens.

I wait as she struggles to find the right words.

"I'm hurt," she says in a rush. "I'm hurt that you didn't come to me, tell me any of this. Don's hurt, too. Nathan never said a word, and he and Don go back over twenty years. We thought you were our friends, our best friends—"

"Nathan's filed for a separation." I don't mean to cut her short, but at the same time I can't bear to be lectured to right now. Maybe it's not a lecture. Maybe it's a scolding. But I'm so raw at the moment, so raw that I can't handle another rebuke or criticism. "We're not just having marital problems, either. We're broke. Beyond broke. We've lost everything. Including the house." I gulp for air, pray I won't break down and cry. "I didn't tell you because I...I..."

Her expression is so bewildered that I want to hug her, tell her it's okay.

"Patti, I didn't know how to tell you. I wanted to tell you. But I didn't know how to say it." My eyes are watering, and I chew relentlessly on the inside of my lip. "I was afraid if I said these things out loud, they'd be true."

"I can't believe it," she answers, her hazel eyes searching my face. She looks so young all of a sudden. Sixteen, seventeen. "You and Nathan are the perfect couple. You two are still so in love."

I thought so.

"Maybe he just needs time," she adds earnestly. "Maybe he just needs space."

I nod, shrug. "That's what I'm hoping."

"So what are you going to do in the meantime? Monica says you have to be out by November twenty-ninth—"

"How does Monica know that?"

Patti's eyes are huge. "What do you mean?"

My heart's drumming hard now, a sickening pace that makes my legs feel weak. "How does she know our move date? I haven't told anyone."

"You know, right?"

It's as though there's a glacier on my heart, a vast white sheet of ice, and it's swallowing me whole. "Know what?"

Patti's eyes water, and she just stares at me.

"Don't tell me," I say, reaching for the banister behind me. "Don't tell me she knows the buyer. Don't tell me—"

"Monica and Doug bought the house." Patti's voice is soft. "She told us all after you left. She's always loved this house, and when Doug heard it was on the market—apparently one of the brokers talked—they made the offer."

My legs crumple, and I sit on the bottom step of my curving staircase. Not Marta, but Monica. Monica Tallman, who already has my hairstyle and took over my book club, now has my house.

My house.

My house.

My hands flail, and then I grab the step on either side of my hips, and leaning forward, I open my mouth in a silent scream. I can't believe it, can't stand it, can't see any justice in it.

Patti stands frozen. "I'm sorry, Taylor. I thought you knew."

I shake my head. "No, but I'm glad to know. It's better that I know."

"Taylor, I don't know what to say."

"I don't think there's anything to say."

Patti's still stricken. "How can I move and leave you like this?"

I can't have Patti feeling bad. Patti has done nothing wrong. I haul myself to my feet. "I'm going to be fine. We'll be fine." But then I groan, "But Monica, of all people! I just wish it wasn't Monica moving into my house."

"You and me both." She looks at me. "What can I do? There must be something I can do to help?"

"How about a hug?" It's my attempt to lighten things, but Patti takes me at my word.

She hugs me fiercely. "Oh, my God, Taylor. I'm sorry. I'm so sorry."

I squeeze her back. "I'm not dying. No one's dying."

She takes a step back but leaves her hands on my arms. "But still. This is...this is...wow."

"Yep." I suddenly laugh. "And you want to know a bigger wow?"

Her nose wrinkles. She's not sure.

I laugh again. I'm so damn tired, all I can do now is laugh. "I'm going to work for Z Design." I can see from Patti's expression that she doesn't get it. My smile is lopsided. "Marta Zinsser is my new boss."

"Oh God!"

Giggling, I cover my mouth. "Oh, yes."

"Get out."

My hand falls away. "Can you believe it? Monica's bought my house, and I'm now working for Marta."

"No, I can't believe it." Patti shakes her head. "The world's coming to an end, isn't it? People just aren't telling me."

I'm laughing again, laughing so hard that I'm leaning against the banister. Maybe that's the answer. Maybe the world is coming to an end. If so, it's one hell of an Apocalypse.

I spend Monday through Wednesday afternoon apartment hunting without much luck. There aren't a lot of older apartments in downtown Bellevue, and the new ones are all luxury towers and outrageously priced, with monthly rents starting at $1,800 for a one-bedroom apartment.

Although I like the idea of secure parking, heated indoor pools, slick workout rooms, and door-to-door dry-cleaning service, I can't justify spending $2,700 a month on a two- or three-bedroom apartment. That used to be our first house's mortgage payment.

Wednesday night I sleep badly, incredibly anxious about my first day of work the next morning. When my alarm goes off at six, I get up, shower, wash my hair, and go make coffee. But drinking the coffee's another matter. I am so nervous.

I dread first days, dread not knowing systems, places, people, things. I dread screwing up and getting things wrong. I dread making mistakes.

With a half hour to myself before I need to get the girls up, I pop in one of my yoga DVDs and go through the thirty-minute routine. It's good. It actually helps. By the time I'm done, I'm calmer, more focused, more optimistic.

The worst thing that could happen, I tell myself as I head back upstairs to wake the girls, is that I get fired.

And honestly, that would be a blessing, so really, there's no reason to stress.

As the girls dress in their rooms, I stand in my closet trying to figure out what to wear today. Today is important. Today I want to be professional but comfortable.

I frown as I study the rows of clothes. It's a huge closet. I know right now that our new place won't have a closet this big. I won't have anyplace for all these beautiful things. I need to go through my wardrobe, get rid of half of everything in this closet. Sell them somewhere, maybe a consignment shop.

In the end, I settle on Michael Kors boot-leg black slacks and a slim black turtleneck that I pair with a belted Max Mara jacket in cobalt. The belt, also cobalt, has a big modern square buckle that saves my outfit from being too staid while still bordering on conservative. The last thing I want to be is overly flashy and fancy.

I get the big girls off to catch the bus, and after tidying the downstairs and starting a load of laundry, I take Tori to school. I haven't told the girls yet I'm starting a new job today, and I'm definitely not interested in sharing that I'll be working for Eva's mom. Jemma is feeling vulnerable enough right now. The last thing she needs to do is worry about the pecking order at school.

But maybe Eva will say something?

My fingers tighten on the steering wheel. I hadn't thought of that.

But maybe Marta hasn't told Eva yet. Maybe Marta is waiting to see how it goes, too.

I relax a little, relinquish my death grip on the wheel, and head back to Yarrow Point. Marta lives just down the street from me, and her office is actually in a converted guesthouse behind her home.

It's strange to think that I'll be working at Marta's house. I feel rather like domestic help as I park on the side of her drive and walk around the back to the guesthouse.

Wouldn't it be weird if she asked me to do little personal things for her? You know, get her coffee, pick up her dry-cleaning, pick up her daughter from school?

I shudder as I walk, my heels clicking on the stepping-stones that lead from the driveway to the office front door.

Heart thudding, I rap on the glass door. A woman who looks like a mom answers the door. "Come on, come in," she greets me even as she offers me her hand. "I'm Susan, the office manager. I'm the one you're replacing.

"Marta's not here," she adds, closing the door behind me. "She's on the East Coast and won't be back until Monday, so it will be a little quieter around here than normal."

"I see a lot of desks," I say, taking in the office. The interior is almost completely open and airy from the walls of windows, skylights, and the overhead halogen light. Drafting-style desks line the walls, while a long white conference table fills the room's center.

"We have five full-time employees, but Marta's thinking about bringing on a sixth. Business is really growing—which is good—but everyone's spread a tad thin right now."

"When does everyone else arrive?" I ask, still clutching my purse and lunch.

"Anytime," Susan answers brightly. "You'll soon see that no one here punches a time clock. Everyone has clients and ongoing projects, along with wooing new clients, so there's a lot of coming and going. I'll show you around, okay?"

There's a small kitchen, bathroom, and supply room as well as a sleek computer on every desk.

"You'll be shadowing me today," she explains as she walks me through her morning routine. "But don't worry if you forget something. Z Design is owned by Marta, but it operates as a team. Everyone looks out for everyone."

We're at her desk, sitting side by side going through the e-mail, when the door opens and the first of the Z Design team arrives.

There's Robert, the artist, who can draw and paint anything and who I'm pretty sure is gay. And Allie, a twentysomething whiz with blue eyes, blond spiral curls, and a delicate chin. Melanie arrives last. She's tall and slim, almost lanky. For some reason, I thought she was southern or Texan until she introduces herself and tells me she's Canadian. Melanie just finished a presentation and is giddy that it's over. Apparently Melanie, or "Mel," as she prefers to be called, replaced someone Marta hired last year to replace some know-it-all named Chris.

I'm still trying to keep all the names and faces straight when Susan tells me it's lunch and asks if I've brought anything or if I was going to go home to eat.

"I brought my lunch," I say. "I didn't know if we were allowed to go home to eat."

Robert and Allie overhear me. Robert leans back in his chair. "You can do anything here," he says, folding his arms behind his head. "Marta can be a stress case, but it's always about the product. As long as we deliver, she doesn't care what we do."

Allie taps a pencil. "What Robert means is that Marta doesn't micromanage. Just do your job and she's happy."

Susan agrees. "And we all do different things for lunch. Some days I go home, some days I eat here. Some days everyone has client lunches—"

"Like me," Mel answers, grabbing her coat and a briefcase and dashing toward the door. "Gotta go, and it was nice to meet you, Taylor."

Robert and Allie decide to go grab a bite and head out together, leaving Susan and me alone.

Following Susan's lead, I pick up my bag lunch and carry it to the conference table. As we eat, we chat about our respective Thanksgiving plans. Susan's taking her kids to her sister's in Olympia. I share that we'll be packing to move. Susan wants to know where we're moving to, and I tell her I don't know, that I haven't found a place yet.

The phone rings, and Susan leaves the table to check the number. She doesn't recognize it and lets it go into voice mail. "During lunch I only pick up if it's Marta, one of the team members, or the kids' school," she explains, sitting back down.

"How long have you worked here?" I ask as she peels the lid off her blueberry yogurt.

"Couple years now."

"You like it here?"

"It's terrific. The team is terrific. I honestly can't complain."

I notice she doesn't mention Marta specifically. "No problems with Marta?"

Susan's expression turns incredulous. "Problem with Marta? Heavens, no. She's...she's..." Her hands lift, outstretch. "She's brave. She's smart. She's...incredible. I wouldn't have my new job if it weren't for her. She helped make it happen. She believed in me. She believed in me when I didn't believe in myself."

Susan must see my look of disbelief because she hastens to add, "Now that doesn't mean she can't be demanding. She has really high standards and works very hard, and sometimes it can be a bit much. But if you're ever overwhelmed or feeling pinched, just talk to her. Marta's the type you can talk to. Straight up. No games. She will listen, I promise."

The phone rings again, and Susan once more goes to her desk to check the number. This time she picks up. "Marta, hi, how's New York?"

I can't help listening as Susan chats with Marta and then picks up a pen and scribbles some notes. "I'll get you on that earlier flight....No problem, and I'll line up the car service, too....Okay. No worries....Talk to you tomorrow."

Conversation finished, Susan writes a few more notes to herself and then returns to the table. "You said you haven't found a place yet?" she asks, dipping her spoon into the yogurt.

"No, and we have to be out of the house by the end of the month. Thank God Thanksgiving is late this year. Otherwise we'd be moving in between bites of turkey and cranberry."

Susan chuckles. "I've done that before. No fun. So what kind of place are you looking for?"

I tell her it has to be relatively affordable (meaning cheap) and preferably in the area because I really, really don't want the girls to change schools.

She understands. She has kids at Points, too. "You know, there's a house on my street for rent. Nothing fancy. But I know the owners and they're looking for a year lease and they want someone trustworthy, someone who won't be having loud parties and lots of people over."

I think about my life and can't imagine loud parties or lots of people over. "How big is it?"

"Three bedrooms. Two baths. Decent-size living room. Kitchen's old, though, never remodeled, but the back-yard's fully fenced and there's a nice little carport."

A fenced backyard and a carport. That's where I am now. Unbelievable.

"Do you know how much the rent is?" I ask, biting into the second half of my very boring turkey sandwich. I hate turkey sandwiches. I don't know why I made me one. Penance, maybe?

"Eighteen hundred a month, plus first and last."

Not cheap for a rental that sounds like a dump. "The house is close?"

"Maybe a mile from here and within walking distance to the school."

I put down my sandwich. "So the girls wouldn't take the bus?"

"No. Unless you drove them, they would just walk together. My kids walk to school. Lots of the neighbor-hood kids do."

I feel a pang. I'm saying good-bye not just to our house, but to our neighborhood and our bus stop. I think about our bus stop and all the moms who stand around with their cups of coffee and their dogs on leashes. If we move, we won't be part of that stop anymore. We won't be rushing to meet the bus. By moving, our whole routine will change.

Everything will change.

A lump fills my throat. I won't be able to eat another bite now, and I put the sandwich in the bag and crumple it up.

"Do you want to go see it?" Susan asks, dropping her plastic spoon in her empty yogurt carton. "It's not far. We could zip over and back in less than ten minutes."

"You think so?"

"I know so. Come on."

The house is a square, squat 1950s-era brick house with the original windows and a moss-covered roof. The front lawn is green but shorn short, and the shrubs have all been pruned into small, hard mounds. One or two cedars stand sentrylike along the driveway. The carport is metal and gloomy. The interior (or what I can see through the living room window) is gloomy. The front door with its screen door is a faded barn red.

It could be worse.

I know it could be worse. And it is just three blocks from school.

Okay, it's on the wrong side of Clyde Hill's hill, the side that isn't officially Clyde Hill, just Bellevue, but lots of new houses are being built up and down the street. If you look past all the construction vehicles, you can see Mt.

Rainier in the distance and a span of the Cascades along with some of downtown Bellevue's skyscrapers.

Susan drove us in her car, and I walk back to her car and glance down the street. "You're sure the owners want a year's lease?"

She nods. "They're going to tear this down and build a new house, but it'll take a year to get the plans done and all the permits approved. They don't want it sitting empty for the next year if they can make some money on it—" She breaks off as a huge truck lumbers by. "It won't be the quietest street. There is a lot of construction going on. It drives me a little batty."

"Where do you live? Which house is yours?"

She points to the end of the street. "The little blue one." She makes a face as if seeing it through my eyes. "Someday it'll be someone's tear-down, but we're happy with it. At least, I'm happy with it. The kids want a bigger house. I think they're embarrassed that we live in a shoebox when their friends all have nice houses, but they don't understand. This is nice. Far nicer than anything I had growing up."

"I understand." And I do. The little shoeboxes on this street still cost a million dollars. Bellevue's not cheap. Great schools and proximity to the Seattle bridges come with a hefty price.

We head back to Z Design's office, and although it was weird this morning pulling up to Marta's house and walking up her drive for my first day of work, I'm not uncomfortable now. I don't know if it's Susan's company or her confidence, but as we walk through the door, I smile at Robert and Allie, who are also back and working at their desks.

Inside, Susan takes my coat and tells me to go ahead and check the phone for voice messages.

I sit at her desk and, lifting the phone, use the code Susan gave me to retrieve messages. Seven. I write down everything I think I need to write down before playing the next message but save each message just in case I get some of the details wrong.

In between answering the phone and making requested copies and faxes, I listen as Susan teaches me how to do the monthly billing. She shows me the program she uses and how to invoice and how to show a payment is made.

Finances aren't my strong suit, but I take notes and remind myself that Susan didn't know how to do this, either, when she first started. I can learn. I can learn anything. I just have to be patient.

We're practicing making fake invoices when the office door opens and shuts. I'm so used to the team coming and going that I don't even look up anymore, so it's a shock to hear my name.

"Mrs. Young?"

My head jerks up, and I look straight into Eva Zinsser's wide green eyes. "Eva."

"What are you doing here, Mrs. Young? Are you working on the auction?"

She's so excited, I think, so pleased to see me here. I open my mouth to answer, but before I can speak, Susan is sliding off her reading glasses. "Eva, I don't know if your mom told you, but Mrs. Young is working here now."

Eva's jaw drops. "She is?"

Susan nods and smiles broadly. "Isn't it wonderful? She's your mom's new secretary."

Chapter Seventeen

The positive is that I survived my first day as Marta Zinsser's secretary.

The negative is that tomorrow I will still be Marta Zinsser's secretary.

But I'm focusing on the positives as I drive away at five-fifteen: that I don't have to go back until tomorrow, and I've also got the opportunity to go see the rental house on Susan's street.

After lunch, Susan tracked down the man who owns the house, and after he and I talked for a few minutes, he invited me to come see the house on my way home from work.

The squat brick rental house is just as forlorn on the inside as it is on the outside, but there are three bedrooms and two working bathrooms and a nice fireplace in the living room, which makes me think we could have Christmas here. I don't know why I always look at a house and try to imagine it at Christmas. Where would the tree go, and how could we hang the girls' velvet stockings?

"I understand you want to rent for a year," I say, returning to the kitchen, where he's leaning against a counter waiting for me. The kitchen must once have been pale yellow, but it is now more putty gray.

"Six months to a year," he agrees.

I cross my arms, thinking. School will be out in six months. The girls and I could move to join Nathan as soon as school ends. If Nathan lets us.

"Could we do a six-month lease, with maybe the option to renew for another six months?"

The owner, a man in his fifties, looks at me. "That would probably work. Are you building a house, too?"

We have a house. A big beautiful dream house, just like the Barbie dream house I had when I was a little girl. Three stories and lots of rooms.

I shake my head. "My husband is working for a new company. There's talk that we might need to move this summer."

"Six months would be fine, then. Just let me know a month in advance if you won't renew the lease."

I nod.

"The house is available now. I just need first and last month's rent, with a five-hundred-dollar cleaning deposit, and you could start moving in anytime. I wouldn't charge any extra if you moved in before the first of the month."

Which is helpful, but doing the math in my head, I realize I'd need $4,100 to move in. I don't have that. "Is the cleaning fee really necessary? I understand you'll be tearing the house down...?"

"Yes, but if I have to rent it out after you, it'll have to be clean, and you'd be surprised at how most people leave a rental house."

I want to tell him I'm not like that, that I'd never trash a place and leave it, but he doesn't know me. Doesn't know that for the past twelve years I've been the ideal wife and mom, cleaning, organizing, making things beautiful and comfortable for my family.

I glance over my shoulder toward the small dining room, which opens onto the living room. Our dining room table will never fit in the dining room here. Our living room couch would take up the entire living room. None of our furniture will fit here. The scale is all off. Our furniture is oversize and grand. Big pieces that make a statement: *This is who we are. This is what we have....*

Our furniture will have to go, too.

I ball my hands, try not to think of what we're losing. It doesn't help to focus on the loss. It's the future I'm concerned with. "If I give you a deposit, would it be possible for you to hold the house for me? I'll need a little time to get the money together—"

"Is money a problem?" he interrupts nervously. "Not to be rude, but I don't want to get into a situation where people can't make their payments. I don't like evicting people. It's no fun being the bad guy."

"I understand." I ball my hands tighter against my rib cage. "Money's not a problem. It's just that my husband's on the road right now, and I'll need him to send you a check." I hate lying, but I'm not about to admit that I can't come up with $5,000, and I want this house. We need this house. It's close to school, close to downtown Bellevue, and close to where I work.

"It's such a great house for the little girls," I add before he can refuse me. "They'll be able to walk to school, and they already have friends on the street. It'll be such a happy place for them."

He takes a deep breath and exhales noisily. He doesn't like being put in this position, but I don't like it, either. I don't like begging. I don't like pleading. I don't like needing handouts and favors from anyone.

"Fine," he says, burying his hands deep in his trouser pockets. "You could have a couple days. But if I don't have the check by Monday for first, last, and cleaning deposit, I won't hold it any longer."

"Thank you." I beam at him, giving him my full megawatt smile. "That's great. Thank you so much. I really appreciate it. You'll have that check soon. I promise."

Driving home, I vow I'll get the money we need for that house. I've got four days to come up with $4,000. I know what's sitting in my checking account, but I don't dare use any of it since I have to pay Annika's salary tomorrow, as well as groceries and the normal household bills like water and electricity, garbage and phone.

We could have another yard sale. This time we could put more out front, drag furniture outside, along with much of my closet. But I cringe at the idea of selling our furniture out from beneath us.

It seems nasty and desperate.

But I am desperate. And my once enormous pride is quickly becoming a thing of the past. Everything right now revolves around cash. Getting it, making it, conserving it.

I let the gardener go last week. He won't be back, but I still owe him a check. I tried to let the cleaning lady go, too, but she was furious and said I must give her two weeks' notice, so she's coming another two weeks and then not again.

So I need $4,000 to get us into a new house. Four thousand is the difference between being on the streets and settled somewhere close for the next six months.

Pulling into the garage, I realize the kind of sale I'm talking about isn't a yard sale but an estate sale, one of those where you hire a company to come in and empty your house.

At least 10 percent of everything would go to the liquidation company—something I hate to see happen—but wouldn't that be better than trying to move it, or store it, or sell pieces off one by one ourselves?

Or maybe we do sell it ourselves, but not piece by piece.

Maybe—and I start smiling—maybe there's someone who loves my good taste so much, she's willing to buy not just my house, but my furniture and lifestyle.

I turn off the ignition and sit in the garage, headlights illuminating the drywall.

Why not? The furniture was designed for this house. Every Kreiss table, every Lee Jofa upholstered couch, every Brunschwig & Fils covered chair, was bought for a special place for a certain room for just this house.

Shouldn't the furniture and glory stay with the house?

I reach for my cell phone, call Patti. She answers immediately, even though I can tell she's in the middle of feeding her brood. "I was just thinking about you," Patti says, raising her voice to be heard over the din in the background. "How are you? How's your week?"

"Fine, you know, as fine as can be." I hesitate, anticipate my request, and hate that I'm actually grinning. "Patti, I have a favor to ask. I don't know if it's something you could do or not, or if it'd make you uncomfortable."

"Of course. Anything." Patti must be walking into a different room because it's suddenly quiet on the other end of the line. "Tell me."

"I've decided to sell almost everything in the house—"

"Taylor, no!"

"No," I stop her, "this is a good thing. It'd actually be less painful for me to sell everything in one fell swoop than try to figure out how to save this or that. When we move we're better off starting fresh. We'll take the girls' things, of course, and maybe the furniture from my room and a few pieces from the family room for the new house, but otherwise, I'm going to sell it all."

"So what can I do?"

"Let Monica know."

Patti's silent a moment. "But won't she just gloat?"

"Not if she thinks she can't have it." I pause. "That's why I need your help. If you can just drop it into a conversation somehow, that some big New York interior designer is desperate to buy up everything for a house he's furnishing for a client in Portland—"

"Taylor!" Patti's choking on laughter. "Monica will hate it. She'll die. She'll want to buy everything herself."

My lopsided smile grows. "Exactly." I open my car door, slide out one leg. "It's a shame everything's going so quickly, too. The designer will be here next Wednesday. He's paying cash. Twenty grand."

"My God, Taylor, you're wicked." She's still spluttering

with laughter. "And brilliant, and dammit, I'm proud of you. You know she'll buy it all."

I slide out of the car and close the door behind me. "Cash," I say delicately. "Twenty-two thousand."

"Twenty-five, for the pain and humiliation of being stabbed in the back, and you can thank me when you put the check in the bank."

Friday morning before I leave for work, the idea that I have a job still achingly new, I shoot Nathan an e-mail, tell him I've found a house for us for the next six months to a year. I tell him I have a job, too, and everything's great and not to worry. The girls are doing great. We're all doing great. And I know his new job will eventually be great, too.

Today at Z Design is easier than yesterday because I know where everything is and know whom I'll be working with. Fridays are also usually half days, but because it's Susan's last day and everyone has so much to do, we all stay until four, when Allie surprises Susan with a going-away cake and Robert whisks a bottle of champagne from an ugly paper bag in the back of the fridge. Everyone's talking and toasting Susan when the door opens and Marta walks in with a travel bag and briefcase.

"Fantastic. Cake and champagne, my favorites," she says, shutting the door and leaving her luggage in the corner.

"You're back early," Susan answers, licking purple-and-white icing from her fingers even as she stands up.

"Sit down, sit down," Marta insists, and as she gestures for Susan to sit, she spots me hovering in the background.

"Taylor." Her eyes rest on me a moment, her expression serious.

I hadn't expected to see Marta until Monday, and I'm thrown for a loop. "Hello," I say stiffly, feeling awkward here all over again.

This isn't going to work, I think, this isn't something I can do.

But Marta's turned her attention to Susan. "Did you open your gifts yet?" she asks, taking a seat at the conference table, too.

"No," Susan answers, yet she looks delighted.

"We were waiting," Mel explains as Allie cuts Marta a piece of cake and Robert pours her some champagne. "We knew you were trying to get back early, so we were holding off in case you showed up."

Marta smiles, dark hair loose, white teeth flashing. "I showed up."

Susan cheers, and I feel even more alien. This is Marta's place. She's in her element here. These are her people. Her family.

I can feel myself tense yet again. I want to go home now, want to go back to my world, the one I understand, but Marta looks up and catches my eye. "Sit, Taylor. Relax. You're part of the team."

Hard to walk out when your boss tells you to stay.

Saturday morning, I wake up with a raging headache brought on by the two glasses of champagne I had yesterday at the office, which I chased with another glass or two of red wine once I arrived home.

I shouldn't have had that much to drink. I don't normally drink like that. I ordered pizza for the girls last night, the disgusting cheap pizza that I hate to eat—which I ate, accompanied by the red wine.

Now, heading for the stairs, I wince as I hear Brooke and Jemma screaming at each other in the bonus room at the end of the hall.

"I hate you!"

"I hate you!"

"You are the worst sister in the world!"

"You are."

"No, you are."

"Stop copying me!"

"I'm not."

"You are."

Time to play referee. I hate being referee. I open the door and stand there as they continue screaming at each other.

"I hate you for the rest of your life!"

"I'll hate you longer! I'll hate you even when you're dead!"

"That's it. Enough!" I shout, but they don't hear me. They're too busy hating each other's guts for the rest of their lives.

"Jemma! Brooke!" I roar their names to be heard.

They straighten abruptly, both falling silent. They most definitely heard me this time.

I feel a grim satisfaction in my capacity to stun and frighten. I haven't stunned and frightened anybody in a long time.

"Both of you, to your rooms. Twenty minutes. Do not come out. Do not speak to each other. Do not speak to me. Do not make a sound. Twenty minutes. I will come get you when time's up."

They march past me, giving each other cutting looks. "Where's Tori?" I ask as they reach their rooms.

Jemma turns around, points to her mouth. Right, she can't talk. Smart-ass.

"Brooke?" I ask politely.

Brooke flashes her older sister a triumphant look. "She's still sleeping."

"Thank you." I gesture toward their doors. "Twenty minutes. Starting now."

Downstairs as the coffee brews, I open the front door to get the paper before I remember it got canceled since we were late on payments.

I feel a momentary letdown, then remind myself the paper was depressing. It was just a daily dose of bombings, carjackings, murders, robberies, terrorist attacks, global warming threats, and growing world debt. And that's just here in America.

I drink a glass of water as I wait for my coffee. I'm going to need some serious Advil today. Passing the powder bathroom, I see that the light is on, and I reach in to click it off and close the door but stop when I catch sight of my reflection.

Good Lord. I'm tragic. And old.

I move toward the mirror, tip my head, check my roots and then my hairline near my ear.

Dark roots and—fantastic—gray hair.

Not a lot of gray, but enough that I know it's time for overall color. I pride myself on my hair. It's gorgeous hair. I want to keep it that way.

But $180 on hair color and finishing isn't really part of my budget anymore.

I check my roots again. They're definitely darker than they've been in a while. If I fluff my hair back and avoid a part line, you can't see the roots too badly, but I never let them go this long. I guess I kept waiting for the cash flow to improve.

The cash flow might never improve.

The dark roots and gray aren't going to wait, either.

I pour my coffee and sit on one of the bar stools. The Salon uses a L'Oréal product. I can buy a L'Oréal product at Bartel's Drugstore. How hard can it be to do my own color?

I've had my light brown hair lightened for years. I could explain the process in my sleep. Mix up the cream, apply it with a stiff brush to the scalp, putting color only on the roots, let it sit, and then rinse it out.

The hardest part will be matching my hair shade, and honestly, all I have to do is put a chunk of my hair against the picture on the box. The box that matches wins.

After the girls are out of time-out, and after they've all been served hot breakfast, we head to Bartel's together. I've explained to the girls what I'm going to do, and I've enlisted their help.

"We've got to find my hair color. Now, there are going to be a lot of boxes and a lot of different shades, but we want the one that's closest to mine."

The girls are excited. We've never done anything like this before. Home manicure and pedicure parties, sure. Play facials, too, where we make our own hair conditioners and facial scrubs using fruits, vegetables, and oatmeal. But hair color? Never. That's always been the Salon's job.

I knew there'd be a lot of hair color boxes. I thought that would be to my advantage, since many boxes means more hair color choices. But suddenly confronted by twelve shades of blond and eight light brown, I'm no longer sure of myself.

Neither is Jemma. "Mom, what's the difference between Natural Medium Ash Blonde and Natural Medium Golden Blonde?"

"Good question." I bend down to look at the two boxes in her hands and then back on the shelves. "Maybe Natural Neutral Dark Blonde is the way to go."

"But what is ash?" Jemma persists.

Brooke turns around with another box. "This one's for gray, Mom. Do you have gray hair yet?"

I put a finger to my lips. Her voice is a little too loud. "Not enough to worry about," I stage-whisper in a cheerful voice just in case anyone from another aisle is eavesdropping.

Brooke puts back the box and finds another. "How about highlights, Mom? You get highlights."

Tori takes a box off the shelf and holds it in both hands, smiling at the picture. "He looks like Daddy."

Brooke snorts in disgust. "He does not!" she says, grabbing the box out of Tori's hands. Her expression changes, and she tips the box back and forth, as if studying the male model from different angles. "Actually he does. A little bit."

Tori gets another box with the same picture and kisses the model on the lips. "Hi, Daddy."

"Okay, that's just weird," Jemma says before turning to me. "So, Mom, what do you think they mean by ash? And why do they call some colors Natural Light Blonde and others just Light Blonde? Why are some of the colors 'Natural' and some aren't?"

I haven't a clue. I'm beginning to have some reservations about doing my hair color this way. "Maybe we shouldn't do this—"

"No. We should. We're going to help you." Jemma looks up at me. "Let's forget all the names. Let's just match your hair to the hair on the box like we agreed."

Why I listen to a ten-year-old is beyond me. But I do.

We head home with Natural Medium Golden Blonde—after Brooke has announced to the senior citizen man working the register that we're all going home to color my gray hair—but as we troop into the house, I'm worried.

I'm not that golden, and Medium Champagne Blonde sounded like a much better fit to me, but Jemma said it's because I like the name "Champagne" more than the color on the box.

The girls crowd around me as I open the box and take out the instructions. There's a lot of instructions but only three steps. Hmmm, something doesn't fit.

Jemma's reading the instructions out loud while Tori is pulling out the bottles and tubes. I'm feeling close to freaking out. This is too chaotic. I don't want to do anything wrong. I like my hair, and it's cost a fortune over the years to maintain.

"Girls, I don't know. I don't think this is such a good idea."

"Mom..." Jemma sighs, looking up from the instructions. "What could possibly go wrong?"

What could go wrong? How about everything? I could have an allergic reaction. My scalp could burn. My hair could fall out. My hair could turn orange.

My hair turns orange.

Okay, not as orange as orange fruit, more like screaming gold. Think hollowed-out pumpkin with a candle inside.

My former highlights are darker, too. Darker orange. On the burnt amber side.

I'm surprisingly okay with it, and I don't know if it's because having Crayola-colored hair is less traumatic than losing your house, but the girls are shattered.

I knew something was wrong the moment I rinsed the color out of my hair and stepped out of the shower and looked into the mirror.

Jemma was waiting on the other side of the shower door with a towel, and she knew it, too, only she didn't want to believe it. This was her pick, after all, and she begged me to blow-dry my hair fast, hoping and praying that once my hair was dry the color would be softer... more apple cider and less tangerine punch.

My hair's dry, and it's still fluorescent.

Jemma's facedown on her bed, crying. She hates my hair almost as much as she hates her sisters, who have ruined her life by being born.

Tori's a little weepy, but not bad. She's more fascinated by my transformation than anything else. Apparently I look like Charmander from Pokémon.

Brooke is quick to point out that being called Char-mander is not a compliment. Charmander isn't just orange but has a weird dinosaur head and spiky teeth.

Looking at myself in the bathroom mirror, I turn my orange head this way and that. I wouldn't even mind the screaming gold if it was more complimentary to my skin tone. But copper and orange is harsh. It makes my skin sallow. Right now I look at least thirty-nine.

I pick up the phone and dial my very expensive, very snooty hair salon. They're going to be livid when they see what I did to my hair.

Why, oh, why do I learn everything the hard way?

Chapter Eighteen

I can't get into the Salon until Monday noon, so I spend Sunday working at the house, getting us prepared for the move, trying not to be overwhelmed by the staggering amount to do in the next few weeks. There's just so much to sort, organize, pack, and toss out.

While the girls play games, I pull down the ladder to the attic and tackle the sea of boxes stored up there. Everything's up there: clothes, small furniture, lamps, pictures, and dozens of boxes of Christmas and holiday decorations. The sad thing is, unless the box is Christmas or holiday decorations, it's just collecting dust.

Tired of dust and tired of stuff, I'm determined to get rid of everything that can't fit into the new house, and since very little can fit into the 1,650-square-foot house, almost everything has to go.

While going through plastic tubs and cardboard boxes, I find a bin filled with old cassettes and record albums from my high school days.

I smile at my collection of music. Keith Green, 2nd Chapter of Acts, Amy Grant, Matthew Ward, Sandy Patti. I was born again in high school, and my dad, despite being a deacon in our church, wasn't thrilled by my evangelical fever. Memorizing scripture and prayer was fine, but joining a "worship group" and singing praise songs for hours was going too far. The charismatic movement made him suspicious. Emotion and passion made him suspicious, but emotion and passion were what I craved.

I needed to feel something good. I longed to feel something hopeful. Brave.

Being deeply religious had its benefits. God took me away from the disaster at home, and believing in Jesus Christ meant I didn't have to believe in me. I didn't have to be perfect because that was the Holy Spirit's job. I just had to show up with an open heart.

I suddenly miss that young me, the one full of fire and grace. I was so sure I'd be a light in the world. So sure that I, Tammy Jones, could make a difference.

Reluctantly, I slide back the box of cassettes and albums and reach for another box, unsure what to do with my Christian music. I don't play the old albums anymore, but I still can't bear to think of tossing them away.

I lift the lid on the next box. A white cotton quilt edged in the most gorgeous blue and white silk ribbon.

Matthew's baby blanket.

I slowly lift the blanket from the box and bring it to my face. I made this blanket.

Matthew was the baby between Jemma and Brooke, the baby boy I lost at seven and a half months.

No one could tell me why I lost him. At the seven-month checkup, he was healthy and moving, kicking up a storm, and then two weeks later he stopped moving.

I knew something was wrong the night he stopped moving. Matthew had always been such a busy boy in my tummy. When I went to sleep, he'd start to play. But that night when I went to sleep, he never did his kicks or somersaults.

I kept putting my hand on my stomach. *Wake up, Matthew. Wake up, Matt, wake up for Mommy.*

I woke Nathan early in the morning to tell him something was wrong, and Nathan put his hand on my belly, and then his cheek and then his lips, as if he could breathe life into the baby.

I had to deliver Matthew the next evening. They induced me, and I went into labor. It was horrible. Jemma was a hard delivery, but this was so much worse. I remember begging for the epidural, but they said they were afraid it would stop the contractions and the baby had to come out. Nathan was with me the entire time. He held my hand. He wouldn't let it go even when I was screaming at God and the doctors for taking my boy.

Thank God Nathan was there. He made sure I got to hold Matthew after he was cleaned up and wrapped in a little blue hospital blanket.

He was small but otherwise perfect, with wisps of gold brown hair on his head.

I'm glad we named him Matthew. Matthew was my favorite apostle.

I tuck the soft quilt back into the box with the crib sheets and bumper. I made everything for Matthew's nursery, just the way I made everything for Jemma's.

I stack Matthew's box on top of the box with my Christian music. These two boxes will go to the rental house.

Although I can't bear to look at either one, I can't bring myself to get rid of them, either.

I'm emotionally and physically flattened by bedtime. I spent nearly five hours hauling boxes downstairs, but the attic is now completely empty. A third of the boxes will go to the new house, another third will go to the garbage, and the last will be dropped off at a Goodwill station.

I shower and, still wrapped in a towel, apply my evening skin repair cream, the one that's supposed to erase fine lines, fade age spots, and even out a blotchy complexion. I hear the phone ring, but I don't answer it. I'm too tired. I just want to get the girls in bed and then collapse in bed, too.

My bedroom door opens and Jemma walks in, carrying one of the cordless phones. "It's Patti, Mom. She has to talk to you."

"Oh, okay." I quickly finish smoothing the lotion over my face and throat and then rubbing the leftover into my hands.

As I take the phone, Jemma whispers to me, "We called Dad and talked to him. He's going to try to come home for Thanksgiving. Isn't that great?"

I hold the phone against my chest. Nathan's coming home for Thanksgiving? "Really?"

She nods and smiles. "He's going to help us move, too."

"That's wonderful." I kiss her forehead and then bring the phone to my ear. "Hi, Patti."

"She wants it." Patti's voice squeaks with excitement. "All of it. Including the art on your walls."

I press the towel to my chin. "She's lost her mind."

"I told her the moving truck arrives Wednesday, so she said she'll bring you a check over tomorrow."

I can get the house. We'll have the rental house. I sag against the counter, overwhelmed.

"But, Taylor, won't it be hard seeing her in your house with all your things?"

"I won't be back. When I walk away, I'm walking from this house for good." But just saying the words brings a lump to my throat. This house has meant a lot to me. It's still so painful to think it'll soon be someone else's.

"Have you started packing yet?" I ask, needing to change the subject.

"No, we have movers doing it. I'm just taking care of personal stuff, putting things in suitcases that I don't want in the truck. How about you? Do you have a company coming in?"

"Not if Monica's willing to buy the house furnished."

It's not until later, when I slide between my covers, replay Patti's call, and think about Monica, that I realize I haven't talked to Kate since book club. I would have thought she'd call. Kate and I have been friends for years. We've gone on girls' trips together and skied together and spent endless hours by the club pool together, too.

Maybe Kate's hurt. Maybe she's uncomfortable. Maybe she just doesn't know what to say. I make a mental note to give Kate a call tomorrow.

After I get my hair color fixed.

Monday morning, I dress carefully, as I'm determined to find an outfit that won't clash with my color, which means orange, red, pink, and coral are all out. Gray, possibly.

Black, too much of a contrast. Brown, no. I settle on a tweedy olive green jacket and cuffed tan slacks. By pinning my hair up in a knot, I hope there's less hair to see.

Monica calls on my cell while I'm driving Tori to preschool. Just seeing her number on my phone makes my hands sweat and my heart race, and I let her call go into voice mail. I know she's calling about the furniture, and it's a call I should take, but I still feel so betrayed.

How could she make an offer on my house without telling me? How could she and Doug do such a thing without being up front?

I check my voice mail as soon as the message appears. Monica's leaving the check under my front door mat now. I've got the money for the rental house, but it comes at a great price.

I walk Tori to her class, kiss her good-bye, and head to work. Everyone's in the office by the time I arrive. I'm flustered to see Marta and her team already working when I walk in. I hate being late, finding it awkward being the last one to arrive.

"Good morning," I say nervously as I close the door behind me.

After hanging up my coat, I slide my purse in my desk drawer just the way Susan did with hers. I sit at my desk. My computer's already on. I check my e-mail first, as that's what Susan said she always did, and there are fifty e-mails waiting for me, at least thirty as forwards from Marta.

For a moment, I feel pure panic.

I can't do this. I don't know how to do this. I don't know anything about advertising, and I've been out of work so long—

"If you have any questions, Taylor, just ask. We know

you're going to need some time to get the hang of things."
Marta's behind me, en route to the little kitchen to refill her
coffee.

I nod. I should be reassured, but I'm not.

This is hard. And scary.

The morning passes with time dragging at points and
then passing in a blur at others. I'm acutely aware of
being new and not knowing basic things. I'm aware that
I don't type as fast as Susan did and that I don't know any
of the names that the team mentions when they're asking for a phone number or a file or a meeting that's being
scheduled.

I can see why I've felt so powerful at home. In the world
I've created at home, I'm the queen. Here I'm the bottom
of the totem pole.

At lunch, I dash into downtown Bellevue for my hair
appointment at the Salon. My stylist is horrified as I am
seated at his station.

*What was I thinking? Didn't I realize my color wasn't single
processing? I have highlights and lowlights and overall color, and
I've ruined it. Ruined it.*

I didn't cry when I messed up my hair at home. I did my
best to keep my sense of humor intact. But right now, my
humor's sadly lacking. I'm just angry. I've got enough to
cope with. I don't need Mr. Marco's attitude.

"What do you expect from me?" he continues, returning with the bowl of color. "You had beautiful hair. Gorgeous hair. And it's ruined."

"You're not helping things, Marco," I answer flatly.

He stirs the color in quick, angry jabs. "I'm not a mira-
cle worker. I don't know why you think you can ruin your

hair and then come in and expect me to make everything okay."

"I am paying you to fix it. You're not doing it for free."

He rolls his eyes. "Everybody thinks they can color their own hair. Everybody thinks they're a professional now."

That's it. I'm done. Suddenly I'm on my feet and ripping the cape off from around my neck. "Forget it. My hair's not that bad after all."

I know I'm emotional. I know I need my hair color. But my God, enough is enough. Can't I make a mistake? Can't I screw up without everyone climbing all over my back?

Marco shouts after me as I walk to the door. He has the color ready. He's got a busy day. I can't waste his time like this.

I don't turn around. I don't stop walking. I just head straight out the door and into the weak November sunshine. I've had it with the lectures. I've had it with the sly, snide comments. I'm doing my best. I'm trying my hardest. That has to count for something.

I'm practically running as I reach the parking garage and nearly trip over Suze, who is heading for the elevator.

"Taylor!" She does a double take and then gives me a tight, perplexed smile as she stares at my hair. "What, uh...what uh, how are you?"

Of course she'd be freaked by my hair. It's hanging like gold and orange streamers down my back. "Just left the Salon," I say, giving my head a jaunty toss. "Change is fun!"

"Yes, well..."

I smile at her, smile as hard as I can, even as I tug on my coat, pulling the lapels up against the biting breeze. "See you soon."

She's still staring at me in shock. "See you soon."

My bravado is all very well and good until I return to Z Design and the first person I meet is Marta on her way back from a lunch appointment.

"Taylor, so what's the story with your hair?"

I should be offended. But at least Marta's open and honest. My shoulders lift and fall. "I tried to color my hair at home. It didn't work. I tried just now to have my usual stylist fix it, but he gave me a lot of attitude, so I walked out."

Marta nods approvingly. "That's right. Don't take shit from anybody. That's my mantra, and it's served me pretty well."

"Yeah. Until you're Ms. Pumpkinhead."

She flashes a wry smile and reaches into her bag and retrieves her cell phone. Skimming through her contacts, she chooses a number. "Monique, it's Marta Zinsser. What's Michelle's schedule like today? Is she just crazy?"

Marta waits while Monique checks Michelle's schedule. "She does sound busy. Is there any way I can talk to her, though? Tell her it's Marta and I'm desperate."

Marta looks at me, covers the phone. "Michelle's brilliant. The only person I let touch my hair. She's the main colorist at Paule Attar. She'll be able to fix your hair without drama, I promise."

Again Marta waits, and then Michelle gets on the line.

"Michelle, sorry to interrupt you, but I've a huge favor to ask. A friend needs an emergency fix job on her hair. She tried coloring her own hair, and her usual stylist had a fit, and my friend doesn't know where to go. I know you'd know what to do. Is there any way you could see her today? Just for a consult?"

Marta's listening again and nodding. "Great. That's fantastic, Michelle. You're the best. Thanks." Marta hangs up and grins. "You've a three o'clock appointment. You're in."

"That's wonderful. But shouldn't I be working?"

"Yeah, you should. But, Taylor, I have to be honest. I won't be able to get anything done, not with you looking like Carrot Top."

Michelle might be a genius with hair color, but she's also intimidating as hell. She's tall and glamorous, with gorgeous dark hair, high cheekbones, and perfectly shaped lips. I slink into her chair, and she fastens a dark cape around my neck.

"So what did you do?" she asks, standing behind my chair and studying my reflection in the mirror.

"Ruined my hair?"

She cracks a small smile. "I guess what I should say is, what do you want to do? I can take out the blond and tone down the orange, but that doesn't solve anything long-term. Four weeks from now you'll have to touch up your roots. What do you want to do with your hair?"

I look at my hair, which hangs past my shoulders in vivid color streaks. "I'd like to be dark blond again without the orange. I had highlights, but they were a lot of maintenance. I used to go to the Salon every four weeks for touch-ups and every six to eight weeks for highlights. But I need easier upkeep. I'm in a different place financially."

"There's no rule that says you have to spend a lot of money to look great," she answers, adjusting my cape. "I have a lot of clients on tight budgets, and a lot of those clients are blondes with great hair."

"Really?"

"Really." Michelle pats me on the shoulders. "It's going to be all right."

"So what will you do?"

"Take out the color you have on your hair right now, change your base color, going darker blond, which will help stretch out your root touch-ups. Then we'll add high-lights, but do them underneath, instead of at the crown to hide grow-out. That way, you'll only need to do highlights twice a year instead of every six to eight weeks."

She does what she said she'd do, but it's not a speedy process. First we strip the color and then put in new color as well as the highlights.

By the time I walk out, I've been in the chair for hours. Fortunately my hair is dark blond again, but the high-lights are more subtle and less "sun kissed," which is fine considering it's mid-November and Thanksgiving is just around the corner.

I call Z Design on my way out and get the answering machine. The office is closed for the day. I'm not surprised, since it's almost five-thirty and completely dark out, but driving home, I keep feeling this funny little tug inside my chest.

Marta isn't so bad, I think, swinging by the house to get Monica's check and head to the bank. Marta might even be nice.

*   *   *

Monday night after dropping a check by the landlord's, I flex my fingers against the steering wheel and grin. Our rent's covered now until June, and we should have enough for my car payment, too. My job will pay for groceries, child care, and incidentals.

I should call Nathan. He'd be proud of me.

I reach for my phone, call him on speed dial. To my delight, he picks up right away. "Nathan, great news," I blurt out breathlessly, "I've just sold all our furniture for twenty-five thousand dollars!"

I'm met by dead silence.

"Did you hear what I said?" I say, a hint of hurt creeping into my voice. "I sold our furniture to Monica and Doug. Twenty-five thousand dollars, Nathan—"

"Taylor, the dining room set alone cost twenty-five thousand dollars."

His voice is chilly and remote. I pull over to the side of the road, lean on the steering wheel. "Are you mad?" I ask incredulously.

He exhales. "You're so impulsive, Taylor. You just don't think."

"That's not fair!"

"It'd cost us a hundred thousand dollars to replace all that furniture. The couch in the living room was more than twelve grand. The two armchairs were five thousand each. How are we going to be able to replace that?"

I press the tip of my tongue to my teeth, press hard, pressing to silence my protest. I can't win with him anymore. Nothing I do is right.

"But we don't have a house it'll fit in," I answer after a

moment when I'm sure I'm calm. "None of the pieces will fit in the rental house, and we can't afford to store it all. Nathan, we have furniture to fill a six-thousand-seven-hundred-square-foot house. The rental house isn't even two thousand square feet. It's itty-bitty. Trust me."

"So why pick that house?"

"Because it's available, it's cheap, and it's near the girls' school."

He's silent so long that I think he's hung up, but then I hear a low, heavy sigh. "You don't even need me anymore," he says quietly.

Something in my chest wrenches. "That's not true."

"It's what it feels like to me."

"You're wrong."

"Yeah. That's what I keep hearing."

Our conversation weighs on me the rest of the night, and I phone him back the next day on my way home from work but then don't know what to say.

Come home, let me support you? Quit your job and live in the ugly rental house with us?

I swallow hard as I drive. Nathan was raised with money, by a stay-at-home mom and a father who made millions in the seventies and early eighties in Silicon Valley. Nathan was expected to make millions and millions, too. Instead we've lost everything, and my handsome quarterback husband is slogging away in Omaha.

There's times I think I have it hard, but looking at the big picture, Nathan has it worse. He's a man. He's supposed to be the provider. He's supposed to be in control. Knowing Nathan, knowing his family, I'm sure he feels like a failure.

*   *   *

Wednesday is a short day at Points Elementary, which means Eva appears in the Z Design doorway at two-thirty in the afternoon.

Robert and Allie are presenting to a client, Mel's on a plane to New York, and Marta's in the house searching for something her mother either wants or needs. Eva in the meantime is in the studio office, spinning in the chair at the corner workstation. It's the extra computer for when Marta has part-time employees, but there aren't any part-time employees right now, just Eva making me crazy.

"I talked to my mom," she says, pausing in her spinning to look at me. "She says you're not her secretary. You're the office manager. Apparently there's a big difference."

I look up from the letter I'm typing. "Thank you, Eva. That's good to know."

She spins once and stops herself by grabbing the edge of the desk. "Did you want to be her secretary?"

Does anyone like to be tortured? "Not particularly, no."

She's hugging her knees to her chest now, her red sweater bright against her blue jeans. "Why are you working here?"

"I needed a job."

"Why?"

It feels as though she has a nail and she's tap-tapping it into my forehead. "Why does your mom work?"

"Because she's smart and she likes it." Eva makes a face. "And because she's a single mom. My dad's a sperm donor."

I'd just reached for my coffee, and I nearly spit the

mouthful all over the computer screen. Wiping coffee dribbles from my chin, I turn to look at her.

She nods matter-of-factly. "Apparently he donated a lot of times, too. He wasn't supposed to, but he went to different clinics and somebody in New York just figured it out. They called my mom and said I probably have ten or twenty brothers and sisters out there." Eva reaches up to rub her cheek. "That's a lot of brothers and sisters."

"Uh-huh." It's a terrible answer, but I don't know what else to say. Eva's not like most little girls around here.

"The thing is," she continues, studying her nails, "I have to be careful I don't marry my brother. It could cause defects." She pauses, frowns. "Besides, it's gross."

The office door opens and Marta appears. She's tugging off her jacket and dropping it on the back of her chair. "You're not supposed to be bugging my staff," she says, crossing to her daughter's side and dropping a kiss on the top of her head.

"I'm not," Eva answers blithely, sliding from her chair to head to the office door. "I'm just telling Mrs. Young about my dad."

She leaves and Marta stands there a moment, hands on her hips, before shaking her head. "That has to be her father's genes. Can't be mine."

"Can't be you," I agree, uncertain if I should be impressed by Eva's nonchalance or horrified. "You're not a rebel."

Marta laughs and drops into her chair, stretching her long legs out in front of her. She's wearing old jeans, a white men's shirt with the tails hanging out, and her hideous combat boots. "God, I'm tired." She tips her head back and rubs her neck before turning to look at me. "I'm not paying you enough for you to work this many hours, Taylor. Susan never worked past three on Wednesdays and twelve on Fridays."

I gesture to the stack of paperwork on my desk. "There's too much to do for me to leave."

Marta lifts an eyebrow. "There will always be too much to do. You'll never get to the bottom of the pile because new stuff will come in. Just do what you can do and when everyone else dashes out, you should, too."

"Well, let me at least finish this letter I was working on. Once it's printed I'll take off."

Ten minutes later, I'm going through the document one last time doing spell check when I feel Marta's gaze. It's incredibly unsettling. I look over my shoulder at her.

"Have you always been such a perfectionist?" she asks quietly.

I frown. "Why do you think I'm a perfectionist?"

"I've been watching you. You've read the letter through at least four times, maybe five. Move on. Be done with it."

"I just don't want a letter going out from Z Design with mistakes in it. It'd look bad—" I break off as Marta laughs. "Why are you laughing? I'd think you'd care about appearances—"

"I do." She's no longer laughing, but she's still smiling a little. "I do, but I also know what it's like to juggle home and work. Go home, Taylor. Your girls had a short day, too, and I'm sure they're dying to see you."

The girls are screaming at the top of their lungs as I open the front door. *"It's all your fault!"*

That's Jemma, I think, closing the door between the garage and mudroom.

"It's yours!"

And that's Brooke. Sagging with fatigue, I hang up my coat on a mudroom wall hook, set my purse on a bench, and head toward the kitchen.

"If you weren't such a spoiled brat, we wouldn't have to move and sell all our things!" Jemma again.

"If you weren't such a jerk, Dad wouldn't be in Omaha!" And that's dear Brooke.

I close my eyes, take a breath, and another, trying to keep from losing my cool. How can this be my family? How can these be my children? How can they be so horrible?

"I'm home," I shout wearily, stepping out of one high-heeled pump and then the other.

The girls don't even hear me. They're still screaming mean things, and now Jemma's shouting at the top of her lungs: *"Well, Mom and Dad never even wanted you. You're a mistake!"*

Suddenly I don't have it in me to yell. I don't have words for anything. I'm just sick of the screaming and sick of the worrying and sick of trying to do it all by myself.

I grab two lids from the pots and pans cabinet and clang them together as hard as I can. It's like cymbals crashing. It's loud. Really loud, and worse, I can't stop banging the tops to the pans.

Suddenly Annika and the three girls are on the stairs, staring down at me. Annika's aghast. She's Finnish, never loud, always civilized. Whatever.

My girls stare at me as though I'm mad. I am. So there.

Dropping the lids onto the counter, I face the girls. "There's no mistake in this family. Each of you was deliberately made, and each of you was very wanted. There were more of you planned, and more of you wanted, but life doesn't always turn out the way we plan or we want. So, get down here, pick up your toys, and help me make dinner."

I glance at Annika. "And Annika, as the Wicked Witch is home, you're now free to go."

Chapter Nineteen

Thursday afternoon, I hand over a check to Mr. Oberon, the owner of the rental house. It's for $5,900, the first two months of rent, the last, and the cleaning deposit. I know he didn't need the extra month's rent, but I do it for my peace of mind, not his. This way, no matter what happens, the girls and I have a home until January 31.

Last Monday night after signing the lease agreement, Mr. Oberon handed me the keys to the house and let me know I could start moving in any time.

Now on Thursday I stand in the middle of the horrid little house that will soon be home and realize I can't move the kids in, not with the house in this condition.

I'll paint the walls. Rip up the stained carpet and have it hauled away. Maybe the floor beneath isn't so bad. Maybe I'll splurge and get us some new remnant carpeting.

Maybe I should have found a different place.

Friday, Marta closes the office at eleven-thirty. I head to Home Depot and buy gallons of white paint. White paint covers a multitude of sins.

At the very least, it'll hide the stains, mildew, and grime.

* * *

I spend all Friday painting, and after arranging playdates with Patti's kids (I called Kate as Brooke wanted to play with Elly but haven't gotten a call back), I spend Saturday painting, too.

By the time I pick up the kids from Patti's, my arms, face, and hair are covered in tiny paint freckles.

Sunday, Lucy has the girls over and I return to the rental house for another painting marathon.

I know we're going to be in the rental house for only six to twelve months, but I can't stand the faded paint, the walls a drab gray and dirty beige that makes leaving our beautiful sunny house even more depressing. I won't be depressed. I refuse to be depressed, so little by little I work my way through the house with a paintbrush, roller, and cans of off-white paint.

The only negative with painting is that it gives me way too much time to think. I find myself thinking about everything. I think about Nathan. I think about his family. I think about my family. I think about those Christian music tapes I found and Matthew's baby box.

I haven't painted a room, much less a house, since before Matthew was born. But then I haven't sewn, either, and I used to sew all the time. I designed and sewed my own clothes, curtains, slipcovers, baby clothes. I made Jemma's entire layette. But I stopped sewing after losing Matthew. I don't know why I didn't sew again other than it hurt whenever I thought about fabric or patterns. It hurt because I could remember Matthew's room and the crib that was already furnished and ready. I remember the padded bumper and the soft quilt that I hung over the rocking chair.

I remember the cheerful sailboat valances, the little throw pillow I'd embroidered his name on.

Matthew Young. Matt Young. It sounded like a quarterback's name. My son was going to grow up and be like his father.

After Matthew, Nathan wanted me to get pregnant right away. He thought it would make the grief better. I couldn't. I couldn't even bear for Nathan to touch me. I hurt too badly.

It was around that time that I began sketching, putting together all my ideas into a dream house. Nathan loved the sketches. He got excited about having a big house on the water, a house we'd fill with more children, little boys and girls, and we'd be this all-American family. We both got so excited by the idea of what we could be that, looking back, I see we lost who we were.

Nathan and I never were about things in the beginning. We were about us. About love. About making our way through life together.

My eyes sting as I paint, and I tell myself it's the fumes, but I know better.

I know I'm incredibly, deeply hurt. And incredibly, deeply confused. I could never love any man the way I love Nathan. He and I just work. We fit.

By the time I'm finished, it's dinnertime and pitch dark outside and I hurt all over. My back, shoulders, and neck ache as I wash out the paintbrushes in the hideous kitchen sink, but at least I've got the living room, dining alcove, laundry area, and kitchen done.

I think I could have picked a better white paint, as this one looks a little chalky, but it's not as if I can't repaint some of the walls later. The hall to the bedrooms would look nice in a crisp green, and the kitchen would be far brighter and cheerier if the walls were more buttery or maybe lemon.

At home, I let the girls order a DirecTV movie and they all climb onto my bed with microwave popcorn to watch. I'm so tired that I fall asleep before the movie ends. And when I wake up, the TV's off and the house is dark except for a light in the upstairs hall.

I go into Tori's room, and her bed is empty. I check Brooke's room, and her bed is empty, too. I hurry into Jemma's, and there they all are, sleeping on the ground with Jemma's blankets and comforters as if they're having a slumber party.

They put themselves to bed.

I stand in the doorway a moment and watch them sleep before heading downstairs to lock the doors.

The doors are all locked. The lights are all off.

They even put their popcorn bowl in the dishwasher and wiped off the counters.

Maybe my girls aren't so horrid.

Monday, Marta lets me leave work at four so I can show the girls the house. I'm nervous about their reaction but want them to see the house and help pick out the paint colors for their rooms.

When I go home to get the girls, Annika asks if she could talk to me. In private.

What cruel thing has one of my daughters said now?

Turns out none of them have said cruel things. Annika's just ready to move on to another family, a family that's more stable and can offer better hours.

I ask if she needs a reference and she says no, she has a job lined up already. She just needs to give me a week's notice, but because it's Thanksgiving this week, Wednesday, just two days from now, will be her last day.

After Annika leaves, I drive the girls to the rental house. Holding my breath, I wait for their opinion.

The girls don't hate the house completely. Tori likes the green "fur" on the roof, says it looks like Turtwig, the green Pokémon with a little leaf on its head.

Brooke gives me a pointed look. "That's a bad thing, Mom."

Yeah, I got it.

Walking through the house, the kids want to know which are going to be their bedrooms. I show them the two at the end of the hall. The rooms are tiny, and the windows are up too high. Great for placement of furniture, but bad if you want light.

Jemma announces she wants her own room (no surprise there), which means Brooke and Tori will share the other. Brooke starts to throw a fit, but I snap my fingers and give them my new, improved don't-or-you'll-die look.

That silences the fighting. Now we just have to decide on bedroom wall color. Jemma wants lavender. Brooke wants lavender. Tori wants pink.

Jemma denounces Brooke for picking her color. Brooke shouts that lavender doesn't belong to Jemma. Jemma didn't make it or buy it, so she can't own it.

Tori wants pretty pink.

Jemma laughs because Brooke—who hates pink—is going to have a pink bedroom.

Tori wants ballerinas.

Brooke wants soccer balls.

Jemma rolls on the ground, laughing, saying that maybe we can find wallpaper where pink ballerinas are playing soccer.

Brooke slugs Jemma. Tori cries because she doesn't want her ballerinas to play soccer. Jemma cries because Brooke hit too hard and she hates everything to do with our family.

I'd like to cry, too, but at this point, it seems a tad redundant.

Time is passing quickly, so quickly that I realize I haven't thought about the auction once, nor have I been sending out my weekly e-mails to the various chairs and committees, checking on progress and giving everyone updates.

Tuesday I use my lunch to send everyone a brief e-mail letting them know that we won't be meeting until after Thanksgiving weekend (how could we meet before? I have to get us moved), but please feel free to e-mail me with any questions, suggestions, or problems.

With that e-mail sent, I'm inspired to tackle more of my to-do list, and I knock off another dozen e-mails, notifying the kids' schools that we're moving and giving the effective transition date and new address. I e-mail magazines, place a change order with electric, phone, water, garbage, and DirecTV. I restart our newspaper subscription, reasoning it'll just feel more homey with a paper arriving every morning in our driveway (in front of our carport). I call U-Haul and reserve a large pickup truck along with a dolly and moving blankets. I inquire about their packing materials and resolve to go by on my way home from work tomorrow (it is a half day, after all) to get everything I'll need for packing up our clothes and our dishes.

I send one last e-mail before wrapping up my business: *Hi, Nathan, Just a quick update re the house and move. I've nearly finished painting the rental house and we're almost ready to move this weekend. The girls are really excited you're coming home tomorrow. It wouldn't have been Thanksgiving without you. It's been a hard couple months, but I know we're over the worst now. From here on out it's going to be better. Love, Taylor.*

E-mail sent and my lunch hour over, I shift gears again, finishing letters that need to be written, resending invoices on statements that haven't been paid, photocopying the color handouts for Marta's presentation in the morning.

Marta's been out much of the day, arguing with one of her big printers. She's not happy with the calendars she designed for one of her clients. The calendar is the client's Christmas gift to their customers, and the dark burgundy wine color isn't the color Marta ordered, and she's not going to take the calendars. She wants them redone. And she wants them done now.

Knowing that Marta is not in a good mood, the other team members have slunk out of the office to avoid potential storms.

When Marta returns at one-thirty with a slam of the door, I know she still hasn't gotten the printer to do what she wants.

"Hi," I say as she slings her purse into her chair.

She grunts a hello.

While the copy machine in the supply room continues copying and collating, I attack filing. A tall filing cabinet is sandwiched between the wall and my desk, and I start finding homes for the huge pile of paperwork that has been accumulating on my desk over the past two weeks.

I'm trying to straighten the files in the second drawer but can't seem to make the folders line up right. Instead of going in horizontal, they are twisting to the side. Sliding my hand to the back of the drawer, I feel something wedged back there. It's a book. With a twist and a yank, I manage to free it.

I blink at the title: *How to Be the Most Popular Girl in Your School*. I had no idea there was such a book, and the bigger surprise is that it's in Susan's filing cabinet.

"Did Susan read stuff like this?" I ask, studying the back cover blurb.

"What?" Marta asks sharply, looking up.

"This." I turn the cover toward her so she can see it. *"How to Be the Most Popular Girl in Your School."*

"Where did you find it?"

"In the filing cabinet, at the back of the second drawer."

Marta shakes her head. "So that's where that is."

My eyebrows arch. "It's yours?"

She glares at me. "It was Eva's. I was her project last year. She was determined to make me popular."

I'm struggling not to laugh. "No offense, but I don't think her plan worked."

"Really?" she answers with a roll of her eyes as she turns back to her computer. But not before I see she's smiling.

Nathan replies to my e-mail that afternoon: *I can't wait to get home. It feels like I've been gone forever. Do you need me to arrange a moving truck?*

Feeling very pleased with myself, I e-mail back: *I've taken care of the truck, but we do need you.*

Two hours later, the phone rings. "Z Design," I answer, picking up the phone without checking caller ID.

"Marta?" a voice quivers at the other end.

"No, this is Taylor. Would you like to speak to Marta?"

The woman doesn't answer. A long silence ensues. I'm not sure what to do next. "How can I help you?" I ask after a moment.

"Marta?"

"No, this is Taylor. I work for Marta. Can I help you?"

The line goes dead. I replace the phone, perplexed. Such a strange call.

"These look good," Marta says, emerging from the supply room where she's been flipping through the handouts that I just finished binding into books. "We're set. Now all I need to do is dazzle them, win the account, and close the deal."

"Piece of cake."

Her eyebrows lift. "How many did you make?"

"Sixteen. A few extra just in case." I glance at the phone, the call still very much on my mind. "Marta, there was just an odd call. Someone asked for you but then wouldn't talk. I'm wondering if we should check caller ID, make a note of the number, just in case."

Marta frowns and picks up the phone from my desk. She hits the last number. Her expression clears. "My mom."

She returns the phone to me, grabs her cell phone, and walks out, heading toward her house. She doesn't return for fifteen minutes, and when she does she sits at her desk but doesn't do anything except stare out the window, troubled emotions flickering over her face.

I've never seen Marta this way. She looks lost.

It's not the way I think of Marta, and even though I'm just an administrative assistant, I feel I should do something, say something, but I don't know what.

Shuffling the papers on my desk, I tell myself to get back to filing, but instead I stand at the filing cabinet, biting my lip, wondering what to say.

"Is your mom okay?" I blurt out.

Marta nods once. She looks even more sad, if anything.

I realize I don't know Marta. I've made snap judgments based on appearances. I suppose I've taken a look at her and labeled her. Long hair, combat boots, motorcycle equals pothead, druggie, outlaw, bad lady.

But seeing her here, knowing what she's already done for me, I'm ashamed.

Marta's not that hard. And she's not that wild. She's actually—surprisingly—not that different from me.

"Marta," I say tentatively, "why did you have Eva on your own?"

A small muscle in her cheek pulls. "I wanted to be a mom." She looks at me, slim shoulders shrugging. "And I didn't want to wait for a man, or try to snare a man. I just wanted to be a mom and get on with my life."

I nod. It makes sense in some ways, but in other ways it doesn't. I can't imagine ever wanting children without Nathan. Nathan made me want to be a mom. I wanted to have his children, raise his children, I wanted something that would always be part of him.

I'm just picking up the next paper to file when Marta's voice stops me.

"My mom has Alzheimer's. That's why Eva and I moved here from New York." She pauses, exhales. "Eva had never spent time with my mom, and I wanted her to before it was too late."

"I'm sorry," I say awkwardly.

She shrugs. "I wasn't close to her for years. Moved to New York to get away from her. But when I found out time was limited…" Her voice fades away, and she sits staring at her computer monitor. "I told myself I moved back for Eva, but it's not true. I moved back for me, too. My mom's a good person. She's just different from me."

I don't know if I want to laugh or cry. "Marta, most people are different from you."

She grins crookedly. "I know." Her grin grows. "I like that."

And looking at Marta, I decide I might just one day really like her.

Nathan calls me later that night to give me his flight details. He'll arrive around seven o'clock tomorrow night on Northwest Airlines and won't return to Omaha until Sunday morning.

He sounds almost like the old Nathan on the phone, and for a moment I believe everything is going to be okay. Nathan and I will be fine. We'll be back together the way a family should be.

Because we're going to do a lot of the move on Thursday morning, I make a reservation for Thanksgiving dinner at McCormick & Schmick's. We've never eaten Thanksgiving dinner in a restaurant, but this year I think it's better to go out, take a break from moving to have a proper meal, even if it is prepared by someone else.

Reservation made, I stay up late Tuesday night packing. Even though I'm leaving most of the furniture behind, and even though I've been sorting and organizing and disposing of things for the past two weeks, I don't seem to be making any headway. It's a huge house, nearly seven thousand square feet, and every room is full of things— trophies, vases, books, picture frames, little figurines. I'm taping boxes as fast as I can, filling them even faster, yet the entire house stretches before me.

The dull panic in the back of my brain becomes a constant roar. How in God's name will we be out of here by the end of the weekend? How will I have the house empty (or empty of "us") before escrow closes?

The next morning I get up an hour earlier than usual and pack until the girls need to get up.

Fortunately, on Wednesday, Z Design empties out by noon, and Marta tells us all good-bye for the weekend. Everyone's rushing off for their holiday weekend. Mel's flying out to Dallas. Allie's meeting her boyfriend's family in Gig Harbor for the first time. Robert and his partner are going to Santa Barbara to be with Robert's partner's family.

Marta, however, is home. She's cooking Thanksgiving for her family. Apparently, Luke wanted her and Eva to go home with him for their first real Thanksgiving together, but Marta was too worried about her parents.

"It's probably Mom's last Thanksgiving at home," she tells me as she walks me out of the office and down the drive. At my car, she says good-bye and continues on to the mailboxes to check for today's mail.

It's just a couple of blocks to my house, and as I drive, leaves swirl and blow. I glance at my watch—Nathan will be home in seven hours—and then at the sky. It's mostly gray, but here and there I see glimpses of blue.

I want the clouds to blow out. I want clear, dry skies for the next few days. I want Nathan to arrive and wrap his arms around me and hug me and never let go.

It seems like forever since he touched me. Forever since he loved me. I can't even remember the last time we did make love.

Did I like it? Was it good? How did it feel to be close to him then?

As I enter the house, I find Annika already set to leave, even though I'm home hours earlier than I expected. "Mr. Young called," she says, handing me a notepad with the phone messages. "And if it's okay, maybe I could go now before the traffic is really bad?"

While I write her a check for the last two weeks of work and add in a $200 bonus as a thank-you gift for her eighteen months of help, the girls crowd around Annika with good-bye hugs. Tori's in tears as Annika slips out the door.

"I don't want her to go," Tori cries, racing for the door. "I don't want Annika to leave."

I catch Tori in my arms and swing her up onto my hip. "A new family needs Annika," I say, kissing her cheek, her nose, her neck. "You're a big girl, and you don't need Annika as much."

"Yes, I do. I need Annika. And I'm not a big girl. I'm still your baby—"

"Yes, you are a baby," Brooke sighs, walking by.

"I'm not!" Tori shrieks, wriggling out of my arms.

"You are, too," Brooke calls back as she walks out of the room and up the stairs, "because you still wet your bed!"

"Girls, enough," I plead wearily as I climb the stairs, picking up scattered coats, sweaters, shoes, and socks as I go.

I'm at the top of the stairs when the phone rings. Dropping the girls' clothes in the hall outside Jemma's room, I head for my bedroom for the phone on the nightstand.

It's Nathan on the line. "Hey," I say, pulling the elastic out of my hair and shaking my ponytail loose. "Shouldn't you be boarding about now?"

"There's no plane to board."

"What do you mean?"

"O'Hare's in lockdown. It's so cold and the ice is so bad they've canceled everything. Planes aren't getting in or out."

"But you're flying into Minneapolis—"

"Our plane is trapped in Chicago."

I sit on the edge of our bed, our big king-size bed that

will fit in our room at the rental house only if we disman-
tle the headboard and footboard and use just the metal
bed frame. I chew relentlessly on my thumb's knuckle.

"I'll call you if things change," he says, sounding even
worse than I feel. "But right now it's unlikely."

Nathan's not coming home. I should have known. I
should have expected this. I should have learned by now
not to get my hopes up anymore.

"Taylor?"

I pull my knuckle away from my mouth. "Yes?" My
voice is husky. I'm close to tears.

"I wanted to be there." He sounds like hell, his voice
strained. "I wanted to get you all moved. I wanted to see
the girls."

I swallow the disappointment. It's so thick that I can
feel it choking me. "Let me know what happens."

"I will. I'm sorry."

"Me too."

Chapter Twenty

It's a hard night. A long night. Nathan phones me every three or four hours with updates, his last being midnight my time to say there would be no way he could get here tomorrow. His best hope would be a Friday night arrival. If then.

He's not the only one stranded, and Chicago isn't the only airport hit. Most of the Northeast is frozen shut, and I can imagine the thousands of families frantic and disappointed that their Thanksgiving plans are ruined.

I don't cry after hanging up at midnight, but my insides are heavy, my heart like a lead weight.

I'm getting good at disappointment. I'm getting good at not having my way.

It doesn't mean it's easy, and I can't imagine it'll ever feel nice, but what is, is, and I'm going to make the best of it. I'm going to count my blessings. Even if it kills me.

I wake early on my own. No alarm clocks needed. After changing from pajamas into sweats, I make coffee and start boxing up the family room, trying not to notice that it's still pitch black out and the house is nearly as dark and cold. After taping two boxes closed, I turn on a few more lights and take a big gulp of coffee.

I'm okay. I'm okay. I can do this.

I can move the girls. I can take care of us. I can manage just fine.

But my eyes burn and I'm so unbearably sad that I use my sleeve to wipe at my eyes. No tears. No crying. No pity parties allowed. I'm a woman, not a child. What's the big deal about moving us myself?

With a hard mental kick, I return to the wall of built-ins that line the family room. Books and photos and knick-knacks everywhere. I have to use the smallest-size U-Haul boxes for the books since they're heavy, but I pack them carefully and stack the filled boxes in a tower along one wall.

At seven-thirty, Brooke races downstairs in her paja-mas covered with little red-haired girls playing soccer. "Is Daddy here?"

I fold down the cardboard top, tape it tightly closed. "No. The storm's too bad. There aren't any planes flying out."

Brooke throws herself on the couch and grabs a pil-low to her chest. "But he said he'd be here. He said he was coming home."

"He can't help the storm. Weather is out of our control."

"He *promised*."

I sit back on my heels and rest the massive roll of seal-ing tape on my thigh. "I'm upset, too."

She kicks the pillow at her feet. "I'm not upset, I'm mad. Dad is supposed to be with us." She kicks the pillow again.

"I hate that he's in Omaha. I hate that we're moving. I hate that you're working. I hate that Annika's going to take care of someone else's kids now. I hate everything. I even hate Thanksgiving."

"Me too." I reach for another box and fold it into shape. "I agree. To everything."

Brooke stops kicking. She lies still for a minute before sitting up. Carefully she wipes a tangled strand of hair from her cheek, tucking it behind her ear. "Did I hurt your feelings?"

I stop taping the bottoms of boxes and look at her, see her, this middle daughter with her long hair and her fierce, competitive spirit. She's my fighter. Dear God, don't ever let me break that fighting spirit.

"No." I smile at her, and my eyes have that itchy, burning feeling again. "I'm glad you tell me what you think. I'd hate it if you thought you couldn't."

"Even if I'm mad at you and Daddy?"

So that's where all these hates come from. She's struggling just as much as Nathan and I are struggling. "Especially if you're mad at me and Daddy. We're your parents. We're a family. If you can't tell Daddy and me how you feel, who can you tell?"

She smiles then, and the shadows lift from her expression, and it's as if the sun has come out. "Love you, Momma."

"I love you, too, Brooke Young."

I've just returned from the garage with an armful of flat boxes and more packing paper when the doorbell rings. My heart leaps and I think, Nathan. But then I glance at my watch and realize it's impossible. It's eight-fifteen in the morning, and at two a.m. his time he was still stuck at the Omaha airport. There's no way he could be here now.

Running my fingers through my hair, I head for the door, unlocking the dead bolts even as I slide a thumb beneath my eyes, trying to catch any mascara smudges. Opening the door, I freeze.

Mom.

Mom and Ray.

I can't speak. I can't move. I just stand in the doorway and stare at her. It's been years since I've seen her. A decade or more. At least.

"Hi, Tammy," she says.

"Taylor," I correct her, thinking she looks even more like Ali MacGraw than ever. When I was growing up, people always did a double take when they saw Mom running errands or at the grocery store. More than once when I was a little girl people approached her, asked for her auto-graph. No one believed her when she said she wasn't the actress.

She nods. "Sorry."

I look at her and then Ray, still unable to find my voice. She sees my bewilderment. She's never shown up at my house before.

"We came to help you move," Mom says, making it sound as though it were the most normal thing in the world. This from my mother, whom I haven't seen in a decade or spoken to in maybe eight years.

I reach for the door, and I don't know what I'm think-ing. I don't know if I'm going to close the door on her or I need support, but suddenly the past is huge and dark between us.

Mom deserted us. Mom left. She found herself a better life, one more suited to her liking, leaving the rest of us to whatever shit life kicked our way.

I pull the door toward me, shutting my house from her view, thinking there's no way in hell I'll let her through. "I don't—"

"Nathan called me. He said he couldn't get back, storms had closed the airport, and he was really worried about you not having help...." Her voice drifts off, and she shoves a small hand in the pocket of her faded jeans.

I just look at her. Her dark hair is streaked with gray, but it's still thick and long, hanging in dark waves past her shoulders. She's remarkably lean for her age, and her plaid button-down shirt looks like a boy's, stretched across her shoulders and breasts.

So this is my mom at fifty-seven. If she weren't my mom, I'd think she looks damn good. But she is my mom, and she's not part of my life for reasons she and I both understand.

"I'm good at packing, Taylor," she adds quietly. "At least let me do the one thing for you I know how to do."

"Yeah," I say, swallowing back the bitterness. I don't want to be bitter, not now, not anymore. The last few months have been too hard. I've felt as though I've lost everyone and everything.

But Mom came.

And that little whisper inside me makes my heart seize up. I swing open the door and step aside. "Come in. The girls will be thrilled to see you."

"Thank you," she says gravely, passing me.

I make eye contact with Ray as he approaches the door. I've met him only twice, and both times we didn't talk. Ray looks like the actor Sam Elliott from the movie *Mask*. Tall, weathered, and lean, with thick gray hair that reaches almost to his shoulders and one hell of a handlebar mustache. I'm sure he has tattoos, too. I just haven't been around him long enough to see them.

Ray nods at me. "Taylor."

"Ray." I can't even fake a smile. Ray is probably my least favorite person in the universe. There's so many things I don't like about him that I don't know where to begin: My mom ran off with him, he's a professional truck driver, he's a gambler, he's a fighter, and he's a convict.

And he married my mom.

While in prison.

I don't know which bothers me more: that my mom ran off with him, that he's a truck driver, or that he's a convict.

But Mom and Ray are inside my house now, and I start to shut the door, but not before I see an enormous big-rig truck parked in my drive.

"You brought an eighteen-wheeler?" I mutter as I close the door.

Ray shoots a glance at me over his shoulder. "Your mom said you had a big house. I figured you'd have a lot of stuff."

I suddenly feel like shit. "Thanks," I say awkwardly.

He just tips his head my way.

* * *

Introducing the girls to my mom and her husband is uncomfortable, but then everything in my life is uncomfortable right now. Fortunately, the girls are less freaked out than I am. They're definitely curious, though, even excited, and they bounce around the family room regaling Mom and Ray with anecdotes about their lives.

I break up the share-fest after about an hour, telling everyone that I've got to get to work. That pretty much ends the party.

Mom tackles the dining room with the tall glass-paned hutch Nathan and I bought in Ireland on our seventh-anniversary trip, visiting an enormous antique warehouse in Rathkeale, a village in the west. The mahogany wardrobe is filled with china and crystal, every shelf weighted with more dishes than we ever needed. The wardrobe is one of the things I'm leaving behind that I will miss. I wish now I'd thought to ask Monica for it.

Ray is in Jemma's room, and he's breaking down the bed. He's already broken down the other two girls' beds and carried the pieces out to his truck.

I'm struggling to disconnect the last of the stereo's elaborate surround sound when Mom passes me, carrying more boxes to be put together, and sees me red-faced and thin-lipped with pliers and a screwdriver.

"Leave it for Ray," she says calmly. "He's good with things like that."

"Okay." Relieved, I drop the tools next to the stereo and watch her return to the dining room.

I rise and tug down my T-shirt. I'm hot and grouchy,

and it's not even noon. There's also still mountains of house, rooms and rooms, and this will take forever. Panic builds in me, and my throat feels too tight.

I'm about to climb the stairs to head for the bedrooms where I started packing the closets earlier, but first I step into the dining room where Mom is working.

Her dark head is bent, the long hair falling on either side of her face, as she carefully wraps stemware after stemware in thick wads of packing paper before adding each piece to the box.

Mom must know I'm there behind her watching, but she doesn't speak, she just focuses on her job.

"I thought you lived in Santa Rosa," I say, my voice tight.

She carefully wedges the paper-wrapped flute in the box. "I do."

I fold my arms across my chest, feeling increasingly jittery. "What time did Nathan call you?"

"Four in the afternoon."

"It's an eleven-hour drive, Mom, and that's without stopping."

"Ray drove all night."

I stare at the back of her head, and I'm flooded with intense emotion, emotion so strong that it nearly buckles my knees. The only thing that goes through my head is *I love you I love you I love you*

And you left me.

You left me. And you left Cissy, too.

I want to ask her how Lawrence, her first lover, or Ray, her second, could have been more important than Cissy and me.

I want to ask her why she couldn't have waited five years, ten years, to leave Dad, as Cissy and I would have been out of the house by then.

I want to ask her if she's been happier with Ray than she was with us.

But I don't. I can't. She made her choice. We didn't have a choice. We had no say, no power, no voice.

No wonder I'm such a control freak now.

Gritting my teeth, I turn and climb up my elegant circular staircase to the second floor, determined to get the kids' rooms emptied today.

I've managed to get only half my closet boxed when the doorbell rings. After opening up another huge wardrobe carton, I tape the bottom, slide the hanging bar into place, and head back into the closet for more clothes. I'm not going downstairs. I'm not answering the door. It's probably one of the girls' friends, and they can do something around here for a change.

I'm just grabbing an armful of hanging slacks, blazers, and dresses when Marta Zinsser appears in my bedroom doorway. I nearly trip over a dropped hanger in surprise. "Hi."

"Hi." She glances around the room, sees the disaster around me. "Having fun?"

"Not my idea of a fun Thanksgiving. What brings you here?"

She smiles, a wry, lopsided smile. "I was hoping I could have some fun, too. Pack. Lift. Work. Carry."

I look at Marta, this disgustingly confident woman I never wanted to like because she was everything I thought I wasn't and couldn't ever be. I wasn't independent, wasn't brave, wasn't strong, and yet I'm finding my feet and my bones and I've got more muscle—and gut—than I expected. Her gaze meets mine and holds. She's not the enemy. I'm not my own enemy, either, anymore. "You're so twisted, Marta, you're scary."

Her expression doesn't change outwardly, but there's something in her eyes, something almost like affection, and I feel a rush of warmth. Love. *Hope.*

It's going to be okay.

We never make it to McCormick & Schmick's for dinner. Marta has invited us—all of us—to her house for Thanksgiving dinner, and when she asks us, I hardly even protest. I think I just asked if she was sure.

She was sure. I accepted gratefully, and Marta went home to finish preparing Thanksgiving dinner.

In the meantime, I cancel the reservations I made and tell the girls to clean up and change into something more appropriate for a holiday meal, then tell them never mind when I see them trying to rip open all of my carefully sealed boxes.

Nathan calls just before we walk out the door for Marta's. I'm so glad he's calling and so hoping he's finally on his way home. "Tell me you have good news for me, honey," I say, shooing the kids back into the house and motioning for them to close the door.

"Nothing today," he answers. "I don't know about tomorrow. Did your mom make it?"

My heart falls, and I glance at the front door where everyone's gathered. Jemma's showing Mom something on her hand, and Mom's looking and listening. It's so strange to see my mom with my girls. They've never met one another, just exchanged photos, Grandma always being a big mystery.

"Yes. She and Ray arrived this morning. They've been really helpful."

"Good." He draws a breath. "I wish I were there, Taylor. I really do. If I could drive there, I would."

"I know."

"You're mad."

"It's just hard without you, Nathan."

"I'm sorry."

"It's okay." I tuck a strand of hair behind my ear. "Happy Thanksgiving."

"Happy Thanksgiving, honey."

We say good-bye, and I hand the phone to the girls.

We get to Marta's a half hour later than I expected, but the girls end up crying after talking to Nathan and I need some time to calm them all down and help them cheer up.

At Marta's, we find that Eva has made us all turkey napkin rings out of colored paper and written our names on little pumpkins in gold and silver felt markers. Candles the color of brown sugar line the table, and a big autumn arrangement fills the center.

Marta's parents sit at the table with us, and as I look around the table, I see two generations of moms and daughters.

I haven't had a mother in so long that I'm not sure what to feel as I look around the table.

Marta gives a small, brief prayer. I don't know why I'm shocked that she'd say a Thanksgiving prayer. You'd think she was a she-devil instead of my boss and, just maybe, my friend.

The food is good, though. Marta has cooked a turkey with a cornbread-and-pecan stuffing that comes from her dad's family since he was a good ol' southern boy. Her dad absolutely dotes on his wife, waiting on her hand and foot, even when she gets up and wanders off and doesn't want to return to the table and seems to think the living room is a good place to take off her clothes.

Tori tries not to laugh as Marta and her dad wrestle Mrs. Zinsser back into her dress. Jemma gives Tori a dirty look before turning to me, her expression devastated. My girls are so sheltered. We don't see Nathan's mom often because she doesn't like me. We don't see my parents because I don't like them. Yet here's Marta and her dad trying to keep Marta's mom home as long as possible when everyone else thinks it's time to institutionalize her.

It hits me how hard this thing called life is and how ridiculous it is to make it any harder than it has to be.

Abruptly I rise and begin clearing plates, as everyone is done and I can't sit at the table and ignore Mrs. Zinsser's tears in the living room.

Poor Mrs. Zinsser.

Jemma and Eva enter the kitchen with more plates. "Thank you," I say, surprised to see Jemma clearing the table without my asking. She doesn't do it at home without a fight.

She obviously wants to impress someone. Eva? Marta? My mom and ... convict?

Soon all the girls are up and clearing plates and glasses. Without waiting for direction, I just begin hand washing. My good china can't go into the dishwasher and I don't know about Marta's, but washing them the old-fashioned way works just as well.

Marta enters the kitchen just as I finish the last of the pots and pans.

"Sorry," she says, glancing around and seeing that the mounds of dishes are now all done. "That wasn't part of the plan."

I laugh a little, rinse off my hands, and accept the dish towel Marta's holding out to me. "What's the old saying? The best-laid plans...?"

Marta slides some of the dried pots and pans into the cupboard next to her stove. "Your mom is pretty cool."

I lean against the counter, my elbows on the edge. "Of course you'd like her. Her husband was a founding member of the Hell's Angels."

Marta laughs and smashes down the garbage. "He was not."

"He did ride with them."

She shrugs. "He does have some great stories."

I exhale hard, blowing wisps of hair from my eyes. "Which are fascinating if the stories aren't told by your mother's convict lover."

Marta's choking on her laughter. "She introduced him as her husband."

"Oh, he is. They got married while he was still in prison. Would love to see those wedding pic—" I break off as I realize my mom is standing in the doorway with the water pitcher in her hands.

She just looks at me and extends her arms, holding out the pitcher.

Wordlessly, I cross the floor and take the pitcher from her. Mom returns to the formal dining room without uttering a word.

Marta looks at me as I carry the pitcher to the sink. Numbly I dump out the water before setting the empty pitcher on the counter.

"Taylor—"

"I was wrong," I cut her off. "I was just trying to be funny, but it wasn't funny." Swiftly I head to the dining room, where everyone's still sitting, waiting for pie. I gaze at Mom, hoping she'll look at me, but she doesn't, and when I return to the table a minute later carrying a pie, I can see my mom's hand under the table. She's holding Ray's hand. Tightly.

We walked to Marta's house for dinner, and we walk home a few hours later, all of us bundled back in our coats. Mom and Ray walk side by side, with Tori holding Mom's hand.

I walk behind Mom and Ray and Tori. Seeing Mom holding Tori's hand reminds me of Mom with my sister, Cissy. Cissy loved to hold Mom's hand.

As we approach the house, Mom turns to tell me she and Ray will probably call it a night. They didn't get much sleep last night, and if they're going to be of any help in the morning, they better get some rest now.

"You can have my room," I offer, as my bed isn't yet dismantled.

"We sleep in the cab," Ray answers, gesturing to his truck.

"I don't mind," I protest.

Mom stops before the front steps, leans down, and kisses the top of Tori's head before letting her hand go. "This is how Ray and I always travel." She looks straight at me as if anticipating an argument.

I don't argue. "You know where the guest bath is. There should still be a couple clean towels out...unless I accidentally boxed everything up."

"We have our own towels." Mom smiles at the girls, then a smaller, more guarded smile at me. "Good night."

The next day early in the afternoon, I drive to the rental house and Ray follows in his truck, the back filled with bedroom furniture. He's going to set up the girls' furniture in their rooms while Mom and I keep packing at the Yarrow Point house.

I take Ray on a quick tour of the house. "Jemma's stuff will go in this room, and Brooke and Tori are going to share this room."

Ray looks around the tiny bedrooms. "How is all of Tori and Brooke's furniture going to fit in here?"

"It's not." I rub the back of my neck, my muscles aching. I'm aching, so tired that all I can think about is lying down somewhere and taking a nap. "I'm getting rid of Tori's set, it's toddler furniture anyway, and Tori will sleep in Brooke's trundle bed."

"Do they know that?" he asks. Having spent the last twenty-four hours with the girls, he's gotten to know their personalities.

"Yeah, but I don't think the reality of it has hit them yet. It will tonight when we spend the first night in our new house."

"You've got your hands full, don't you?" He's a big guy, a tough guy, and yet his voice is so sympathetic that I don't know where to look or what to do.

"We're getting by," I say at last.

He nods. "Okay, then. I know what to do here. I'll be back soon as I'm done."

I'm just heading out the front door when Ray's voice stops me. "Your mom's a good woman, Taylor. She did try to make it work with your father."

I slowly turn to face him, take in his black thermal shirt, his shaggy gray hair, his weathered complexion. He has a good face, a kind face, and he strikes me as pretty decent, but he and I aren't going to see eye to eye on Mom. "No offense to you, Ray, but she had kids. You don't leave your kids just because you don't love their father."

"She didn't leave you. She left him."

I give him another long look. "When you're a kid, it's the same thing."

"But you're not a kid anymore."

I open my mouth to say something smart, something that will put him in his place, but no words come. Maybe because there's nothing I can say.

He's right. Ray, the trucker convict, is right.

At least in this case.

I don't mention my conversation with Ray to Mom when I return to the house to continue packing. And although Mom and I tackle the kitchen together, we don't say much to each other. It's hard to erase a lifetime of hurts in one day, but I appreciate her help and I'm glad she's here. I'm also grateful to Nathan for thinking to call her when he realized I'd be alone trying to get us moved.

Nathan's trying, I think.

We're all trying.

In the kitchen, we empty the refrigerator and freezer into boxes, and while I drive the cold things to the rental house to transfer into the fridge and freezer there, Mom starts in on the cupboards and pantry.

Dinner isn't fancy. As I transfer all the perishables and unload the kitchen foodstuffs, Ray and Mom hit Kentucky Fried Chicken for a big fast family dinner.

We sit on the floor of the rental house, Mom and Ray, the girls and me, eating our bucket of Original Recipe KFC, sides of biscuits, coleslaw, and mashed potatoes, and I realize I'm lucky. Lots of people have no one. I've got my kids. And whether I want to admit it or not, Ray and my mom.

Chapter Twenty-One

Saturday late afternoon, I'm unpacking towels and sheets into the rental house's tiny hall closet when my cell phone rings. I can hear it ringing in the kitchen but can't find it beneath the mounds of paper from the glassware Mom's been unwrapping.

Mom's the one who uncovers it. She digs through the paper, finds the phone, and hands it to me.

It's Lucy on the other end of the line. "Taylor, where are you?" she asks, her voice barely audible over the sound of voices and music.

I push a wave of hair off my face. "I'm home unpacking. Why? Where are you?"

"Patti and Don's good-bye party."

My stomach falls. "What party?"

"Their good-bye party. The invite was sent weeks ago. I'm sure you got one—"

"I didn't!"

"Well, come anyway. Come now."

I tip my head to hold the phone between my cheek and shoulder as I grab an armful of paper to carry out to recycling. "I can't leave everybody here," I protest.

"But you can't miss saying good-bye, either," she answers.

Ray sees me coming with my arms full of paper, and he opens the front door for me. I scoot past him and dump the paper outside in the carport's recycling bin.

"Just come," Lucy insists. "I know how close you are with Patti."

"Where is the party?"

"The Belosis'. It was a surprise party for Patti and Don. But you should come over and say good-bye. Patti and the kids leave early in the morning."

I glance at my watch. Five forty-five. "What time does the party end?"

"Six. It started at two. It was an open house. But come now. I'm still here, and so is Patti. I'll wait for you."

After disconnecting, I go into the house and head straight to the kitchen. Mom's still unwrapping dishes and putting them on my freshly painted cupboard shelves. "Mom, can I—" I break off, thinking how weird that sounded. *Mother, may I?*

She looks at me, startled, too, and then we both laugh. "I haven't said that in a long time, have I?" I say.

She smiles wryly. *"No."*

"One of my best friends is moving tomorrow. Today was the going-away party and it's almost over. I don't know why I didn't know about it, but would you be all right here with the girls if I dashed over to the party for a bit? I won't be long. A half hour or so at the most."

"Go. We're fine with the girls."

I rummage in the wardrobe boxes that fill my new bedroom, pulling out a long-sleeved peasant-style blouse in a gorgeous blue gray satin. I pair the blouse with dark skinny jeans, a black belt, black boots, and good hoop earrings. With some lipstick and mascara, I look almost presentable, and I do it all—clothes, hair, and makeup—in less than ten minutes.

The Belosis' house is in Clyde Hill, facing Seattle with unobstructed views of the Olympic Mountains, the Seattle skyline, and Lake Washington. Their property is so big that it qualifies as an estate. It's a Mediterranean-style home with a high wrought-iron fence.

There are only a few cars in the circular driveway when I pull up, so I park on the right-hand side between a silver Mercedes SUV and a white Hummer.

I hurry into the house and discover Lucy hovering in the marble foyer, waiting for me. "They've just left," she says, hugging me.

I've been trying so hard lately and fighting the good fight, but all of a sudden there's no more fight left in me. "How could they leave? Didn't they know I was coming?"

"Kate and Bill were taking them out to dinner. They had a six-fifteen reservation at Canlis and couldn't wait." Lucy sees my expression, and she gives me another hug. "It wasn't you, Taylor, it wasn't. They had plans they couldn't change."

I take a frustrated step back. "But why didn't I know about the party? Why wasn't I told?"

Lucy shakes her head. "It was an oversight, I'm sure."

"Is everything going to be an oversight now?"

"I don't know," she says. "But let's go. We'll get coffee now, and you know you'll see Patti before she goes. There's no way she'd leave without seeing you."

"But what must she think? I didn't even show up at her party!"

"She knows you're moving. She knows you're under tremendous pressure. So stop beating yourself up. Okay?"

We agree to meet at the Tully's on Main Street. It's farther away than the Tully's on Points Drive or the various Starbucks downtown, but it's small and private, and parking is easy since you don't have to deal with the congestion on 8th and Bellevue Way.

As I park it starts to rain, and by the time I'm inside, it's coming down hard. I stand next to the front doors, trying not to feel overdressed, when I spot Monica at a table in the corner with a man who isn't Doug.

I watch as Monica and the man lean in close as they talk. Their heads are very near, and their hands are also on the table, ostensibly holding coffee cups, and yet their fingers are almost touching.

It isn't until the man shifts that I recognize him. It's that new dad, the one who moved with his surgeon wife from the East Coast.

Maybe they're having a committee meeting. Monica did say she'd gotten him to agree to co-chair Fun Day with her. But their body language doesn't say school business. Their body language says personal. Intimate. But not sex. At least not yet.

The front door opens and Lucy dashes inside, chin tucked down against the rain. She's wearing just a black blouse and black slacks without a coat, and she's shivering as she pushes her damp blond hair back from her face. "Sorry I'm late. I shouldn't have taken Bellevue Way. I don't know why I did that. Traffic is horrible around the mall, especially this weekend with everyone out shopping."

"How was your Thanksgiving?" I ask after we've finished ordering.

"As good as one can be. I had the kids this year. Next year I won't."

"Next year you come to my house for Thanksgiving, then," I answer, reaching over to give her a hug. I'm surprised at how thin she is. You can feel the vertebrae in her back.

"Are you eating?" I ask her.

She shrugs. "I'm just not hungry."

"Just make sure you take care of yourself."

Coffees in hand, we go in search of a seat. Lucy freezes just in front of me. "Monica's here," she whispers.

"I saw."

"Who is she with?"

I glance at Monica and the dad. Their hands are so close, they're practically touching now.

"He's a Points Elementary dad. I think he's co-chairing Fun Day with her."

Lucy watches them a moment, than shakes her head. "She should be careful."

We find two big armchairs on the opposite side of the café.

"That's how it starts," she adds, sitting in the leather chair and curling her legs up beneath her. "You talk, and he listens. The guy...the one I ruined my life over...he hooked me by listening."

She makes a soft sound of disgust. "I didn't realize how badly I wanted someone to talk to me, to listen. Pete stopped listening years ago, and I guess I got lonely. I didn't even know how lonely I was until this other man paid me attention. He really looked at me when I talked, he really listened to what I said, and it made me feel so good. More beautiful than all the nips and tucks in the world. That's what love does. It makes you feel beautiful from the inside out."

Now Lucy darts a glance in Monica's direction. "Do you think she's having an affair?"

"I don't know, nor do I want to know." I deliberately turn my body so that I can't see Monica or her table. "Between book club and my house, she's not on my popular list right now."

"That's what I wanted to talk to you about. I was at the gym yesterday when I had an idea. Let's start our own book club—"

"Noooooo."

"I heard about it on the Internet. This lady in Texas started it, and all we have to do is read the book, wear a tiara, and dress in pink and leopard skin."

My jaw must have smacked the ground four times while Lucy was talking. "Lucy Wellsley, you've lost your mind."

"There'd be no diet foods," she continues cheerfully, "just good food, and no negativity."

"Perhaps," I say grudgingly, as I'm not ready for another book group, but I like seeing Lucy happy like this. "Do you still love Pete?" I ask abruptly. I don't know why I ask the question or where it comes from, but I suddenly need to know.

She clasps her coffee and thinks a long moment. "We made three kids together, so part of me thinks I should love him, but I don't like him. He's been so ugly. It's not just that he's going after custody, but the things he says...I'm not a fit mother, that I'm a bad person, a bad woman...it's so unnecessary. It's as if he can't help hitting below the belt, over and over. I can handle a lot, but the constant attacks wear me out."

A shadow passes and then stops. Lucy breaks off, and we look up to see Monica standing directly in front of us with the PTA dad almost right against her side.

"Oh!" Monica exclaims, flushing. She takes a swift, self-conscious step away from the PTA dad. "I didn't know you two were here."

"We saw you when we came in but didn't want to bother you," Lucy answers.

"We were just having a meeting." Monica takes yet another step back. "Taylor, Lucy, do you remember Leon Baker? He and his wife moved here from Philadelphia over the summer. Leon's organizing the Fun Day with me this year."

"Yes, I do remember you, Leon. It's a pleasure to meet you." Lucy extends her hand. "I'm Lucy Wellsley, my younger two children attend Points Elementary. My older son is a seventh grader at Chinook."

"Nice to meet you." Leon shakes hands with Lucy, then turns to me. "And I remember you from Back-to-School Night. You gave one of the welcome speeches."

"I did, yes."

"You're the auction chair, right?"

"I am, and at this point I'm not sure if it's a good thing or bad thing. My auction co-chair is moving."

Monica claps her hand to her head. "Patti's party. I forgot. We were so busy talking about our ideas for Fun Day that I totally forgot to stop by the Belosis'."

"I better run," Leon announces. "I've got to get home to the wife and kids. We're seeing Santa tonight. He's apparently arrived here at the mall." He lifts a hand in farewell. "It was nice to meet you. Monica, I'll be in touch." Then he's gone.

Monica watches him leave for a moment before turning back to us. "So..." She struggles to smile, but she looks almost bereft. "How are things?"

"Fine," Lucy and I answer simultaneously. Monica nods, and it's awkward at best.

"Well, happy Thanksgiving," she says.

"Happy Thanksgiving," I answer, with Lucy chiming more or less the same. Monica leaves, and Lucy and I get up to go, too. As I dash through the rain to my car, I reach into my purse for my keys and my phone. Must call Patti. Must make sure she'll stop by or meet me for coffee in the morning before she leaves.

Patti swings by the Yarrow Point house Sunday morning en route to the airport, with her kids and a tray of lattes and bag of warm, freshly baked bagels. "I got your message," she says after I've introduced her to Mom and Ray and her kids disappear with mine to the now empty bonus room. "I'm so sorry I wasn't at the Belosis' when you arrived. But you know I'd never leave without seeing you first."

I've been pretty damn stoic about her move until now, but suddenly I can't do it. I can't let her go. Tears fill my eyes, and I just look at her, shake my head. "Don't go."

"Taylor!" Tears fill Patti's eyes, and she's suddenly hugging me. "I can't believe I have to leave you like this. Your life has gone to shit."

I'm crying and laughing against her. "It sucks. It's a nightmare."

"You'll get through it."

"I know." I step back, wipe my eyes on the back of my wrist. "Maybe that's the part that makes me the craziest. I know I'll survive. I've been through too much."

"What's the saying? That which doesn't kill us makes us stronger?"

We laugh some more and sit with our coffee on the staircase and talk about everything and nothing for a half hour until she has to go.

When we say good-bye this time, there are no tears. She's my friend. I love her. I'll miss her. But as women, we do what we have to do.

Mom and Ray leave Sunday afternoon. They have a 770-mile drive back to Santa Rosa. I had hoped they'd leave earlier, but Mom refused to go until all the boxes were out of the house and everything at the new house looked like home.

The kids hug Mom and Ray good-bye, and then I walk them out to their truck. "Thank you," I say again. "There's no way I could have done this without you."

"Happy to help," Ray answers, climbing into the truck.

Mom stands facing me. I look at her for what seems like forever. I haven't seen her in a decade. How long will it be until I see her again?

"Sorry it was such a lousy Thanksgiving, Mom."

She half smiles, her eyes a lighter shade than mine. "It was a good Thanksgiving, Taylor."

"You had to work hard."

"I got to see you and the girls."

"Thank you."

"Anytime, Taylor. Just pick up the phone."

I look at her a long time, trying to remember her, trying to remember this. This is a good feeling. No anger, no resentment, no bitterness. "Drive safely," I whisper.

Her eyes search mine. "We will." Then she swings herself up and into the passenger side of the truck.

The girls come running out of the house as Ray starts the truck, and the four of us stand on our little lawn and wave them off while Tori blows kisses.

"I like Grandma," Tori says wistfully as the truck disappears down the street.

"I like Ray," Jemma adds.

Brooke grins. "I like Ray's tattoos."

It's a battle getting the girls ready for bed tonight. As I make them take baths in the little bathroom with the hideous tub and sink (I couldn't paint those), they realize for the first time that we aren't going back to our house.

The rental house is home now. There's no going back to the big, beautiful house on the lake. This dark, little house with low ceilings and narrow aluminum windows is where we live.

Wrapped in bathrobes, the girls huddle on my bed, crying as I comb out their long, wet hair.

"It's only for six months or a year," I say, trying to cheer them.

"But that was our house, Mom. That was where we lived," Jemma protests.

"I know," I murmur, carefully working at a knot in Brooke's hair.

"Will we ever go back there again?" Brooke asks, wincing as the comb pulls on the knot.

I take the comb out of her hair and try to pull apart the knot with my fingers. "I don't know." Finally the knot's out and all the girls' hair is tangle-free. "Let's try not to think about that house, not if it makes us sad."

Brooke turns to look at me. "Does it make you sad?"

I look at their free, young faces. God, they're still so young. "Yes, if I were to think about it too much. So I try to think about other things instead."

"Like what?" Tori asks, scooting closer to me so she can claim my lap.

"This house," I say.

"Ick," Jemma answers, curling her lip.

"And Christmas in this house," I continue. "And how the mantel on the fireplace is big so we won't have any trouble hanging your stockings."

Jemma's still not happy. "But what about when Christmas is over?"

I shrug. "I'll think of something else then. Something nice to think about, something that makes me feel good."

"Like what?" she insists.

Struggling to think of something on demand, I look around the room, at the odd putty color I painted the walls in here. The color wasn't supposed to be putty, it was supposed to be a toasty taupe, but for some reason it didn't turn out that way. "Well, look at these walls. They remind me of graham crackers—"

"Gingerbread!" Brooke cries.

"Gingerbread, yes, that's even better," I agree. "We're now living in a little gingerbread house. And if we tell ourselves it's fun, and if we make it interesting, then living here will be fun and not sad."

"But it is sad," Jemma says with a shake of her head. "It is, Mom. We don't have any of our furniture anymore. We can't have most of our toys. We only have two TVs—"

"We didn't need all the TVs," I interrupt.

"Still. I don't like it. I don't like not having our own house. I don't like knowing we have to move again at the end of the school year. I don't like knowing we can't have people over—"

"Now that's just silly. Of course we can have people over. Our friends don't care if we have a big house or not." I pause and see the way Jemma's looking at me, so I hurry on. "And our friends will like coming here for dinner. In summertime we can still barbecue."

"But how can we barbecue without Dad?" Tori asks.

The girls all look at me and wait for my answer. I wait, struggling to come up with a good answer.

"Dad will be back," I say at last. "He'll be here by summer."

Tori looks happy. Brooke looks hopeful.

Jemma's just suspicious. "How do you know?"

I think about it, and I listen to that little voice inside me, the one I haven't listened to enough these past few years.

"I just know." I look at them and smile, and it's a real smile. "Daddy loves us too much to not come back."

*   *   *

An hour later, I finally have the girls tucked in their beds in their new bedrooms. They're asleep, and I close all the blinds, lock the front and back doors, and turn off the lights except for the light in the hall that connects our bedrooms.

In the tiny bathroom that adjoins the "master" bedroom (an inane description of our minuscule bedroom if I ever heard one), I wash my face and brush my teeth and put on my antiaging lotion, but a thinner layer than I used to since the bottle's almost empty.

This has been my bedtime routine for years. It's as much a part of me as chatting with Nathan as he settles into bed to read.

I smile crookedly as I think about Nathan trying to read and me standing in the doorway trying to talk to him at the same time.

He would always put down his book, too. He'd always set aside what he wanted to do to listen.

My smile fades.

I miss him. I miss him so much.

After turning off the bathroom light, I climb into bed, turn off the table lamp, and lie in the dark in my new room and listen to the sounds of an unfamiliar street. A car horn blares outside, and a truck rumbles past. Lights shine through the cheap miniblinds at the windows.

I don't know this room. I don't know this house.

I feel like the girls right now. I miss our old house. I want our house. I want that life back.

The losses hit me so hard, I have to fight back to keep from falling apart. It's going to be okay. Tomorrow it'll be okay. Tomorrow it'll be fine. The girls will go to school. Annika will pick them up—

And then I go cold all over. I knew I was forgetting something.

I don't have Annika anymore. Annika's gone. I have no child care.

Chapter Twenty-Two

I wake up to find an e-mail from Nathan. He wants to know how the move went and how our first night in the new house went. He hopes the girls' furniture fits okay in their new rooms, and he wants me to have a locksmith come in and check all the locks and install dead bolts on the front and back doors.

I read his e-mail twice through before answering. *The house is fine. Ray checked out the locks when he was here and the windows, too. Maybe you can come see the house this weekend since you missed last weekend?*

I spend my lunch researching prospective sitters and screening them before selecting three to interview, and then Marta lets me leave early Monday afternoon to pick up Tori from preschool. I bring Tori back to the office for a half hour, where she colors at my feet before we race back to school to pick up Brooke and Jemma.

I've scheduled interviews with the three sitters that evening, and I hustle the girls to their rooms after a hasty dinner of buttered noodles and carrot sticks. It's a pathetic meal, but they're kids, they're full, and for now they're happy.

The first sitter is a college student, and she seems sweet but arrives late, complaining of bridge traffic. "It's such a long drive in traffic," she adds. "Is there always traffic?"

I mentally cross her off the list.

The second sitter is a professional nanny looking for a full-time position. She also charges a minimum of $20 an hour and needs at least thirty-five hours a week.

Basically she wants more an hour than I earn.

I cross her off the list.

The third woman is a tall, large-boned, gray-haired Russian woman somewhere between forty-five and sixty. She's sat for a lot of the families in the area. She doesn't mind doing laundry, grocery shopping, or making dinner. She's happy with an afternoon-only job, as she still takes care of a baby for another family in the mornings. She charges $14 an hour, but she has her own car and insurance.

She also has a mustache and a unibrow, but she's available tomorrow afternoon to pick up Tori.

"What if we give it a try for two weeks and see what you think?" I say, realizing that maybe I need the two weeks to think.

She's sitting on the slipcovered couch that I brought over from the bonus room of the Yarrow Point house, and she folds her hands in her lap. "You pay me every Friday."

God, I'm desperate. "Yes."

"Cash. No checks."

I'm so desperate. "Yes."

"Your girls. Can I meet them now?"

Oh, Lord. The girls aren't going to be happy about this. "Yes."

I go to Jemma's bedroom, where Jemma's lying on her

bed and the two younger ones are on the trundle, watching a DVD movie. "Hey, girls," I say, switching on the light. "Do you want to come meet Mrs. S?"

Jemma's nose wrinkles as she sits up. "Mrs. S?"

"She seems very nice, and she's taken care of a lot of children in Bellevue."

"Did you hire her?" she persists.

I swallow my sigh. "Just come meet her. Please?"

The girls trail after me into the living room, walking single file with Jemma in front and Tori bringing up the rear. It's not a long way, but I feel dread weighing on me with every step. Mrs. S isn't what the girls are used to. They're used to young and fun, blond and bubbly. Mrs. S is none of the above.

Hopefully the girls won't notice.

Mrs. S remains planted on the couch as the girls walk in, her brow furrowing as she studies each of them in turn. "Hello," she greets them soberly. "I am Mrs. S. I am your new child minder."

"Child minder?" Brooke asks, glancing at me.

"Baby-sitter," I whisper, but Mrs. S overhears me.

"But I am not a baby-sitter. There are no babies here," Mrs. S answers, rising and extending her hand to Jemma. "And your name is...?"

"Jemma Taylor."

"It is good to meet you, Jemma. You may call me Mrs. S."

"S?" she asks.

"Slutsky."

"*Slut*sky?" Jemma chokes on muffled laughter.

I give Jemma a don't-you-dare look and press Brooke forward for her introduction.

By the time Mrs. S leaves, the girls are thoroughly unhappy with me.

"Why her?" Jemma demands the moment the door closes.

"She's available the hours we need, she's experienced, and she's...cheap."

Jemma glares at me from across the living room. "You know she's going to make us eat beets and borscht, don't you?"

"No, she won't."

"Yes, she will. Devanne had a Russian housekeeper, and when her baby-sitter wasn't there, the housekeeper made Devanne eat all kinds of weird things like cabbage and sausage and borscht."

I check my smile. "You don't even know what borscht is."

"I do, too. It's potato and cabbage soup with beets and beet juice and sour cream."

Tori's near tears. "I don't want to ear borse. I don't like borse—"

"It's borscht, Tori," Jemma flashes before turning on me. "Mom, you can't hire her. You can't. You've already ruined our lives enough."

"I haven't ruined your lives—"

"You sold the house. You made us give up our things. Kids are already talking about us. They're saying we're poor and our dad left and isn't coming back—"

"That's not true," I protest.

"Now we have a hairy old Russian nanny?" Jemma, who never cries, has tears in her eyes now, and she balls her hands into helpless fists. "People will laugh at us even more, Mom. They'll make fun of her name and her hairy lip and her funny dress."

"But people won't see her. She's just going to watch you for a couple hours after school until I come home from work."

"People will see her. My friends will see her. Brooke's friends will see her. She'll pick us up from playdates, or if our friends come here, they'll see her here. They'll smell the borscht and they'll say our house smells funny." Jemma takes a huge breath. "Mom, please. Think about us."

I look at her and then Brooke and finally Tori. They're children. They don't understand. There are worse things than having your dad take a job out of state. There are worse things than moving into a smaller house. There are worse things than having a mom who works. There are worse things than having a caregiver who speaks English with a thick Russian accent. There are.

But right now, looking into the girls' tear-streaked faces, I can't remember what they are.

The girls are on the sullen side when I take them to school the next morning. They don't want me to work anymore. They don't want Mrs. Slutsky coming to the house in the afternoon. They just want me there.

Frankly, I'd like to be there, but I need the income. We need the income.

Nathan calls during my lunch to see how the move went. He called a few times over the weekend, but we could never say more than hi and bye, as I was always in the middle of something like loading boxes into the truck, or away from my cell, or just about to feed the girls Sunday night.

Now I start to tell him about the new house and the new sitter when Marta beeps in from Los Angeles, where she's presenting to a commercial real estate company. "Nathan, I have to take her call. She only calls if it's important."

"Taylor, we really do have to talk."

"I know."

"When can we?"

"I don't know. It's so busy here. I'm so busy." I can hear the beeping of Marta's call still, and I'm panicking that she might hang up. "I'll try you soon."

"I'm heading into a meeting, Taylor—"

"Okay. Then we'll talk after that. Sorry. Bye." I hang up quickly and take Marta's call, but the cloud of doom and gloom is on me again.

I've learned now that when Nathan says we have to talk, it means he has something to tell me, and it's never good news.

I try to call Nathan back before leaving work, but I don't reach him. He calls me while I'm making dinner. "Sounds like you're busy," he says, and I immediately feel defensive.

"I've just got three hungry little girls here," I answer, trying not to be short and yet wanting to throw the phone. I'm tired. I really am. "You said you had something important to tell me...?"

He hesitates. "I do."

"So?"

"Maybe now is not a good time."

I can't hide my exasperation. "Will there ever be a good time?"

"I don't know."

His voice is so low and heavy that I immediately feel guilty. "Nathan, are you okay?"

He doesn't answer, and the silence seems to stretch forever.

"Nathan?"

"Maybe we should just do this in person."

Do what? Panic replaces my guilt. "What, Nathan?"

"I miss you, Taylor."

I have never heard so much sadness or hopelessness in his voice. My eyes burn and my throat aches. "Come home, Nathan. Please. Because if you don't, I'm getting on a plane and going there."

"Okay."

"Okay what?"

"I'll come home."

"When?"

"Soon. As soon as I can. I promise."

The rest of the week passes in a frenzy of activity. I wake up, tumble into clothes, hurry kids into theirs, and rush them out the door before hustling to Z Design; and then I'm rushing home, and it's another frantic couple of hours of homework, housework, laundry, and dinner before bed.

For the first time, I understand what single moms and working moms go through. I'm so busy, I find myself looking at mail as I brush my teeth and leafing through new magazines while peeing. I've always been good at multitasking, but multitasking takes on a whole new meaning now.

But even though I'm busy, Nathan is never far from my mind. I think about him first thing when I wake and last thing before I fall asleep, and at night I dream about him, about us, I dream we're together, we're over, we're strangers. I dream the girls miss him. I dream he's dead. I dream it's all just a dream and we're really still in our house and together like we were. In the mornings, I wake up and lie in bed feeling flat, low, depressed.

I need to go to Omaha. I need to go see Nathan.

Marta's back from Los Angeles, and she returns with a two-page to-do list that she wants taken care of before the holidays, and that's only my list. She has lists for everyone on the team.

Friday, as it's a half day, the others leave at noon, but I stay on, determined to get at least half of the company Christmas cards addressed this afternoon. Marta sends cards to 350 customers, colleagues, and contacts; she doesn't believe in computer-generated labels, and the only way I can do a job like this is by breaking it down in chunks.

With a cup of coffee at my elbow, I work on the stack of envelopes in front of me. I try not to look at the size of the stack; instead I focus on one envelope at a time.

I've been working for only forty-five minutes or so when Marta enters the office, slides off her coat, and pulls a paper bag from her purse.

"Here," she says, pushing the paper bag across the conference table toward me. "An early Christmas present."

I look in the bag. I pull out a black-and-pink box. There's

a big-breasted blonde on the side and fancy script on the top. I turn the box over to the window and see what's inside: a gigantic purple penis with silicone veins and a battery end.

Marta's watching me. "It has great texture. Feel it."

"What is this?"

"It's a vibrator."

"No, I know it's a vibrator, but...what kind of gift is this?" Disgusted, I shove the box back in the bag and crumple it closed.

Marta leans across the table, takes the bag, and dumps out the contents. The box with the silicone penis falls out, along with a smaller box, this one silver and black with a hot pink font.

"And the pocket rocket," she says, tapping the smaller box. "Every woman has to have one. I love it."

"Yuck. I don't want these."

"Yes, you do. They'll make you feel better and maybe help you stop pining for Nathan. A man who doesn't even deserve you, I might add."

"How can you say that?" I demand, grabbing the boxes and shoving them back into the crumpled bag.

"Because I see what I see. He's not here for you, he's not trying to be here for you—"

"Maybe I chased him away. Have you thought about that? Maybe I blew it. Maybe I was the one who messed everything up."

"How?" She bends down low and looks me hard in the eye. "How did you mess everything up?"

"You don't know the situation, Marta. You don't know what Nathan had to put up with—"

"Put up with? Taylor, were you some psycho bitch?"

"No!" I cry, incredulous.

"Did you fly around your house on a broomstick?"

"No."

"So what did you do that made you so awful?"

I know she's trying to help me. I know she's trying to make me feel better, but she doesn't understand. I do screw up. I have screwed up. I've chased Nathan away. And I don't even know how, as I've spent the past twelve years trying to improve me. Trying to be a better woman, a better wife. I have dieted and exercised, I've studied fashion and interior design. I've taken cooking classes and sailing classes and even joined a wine group so I could appreciate wine with him.

Yet it wasn't enough. Nothing I do is enough.

"What makes you the villain in this story and Nathan the good guy?" Marta persists.

I shake my head.

"No, I don't accept that." Marta is bent so low that we're eye to eye, and it's scary as hell. "Tell me. Why are you the bad guy?"

"I...have problems."

"Taylor, everyone has problems. That's why we have religion. To redeem and save us. To make us whole."

"But I wasn't always easy to live with—"

"So who is? And for that matter, did he ever complain before you had money troubles?"

"No."

"I didn't think so." Marta returns to her desk, drops into her chair, and crosses her legs. "And I'll tell you why. Because, Taylor Young, you're beautiful. You're smart and hardworking and a great mom and all-around successful. Everyone in the community knows you, and therefore knows him. Nathan isn't what's made your family the family it is. It's you. You've created this gorgeous, beautiful family. You carried the babies. You designed the house. You furnished the house. You took care of yourself. You volunteered endlessly at school. You did everything asked of you. And more."

I grab the Christmas cards and the green envelopes and jam them into my bag. "Maybe I could do these at home—"

"Why can't you see the good you do?"

"I do," I say, my heart thumping wildly. "I do. So do you mind if I go?"

The weekend is quiet. In fact, the entire next week is quiet. I don't know if Marta is more distant at work or if it's me, but we don't speak to each other unless there is something specific to say. I'm still agog that she'd think vibrators were a solution to anything.

But the office isn't the only quiet place. Life at home is more silent, too. The phone doesn't ring as much, and I've realized that in the last month people don't invite us over or out as often, either.

After having so many friends and such a busy social life for so many years, it's hard to believe my world has shrunk so dramatically.

What are people afraid of? Nathan isn't dead or dying. We're not getting divorced (at least not that I've heard). We just sold the house. Downsized. Tightened the belt, so to speak.

It shouldn't matter to anyone but us. Money troubles aren't contagious. You aren't going to lose your blue-chip stocks just by having dinner with us.

But people are scared anyway. They stay away. They don't call, they don't return my call, leaving the girls and me more isolated than ever.

It's so confusing, too. You'd think people would want to rally around, give us the good old pep talk, the one about life being difficult but you can do anything if you just set your mind to it.

People don't give that pep talk here.

Maybe for most people life isn't so difficult here.

It had never been difficult for us, either. Maybe that's why Nathan couldn't come to me when he lost his job. Maybe he didn't expect that he—the golden boy—would ever have anything bad happen to him, and maybe he thought if he didn't talk about it, it wouldn't be true.

It's finally Friday noon, and I leave Z Design for the post office, where I mail all 350 cards now that they're signed and sealed.

I have an auction chair meeting at Tully's at one.

I arrive early, and as I always do, I grab chairs and create a little cluster. It just seems easier to have everything ready when everyone arrives. I suppose it also gives me something specific to do. I like having something specific to do. Gives me a sense of purpose.

As I wait with my coffee for the others, I spot a group of women at the conference table. I've seen them before, they gather here on Friday afternoons once or twice a month.

They're former teachers and librarians, smart women who love books and ideas and living. I never paid them much attention in the beginning—they weren't dressed to the nines and didn't care about good wine or the newest advances in technology—but today they're discussing the movie *Thelma & Louise*.

"A cop-out, the ending was a cop-out. Just going over a cliff like that."

"It's because they made so many mistakes."

"Too many mistakes. They made mistakes all along the way."

"But you don't drive off a cliff just because you screw up."

"No, but they should have reported the rape. That's the thing."

"Driving off the cliff holding hands. Ridiculous. What a waste."

"I thought it was funny. I laughed the entire movie."

"Laughed because it's foolish," another shot back.

My attention is interrupted by the arrival of the committee. They've come in one big group, and I smile and greet everyone enthusiastically. Kate's here, too, and I rise to give her a huge hug. God, I've missed her. I've missed everyone.

"How was everyone's Thanksgiving?" I ask, smiling and looking around.

"Good, good," they answer, but it doesn't take me long to realize that no one's making a lot of eye contact. In fact, no one's really looking at me at all.

I feel a pain in my gut, a sharp pain that makes it hard to breathe. "Everything okay?" I ask quietly.

My question is greeted by silence. There's my answer, I think as the pain in my gut spreads, radiating out, making me feel sick. Panicked.

Finally Kate looks at me. "The PTA board is worried about this year's auction. The auction is just three months away, and the board is concerned that the auction is floundering."

"But everything is right where it should be," I answer, a little surprised by Kate's comment but not unduly troubled. The auction's stressful. Every year we have little dramas and disappointments during the planning. "Our procurement is right on target, and when the invitations go out in the mail after the holidays, we'll work with the PTA board to push the ticket sales."

No one says anything. These women, people I think of as friends, just stare into their coffee cups.

"Taylor, they've asked me to step in." Kate sits tall. "They want me involved."

I try to overlook the vote of no confidence. "That's great, Kate. I'd love to have your help. The auction's a huge project, and with Patti gone, I could use a co-chair—"

"They're not talking co-chair."

My heart hammers harder. My smile slips. "I don't understand."

"Taylor, you don't have the big corporate sponsors yet, and usually at this point we have the corporate underwriting in place."

I look steadily at Kate. "I'm confused. You and your husband are usually the auction's biggest underwriters. You've underwritten the auction for the past five years. Are you saying you're not underwriting the auction this year?"

"No, we're not." Kate gives me my answer while looking past my shoulder rather than in my eye.

"Why not?"

Her eyebrows pull. She looks pained that we're even having this conversation. I'm pained, too. Kate's my friend. We've been friends for years. "It's a lot of money, Taylor."

I know it's a lot of money. It's close to twenty thousand dollars. But they do it every year. They're our Gold Sponsor, our Points Angel, every year.

When I say nothing, Kate is forced to continue. "Bill and I have discussed it, and we're not comfortable underwriting the auction as it stands. We're not sure it's a wise investment."

"*What?*" I choke, flushing.

"Taylor, there's concern about your ability to manage such a large fund-raiser—"

"That's absurd. I've been involved with fund-raising for years."

"People are talking, Taylor, you might as well know it. The consensus seems to be that if you can't manage your personal finances, how can you be responsible for the school finances?"

"But we're working as a group. We work by committee."

Amelia now clears her throat. This is Amelia's first meeting. "The board felt it wasn't wise to have you chairing an auction of this size."

"*What?*"

Amelia presses on. "Now if Patti were still here—"

"But she's not," I interrupt fiercely.

For the first time, Kate looks sympathetic. "I'm sorry, Taylor, the board is asking that you step down as chair and allow someone else from the committee to assume the leadership role."

I can't believe it. Can't. Kate's my friend. She's been my friend for years. "And if I don't?"

Amelia, Kate, and Louisa exchange quick glances. "The committee chairs met last night, and we put the issue to a vote. The school administration has already been noti-fied. You've been removed from your position."

"So it's done? Decided?" I look at them, not able to believe that women I know, women I consider friends, would go behind my back to have me removed in a vote of no confidence.

"If we can just have your binder and notes," Barb says terribly gently, "it'll help the transition process and ensure we don't lose further momentum."

I still haven't accepted it. I can't accept it. This is such a huge power play, and I won't be played. "No momentum has been lost. We're still right on target, if not ahead—"

"We need the Gold Sponsors." Amelia cuts me short. Her tone is crisp, no-nonsense, and I suddenly remember where we met and why I'm not comfortable with her. Her husband works at McKee Holding Company, Nathan's former company. Her husband may have even replaced Nathan.

"Without the Points Angel," she continues, "we don't have a successful auction."

I look at Kate. Her expression is pinched. "Kate," I say softly, pleadingly, "you're the underwriter, you're the Points Angel. Work with me."

Kate shakes her head. "I would, but Bill won't. He's not comfortable." Her voice drops. "Taylor, you must understand...so much has happened in the past few months, so much has changed..."

I reach for her hand, clasp her fingers. "But I haven't changed. I'm still me."

Kate squeezes my fingers. "People are worried."

"About what? That I'd embezzle money?"

"No, God, no." Kate looks stricken. "It's just that to effectively chair the auction, one has to be a good leader."

"I'm not?" When she doesn't answer, anger surges through me. Nathan and I are trying to be responsible. We're trying to do the right thing. How else would people have us handle our mistakes? What would they have us do? Just continue to fake it? Digging deeper and deeper into debt?

Maybe the right thing doesn't look all glossy and interesting, but it's real.

Kate squeezes my hand again. "I'm sorry," she whispers. "I am. If it were me, I'd do things differently."

Louisa puts her hands on the table. "I think that covers it."

Amelia nods, rises, and, as she leaves, nods at me again.

The meeting ends and they go, but I don't. I sit at the small rounds I pushed together earlier, back when I was excited to see everyone and anticipating a good meeting.

As I sit there, I want to quit. I really do. I want to lie down right here in the middle of Tully's and just give up.

But then I glance at the group of older ladies. I remember their scathing assessment of *Thelma & Louise*. *You don't drive off a cliff just because you screw up.*

No, you don't, I think, getting to my feet. And I'm not, either.

*   *   *

But once I'm back in my car, my anger dissolves into pain. I sit locked in my car outside Tully's for nearly ten minutes without moving, staring blindly at the big bare trees lining Points Drive.

How could they kick me off the committee? How could they yank it all away like that?

How could people I view as friends lose confidence in me?

Maybe I've always felt like a faker, but I'm a hardworking faker. I have poured myself into Points Elementary, have done anything and everything to show I'm dependable. Maybe even indispensable.

Yet with one yank of the rug, I'm off my feet and on my butt.

Kicked out. Dismissed.

It hurts so much, I can hardly breathe. It hurts so much, I can't even cry. Kate, *Kate*, booted me.

Hands shaking, I reach into my purse for my cell phone. I call Nathan. Even if he hates me, he'd still understand how devastating this is.

The fact that he doesn't answer nearly sends me over the edge. I start crying as I get directed to voice mail, and I can't stop. I'm not even coherent as I tell him that I've been kicked off the auction committee. That no one trusts me anymore. That people are concerned I'd maybe embezzle their money. That I, Taylor Young, would steal from anyone.

Just saying the words out loud makes me cry harder. I don't even finish the message. There's no point. I hang up.

There's nothing to say, nothing that can make any of this better.

It takes me another five minutes to calm myself enough to try to drive home. I hurt as I start the car. I feel as though I've been physically beaten, pounded. My bones ache. Even my insides feel bruised.

My phone rings as I drive. I see it's Marta, and I answer. "Hi, Marta." My voice sounds thick and rough. I can only hope she doesn't notice.

"Taylor, sorry to bother you, but I was trying to find the Clendon Winery folder in the filing cabinet but can't locate it. I hoped you might know where it is."

"It's actually on my desk, underneath the invoice folder."

"Ah...yep, found it. Thanks." She hesitates. "You all right?"

The question alone makes my chest squeeze, my stomach feel on fire all over again. I've tried so hard. Tried my best. "Yes."

"But something's happened. I've never heard you cry before."

"I'm not crying." Tears well up all over again.

"Is it Nathan?"

"No, it's not Nathan. It's everything." I gulp air, fight for control. Try desperately hard to get my voice back to normal. "And I thought I was doing okay, handling everything that's come up in the past couple of months, but apparently not." I take a quick breath. "I was just booted off the auction committee. Removed in a vote of no confidence."

"Can they do that?"

"They did." I hold my breath. God knows I don't want to be overly dramatic, but it is humiliating and painful. I've never been fired before. From anything.

"But who did it? And why?"

"Kate."

"*Your* Kate? Kate Finch?"

My throat feels raw as I swallow. "I don't think she's my Kate anymore. She said as long as I remain auction chair, she and her husband won't underwrite the auction as corporate sponsors."

"Is that a big deal?"

"They've been our Gold Sponsors for years. They donate the most money. Twenty thousand or more to help cover operating expenses."

"Do you want to come by for a coffee or glass of wine?" Marta asks. "Luke's out of town this weekend, and Eva's at Jill's for a sleepover."

I'm flooded by gratitude. Unconventional Marta has been more of a friend to me than almost anyone. "I wish I could," I answer honestly, "but my sitter has to go. She's a bit fierce."

Marta laughs. "You're intimidated by your own sitter?"

"Meet her. You'll see what I mean." I pause. "But maybe you'd like to come to dinner at our house tonight? I can't promise you that it'd be fancy, but it'd be food and you wouldn't have to make it."

"What time are you thinking?"

"Anytime. Five-thirty. Six. Six-thirty. It's up to you."

"How about sometime between six and six-thirty? That way I can finish up the project in front of me."

"That sounds great. You know where the new house is?"

"I do. See you soon."

Entering the rental house, I stop and sniff. The house has a heavy, sour smell. Like onions and boiled cabbage. Mrs. Slutsky must be cooking.

"Hello," I call out, setting my purse on the couch and then taking off my coat and dropping it there, too.

Mrs. Slutsky emerges from the kitchen with laundry beneath her arm. She looks at me and then my coat. "I cannot make the children responsible for their things if you do not set a good example," she says disapprovingly.

I glance at the couch, see my coat. "I'll put it away—"

She shakes her head and with a *tsk-tsk*ing sound walks out.

I make a face at her back. My girls aren't the only ones missing bubbly, blond, and fun.

Chapter Twenty-Three

It takes me fifteen minutes to get rid of Mrs. S, a half hour to get rid of the smell of cabbage and potato soup, another twenty minutes to get a dinner of shrimp risotto going, and then fifteen for me to shower and wash my face, reapplying makeup to repair the damage done when I cried.

I'm working on opening a bottle of wine when Marta arrives.

"Perfect timing," I say, answering the door with the bottle of wine in my hand. "Come in."

As she enters the house, she slides off her black leather jacket. It's a biker jacket, something a Hell's Angel—or Ray—would like. "Thank God it's Friday."

With the wine under my arm, I hang up her jacket and lead her into my itty-bitty kitchen. Marta looks around and examines the changes I've made.

"This house is amazing. It smells amazing, too." She takes the glass of wine I've poured her. "What is that? Saffron?"

"I'm making shrimp risotto, and if you'd been here an hour ago you would have smelled something very different."

Marta grins. "Well, you should be proud of yourself. You've turned an ugly house into something charming. I'm pretty good with basic design, but I couldn't have done this. This required some serious imagination, never mind a lot of elbow grease."

I shrug off the compliment and head for the dining room table, where I've put out small dishes of olives, hummus, goat cheese spread, and crackers. "I like making things pretty. It's easy for me."

"It's not easy for everyone." Marta sits at the dining room table and takes a cracker. "You can do things most people can't do."

"They could if they tried."

"You can't be nice to yourself if you tried."

I groan, rub at the bridge of my nose. "You're already my boss. It'll give me nightmares if you're also my shrink."

She laughs and runs a hand through her long dark hair. "I hate shrinks. But that's probably because I need one more than anybody." Then without skipping a beat, she changes the topic. "So what did you do to deserve being excommunicated from the Points auction committee?"

The lump returns to my throat. I shake my head.

"They had to have a reason," she persists.

I struggle to get out the words. "I haven't been financially responsible."

"With the auction money?"

"With Nathan's and our money."

"But that's your money. That's personal. You haven't been irresponsible with anyone else's money. You're not irresponsible with people's time."

"But it doesn't work that way, and the horrible thing is, I knew it, too. I learned when I was growing up if you goof in your personal life, you'll suffer in your public life. One mistake and you're labeled."

"Only if you let yourself be labeled."

If only that were the way life worked.

"Taylor, if you have a fault, it's that you give people too much power. People aren't that powerful. They can't hurt you—"

"Yes, they can. They can and they do."

"Because you let them!" Her voice rises with frustration. "You've told yourself that others are more important and more valuable than you—"

"I haven't."

"Then why does their opinion matter more to you than your own?"

I don't have an answer.

"It seems to me that you've decided if people have money, they have more power, and clout—"

"Well, they do," I say shortly. "People with money are respected. People with money are listened to."

"You think you need money to be respected?"

I think of South Pasadena, where I grew up. I remember how my dad's business suffered when Mom left, I remember the gossip and scandal. Cissy and I were mocked. Teased. Dad was demoralized. He hid.

"Maybe."

"You know, Taylor, if money brought respect, why do I respect you more now than when you were the head honcho of everything?"

She must see my expression because she nods. "And I don't just respect you, Taylor, I've realized I like you. I even admire you."

"*You* admire *me?*"

Her gaze holds mine. "You do things many women are afraid to do. You tackle enormous projects, hard-core projects. Someone needs help, you offer your time. Someone needs a hand, you're there in person. You do something lots of people don't do anymore. You give. You give of yourself, and you don't ask for anything in return."

There's something so honest and kind in Marta's voice that I look down into my wineglass before she can see how much her words touch me. She doesn't realize how much I needed to hear something good about me, something positive.

"You're a lot like my Eva," she continues. "Eva really wants everyone to like her. Eva wants everyone to approve of her. Not because she isn't wonderful, and not because she truly needs approval. It's because she's sensitive. She cares about other people. She likes making other people happy, but as I'm trying to teach her, you can't hinge your happiness on other people's. It's impossible to always make others happy. Some people just don't want to be happy. Others are looking for someone to blame."

Her expression is concerned. "Perhaps it's time you stopped listening to that little voice in your head and grew a new voice. One that's nicer to you than the one you've got talking at you now."

"Marta," I protest, but she looks at me so long that I squirm.

"We're not so different. I actually don't think women are all that different. Somehow we've all ended up with mean little voices in our heads. Voices that say we're not good enough and we'll never be good enough."

"You have those, too?"

She grimaces. "*Yes*. And one day I just got sick and tired of all that crap in my head, so I stopped letting the voices yap away. I kicked them out, and I think you need to do that with the nasty voices in your head, too."

I look at her skeptically. "What did your voices say?"

"I was unlovable. I was bound to fail. That no one would ever want me. That no one would ever be faithful." Her shoulders shift. "They're not uncommon fears. But I was just sick of them. Sick of them making me feel bad all the time." She leans forward, taps my arm. "Maybe it's time you stopped focusing on what you do wrong, Taylor, and start celebrating what you do right."

Later that night after Marta leaves and my girls are in bed, I stand in the kitchen at the sink, finishing the dinner dishes, and think about everything Marta said.

Marta said a lot.

She said so much that my brain still hurts.

But one thing stands out: I don't trust myself right now, and I don't trust the little voice in my head because it is warped. It does say mean things...it says mean things about me. And it talks endlessly, a constant dialogue critiquing everything I think and feel and do.

You blew it.

You did it wrong.

You always do it wrong.

You messed up.
You can't get it right.
You can't get anything right.
You're stupid.
You're lazy.
You're foolish.
You're dreamy.
You're impractical.
You're selfish.
You're bad.

You're bad. I silently repeat the last one as I load the dishwasher, knowing these voices are part of that horrible, hollow feeling inside of me. Knowing I've somehow created this horrible, hollow feeling inside of me. But I'm not hollow, and I'm not horrible. For all my mistakes, I do love my girls, and I try my best to take care of them. For all my flaws and my vanity and my pride, I do love Nathan, and I love him with all my heart. The truth is, I do try. I always try.

Maybe Marta's right about something else. Maybe trying your best, and doing your best, even if it's not perfect, is enough.

Maybe it's unrealistic to think I can be perfect.

Or to put it in Marta-speak, that's why we have religion. God's perfect. We're human.

As I turn off the water, I reach for a sponge. Wouldn't it be amazing to stop expecting perfection and focus more on being real? Being human?

Wiping off the counters, I have another thought. Maybe Dad's biggest mistake wasn't being left by Mom, but cowering. Apologizing. Hiding.

My fingers grip the sponge so hard, I squeeze water all over the counter.

I'm so sick of apologizing.

So sick of feeling less than. I want to be happy with me. I want to finally like me. Would that be so wrong?

"Mommy, I'm thirsty," Tori says, suddenly appearing in the kitchen doorway in her pink princess sprigged pajamas.

"You're supposed to be asleep," I say, dropping the sponge in the sink and turning to face her.

"I can't sleep. There are too many spiders in my room."

"There aren't any spiders," I say, fighting exasperation.

"Yes, there are."

"Tori."

"Come see." She holds out a hand to me, her expression determined as well as resigned.

I take her hand and we walk back to the little room she shares with Brooke. A small night-light is plugged into the wall, illuminating one wall with soft yellow gold light. I look around the room and see nothing. "There's no spider," I whisper. "Now go to bed."

"There is a spider."

"Tori..."

"Look." She slips her hand from mine and walks to the foot of the trundle bed and points at the wall. "See?"

I go look and see. A spider not quite as big as my palm sits on the wall just a few inches above the heating vent. It's big. It's blackish brown. It is not—on the plus side—hairy.

"See?" she repeats.

Bless her. "Yes, I do. Just a sec." Back in the kitchen, I get a wad of paper towels, then I grab the spider and take it outside and dump it in the bushes next to the front door.

My arms are covered in goose bumps as I close the door, but Tori's beaming at me. "You did it! Hooray!"

I lift her onto my hip. "Do you think you can sleep now?"

She wraps her arms around my neck. "If I can sleep with you in your bed."

She looks at me so hopefully that I can't tell her no. "Only if you promise not to pee the bed."

In the morning I wake up and slide quietly from beneath the covers so I don't disturb Tori, who is still asleep and sharing my pillow. After closing my bedroom door, I check on the other two. They're still asleep, too.

I make coffee, then sit at my computer at the dining room table, check e-mail, and see that I've got two messages, one from Nathan and one from Marta.

I open Nathan's first. *T, I'm sorry I missed your call. I want to talk. N*

I read and reread his e-mail. He wants to talk...he wants to talk...he wants to talk. What does that mean?

I type a brief answer: *Call when you can. I'm just home hanging out with the girls today.*

Next I read Marta's e-mail. *Taylor, do you want to be auction chair again? Marta*

Wow. Interesting question. A good question, too. I get up from my chair, pace the kitchen and living room.

Part of me would jump at the chance to be auction chair again. I started working on the auction months ago, before school even ended last year. Our first meeting was last August, and Patti and I poured ourselves into organizing and motivating the committee.

Being auction chair meant so much to me then. It doesn't mean as much now. Having my family together again, that's what's important now.

I sit back at my computer, answer Marta's e-mail: *If I could have anything, I'd have Nathan home with us again.*

After pushing send, I get up and pace again as the old fear comes back at me, the fear of being less than, the fear of being forgotten, abandoned. But instead of running to my beloved box of Cheerios, I face the fears that I'm no one and nothing and realize it's not true. I am someone. A very flawed someone. But flawed or not, I matter. I matter to a lot of people. Even more important, I matter to me.

The girls end up sleeping in, and after they wake up we just hang out, enjoying being lazy. I'm glad. It's Saturday and a gorgeous day already, too, with clear blue sky and morning sunlight streaming through the kitchen windows and bouncing off the small antique crystal chandelier I hung in the kitchen light fixture.

Delicate rainbow prisms splash on the opposite wall. Little crystal knobs I rescued from a thrift store catch the light and dress up the creamy white cabinet doors.

Brooke enters the kitchen with my box of Cheerios under her arm and sees the splinters of light shimmering across the narrow room. "Rainbows, Mom."

I'm standing next to the counter, making a grocery list. "It's pretty, isn't it?"

"I like this house," she says, putting down the box and coming to stand next to me. "It's little and old, but you made it nice."

"Thank you." Someday, I think, I'll miss our old house, but for now, I'm determined to focus on the things I can do, the things I can make, and the things I can paint. "Did you and your sisters still want to get out some of the Christmas decorations today?"

"Are we going to get the tree, too?"

"Maybe."

Jemma enters the kitchen with a stack of catalogs that came in yesterday's mail. "I don't want to do the tree today. I want to start our baking. We haven't made anything yet."

I add peanut butter to the list before looking up at the girls. "Maybe we can do the tree today and the baking tomorrow."

"Or maybe we can do the baking today and the tree tomorrow," Jemma answers, hauling herself onto the kitchen counter to look through the new Victoria's Secret catalog. She loves all the catalogs, always on the lookout for something interesting or new. I used to be like that. I loved the opportunity to browse and shop. Every glossy catalog filled me with ideas of how life could be. Every purchase hinted at the person I wasn't yet but hoped to be.

"Some of the girls in my class are already wearing a bra," Jemma says, studying pictures of the world's supermodels in delicate bra and panties sets.

"Girls develop at different ages." I chew on the end of my pen and wonder if I'm going to finally have to give the birds and bees talk, something I've carefully avoided almost as much as Jemma has. She never asks questions about how babies are made, and I've never tried to explain...yet. But I should. My mom never explained it to me, and I found out through trash talk from friends.

"I know girls develop at different ages," she answers, "I was just telling you that some are wearing bras. And Katherine Kelley is already big, really big. Everyone's always watching her when she has to run because her...um"—Jemma puts a hand out in front of her small chest—"they go up and down. A lot."

I put down my pen. "Do you stare?"

"No." She pauses. "Maybe. It's just...weird. Last year nothing, and now these big...breasts...and people treat her different. One boy, I don't think he was a fifth grader, tried to kiss her and grab her there, and he got suspended. For a week."

"That's sexual harassment," I say, surprised that such things are even happening at Points Elementary.

"What's sexual harassment?" asks a deep male voice from the living room.

Nathan?

Jemma lets out a scream and leaps from the counter. "Dad!"

Brooke chases after, and Tori comes shrieking from her bedroom. *"Daddy, Daddy!"*

Stunned, I follow a little more slowly, emerging to see three little girls throw themselves onto Nathan. Within seconds he's covered in arms, legs, and kisses.

I don't think he's even aware of me there with all the shrieks and hugs and love, but then his head lifts and he looks at me. He is shockingly thin, with deep creases and shadows beneath his eyes. He looks at me for a long moment. "Hello, honey."

Honey.

Honey.

I try to smile, but I can't. I sag weakly against the wall, my heart so tender that it hurts to speak.

The past rushes over me, the girl I was, the years we shared, the babies we had, the baby we lost, the house we built to fill the emptiness. And looking at him, I feel no anger, no sadness, just peace. Here is my man. Here is my partner. "Welcome home."

Nathan takes the girls to pick out the perfect Christmas tree. I was asked to come, but I said I'd stay home and drag out the boxes of decorations from the storage unit (decrepit shack) that's been attached to the carport in the backyard and start untangling all the lights.

Nathan and the girls are back within the hour with a tree that's way too tall for the living room. I don't even have to say anything to Nathan. He walks into the house, looks up at the ceiling, then sighs. "They are eight-foot ceilings, aren't they?"

"Yep."

Fresh lines run from his nose to his mouth. The furrows in his forehead deepen. "I should have called you."

"It's okay."

"Dammit."

I glance at the girls, who are hovering in the doorway. "We have a saw. We'll just cut the bottom off."

He turns away, stares out the living room window. "I can't—" He breaks off, shakes his head, his expression infinitely sad.

My insides squeeze. Not this, not this, not this.

"Nathan," I say quietly, calmly, as much for my benefit as his.

"It's too much, Taylor." There's anguish in his voice, anguish and heartbreak, and my eyes burn, my throat tightening. *Something bad is coming. Something bad.*

"Mom?" Jemma asks uncertainly.

I look at the girls again, make a shooing motion to send them away. "What's too much?" I ask once the girls have disappeared into their rooms.

"Everything." He turns to look at me, and he's so pale there's a grayish tint to his skin. "I don't know how to do this anymore." He makes a rough sound in the back of his throat. "I don't know that I can."

My legs suddenly don't feel strong enough to support me, and I sit in one of the living room chairs. "Maybe it's time you told me whatever is it you've needed to tell me. Maybe it's time we just got it all out."

He gestures toward the hall. "But the girls are waiting to do the tree."

"They're okay."

I wait for him to speak, but he doesn't say anything. Instead he stands, hands on his hips, his gaze fixed toward the fireplace. He runs his hand over his jaw with its day-old shadow of a beard.

"I'm not in a good place, Taylor," he says at last. "I haven't been in a good place for a long time, and I keep trying to protect you from this...whatever this is...but I can't anymore.

"I was in trouble," he continues wearily, "crashing and burning, and the worst part was I couldn't tell you." He looks at me, damning shadows beneath his eyes. His exhaustion is real. He seems to have aged ten years in the past two months. "I couldn't tell anyone. I didn't know how to tell anyone. It's still something I'm ashamed of."

"I'm so sorry."

He stares at his hands. "Playing football, you never blame anyone else. You learn mistakes cost games. You learn to suck it up, take the hit, and get back out there. I've been trying to do that, but it's not working. I'm back out there, but I'm not the same. We've lost so much. We're out of the game—"

"No, we're not. We don't have the big house, but we don't have the debt anymore, either. We both have jobs, we're both working, we'll soon be able to have another house. It's just a matter of time."

He just shakes his head. "But none of this needed to have happened in the first place. If I'd been more of a man "

"That's not fair, Nathan," I protest, my throat tightening. Nathan's a perfectionist just like me.

"Yes, it is. I invested badly in the stock market, and I didn't want anyone, much less you, to know. I didn't want you to know I couldn't do everything. I didn't want you to know that I'd screwed up." Self-loathing gives his words a hard edge. "Taylor, I hate myself. I hate what I did to you. I hate what I've done to the girls, and I went to Omaha to try to fix things, to try to save things, but now I can't even save myself." Tears fill his eyes. "I can't do this, honey. I can't. I can't do this without you. Please, Taylor, forgive me."

I go to him, put my arms around him, and hold him tight, as tight as I hold the girls after they've had a nightmare. "There's nothing to forgive—"

"Yes, there is. I've got it all wrong. Tried to do it all on my own. Thought that's what a man was supposed to do. But I can't face who I am, or what I am, without you."

I hold on. "You don't have to."

"Tell me we can make it."

"We can make it, Nathan. We can and we will."

In between decorating the tree, a trip to the mall for the girls to see Santa, and a visit to Kirkland's Houghton Beach Park to see the Christmas ships, Nathan and I talk. And talk. And talk some more.

He hates his job in Omaha, hates it with a passion. The work is boring, the management is unstable and petty, but that's not what's making him unhappy. He can't stand living apart from us, can't stand feeling as though he failed all of us.

That evening after the girls are in bed and Nathan and I keep yawning, we agree it's time to sleep, too. I wonder, though, where Nathan will want to sleep. We haven't slept in the same bed in months and months.

He looks just as puzzled, too, standing in the hall between the living room and bedroom. "Where...what... should I do?"

I stand in the doorway of our room. "What do you want to do?" I ask gently.

"Be with you."

"Then come be with me."

In bed, he lies close, wraps his arms around me. He's silent, but I can tell he's awake and something else is on his mind. I wait for him to speak, but he doesn't and yet his misery is tangible. After another ten minutes, I can't take it anymore. "What's wrong, honey?"

He takes a deep breath, exhales. "I said some terrible things to you before I moved to Omaha. I said things I regret, and then I just kind of abandoned you."

"It's okay. I survived."

"How?" he asks, genuinely bewildered.

I let out a breath. "I had to. The girls needed me."

He hesitates. "Have you...been making yourself sick? You know...that eating disorder thing?"

"I don't throw up anymore, anyway. I haven't in years. But I still binge-eat a bit. But now instead of a whole bag of chips, it's a half. Instead of a carton of ice cream, it's a half box of Cheerios."

"That's progress."

"Yeah." And it is. I'm not "cured." I'll probably battle with food for a long time, but I'm learning to make better choices, and I just try my best every day. That's all I can do.

"And you're not shopping?" he persists.

"Definitely not."

"Why not?"

"I don't know. Maybe it's like the eating thing. I realized I don't have to be self-destructive. I realized I can take a hit and be all right. I'm not afraid to take a hit, either. I might get knocked down, maybe even knocked out, but I know as long as I get up again it's okay."

Nathan draws me even closer to his chest. "You sound like a quarterback."

I laugh softly, and lifting his hand, I kiss it. "I just love my quarterback, that's all."

He kisses the top of my head. "Your quarterback loves you."

"I know," I whisper. "I've always known."

By the time Nathan catches a flight back to Omaha Monday morning, we've agreed on three things: 1) He's taking a full week off between Christmas and New Year's Eve to be home with us (which reminds me, I've got to cancel our Sun Valley tickets). 2) He's going to start looking for a job in the Seattle area again. Immediately. 3) And if he can't find a job in the Seattle area by June 1, we will move to Omaha to join him until he finds a job in Seattle.

I arrive at work late Monday morning, as I had to drop Nathan off at the airport first and traffic was a bear on the 405 heading north toward Bellevue. I don't do the commute that direction, so I was shocked that it took forty minutes for what is usually a twenty-minute drive.

Fortunately, it's quiet at Z Design when I arrive. Marta's not in the office. She apparently had a doctor's appointment. Robert and Allie are at their desks. Mel is traveling. Mel spends almost half her time in Chicago and New York with two of Marta's biggest accounts, accounts that seem to require endless hand-holding.

When Marta appears it's close to noon. Her cheeks are flushed, and it looks as though she may have been crying.

Knowing that she's been at the doctor's, I'm worried but say nothing to respect her privacy.

At noon Tiana Tomlinson, Marta's famous TV anchor friend from Los Angeles, calls on the office line. I step into the supply room, where Marta's hunting down a legal pad, to hand her the phone. Marta takes the phone and walks outside with it. I can see her pacing the yard as she talks to Tiana. I can't really see her face but know something's up.

Later in the afternoon, when I see Marta just sitting at her desk, staring off into space, I ask her if everything is all right. She answers a blunt yes. I don't press.

At home that evening, I'm just about to sit down with the girls and watch *Rudolph* on DVD for what feels like the hundredth time when the doorbell rings.

I open the door to discover Marta and Eva on our doorstep with a cake and a gift wrapped in festive purple-and-gold paper.

"It's a housewarming gift," Eva explains, handing it to Jemma. "We thought we'd get you something for your new house for the Christmas holidays."

Jemma slowly takes the gift. "You celebrate Christmas?"

Eva's frowning. "Yes, of course. Why?"

Jemma shrugs. "I just thought you didn't believe in religious holidays."

"The cake looks wonderful," I say, a little too enthusiastically.

Marta's smiling as they enter the house, and I close the door. "Eva made the cake. It's a one-two-three-four cake," she shares as the girls run down the hall to the bedrooms. "It was a favorite recipe in my mom's family."

"Well, thank you. Can I get you some coffee, or wine?" I ask, taking the cake and carrying it to the dining room table.

"Just water," she answers, rubbing her nose. It's then I see the glint on her finger. It's not a little sparkle, either, but a brilliant sparkle from an enormous stone.

"Marta..." I look up at her, into her face, and she's smiling crookedly. "Marta," I repeat. "On your finger...the ring..."

Rich, dusky color floods her cheeks. "Luke asked me to marry him."

"No!"

"Yes." She smiles at me, and all the tension disappears from her face. She looks absolutely radiant.

"Have you set a date?"

"February seventeenth, during Eva's winter break. We're going to have the wedding at the Fairmont Springs in Banff."

"That's only two months away."

"We decided not to wait too long." She hesitates, picks her words with care. "It's better to do it sooner, before I show too much." She waits, sees comprehension dawn on my face, and then nods, shyly blushing and smiling simultaneously. "We're expecting a summer baby."

"You're pregnant."

She nods again, blushing, glowing. "I haven't told Eva yet. She knows about the wedding, but I can't figure out how to tell her about the baby." Marta stumbles over her words. "I was thinking you might have some ideas for me, maybe help me come up with a way to break the news."

I grin. That's something I can definitely do.

Chapter Twenty-Four

A month has passed. A low-key Christmas came and went, along with our equally low-key New Year's. In the past, we've had half a dozen parties to choose from, and this year we were invited to one party, but neither Nathan nor I could put a face to a name so we declined, choosing to stay home with the girls instead.

Now the girls have been back in school for two weeks, and Marta's wedding is only a month away. It's a small wedding, less than one hundred invited with maybe fifty attending. I'm both surprised and delighted to be on Marta's guest list. She said the girls were welcome to come but there wouldn't be any other children attending except for Eva. After talking about it, Nathan and I decide he and I will go without the girls. We haven't had any time alone in months, and four days in Banff sounds unbelievably good.

I call Horizon Airlines to see if they'd allow us to exchange two unused Sun Valley tickets for tickets to Calgary. They agree, although there is a nominal service charge.

I'm so excited about the wedding: thrilled for Marta, thrilled for Eva, thrilled about the new baby. Eva knows about the baby, too, and she's over the moon. She talks about being a big sister all the time. "It's what I always wanted," she tells me earnestly one day in the office as she sits at the conference table, poring over the most recent issue of *Town & Country Weddings* magazine.

In the weeks leading to the wedding, Lucy hosts the first get-together for the brand-new book club. There are just four of us for that first meeting. It's Lucy, me, Marta, and Marta's friend Lori Johnson, who owns the restaurant Ooba's.

We discuss the book that Lucy has picked, *The Pulpwood Queens' Tiara-Wearing, Book-Sharing Guide to Life*, and it's the perfect book with which to start our new group, warm and bighearted. Reading the book makes you feel as if you're sitting with a close girlfriend talking about life and what we women need.

It's also the antithesis of the books we read in our former book club.

"I think my favorite part of the book is when Kathy Patrick writes that women shouldn't feel bad for choosing to be stay-at-home moms." Lucy flips open her book. "I think it's on page eighteen where she says that serving others is a calling."

"I liked that section, too," I agree. "I've always felt a little apologetic for wanting to volunteer and working at school, but I like being involved at school and with the girls. It makes me feel good to volunteer. It makes me feel good to help others."

"You know, Taylor, when I read those passages I actually thought of you," Marta says. "I don't remember the words verbatim, but it was something along the lines that women tend to hide their passion for everyday things, thinking people will think less of them for enjoying these things. I've said to you before, that we need people like you to care about our schools and our fund-raisers. We need women who love the everyday things as, God knows, there are women like me who don't."

Lucy's nodding. "We're all called to different things, and one isn't better than another. They're just different."

"Different but equally valuable," Lori sums up.

A week later, Lucy calls me on my cell, but as I'm working I don't check for messages until my lunch. Her message is so shocking, I call her back immediately.

"I wasn't sure I heard you right," I say as soon as she answers the phone. "Tell me again."

"Peter and I are going to counseling. Together." Her voice is excited and more than a little hopeful.

I hear so much happiness in her voice that I'm almost afraid for her. I don't want her hurt, and I don't want her disappointed. "What does this mean?"

"We're going to see if we can work things out. Maybe get back together."

I'm silent, trying to digest this surprising turn of events.

"Taylor, it's a good thing. I love him. I love my family."

"But Thanksgiving weekend when we had coffee at Tully's, you said he'd been so mean—"

"He was hurt and angry." She takes a deep breath. "And he's still hurt and angry, but we have the kids to think about." Her voice drops an octave. "We both love them so much, Taylor, neither of us can stomach having them only part-time." Now her tone turns persuasive. "Be happy for me, Taylor, please."

"I am."

"Really?"

"Yes."

She's silent for a moment. "I know it might not work, Taylor. I know we might not be able to pull it off, but I've got to try. I owe my kids that much."

"You owe it to yourself, too."

We say good-bye, and I hang up. I've just put my phone back in my purse when it suddenly rings. It's Lucy again. I pick up.

"Oh, Taylor, I can't believe I forgot. But you'll never believe what I heard today." She takes a deep breath. "Your Yarrow Point house is for sale."

"*What?*"

"It's true. I drove past it to make sure. There's a sign in front. Your house is back on the market."

"Why?" I ask, thinking it's been only two months since Monica and Doug moved in.

"I don't know, but if I hear anything, I'll call you right away."

We hang up again, and this time I just leave the phone lying on my desk.

My house ... my house ...

My house could be mine again.

My house could be mine again.

I close my eyes, picture us the way we were, the beautiful sunsets, the barbecues, the little dock where the girls jumped off to swim in the lake.

We could buy our house back. We could pick up our

lives, be Nathan and Taylor Young with a gorgeous house and three model-perfect daughters...

Then I remember. We can't afford the house. We can't afford a million-dollar house, much less four or five million.

The excitement turns to disappointment, and then the disappointment transforms into quieter acceptance. Acceptance isn't as fun as excitement, but it's not so bad, either.

I'm just wondering if I should even bother to call Nathan to tell him about our house when once again my cell phone rings. It's Nathan. How weird. He must have read my mind.

"I was just thinking about you," I say, answering.

"How's your day?" he asks.

I look at the stack of receipts and expense reports in front of me. Marta and Mel have been traveling a lot lately. "Good."

"You sound tired."

"I am. A little." Allie enters the studio and nods at me. I lift a hand in greeting. "But it's fine. Everything's fine."

"Feel like a date night Friday night?"

"Are we talking a real date or phone sex?" I tease, trying to be funny.

I get a laugh. "A real date," he says, pausing. "I'm being flown in for an interview. One Friday morning, and another Friday afternoon."

"How? What? When did this all happen? And are they good companies?" I'm tripping over my tongue. I can't get my questions out fast enough. "Would you want to work for either of these companies?"

"Yes. I'd love to work for either of them."

"Nathan, this is wonderful. This is...unbelievable. Who are the companies? Would I know them?"

He laughs. I hear eagerness in his voice, and optimism. It's been so long since he's had anything to be really excited about. "Microsoft, and a company called BioMed. So how about a dinner date Friday? Somewhere nice, you and me?"

Unwillingly, I flash back to all the years we ate out, all those thoughtless, careless meals in expensive restaurants. Fifty-dollar bottles of wine. Appetizers and salads and lobster at market price and dessert along with an after-dinner drink.

Filet mignon, crab-stuffed mushrooms, pan-sautéed Chilean sea bass...

"I'm happy eating at home, honey," I answer firmly, because I don't want to think about what we lost anymore, but what we have. And that's love.

Courage.

Grit.

Balls.

I sit taller in my chair. "Home's great, baby, really."

"That may be so, but I'm taking you out. It's time I took you out—"

"Nathan, we don't—"

"Please, Taylor, don't fight me on this. We can afford this. We can spring on one night out."

A night out would be fun. My lips curve wistfully. "Okay," I concede.

As soon as I'm off the phone, I Google BioMed. They're located in Bellevue (awesome), they're a huge international company with offices in Australia, Germany, London, Dublin, and Japan (impressive), and their founder and CEO is a thirty-nine-year old billionaire named Luke Flynn.

Luke Flynn.

I sit back in my chair. Marta's Luke.

My excitement over the two interview possibilities fades. I don't think Nathan knows that BioMed's founder is Marta's Luke. I don't know if I should talk to Marta about Nathan's interview. I'm worried she was behind the interview, worried that she went to Luke. It's possible that Luke has connections at Microsoft, too, and helped set up both interviews.

If he did, what does it mean?

As the day goes on, I'm increasingly troubled. I'd love nothing more than to have Nathan home with a great job with a local corporation. I'd love to have him home, making great money, would love for him to be happy again. But how will he feel when he finds out that Luke Flynn, CEO and president of BioMed, is Marta's Zinsser's soon-to-be husband?

Will he feel awkward?

Worse, will he feel pitied?

Thursday morning, the same day Nathan's set to fly home for his Friday interviews in Bellevue, I get a phone call from Marta's friend, TV personality Tiana Tomlinson. Tiana's flying into town Sunday morning to throw a surprise bridal shower for Marta on Sunday night. She hopes I can attend and would love it if I could put together an invite list for her of people Marta would want at the shower.

I promise to e-mail her an invite list within the next couple of hours. Since Marta's not in the office at the moment, I confer with Allie and Mel to get their input on whom Marta would want at the shower.

Nathan will still be in town Sunday night, so I won't need a sitter for the girls, but I will need to get a gift. I use my lunch to head to the mall to see if I can't find an appropriate present. The shower doesn't have a theme, it's just a chance for everyone to let Marta know how happy we are for her, but still, I want a great gift, the perfect gift. Marta's been so good to me. I want her to know how much I appreciate everything she's done for me.

At the mall, I start at Nordstrom but can't find what I'm looking for (maybe because I don't know what I'm looking for), so I leave and walk the rest of Bellevue Square without finding anything that screams "perfect present." In the end, I return to Nordstrom and buy a beautiful Italian negligee and robe for her honeymoon.

It isn't until I'm back at the office that I remember that being pregnant, Marta might not want a sexy negligee.

Frustrated with my inability to be unique or creative, I type up the list of names for Tiana and double-check the phone numbers and e-mail addresses before sending them off.

As I push send, I can't help but think back to the beginning of the school year, a year that started so promisingly with Patti co-chairing the auction with me and great teachers for the girls. I didn't know then that Nathan had been having some midlife crisis and was still blissfully unaware that our personal lives were in the toilet bowl.

But the toilet bowl taught me lessons, and I'm far stronger, and maybe happier, now than I was then.

Nathan arrives home at dinnertime. The girls and I fight the traffic heading south to the airport to pick him up and then stop at Rainforest Café at the South Center Mall for dinner. Tori loves the Rainforest Café. It's her favorite restaurant on earth, and suddenly dinner with Nathan is a festive celebration with loud elephants, noisy gorillas, thunderstorms, and birdcalls.

The restaurant lights flash and the thunder booms, and Tori shrieks with anticipation. Nathan looks across the table, catches my eyes, and smiles.

"I feel good about tomorrow," he says as the thunder and rain finally let up.

"That's great," I answer.

I want him to get a job here. I want him to be home with us. But I also know that he needs the right job and job offer, one that will build his confidence and not destroy it.

Friday, Nathan is up early to prepare a little more for his interviews. While he sits at the dining room table researching the companies on the computer, I get the girls up and out the door for school.

Nathan calls me while I'm driving Tori to preschool. "Luke Flynn," he says so bluntly that I know he's figured out the Marta connection. "Marta's fiancé, right?"

"Yes."

He's silent a long time, and then he exhales hard. "Did you put this together?"

"No."

"Did she?"

I've asked myself that a dozen times easily. "I don't think so," I finally answer. "Would you not want to interview with them if she did?"

"I don't know." At least it's an honest answer. "I guess I just have to interview and see."

Marta is in and out of the office all morning, and I can't seem to find a quiet moment to ask her if she had a hand in Nathan's job prospects. I'm not even sure I should ask. Would it be so awful if she did put in a positive word for Nathan? Would it be so awful if something good happened to us?

Just before I leave work at one, I get a call on my cell. Mrs. Slutsky, who had originally promised to stay and watch the kids tonight, is canceling. Apparently she's needed somewhere else, and she has to do that instead of be at our house.

I'm disappointed that Nathan and I won't have our special dinner out, but at the same time I'm a little relieved that we're not spending money we don't have to spend. On the way home I call Nathan to give him a heads-up, and he's remarkably upbeat. "Sounds like it was a good day," I say.

"Very good," he agrees. "I actually ended up having a third interview today, meeting with the executives from Hal-Perrin Technology at lunch."

"Aren't they a rival of the McKees?" I ask.

"They are, and they're doing a lot of international growth right now. Lots of exciting things happening with them."

"Their office is in downtown Seattle?"

"Their headquarters, yes."

"So what do you think? Any one interview stand out? Is there one job you'd want more than the others?"

He takes a moment to consider his answer. "You know, I think I could be happy working for any of them."

"Really?"

"Yeah. They're all great companies. They'd all be wonderful opportunities."

I hang up as I'm almost home and want to hear the rest in person. Nathan decides to barbecue for us tonight, so despite the freezing temperature outside, he heads to the store, picks up some steaks, and then grills for us on the little charcoal Weber in our backyard.

I make twice-baked potatoes and a Caesar salad and set the table using a bunch of candles to make our minuscule dining room as pretty as possible.

Sitting at the table eating, the girls chatter a mile a minute, and I glance up to see Nathan smiling at Brooke. It's his old smile, his real smile, the one that made me fall head over heels in love with him.

I know I told him in December we'd be okay, but now I know it.

We're going to be okay. In fact, we're going to be better than ever.

Sunday morning, Nathan gets an e-mail from Omaha that he has an early Monday meeting, so two hours later I'm driving him back to the airport. The girls are upset the entire drive, begging him not to leave. I keep it together until we pull up to the departure curb at the airport.

Fighting tears, I get out of the car and hug Nathan on the curb.

"It's only a couple of weeks until I'm back for Marta's wedding," he says.

"Still."

He hugs me harder, then lets me go. "I'll call you when I land."

"Please do."

"Love you."

"Good. I need it."

Back at the house, I call around trying to find a baby-sitter so I can attend Marta's shower.

Jemma hears me on the phone and comes to stand next to me at the dining room table. "I can baby-sit tonight, Mom."

I cover the phone and look at her. "Honey, you've never baby-sat your sisters before."

"Only because you've never let me. But I'm almost eleven, and lots of girls my age baby-sit. I can do it, too. Just keep your cell phone with you, and I'll call you if there's a problem."

"You wouldn't be scared?"

"Being with Mrs. Slutsky is scarier than being on our own."

I laugh, hard, and wrapping Jemma in my arms, I give her a hug. "I guess we can try. I'm only down the street in downtown Bellevue."

"Mom, knock it off. I'll be a teenager soon."

The surprise bridal shower starts at five-thirty p.m. at Daniel's Broiler, which sits on top of the Bellevue Place Towers. Tiana's managed to reserve one of Daniel's small private dining rooms, and between Jon, the florist downstairs, and Oh Chocolates, they've transformed the restaurant's private room into a lush bower of red roses. Elegant black-and-cream cards are at each plate, and on top is scripted "In Celebration of Marta & Luke," with tonight's special five-course menu printed below.

I'm curious to meet Tiana Tomlinson. I've watched her on television for years. She's the news anchor for a show that's on at the same time as *Inside Edition*, and she's even more beautiful in person than on the TV screen. She's small, maybe five feet three, and fine-boned, with a heart-shaped face, dark hair, deep dimples, and gold brown eyes. I'm stunned to learn she's my age. She looks easily ten years younger.

Allie, Mel, and Susan all show for the shower, along with Lucy and Lori Johnson. Luke's secretary arrives, too, as she's become good friends with Marta over the past year and a half.

Marta arrives last. Luke actually walks her to the door, and when she sees everyone inside, she just stands there confused. "Tiana?" she says, frowning as she takes us in. "What are you all doing here?"

"Celebrating you," Tiana answers, moving forward to give Marta a hug. "Now say good-bye to Luke, as this is a girls-only shower."

Marta's still stunned. "Shower?"

Tiana laughs at Marta's expression. "Yes. You *are* getting married soon, aren't you?"

Lucy sits next to me at the table. She, like the rest of us, is fairly star-struck by Tiana.

"She's so normal," Lucy whispers. "Well, for being a celebrity."

I look across the table, see Marta and Tiana giggling like two sixteen-year-olds, and smile. "I guess they've been best friends since high school."

"That's nice, isn't it?" Lucy watches them for a few seconds, then turns back to me. "I just remembered. I found out why Monica and Doug are selling your house."

"They're not getting divorced, are they?"

Lucy shakes her head. "Doug's sick. Prostate cancer. They decided to scale back while Doug goes through treatment."

I'm sorry to hear that anyone's ill, much less Doug, who is really a very nice guy. "That's terrible."

"Pete's really upset, too. It's made him realize we're not going to live forever. As he said last night, maybe it's better if we counted our blessings sooner rather than later."

Chapter Twenty-Five

Marta and Luke's choice for a winter wedding at the Banff Springs Hotel is beyond romantic. I've never been there, but after poring over the Fairmont Hotel's brochure, I can't wait to go.

It's a short flight from Seattle to Calgary, where we rent a car and drive an hour to Banff. Although it snowed heavily the last few days, the roads are clear and the majestic mountains glitter white and bright against the late morning's clear blue sky.

If we kept driving instead of taking the Banff exit, we'd hit Lake Louise and then Jasper. Instead we head into Banff, where the downtown is just ten blocks long and five blocks wide. It's bordered by mountains, mountains, a little river, and more mountains.

The Fairmont Banff Springs Hotel is even more magical than its setting. It's a huge turn-of-the-century hotel, with so many turrets and towers that Nathan nicknames it Hogwarts.

Marta has arranged the schedule so everyone is free to ski during the day and then meet for evening activities.

The first day, Nathan and I ski until I can't go down the mountain one more time. After returning to the hotel, we change out of our ski stuff and into jeans and T-shirts, heading with our swimsuits for the hotel's heated pool and spa.

Later tonight we'll meet up with everyone for drinks and dinner, but now we soak in the bubbly hot tub, letting the jets work away the kinks and aches.

"That was so fun today," I say, leaning against the rock wall. "The conditions were perfect."

"You've become a really good skier."

"You taught me, and it only took sixteen years."

"So you're saying I'm a really bad teacher," he teases.

"I'm saying you're a very patient teacher."

He smiles, and then his smile fades. I can see the moment the shadows return, his expression darkening, his eyes clouding. "What's wrong, Nathan?"

He shakes his head, but I don't accept that. "I can see something's wrong. Talk to me. Please?"

"I went to my mom last October and asked for a loan." He must see my surprise because he nods, grimaces. "I told her about our situation, told her how devastating it was for us to lose our house."

"She said no."

"No. She said yes." He draws a breath. "She said she'd been waiting for this moment for fifteen years—"

"What?"

He makes a rough sound. "Mom said she knew I'd never be successful like my dad. Said the only thing I'm good at is making bad choices."

"Your mom is evil."

"And then she wrote out a check for one hundred and fifty thousand dollars."

"You didn't take her money."

"No. I'd have no self-respect then." He pauses, reaches out to clasp my hand and tug me through the water toward him. "I wish I weren't so proud, Taylor. You might still be living in the lap of luxury."

I inhale as his chest brushes my breasts. "The lap of luxury was boring."

His hands circle my waist, and he draws me between his legs. "Have I ever told you you're one hot mama?"

"A couple times."

His head dips, and he kisses me. "Maybe it's time to tell you again."

I wrap my arms around his neck and kiss him back. It's a long kiss, sexy as hell, and Nathan lifts his head only when another couple enters the hot tub.

"How about we try the outdoor pool?" I ask as the man splashes past us.

"Good idea."

We climb out of the hot tub and duck through the plastic flaps that separate the inside from the outdoor pool. The pool is hot, the night is cold, and steam rises. A few people float in the darkness, and Nathan and I join them, floating silently side by side. As we float, it begins to snow, tiny flakes that grow until they're huge white fluffy things falling harder and thicker from the sky.

With the shadow of the giant mountains in the distance and the hotel's spires and turrets soaring above us, I think this is the most beautiful, magical moment of my life.

I've never loved Nathan as much as I do now, and I reach

for him, feel his arms come around me, and together we watch the snow fall.

It's all good. Life is good. Life is meant to be lived, and by God, we're living it, every hour, every minute, every second.

It hurts, but it also heals, and as hard as this year has been, I wouldn't have it any other way.

I love my Nathan and my girls. I love my family. I love my life.

I even love me.

Marta and Luke's wedding is held late in the afternoon in one of the huge historic rooms before a massive fireplace. She wears a surprisingly traditional gown, not the sexy satin sheath I would have imagined, and even her dark hair is pinned up in an elegant twist beneath a long lace veil.

Luke's in a black tuxedo with a crisp white shirt and white bow tie. Eva is her mother's only attendant and wears a dusty rose dress and holds a bouquet of beautiful roses and lilies, a smaller version of her mother's bouquet. The ceremony isn't long, but by the time it's over nearly all the women are crying.

Marta's crying.

I can understand why. She's spent the past ten years thinking the world was one way, only to be surprised by Luke.

But isn't that the way it should be? We should never think we know everything. We should never imagine we see the whole picture or know the whole story.

Life's full of surprises. Life has to have those surprises or we'd be bored out of our minds. We'd fall asleep partway through and forget to really think and hope and love and feel.

I slide my hand into Nathan's as the minister pronounces Marta and Luke husband and wife. Nathan squeezes my hand and points out the wall of windows toward the valley. It's snowing again, big fat feathery flakes. Goose bumps cover my arms.

I feel. I feel. I feel.

A half hour later, the cocktail party is in full swing in the Rundle Lounge. Dinner isn't for another couple of hours, so the appetizers are plentiful and the drinks flow freely. Marta and Luke are in and out of the second-floor lounge, taking pictures with Eva and various family members.

Nathan and I are sitting in the huge picture window, where the snow-covered valley is framed by jagged granite peaks. It has to be the most beautiful view in the entire hotel, and I'm so happy I'm here with Nathan and a flute of unbelievably good champagne.

As we sit at our window table, Nathan's phone rings. He reaches into his coat pocket to silence the ringer but stops when he notices the numbers. "It's a 206 area code."

"That's Seattle. Could be the kids."

"I better take it." He walks away from our table to find a quieter spot on the lower level. He's gone a long time, so long that I'm beginning to think there might be a problem. But then he returns and sits across from me at our window table, signaling for a waiter and ordering us two more glasses of champagne.

"That was interesting," he says as the waiter walks away.

"Interesting as in good, or interesting as in...?"

"Good."

I look at Nathan a long time, and he's got half a dozen more lines in his face than he did last year at this time—a deep wrinkle in his forehead, another between his eyebrows, and short but deep creases at his eyes—yet he looks more handsome than I've seen him in a long, long time. "I love you."

"Why?"

I open my mouth, but the only answer that comes to me is, "You're mine."

"It hasn't been easy."

My shoulders lift. "It's been a tough year. But it's getting better."

He reaches out and covers my hand with his. "It's going to keep getting better, too."

"I know it is."

"I do, too."

There's a light in his eye, a sheen I haven't seen there for a very long time. It's as if someone's flipped a switch and turned something on.

"So tell me about this interesting call."

Deep grooves form on either side of his mouth. "I've been offered a job."

"Fantastic!"

"But it's not in Bellevue."

My expression falls. For a moment I can't speak, too bitterly disappointed. "I thought you wanted to be back in Bellevue."

"I do." He hesitates. "But this is a pretty exciting position, and the salary is amazing. There'd be a huge signing bonus, too."

"That's good."

"Very good."

"So where is the job?"

He takes a deep breath. "Sydney."

"Sydney?"

"I'd head Hal-Perrin Technology's Australia office."

My mouth dries up. I can't even imagine moving halfway across the world. Leave the United States to live overseas? Raise our kids in a foreign country? "Wow."

"I know. Pretty huge."

"How huge?"

"The salary and bonus package would double what I was earning at McKee."

"That's some serious money."

"I know. My thoughts are going a mile a minute."

But as I look at him, he doesn't look troubled, he looks thrilled, like a kid who got his first bike for Christmas. Nathan's excited. He's got that light in his eyes, the confident, sexy glint that has always made me believe in him. "What did you tell them?"

"I told them I needed to visit the Sydney office, meet with the different executives and staff there before I could give them an answer."

"That's smart."

He covers my hand with both of his. "I also told them I needed you to come with me. I couldn't take a job if you weren't comfortable—"

"Nathan—"

"I mean it, Taylor. I won't ever take another job without talking about it with you first. You mean too much to me. You're not just my wife, you're my best friend, and I need you on my side."

"I am on your side."

He reaches across the table to brush a tendril of hair back from my face. "Do you feel like making a trip to Sydney with me? They're flying us first-class. Will put us up for a week at a five-star hotel right next to the Harbor Bridge."

My heart's thumping, and it has less to do with the first-class tickets than Nathan's happiness. I love this man. "Yes."

"We'll look at neighborhoods, check out schools, meet some of the Hal-Perrin executives, their wives and families. Most are Australian, although they've got a couple of engineers from India and some marketing people from London and Auckland. But there's no pressure, Taylor, none at all. If this isn't the right job, another one will come along."

"I promise to go with an open mind."

He leans across the table, kisses me. "I love your mind. And your courage." He kisses me again. "And your creativity." He gives me one last kiss, a slow, lingering kiss. "Not to mention your very sexy body."

I grin at him. He's given my body some very nice attention this trip.

Not that I wouldn't like some more.

"Do you think anyone will notice if we sneak out? Head up to our room?" he asks huskily.

I look up, glance around, catch Marta's eye. She and Luke have just returned from more photos, and Marta's smiling at me.

"No," I answer, gathering my small silver clutch. "Let's sneak out while we can."

About the Author

I love being a mom. I've wanted to be a mom since I was a little girl. But that doesn't mean I always do it right. Sometimes I feel as if I've inadvertently enrolled my boys in the Jane Porter School of Big Mistakes and Lots of Trial and Error. Fortunately, they're still alive and, even better, thriving.

When *Odd Mom Out* was first published in September 2007 a lot of folks, including my Bellevue neighbors, assumed Marta was me. The truth is, I am as much Taylor as I am Marta. Like all women, I'm fierce and fragile, hopeful and fearful, sunlight and shadow.

I loved writing *Odd Mom Out* and *Mrs. Perfect* because I was able to get inside the heads of what appear to be very different women, and yet once I started scratching at the surface, I discovered that Marta and Taylor weren't so different. Like all moms, they're both passionate about their children, their purpose, and the future.

These last four years writing my novels for 5 Spot have been among the happiest of my life. I am very blessed with wonderful children, fulfilling work, and people I love who love me and support me in return. As I've learned, life isn't about waiting for good things to happen but making good things happen.

Seize life. Love fully. Live joyfully.

For more on *Mrs. Perfect* and my 5 Spot novels, visit me at www.janeporter.com.

5 WAYS TO KNOW
YOU'RE MRS. PERFECT

 You volunteer for everything because no one else volunteers.

 You hate relinquishing control because you can do the job better than anyone else.

 You wouldn't dream of showing up late for Back-to-School Night.

 You know when your kids' reports are due, even if they don't.

 Your Christmas cards are already addressed and stamped by December 1.